the burning island

ALSO BY HESTER YOUNG

The Gates of Evangeline

The Shimmering Road

the burning island

Hester Young

G. P. Putnam's Sons
New York

G. P. PUTNAM'S SONS
Publishers Since 1838
An imprint of Penguin Random House LLC
penguinrandomhouse.com

Library of Congress Cataloging-in-Publication Data

Names: Young, Hester, author.
Title: The burning island / Hester Young.
Description: New York, New York : G. P. Putnam's Sons, an imprint of
Penguin Random House LLC, 2019.
Identifiers: LCCN 2018038078| ISBN 9780399174025 (hardcover) |
ISBN 9780698190795 (ePub)
Subjects: | BISAC: FICTION / Suspense. | FICTION / Psychological. |
FICTION / Contemporary Women. | GSAFD: Suspense fiction.
Classification: LCC PS3625.O96435 B87 2019 | DDC 813/.6—dc23
LC record available at https://lccn.loc.gov/2018038078
p.   cm.

Printed in the United States of America
1   3   5   7   9   10   8   6   4   2

BOOK DESIGN BY KATY RIEGEL

For my mama

the burning island

In the dream, I wear his eyes like a pair of sunglasses. His gaze colors my own. His thoughts—so focused, so clouded with desire—overpower mine.

I leave the woman that I am behind and become him.

The first thing I see is the girl, her face and chest lit up by the flashlight in her lap. She's stretched out on a hammock, arms splayed above her head in a posture that communicates boredom, a certain impatience. A slouchy teenager, Asian, with a ponytail and a thin, delicate nose. Her dark, thick eyebrows hang like marks of punctuation above her seemingly pupil-less eyes. She wears a gauzy white shirt with buttons going down the front. Even in the dark, I can see her bra beneath the fabric.

The girl sways side to side in her hammock, suspended between trees, surrounded by warm, dense forest. The rocking beam of her flashlight makes me feel seasick. Around us, the night is alive with the sound of frogs, but I scarcely notice their chirping, scarcely register the plants tickling my arm or my knees caked in dirt as I crouch on the ground, watching.

Watching *her*.

She rocks back and forth, waiting. When nothing happens, she rolls off the hammock, annoyed. Points the flashlight to the sky and then switches it abruptly off. For a moment, we're in total darkness.

The light blinks on and off again. On and off. Three times, in slow succession. A signal, though not to me. She isn't expecting *me* here, though she should be.

It's all been leading to this night. Her and me. Alone together at last.

My feet are beginning to tingle, deprived of blood too long by my awkward position. I rise slowly to my feet. Giant leaves brush at my cheeks, and a mosquito pierces my neck. I dispatch him with a quick, silent pinch. Listen for any indication that someone is coming, responding to her flashlight. The forest remains still but for the song of the frogs.

She flips off her light with a sigh.

This is your chance, I tell myself. *If you're going to do this, it will be here and now.* I push slowly through the brush, advance on her in the dark. Her flashlight flicks on when she hears me coming.

Hey! Her beam bounces around the trees, trying to get a lock on me. *I've been waiting forever. I didn't think you'd—*

And then she sees me. Sees who I am. Her lips part, and we both know what will happen.

Oh, she says. *Oh, shit.*

I let it sit between us. "Oh, shit" is right. There's no turning back. It's going down now. I have fought against my urges long enough.

She points the flashlight at the ground, so that I can't see her expression. *I guess . . . you knew I'd be here.*

I nod. Of course I knew. I didn't know if she'd be alone, but I knew exactly where she'd be. How many times have I watched her out here, watched her laughing, arguing with her sister, hanging on her stupid boyfriend? I've tried to keep my distance, to do nothing more than watch, but it isn't working anymore.

I move in toward her. Her shape is so strangely familiar. The height, the slope of her shoulders, the texture of her hair. But she smells different, like baby powder and something floral. I wind a lock of her hair around my finger.

It's just us now, I say. *What are you going to do about it?*

You should let me go, she whispers, but my hand cups her face and my lips graze her forehead and she knows she's not leaving.

Stay, I say, stroking her ear with my thumb.

She goes perfectly still. Considers her options and realizes, as I have, that there is only one way this can end. That it's pointless to fight.

You'll regret this, she says. *You're going to hurt a lot of people.*

She's right, of course. I will hurt a lot of people, and probably me, too, in the end. But people get hurt, that's just a fact of life. If I worried about who I was hurting, I'd never get what I want. And I want this.

I undo the top button of her shirt. *What else can I do?* I tell her. *I think about you all the time. I tried to stop.*

She says nothing. I wonder if she can feel it, this electricity that runs through me whenever she gets close, this crazy, giddy feeling where I want to touch her so badly. I'm not supposed to want that, but I do. Maybe this is the way to do it. Maybe this will get her out of my system.

I lean closer, inhaling her hair, and undo another button.

before

Tucson, Arizona

one

"W e gotta turn around, Charlie."

I jog ahead, pretending not to hear Noah, although I know he's right. I know from the chilly air, the canyon's lengthening shadows, and the beleaguered glances he keeps casting me that we can't go on much longer. The dark is coming.

I take a sip from my canteen and feign optimism. "This looks familiar," I call, although the rocks and scraggly trees around us look like all the other rocks and scraggly trees we've seen today. "I think we're getting close."

Behind me, Noah groans and wipes his forehead. His dark hair is getting long, edging toward his eyes, and the man needs a shave.

I wait, listening for the slow trudge of cowboy boots through rock and dirt. When it comes, I can't help but smile. My fingers go reflexively to the engagement ring he gave me three years ago.

This man would follow you anywhere, I think. *You guys should really get around to making this official.*

One glance at the sky, and my smile fades. The sun hangs low over the canyon, a glowing orange period that moves ever closer to the end of an irrevocable sentence. Soon, I will have to admit defeat. I dart uphill to get a more commanding view and begin to scan the land below me.

"We gotta get back to the trail before dark," Noah says, and his Texas twang suits the rugged landscape. "Last thing we need is to get lost out here."

I squint down at the ravine. "I just need a few more minutes."

"We don't have a few more minutes," Noah tells me. "It's almost dusk. That's huntin' time for cougars. If we had any goddamn sense, we woulda left an hour ago."

I can't argue with Noah's logic. If we had any sense, we wouldn't be here at all. Sabino Canyon has been closed to visitors for a week now after aggressive behavior from the local mountain lion population. Normally, that would be quite enough to dissuade me from setting foot on any piece of land. I have a healthy respect for authority and zero interest in a mountain lion confrontation.

But there's Alex to consider.

Twelve-year-old Alex Rocío, missing four days, his face splashed all over the Tucson news. Last seen biking furiously from his home after a fight with his parents. *A runaway,* authorities thought. *Just trying to scare Mom and Dad.* But when he didn't come back, the possibilities began to darken. Ominous words began appearing in the newscasts.

Kidnapping.

Abduction.

Conventional wisdom says Alex Rocío shouldn't be anywhere near Sabino Canyon, a full ten miles from his house in Casas Adobes.

But I know what I saw last night.

I dreamed of these familiar rocky gorges, these desert foothills, recognized them from half a dozen hikes I've taken in the park. I dreamed of a boy's bicycle lying abandoned in a ditch, an orange Mongoose Ledge, just like in the newscast. I dreamed of his Nikes, blood-red against the mountains' muted greens and browns.

I felt his fever. I felt his thirst. And after years of seeing and feeling things with unsettling accuracy, I could not dismiss this dream.

It's Saturday, and Noah and I have plenty to do without traipsing illegally around a cougar-infested park. We have two girls at home, a household to manage, and strange new professional paths to navigate. Noah's missing a board meeting tonight for Desert Garden, the non-profit he founded last year to bring urban farming to low-income kids. And I need to get started on my next article for *Outdoor Adventures* magazine, to prove I'm worthy of my recent upgrade to contributing editor.

You want an outdoor adventure? I think, gazing out at the mountains. *I'll show you an outdoor adventure.*

But I can't write about this. The twisted paths my dreams lead me down—this is not a side of myself that I want the world to know.

I don't want to be clambering around this canyon any more than Noah does, but I can't return to the trail, not without Alex. Not after we discovered his orange mountain bike a couple of miles back, its front tire blown out. Whatever doubts I had about our slapdash search party evaporated in that instant.

There's no one else coming for him. We're all this boy's got.

I peer down at the ravine, my eyes suddenly drawn by a brief, flickering motion.

"There. Did you see that?" I point to a trio of trees about a hundred yards off. "Something moved."

Noah's hand goes to his side, feeling for his nine-millimeter. "Could be a cougar," he says grimly. "We need to get outta here. Now."

"No, wait." I crouch down, trying to escape the sun's glare. "Right there. Look."

Though it's hard to tell with the encroaching shadows, I think there's a spot of red down in the brush. *Two* spots of red, in fact, like a couple of cactus fruits growing out of season.

"I don't see anything." Noah's already consulting his compass, trying to determine the quickest way back to the trail.

The temperature is dropping as fast as the sun. I shiver. My hand drifts to Noah's sleeve, and I think about our girls, safe at home right now with our friend Pam. "There," I say, pointing again. "Use your binoculars. That half-dead tree in the middle. Look just below it."

Noah sighs and holds up the small pair of field binoculars that dangle from his neck. "What am I even looking for?" he begins irritably. And then stops.

"The Nikes," I say. "Those are the red Nikes, right?"

He releases a breath. "Not just the Nikes, Charlie." His voice has gone hoarse. "The boy's still wearin' 'em."

That's all I need to know. I take off, ignoring Noah's warnings to be on the lookout for cougars. I have to get to Alex, have to take advantage of the sunlight while we still have it. The only question that remains in my mind is what state I'll find him in.

A living, breathing twelve-year-old boy? Or a body? That movement I saw beneath the tree could've been a scavenger.

Only one way to find out.

My feet are nimble and steady as I scramble across the craggy earth. Adrenaline kicks in, erasing whatever exhaustion I might feel after a day spent trekking around the canyon. Bounding over the rocky terrain, I realize I am not the New Yorker I once was, a woman who jogged for fifteen minutes along the paved roads of Central Park and found herself winded. Three years of living in the desert—shaking your shoes each morning for scorpions, braving temperatures of 115 degrees—will toughen up even the softest of city girls.

That doesn't mean I'm tough enough for whatever's waiting.

Please be alive, Alex, I think. *Please be alive.*

I have two young daughters. Less than five years ago, I buried a son. I know what it means to lose a child. I don't want Mama and Papa Rocío to learn.

As I draw closer, I get a better look at the red shoes. Black laces. A stripe that identifies them as Nikes. And somewhere, barely visible through the trees, a flash of jeans against the ground. A gray sweatshirt. My pulse quickens.

Did Alex crawl under the tree seeking shade? Or was he dragged there? Was he abducted by some sick stranger and left for dead? Mauled by a mountain lion? What gruesome sight is waiting for me?

"Alex?" I shout. "Alex, can you hear me?"

There's no reply, but his foot twitches.

I break into a run.

When I arrive, he's curled up on the ground, huddled in the shadow of an ash tree. I scan the surrounding dirt but find no signs of a water bottle. If it were a summer month, he'd already be dead. Southern Arizona has no pity. Even in early November, his face and neck are pink with sunburn, his lips cracked and bloody. Dehydration has left him delirious and barely coherent, and the crisp desert nights haven't done him any favors, either.

"I saw one," he mumbles as I lift him up. "I saw a mountain lion take down a deer. You have to tell my friends."

I unclip my canteen and remove the cap. Press it to his lips. "Short sips, okay? You don't want to choke."

He drinks like an animal, his swollen tongue probing for water. I try not to think about how much longer he would've survived out here, try instead to think of his parents, how their boy will grow to be a man. Still in rescue mode, I search the kid for any signs of injury— dried blood, an arm or leg bent at a wrong angle, anything the medics might need to know about.

Noah appears behind me, having finally slogged through all the rocks and ground cover. At the sight of Alex slurping greedily from my bottle, his broad shoulders slump with relief. "Thank God." He watches the boy drink, touches the kid's greasy hair, and turns to me with the kind of expression some people reserve for prayer. "You found him," he says. "You were right."

I don't know why, at this stage of the game, Noah's still so awe-struck. We've seen it plenty of times these past few years: messages about children that come to me in waking dreams. Sometimes, under their guidance, I can make the difference. I can stop the little girl in Walmart from leaving with a hovering older man. I can break a win-dow and call police when I find the toddler crying in a hot car. I can show up at a teenage boy's house, pretending to represent a local youth group, before he ends his life over a breakup. Those are the good days.

But sometimes my dreams are not enough. One night a boy took my hand and led me through the wreckage of a car accident, word-less and frightened. I knew the intersection—it was less than a mile from my house—and when I awoke, I went running off into the night trying to prevent the crash. It was too late. Emergency re-sponders had long since cordoned off the site, and the two vehicles involved had already been towed. I learned later that the boy was pronounced dead at the scene. There was never any way for me to save him, and yet as I stared at the twisted metal that littered the street, watched the road glitter with broken glass and the flashing lights of a police cruiser, I felt myself a failure.

Those are the hardest dreams, the ones that leave me powerless to change a brutal outcome.

My vision of Alex, thankfully, has proven itself to be the good kind. I've won this round, solved this puzzle, and my actions have real-world consequences. I'm glad the day has turned out as well as it has, although the boy is in bad shape.

Concerned by the glazed look in his eyes, I transfer Alex from my arms to Noah's. The kid needs medical attention, sooner rather than later. I dig out my cell phone, see a stream of texts from my friend Rae and a photo Pam sent of our girls. Grateful for the strong signal and the pure desert air, I dial 911.

THE FOREST SERVICE has plenty of questions for us. *What were you doing in Sabino Canyon? Don't you know the park's closed? There were reports of mountain lions stalking visitors! Why did you veer off the trail?*

With Alex off receiving medical care, I deflect these inquiries with vague answers and questions of my own. "We were just out hiking," I say, speaking to a point somewhere above the ranger's left ear. "We found the bike and thought we'd better have a look around. Is the kid going to be okay?"

Noah says nothing, but I can tell from his shuffling feet and the constipated look he keeps giving me that he disapproves of my attempts at subterfuge. He's the kind of misguided sweetheart who really believes that honesty is the best policy, that you can look a law enforcement officer in the eye and say, "Alex Rocío came to me in my dreams, sir," without any ill effects.

Later, when the Pima County sheriff's department steps in and we're asked to provide a statement, I know our situation has taken a more serious turn. This is not my first rodeo when it comes to facing the bureaucratic aftermath of a missing child, but there's something in the female deputy's face that I don't like—an undercurrent of distrust beneath the polite veneer. The small white room she's got us in, bare except for a metal table and two chairs, looks suspiciously like an interrogation room.

Her sergeant, a middle-aged fellow with bushy eyebrows, quickly moves to get Noah alone. "You come on with me." He taps Noah on the shoulder. "We'll take your statement while your memory's still fresh."

"Can't I do that here?" Noah glances at me, nervous about answering questions on his own.

If they're hoping to tease out the discrepancies in our accounts, they won't have to try hard. Noah and I should've spent more time getting our story straight, eliminating any bizarre psychic elements from the telling. Not that it would save us. The truth is all but burning a hole in Noah's tongue. In some inexplicable way, he's proud of me. He wants to tell people about my freakish abilities. He doesn't understand the damage these dreams would to do my credibility as a journalist.

The sergeant scratches his head. "Memory's a funny thing," he tells us. "People remember different details about the same incident, and you never know which ones are gonna matter." He leans against the door and regards us with a yawn that feels intentionally casual. "We always keep folks separate when they give their statements.

Who knows? Maybe something you give us will help us figure out what happened to that boy you found."

I stare at the metal table, only just starting to absorb the full extent of how screwed I am.

It's clear this department believes Alex Rocío was abducted and we were somehow involved. And I get it. Our story sounds shady as hell. Who goes for a stroll in a park that's been closed for mountain lions? They must know we haven't exactly been paragons of candor. Noah is a god-awful liar, and I'm only slightly better. Any detective worth his or her salt could tell we're hiding something.

I should've realized what we were getting into. I was so intent on helping Alex, I never stopped to think about the repercussions.

If the sheriff's department would just talk to Alex, this whole mess could be cleared up. Whatever happened out there, that kid must know we had nothing to do with it. But Alex is at a hospital now getting medical treatment, only half-conscious. They probably won't chat with him until tomorrow. And tomorrow is too late. I know Noah. The man's best and most endearing qualities are also his greatest liabilities. All it would take to elicit the whole truth and nothing but the truth from Noah is a "please."

Later, I will kick myself for not demanding a lawyer. I will wonder why we didn't just insist upon going home. I will learn that legally, we could've left at any time. But at this moment, after a long day in the canyon, after all the fear and elation of finding Alex, I have no fight left, no objections I can think to raise.

When the bushy-eyebrowed sergeant presses a hand to Noah's back and says, "Let's get this sorted, huh?," I say nothing. I press my forehead to the cool metallic table. I think, *This will end badly.*

𝖐

THE FULL DETAILS of Alex Rocío's canyon debacle emerge the following afternoon, after the newly restored twelve-year-old gets chatty. We are absolved by the boy's words, of course. The female deputy comes by our house that afternoon to tell us in person—an indirect apology, I think, for the energetic grilling we received in the early hours of the morning. Noah and I stare at our coffee, bleary-eyed, too exhausted by the whole ordeal to feel any sense of vindication.

In an account that was sheepish but largely unrepentant, Alex admitted to riding off on his bicycle Tuesday afternoon following a fight with his parents. He was mad, he said. Thought he'd disappear awhile and leave them to sweat it. He didn't set out for Sabino Canyon at first, just started pedaling, and ended up in that direction. He'd hiked the canyon before with his Boy Scout troop, and the signage announcing the park's closure and aggressive mountain lions only served to pique his interest.

"He wanted drama, and he got it," the deputy observes wryly, but I don't smile.

Alex hit the trails on his bike, hoping to see one of the animals for himself and earn some bragging rights with his friends. Even this particular act of foolishness might've turned out okay if he'd stayed on the path. But, continuing a pattern of poor decisions, he did not. Pursuing what he thought were mountain lion tracks, he went careening off the trail on an ill-advised hunt, eventually rupturing his front tire and ending up lost, frightened, and very, very thirsty. The kid would almost certainly have died if we hadn't come along.

His tale exonerates Noah and me entirely, even casts us as

heroes of a sort, but by then it's too late. By then, Alex's story is a consolation prize, nothing more, because Noah has already spilled his guts.

I never do learn which enterprising member of the sheriff's department first begins digging into my past, but someone does. Someone unearths my name from a case years earlier, another child abduction in Tucson. Someone tracks down a story about my saving a child in Louisiana. Someone contacts Pam and my old friend Detective Remy Minot, seeking answers. By the next day, Alex's misadventures in the desert are no longer the story.

The story is me.

two

Kneeling on the living room floor, I try to manhandle my daughter out of her soaking clothes. Tasha's lack of cooperation stems less from rebelliousness and more from her indifference to the fact that she's covered in milk. Once undressed, she darts out of my arms and makes a lunge for the window, hoping to get a peek at the news truck parked outside.

"I want to go on TV, Mommy!" she announces. "I want to see the man with the camera, and he can take a video and put it on TV."

At three, Tasha is the only member of our household enjoying the sudden media presence in our lives. My phone has been ringing non-stop for a few days now. Strange cars come and go and stop at the foot of our driveway. Reporters knock on the door, seeking sound bites. While I pass briskly from house to car, hands covering my face, Tasha mugs for cameras, reporters, and anyone else who shows an interest in her antics. You'd think the child has been raised on the set of a reality TV show with all her grandstanding.

Despite all the unwelcome attention—thank you, Associated Press, for picking up what could've remained a local story—I'm making a play for normalcy tonight. I've switched off the ringer on my cell, drawn the curtains so I can't see the news truck waiting to get footage of me, and planned a pleasant evening indoors. However ridiculous it is, I'm determined to pretend this is just an ordinary Wednesday evening with my family.

Micky, my nine-year-old, is having none of it. "When will they go away?" she grumbles. "I want to go *out*." She sits sulking in the corner of the living room, mouth stitched into an enduring frown. Earlier this week, before the Alex story broke, I'd promised to take her to Tucson Mineral and Gem World so she could purchase some new rocks for her collection. The arrival of the news crew changed all that. Instead of rocks, she gets mandatory Family Night, which I invented mainly as an excuse not to venture out of the house.

On the coffee table, my phone lights up with a text. I catch Tasha from behind and slide a clean shirt over her head. "Can you check that text, Mick? See if it's Daddy."

"Don't you know who it is?" Micky asks with a smirk. "You're psychic, aren't you?"

"Michaela. Please check my phone."

She rolls her eyes but complies. "It's Rae," she informs me. "You're supposed to call her about Girls' Weekend."

My best friend, Rae, is just another casualty in this humiliating affair. I've owed her a call for days now. We're supposed to hold our annual get-together in nine days, to continue our tradition of a kid-free weekend in whatever city offers the cheapest last-minute airfare. *This is it*, Rae jokes every year. *We're going to Hawai'i.* Then we check the ticket prices and end up in Cleveland or some such place—and have a fabulous time.

Ordinarily, the ritual adds some much-needed spontaneity to my life and marks a rare chance to see Rae, who lives in Connecticut. But I just can't see it happening this year.

"I'll call Rae later," I say, wrestling with my three-year-old's left leg, which seems determined to cram itself into the same pant leg as the right. "Tasha, would you stop squirming? You're making this much harder than it needs to be."

Tasha finally relaxes and, with the languid imperiousness of a pre-Revolution French aristocrat, allows me to dress her. When at last I snap her pants and pronounce her done, she looks down at her jeans, as if seeing them for the first time, and lets out a high-pitched wail.

"They're boy pants!" she exclaims. "You put me in *boy* clothes!"

The statement dismays me on many levels. We're supposed to be a progressive household, not one that divides the world into boy and girl stuff. Also, *jeans?* What kind of fashion Nazi am I living with?

"Mommy's wearing jeans right now." I gesture to my own legs in exasperation. "Is Mommy a boy?"

"No," Tasha sniffs. "But you wear clothes like one."

From her corner, Micky snickers.

I feel an irrational urge to defend myself, to point out how good my butt looks in these jeans, to inform Tasha that no man could rock a hoodie the way I do, but that probably doesn't send the right message. And she isn't altogether wrong. The sweatshirt I'm wearing belongs to Noah. A little behind with the laundry, I lifted it from his closet this morning.

"*Please*, Tasha." I'm reduced to begging. "Daddy's going to be back from the nursing home any minute. I want you dressed when Great-Grandma gets here."

"But I want the stripey pants," Tasha whines.

"Your striped pants are dirty, hon," I explain. "You're down to jeans and pajamas."

Micky, who has mercifully never displayed any interest in clothing whatsoever, casts me a knowing look. "You need to do the laundry," she says, an observation so obvious and true and infuriating that I almost assign her the task as punishment.

"I want my stripey pants!" Tasha tugs the jeans down to her ankles, accidentally dragging her underwear along with them. "Wash them, wash them!"

"Your striped leggings are *not a choice*, Tash. It's time for you to—"

But it's too late. I hear the front door open, Noah speaking in that courteous, 1950s-boyfriend tone he always uses in the presence of my grandmother. He's making an awkward joke, something about the paparazzi and my newfound celebrity, but I can't make out all the words. Tasha senses my distraction and makes a dash for her great-grandmother. Jeans and underwear still bunched around her ankles, she greets the woman with outstretched arms and fresh tears.

"Great-Grandma!" she cries. "Mommy won't let me wear my pants!"

The rest of the evening proceeds in a similar vein. Both girls complain about the dinner I make. Afterward, Noah flips on the television and watches the basketball game on mute. Micky plants herself in the corner with a book. Tasha, having moved past the jeans fiasco, quietly dismantles our couch, stacking all the pillows and cushions in a tower that threatens to collapse onto my ninety-one-year-old grandmother.

"Tasha!" I snap when I realize what she's doing. "That's not safe. Pick that up!"

"But I'm building," Tasha says, as indignant as if I've halted work on the Great Pyramid. "I'm making a castle, Mommy."

My grandmother looks up from her crocheting and smiles. Though she's still mobile and perfectly lucid, it's impossible not to observe her age in all her movements now—the hand tremors she battles as she works, her slow and painstaking stitches.

"Your castle is about to fall on Great-Grandma," I tell my daughter. "Can you find a better place to build it?"

"It's not going to fall," Tasha insists.

"Yes, it is," Micky pipes up from her corner. "And then you'll mess up Great-Grandma's knitting."

"She's crocheting today, not knitting," I correct her, although Micky knows the difference and is probably getting it wrong just to annoy me. "Single hook, remember?"

"Knitting, crocheting, whatever. Who even cares?" Micky delivers an eye roll quite advanced for her almost ten years. On another day, when my patience wasn't wearing paper-thin, I'd rejoice in her apparent normalcy, remind myself that an occasionally mouthy tween is a vast improvement from the quiet, traumatized child Noah and I took in three years ago. Today, however, I have few inner reserves to draw upon.

"Lose the attitude or go to your room," I say.

"I choose my room." She stalks off.

Noah, completely oblivious to what has just transpired, leans forward in his seat, transfixed by the basketball game. As Tasha goes to place the final pillow on her pile, he lets out a loud and startling cheer. Tasha's hand jerks back. The pillow tower falls, knocking my grandmother's glasses from her face.

"Tasha! I told you to take that down!"

At the sound of my yelling, Tasha makes a dash for Noah's arms. "Daddy," she whimpers.

"It's okay, baby," he murmurs into her hair. "Mommy's been having a hard day, that's all."

The suggestion that I am somehow at fault is more than I can stand. *"Would you stop undermining me?"*

Noah's glance holds no anger, just mild curiosity. "I'm not undermining you, babe. I think you're a little stressed, that's all." He takes Tasha's hand and leads her into the kitchen. "Come on, muffin. Let's give Mommy a few minutes with Great-Grandma."

So much for Family Time.

I drop to my knees, trying to locate my grandmother's fallen eyeglasses. I lift cushions, peer under chairs before finally discovering them in the lap of Tasha's stuffed hippo. "I'm so sorry, Grandma." I hand her the glasses. "I don't know what's got into them."

Grandma waves off my apology. "It was an accident, Charlotte. Children being children."

"Well, they're driving me crazy, the three of them. The girls are being so rude. Maybe if Noah could stop drooling over the basketball game for five minutes—"

"But that's not what's bothering you, is it?"

I don't reply.

My grandmother lives in a nursing home, but she doesn't live under a rock. She saw the situation outside, and I'm sure she saw the article in the *Arizona Daily Star*, which she's read nearly every issue of since moving to Tucson a couple of years ago. I've already told her what happened in Sabino Canyon, how my dream led us to Alex Rocío. But Grandma must've heard other versions of the story as well: TWELVE-YEAR-OLD RESCUED FROM GRUESOME DEATH BY PSYCHIC VISION, and all the other sensationalist headlines floating around.

Despite my refusal to grant a single interview or offer any statement whatsoever, the articles persist, all identifying me by name, most running a photo of me from a charity event that somehow slipped into widespread circulation. Yesterday, kids at school began asking Micky about me. *It'll be great for your book sales!* my editor, Isaac, raved in an email. *We need to discuss your next big project! Something with a clairvoyant angle, obviously.*

That was when I knew. There was no hiding from this anymore. I'd been outed.

I don't blame the reporters, not really. I've been the intrusive journalist myself. It's a job. You do what you have to do. But this is not the version of Charlotte Cates I wanted the world to see. I've always been the woman who deals in facts, who verifies her sources, and now here I am, exposed to everyone as some nutcase who follows her dreams— literally. That my dreams/visions/whatever-you-want-to-call-them have proved eerily accurate on multiple occasions only enhances my reputation as a Grade-A Weirdo.

I meet my grandmother's eyes, squirming under their slate-gray gaze, and wonder how much of this she knows, how much she has guessed. In her younger days, my grandmother had premonitions of her own, visions of past and future events just like I do, but she managed to keep them under wraps. Her unusual ability never came to define her, never swallowed her up whole.

"The media attention has been a challenge," I admit.

"It won't last. They'll find another story. They always do."

I fold my arms across my stomach and stare down at the toy-strewn carpet. "The damage is already done, isn't it? Google my name, and all this crap comes up. That won't change."

She shrugs. "It's not wrong, most of it. You see things most people don't, Charlotte, and that's a fact. Maybe it's time to stop worrying over it and just . . . settle into your own skin."

"Easy for you to say. No one ever knew about *you*."

She spreads her handiwork across her lap and loops yarn around her crochet needle with an unsteady flick of the wrist. "That's true. Your grandfather and your father both died without any idea that I saw things. I didn't talk about it with anyone."

"Not *anyone*?" I raise an eyebrow. My grandmother has always been tight-lipped with me about her abilities, sharing a few meager details of her experiences only when confronted with my own. Still, she must've spilled the beans to a few other folks along the way. "Come on, Grandma. I'm sure you mentioned it to someone. I mean, you told me."

"And I'm glad I did," she says. "It was . . . a relief. It's a burden, always trying to hide yourself, isn't it?"

I can feel this turning into some illustrative tale about self-acceptance and living in the light, but that's not a story I want to hear. "The point is, you had a choice," I say. "That's all I wanted. A choice about who to tell and when."

"Oh, honey. You must know by now, we don't choose what happens, only how we react."

"And how am I supposed to react?"

"Don't," she says simply. "They're saying good things about you, don't you know that? That you have a gift. That you use your gift to help children." Evidently, my grandmother hasn't been reading the online comments sections of these articles, which accuse me of being a fake, a flake, and a "shameless publicity whore." Still, it's comforting to know that she's not embarrassed by me.

"They've been writing about Keegan," I say softly. "I wish they'd leave him out of it."

That's the worst part of the reporters: they keep asking me about my son.

Your first child died of a brain aneurysm at the age of four, Ms. Cates. Did that impact your decision to focus your abilities exclusively on helping children?

Like I can control it. Like my visions are something I can summon at will instead of a frightening, unwelcome visitation.

I could tell them that I never wanted this. That if I could choose between an ordinary, boring life and one filled with images of dead or endangered children, I would choose ordinary and boring every time. But speaking to the press would only prolong my time as clickbait— and I'm certainly not speaking to them about my son.

"I need some coffee," I tell Grandma, rising to my feet before the lump in my throat can overtake me.

In the kitchen, I find Tasha and Noah playing with alphabet magnets on the refrigerator. Noah places an A next to Tasha's R, and she bashes it with a violent L. "This is the bad guy," she explains, prying the A from the fridge and tossing it to the tiled floor on wicked L's behalf.

"That is one mean dude," Noah agrees, glancing over as I pour the last of the coffee into a mug. "Rae just called," he tells me.

"Called *you*?"

"She says you haven't been answerin' your phone."

"Oh. Yeah." I take a sip of coffee and decide that it is old and luke-warm enough to require milk. "I guess I should call her back. Cancel our Girls' Weekend."

Noah takes a Y magnet and dances it across Tasha's knees. "Why would you cancel on her?"

"What, you still want me to go? And leave you guys here with all these reporters?"

He shrugs. "The reporters will clear out faster if you're not here. Anyway, you don't need a Girls' Weekend. You need a Girls' *Week*."

"What?"

"I just spoke to Rae about it. It's last-minute, but that's how you guys always do things. She says she can get the time off. You should do this, Charlie. Take a week."

I'm too floored to fully comprehend the gift he's offering. "You really think I can just walk away from the household for a whole week? Noah, I don't think you know what I *do* around here."

He looks down at his feet, which I see now are clad in mismatched socks, and wiggles them playfully. "Whatever it is, it's sure not laundry." He offers me a good-natured grin. "Look, I'll handle it, okay? It might be a li'l messy, but I'll handle it. You need the time away. This whole situation is gettin' to you."

I'm not an idiot. Noah's sending me off on a sudden vacation with my bestie isn't just a loving gesture—it's atonement. He feels guilty about his role in all this. "You don't have to do this," I tell him. "I'm not mad at you, okay? God knows, I'd love to get away, but you don't owe me anything."

"Maybe I do. Me and my big mouth landed you here, after all." He crosses the kitchen and takes my hand. "I had this dumb idea the truth would set you free. Instead, you're stuck in the house hidin' from reporters. I never meant for that to happen."

"It is what it is," I sigh. "Even if you'd kept your mouth shut . . .

sooner or later, someone would've figured it out. I couldn't keep it under wraps forever." I'm not actually convinced of this, but there's no sense guilting Noah, not when he's doing a perfectly good job of guilting himself.

"Maybe it's a good thing," he says. "Next time you have a dream, people will listen." He strokes my fingers with his thumb, traces the circle of my engagement ring. "I still think you should take a vacation, baby. Recharge for a week. Get your head in the right space."

"Noah, I have three weeks to get *Outdoor Adventures* a feature article. I can't just disappear." But I'm already warming to the idea, imagining a warm blue ocean and verdant island. I can hear Rae's voice in my head: *This is it. We're going to Hawai'i.* And I realize that's exactly what we need to do. "A working vacation maybe," I say slowly. "I think I could swing that."

I smile. Nestle my chin upon Noah's shoulder. It's a fantasy Rae and I have entertained ever since we were new mothers back in Connecticut, sleep deprived and juggling the relentless demands of our work and family lives. And it just might be far enough to escape the media circus I'm currently engulfed in.

"Hawai'i," I say. "We'll go to Hawai'i."

"Hawai'i?" Noah repeats. "Really? But . . . you've been there before, haven't you? You don't want to try somewhere new?" From his expression, he was expecting something less glamorous—another Cleveland, perhaps. Some random place he'd never want to visit so he could feel benevolent but not jealous.

Nope. When a mother is cut loose from her duties for a week, she's got to go whole hog.

"Hawai'i," I say firmly. "Final answer."

three

Outside our gate at the San Francisco airport, Rae flips idly through a celebrity gossip magazine, her brow furrowed over some finely chiseled Hollywood actor or whichever *Bachelor* contestant is currently seizing headlines. Age will never diminish her style. Her clothes remain chic, her springy Afro curls effortless. My heart lifts in happy recognition. The fact that we've both made it this far—meeting on a layover so we can share the flight to Hilo together—means we've already achieved the most important part of our plan. We're together.

"Rae!" I call, but she doesn't hear me amidst the whining children, loud cell phone conversations, and flight announcements. I send her a text. *Look up.*

She squeals at the sight of me, a high-pitched middle-school-girl squeal, and leaps to her feet. Several passengers glance over, probably expecting Justin Bieber or at least some paunchy, washed-up member of a nineties boy band.

"You made it!" Rae exclaims, not the least bit concerned that we're making a scene. "Oh my God, get over here!"

I drag my carry-on past a series of unmoving legs, apologizing when I bump a pair. Rae practically bounces as she waits for me, her face somewhere between thrilled and incredulous. I know the feeling. A weeklong Hawaiian vacation with your best friend is not a luxury most moms will ever get, and yet here we are, unencumbered by children or spouses. I'm still struggling to comprehend our outrageous good fortune, still half-expecting our flight to be indefinitely delayed for mechanical failure, because how can this be real?

I ditch my bag and meet Rae in a giant, squishy embrace. "We did it! This is happening!" Hugs aren't normally my thing, but she has worn me down over the years, has pushed past my stiff reserve and bestowed her affection so warmly, I can't help but reciprocate. "How the hell did you get away from work?"

She wrinkles her nose. Rae works in chemical sales, and though she regularly closes big deals and earns impressive commission checks, her job always seems to be last on the list of things she wants to talk about. "I told them I had a funeral to attend," she says. "They were very understanding."

"A funeral? For who?"

"My favorite aunt," she replies without skipping a beat. "Lung cancer. All those years of smoking finally caught up with her. The doctors thought she'd have more time, but it took her down fast. Probably a blessing." Rae has always possessed the kind of clear-eyed and straight-faced lying skills Noah and I can only dream of. "Auntie didn't have any kids, so it's on me to handle her affairs this week."

"You're a wonder," I declare, shaking my head in both envy and admiration. "Soon as we hit the Big Island, I'm buying you the fruitiest, girliest drink we can find."

"Says the woman who won't touch alcohol." Rae laughs and

nudges one of her curls back into line. "Are you really gonna leave me drinking all by my lonesome?"

"Someone has to stay sober to fend off all the drooling men. I mean, look at you."

This is not flattery. At forty-five, Rae looks ten years younger, with smooth, coffee-colored skin and a backside that rivals that of any Kardashian. When she walks into a room, males of all ages take note, and the ring on her left hand—a ruby, not the traditional diamond—does little to discourage their attentions.

"Hmph," Rae says with a pout, "I was hoping for a partner in crime, not a chaperone."

I grin. "Guess that depends on the crime. You know I'll always have Mason's back."

We're joking, of course.

Despite her talk and flirty attitude, Rae's been happily married for fifteen years. She and Mason are my model for monogamy. They saw me through my own predictable-in-retrospect divorce, held me together after the death of my son. Whenever Noah and I hit bumps in our relationship, I look to Rae and her husband as a reminder of what's possible.

"Mason knows I need this," Rae says, settling back into her chair. "Not gonna lie, it's been getting to me, the whole work-life balancing act. The money's too good to leave my job, but . . . some days I kinda wish they'd fire me." She grabs her water bottle and gossip magazine from the seat beside her, clearing me a space. "Noah said you're a little frayed at the edges yourself."

"Yeah. Hawai'i could do us both a world of good."

"Just don't go posting photos of us all over Instagram," Rae says. "Wouldn't be respectful to my dead auntie."

I laugh. "That sounds like me, exposing all your secrets on the Internet." Rae knows perfectly well my Instagram account is set to private and I haven't used it in ages—she's always after me to post more. And Noah doesn't even have an account. We are, according to Rae, the most social media–shy couple she knows. "If you don't blow your own cover, I think we've got this one in the bag," I tell her.

"I'm on it." She rubs her hands together. "Kalo Valley, here we come."

"You know it's not all play for me this week," I remind her. "I have that piece I have to do."

Rae makes a face. "As long as you *have* some outdoor adventures instead of just writing about them. What's your article on, anyway?"

"I'm profiling Dr. Victor Nakagawa."

She gives me a blank look. "Who?"

"He's a volcanologist who runs triathlons," I explain. "I got his name from my editor at Meyers Rowe."

Eager to ride the wave of my recent publicity, my editor Isaac called again on Wednesday, pushing hard for another book. "A memoir," he suggested. "About visions and kids and all that. It'll be a huge hit." I hedged, told him I was headed for Hawai'i, that I had to knock out a big *Outdoor Adventures* article and hadn't even chosen the topic. I wasn't ready to talk book deals yet, I said. The next day, in a helpful-with-ulterior-motives move, Isaac sent me a name.

Victor Nakagawa, he texted. *There's your article. Now let's get started on your next book!!*

Isaac, with his typical nose for a story, was onto something. Last month, fifty-year-old Victor Nakagawa placed first in his age category in the Big Island's Ironman competition, making him a local hero.

Add to that a day job at the Hawaiian Volcano Observatory, and he's perfect *Outdoor Adventures* material. All I need from Dr. Nakagawa is a couple of good lava anecdotes to nail the swashbuckling-scientist angle, and I can knock this story out of the park. The only downside is knowing that I'm in debt to Isaac—sooner or later, he'll come to collect on the favor.

Evidently I'm not the only one impressed by Dr. Nakagawa's bio, because Rae perks up at my description of the man. "A scientist who does Ironman? That swimming, running, biking thing?"

I nod. "I talked to him on the phone yesterday. He was flattered I wanted to write about him. He put me in touch with our B & B and promised us a behind-the-scenes tour of the volcano observatory. We're supposed to meet him tomorrow."

"Huh." Rae strokes her chin. "I'm into the volcano thing, but those super-athletic dudes can be a little much."

I shrug. "He's obviously very accomplished. Shouldn't be a hard article to write."

Though I haven't had a lot of time to research Dr. Nakagawa given the haphazard nature of our trip, I've done some basic digging. Run his name on Google, and you're inundated with legions of his scholarly articles and competition results, charts citing his work for the U.S. Geological Survey, images of him presenting at conferences and crossing finish lines. The only downside to Nakagawa is my own ignorance of his field. After wading into a few of his baffling papers, I've had to brush up on my Earth science, cram for our interview like it's a test.

"Star athlete and badass scientist—sounds like a good story," Rae says.

"Not as fascinating as *your* reading material, though." I gesture to the gossip mag on her lap. "What are you reading the *Squealer* for? Did Jennifer Lawrence get a boob job? Is Ryan Gosling behaving badly?"

Rae gives me a long look. "You want celebrity news? Page twelve." She slaps the magazine into my hand.

My heart sinks as I flip through the pages. I know what I will find. Not Rihanna or One Direction or Ariana Grande. Not even the latest nanny to break up a Hollywood marriage.

It's me.

Psychic Mom Just Wants to Be Left Alone, the caption says, which is both accurate and ironic. There's a picture of me stepping into my Prius, one hand up to the camera, though you can still see my face, dark hair framing green eyes and a sharp chin. Not a terrible photo, at least. The grainy image masks my crow's-feet and flyaway hairs. I scan the article quickly.

> Her amazing abilities have saved the lives of three children and attracted national attention, but Charlotte Cates, 42, prefers the quiet life. "It's not easy for her, having this gift," a source close to the mother of two reports. "She wants to be there for her children, but there are other children out there who need her. That's a big responsibility."
>
> For years, Cates tried to keep her powers on the down-low, but her uncanny ability to help kids in trouble made headlines this month after her daring rescue of a twelve-year-old boy in an Arizona canyon. The story has surprised several of Cates's friends and colleagues, who say they didn't know about her psychic skills.
>
> "She never talked about it," a former coworker told the *Squealer*. "This is a whole other side of her nobody knew."
>
> A secret identity and a superhuman power? Sounds like a real-life superhero to us!

I look up at Rae, cringing. "Oh, God. The *Squealer*'s covering me now? This is worse than I thought."

"Can't say I'm too thrilled about it myself," Rae says pointedly. "I mean, really? I have to read about your special 'gift' in the freaking *Squealer*?"

I stare at my feet. Rae has every right to be upset. I've never discussed my abilities with her, not in so many words, but I should've. "I'm sorry. This isn't how I wanted to have this conversation."

"Which conversation is that? The one where you finally flat-out admit you've got some cool psychic shit going on?"

My voice drops several decibels as I glance around the gate to see who might be listening. "Yeah, that one."

"You could've just said," Rae tells me. "It's not like I haven't had an inkling. You're always dropping these little hints, but whenever I try to bring it up, you get all squirmy. I pretty much knew, though. Ever since that time with Zoey, I knew. Remember that? When my baby girl broke her ankle? You saw it coming. You dreamed it."

"Then you've known since the beginning," I say, and it makes me feel a little better. My premonition about Rae's daughter was the first, a dream that came just months after my son died, when I finally stopped taking sleeping pills.

"Why didn't you ever talk about it?" she asks reproachfully. "It's *me*. You know how much I love paranormal stuff. You didn't have to hide it."

"It's just embarrassing," I mumble. "I sound like a kook, like a—a mentally ill person." I snatch her copy of the *Squealer*. "Look at this. I'm a laughingstock. It's awful."

"Awful? Nah." She chuckles. "I can't wait for the TV movie."

I shudder. "I am so not ready to become a Lifetime original."

"I don't see what you're worried about," Rae says. "You're the good guy in this story. A real-life superhero, they said. Super Charlie! Or no, um . . ." She flounders for a better name. "The Protector. WonderMama, defender of innocents." When I fail to look amused, Rae puts an arm around me and leans her head against mine in an awkward sideways hug. "Okay, okay. Being in a trashy airport magazine is not, like, the fulfillment of a lifelong dream for you, I get it. One more way we differ."

It's not simply the unwanted publicity that has me down, though. Rae won't be the only person I care about to learn of my so-called gift from the *Squealer*. There will be a lot of people reevaluating their relationships with me.

"I'm so, so sorry, Rae. I should've talked to you about it, all my weird visions and stuff." I swallow. "I just didn't want you to look at me differently."

"Too late," she says. "From now on, I will look at you differently. Because having crazy mind powers is awesome, and I am totally jealous. Speaking of which, I heard there's a really good psychic adviser in Kalo Valley, not far from our B & B. Marvel Andrada—what a name, right? I can't wait to check her out. Unless *you* want to give me a free reading, of course."

Rae's abrupt subject change doesn't fool me. I know my bestie. Her tendency to keep things light and avoid conflict can conceal all kinds of hurt.

"You have a right to be mad," I tell her. "I owe you more than just an apology, I know that."

"Yeah, well." Rae kicks up her feet and rests them on her suitcase. "You've got a week to make it up to me. In Hawai'i, no less. Who could screw that up?"

I smile, but I'm pretty sure that she's just jinxed us.

four

By the time we land in Hilo's tiny airport, it's getting dark. The sky glows a smoky purple, but there's no sunset—we're on the eastern side of the island. Rae and I make a dash for the car rental, hoping to avoid night driving, but by the time we leave the lot, evening has arrived in full force.

Rae punches the address of Koa House, our B & B, into an app on her phone. A male voice dispenses directions with a refined British accent, sounding both polite and knowledgeable, if a little bored.

"I call him Nigel," Rae says with a yawn. "Makes me feel like I have a butler."

With about forty thousand residents, Hilo is the most populous city on the Big Island. On a sleepy Sunday evening, that's hard to believe. After passing a couple of strip malls with generic mainland chains, civilization dwindles. Trees rise up along the one-lane highway and form dark shapes against the dimming sky. Exhausted from her day of travel, Rae leans her head against the window, drooping.

"Go to sleep," I prod her. "I'll wake you when we get there." Our B & B is, by its own admission, "off the beaten path," but if Nigel's not sweating it, why should I?

"Nope." Rae props her head up with one hand, although her eyes are still half closed. "I'm good. Totally awake. Let's do this."

Living in Tucson, I'm used to unlit, winding roads, but the lush jungle-scape of eastern Hawai'i is quite unlike the barren desert lands of home. And the *air*. I roll down the window, breathing in that damp, earthy smell.

On its website, the Koa House Bed and Breakfast proclaims itself a "tropical hideaway nestled between sea and fire." That poetic turn of phrase, coupled with a recommendation from Dr. Nakagawa, made my scramble for last-minute lodging an easy one.

Situated in the Puna district, on the southeastern side of the Big Island, Koa House promises something more authentically Hawaiian. Granted, that includes a rather lackluster nightlife, but I figure Rae and I can cram our days with adventure enough.

The whole plan seemed brilliant and exciting when hatched in Arizona, but as fatigue sets in and the B & B proves more remote than I anticipated, I feel pangs of doubt. The unlit road dips and curves and the plant life lining the highway swells, growing both taller and thicker. Periodic breaks in the flora give way to unpaved driveways, barely visible in the dark, but few of these properties have obvious signage or clearly marked street numbers. Even more disconcerting, the GPS loses its signal at various points in the drive.

"Don't leave me hanging, Nigel," I beg as Rae snores beside me.

Despite technical lapses, Nigel manages to get me all the way to Kalo Valley, the small town of about twelve hundred that Dr. Nakagawa calls home. At first glance, the village is a little disappointing. I see a gas station and something called the Rainbow Drive-In, but not much else in the way of commerce. Occasionally, I pass a side street to a residential area, but the main road forks only once, at Kanoa Drive.

Beneath the street marker, a sign with an arrow indicates the way to the School for Free Thought. *Weird name,* I think. Per Nigel's instructions, I don't turn.

The houses thin, leaving nothing to indicate human inhabitants but a few dirt paths that stretch into the dark. Nigel's claims that we are very nearly there concern me. We are very nearly nowhere. Perhaps Kalo Valley was a mistake.

Rae and I didn't have to stay here. We could've opted for Hilo, Volcano, or the vacation-friendly Kona coast with its expensive resorts, exclusive golf courses, and pretty beaches. I chose Kalo Valley not just for its proximity to Dr. Nakagawa, but because I wanted a taste of the *kama'āina* experience: the unhurried pace of a Big Island village, the feeling of a home, conversations with locals and not drunken hotel guests. Rae agreed. *None of that standard tourist crap,* she said. *We'll have an adventure!* Now I wonder about our decision. A tacky hotel might not be so bad.

"Arriving at destination, on right," Nigel informs me, although there's nothing outside but unchecked vegetation.

Rae bolts upright and shakes herself awake. She presses her face to the window, trying to discern some hint of our B & B. "Where *are* we?" she asks with a yawn.

"Koa House, supposedly." I gesture uneasily at the woods. "But I don't see anything out there, do you?" In truth, it's not the things I see that unsettle me. There's a stifling thickness that emanates from behind those trees, something potent and unnatural.

Rae rubs her eyes. "Slow down. It's got to be here somewhere."

I pull into the next dirt road I find. A rusted metal gate extends across the path, blocking all vehicle entry, and a hand-painted sign nailed to a tree announces, WAKEA RANCH. PRIVATE, NO TRESPASSING. Anxiety coils in my gut. This place is all wrong. Nothing good will happen here. For a brief second, I catch a whiff of spoiled milk, and my stomach turns. Have we been swindled in some elaborate Internet ruse? Is Koa House's proprietor, David Kalahele, a phony, just another Nigerian prince promising to wire money? Or worse, a guy who lured us out here with bad intentions?

Whether it's gut instinct talking or just my overactive imagination, I want out.

"Turn around," Rae says. "We must've missed it."

As I execute a clumsy three-point turn at the foot of the Wakea Ranch driveway, something moves behind one of the trees. My skin begins to crawl. On the other side of the rusty metal gate, half-hidden from view, a figure stands observing us.

Someone must've been out there crashing around the woods at night when our car pulled mistakenly into the drive.

"Jesus," Rae mutters under her breath.

Our headlights sweep across him, and in that fraction of a second, I catch a visual. A boy, probably a teenager, with straight black hair and bangs that half-cover his eyes. He ducks away from the light, one arm shielding his face. Then he's gone, swallowed up by the shadows.

I can't shake my bad feeling as we pull back out onto the road. "He didn't even have a flashlight, Rae. What if he was an intruder?"

She pats my arm. "Relax, you. I have no clue what that dude was up to, but he must know that land pretty well if he's roaming around in the dark. Let's just find the B & B."

On our second pass, we spot another small dirt road about a quarter mile up from the forbidding Wakea Ranch. Wrapped around a post at the foot of the drive, a cluster of flowers heralds an otherwise imperceptible path. I turn down the drive, my misgivings about the boy, our accommodations, and the entire trip not yet quelled. Rae has no such reservations. Her body tilts forward in the passenger seat, eager for whatever's coming.

Eventually the forest gives way to a buttery yellow house. Lit up against the night, the glowing windows and plant-lined front patio convey all the warmth and welcome one could hope for.

Our hosts, who appear to have been enjoying a pleasant night on their porch, rise to their feet, waving. David Kalahele and Thom Marcus, our smiling proprietors.

"Aloha! You found our little hideaway!" The taller of the two men comes to greet us, strings of flowers spilling from his arms. "I'm David." He's slim and barefoot, with gray-streaked hair and bright black eyes—likely of Hawaiian descent, judging from his surname. "So," he says, eyes moving from me to Rae. "Which one of you is Charlotte?"

I raise a hand, my apprehensions rapidly subsiding. "That's me. Thanks for hosting us on such short notice."

"Happy to do it." David places a lei of purple and white orchids around my neck. "Welcome! I hope you'll enjoy your stay at Koa House. And you . . ." He turns his attention to Rae.

"Rae Shapiro." She beams as he bestows a second lei upon her.

"This is my husband, Thom," David says, and Thom grins. He's already all over our suitcases. A solid white guy of average height, Thom has embraced his hair loss and shaved his head completely. A neatly trimmed goatee and rectangular silver spectacles offset his pale dome. His T-shirt reads, *There are only two kinds of people in the world: those who can extrapolate from incomplete data.*

I break into a smile in spite of myself. Nerd.

"I'll just get these up to your room while David shows you around," Thom says.

The tour takes only a few minutes. Having spent most of my life in the Northeast, I'm accustomed to sprawling Victorian bed-and-breakfasts with antique furnishings and stiff, vaguely oppressive décor. Koa House is entirely the opposite. Light wood floors, yellow walls and splashy upholstery, thriving floor plants, large windows with sheer curtains, and sliding doors. Rae swoons at the private outdoor bath, a fenced-in area with a claw tub and strings of Christmas lights woven through an avocado tree. In the living room, I ogle the shelves of awesomely trashy beach reads and smile at the pair of cats, one black and one orange, who lie snoozing together in a furry pile. Everything looks neat, comfortable, and unpretentious.

"This already feels like a vacation," Rae says, grabbing a Michael Crichton novel from a shelf and clutching it rapturously to her chest.

Upstairs, our suitcases wait in adjoining bedrooms. I get the Bamboo Room, and Rae the Tree Fern Room, designations that I think my horticulturally minded fiancé would appreciate. A pair of newlyweds will arrive tomorrow to claim the more extravagant Paradise Suite, David says, but tonight we have the place to ourselves. The Bamboo and Tree Fern Rooms are decorated according to their names and share a balcony that overlooks the backyard. In daylight, the surrounding jungle probably makes for a peaceful retreat, but at night, the dense growth appears forbidding. Around us, hundreds of unseen creatures chirp a dissonant two-note song—a tropical insect, maybe, or some kind of night bird.

"I can't get over how dark it is." Rae leans out over the railing. "I don't see any lights. Don't you have neighbors, David?"

"The lot to the east is for sale," he tells her. "All that forest to your left is part of Wakea Ranch."

I look at Rae, and I know both of us are thinking about the boy we saw wandering around the property at night.

"Don't they have electricity?" I ask.

David smiles. "You're in Puna. A lot of people out here live off the grid. Thom and I use solar energy and a rainwater catchment system, but some folks make do with a lot less. Buckets instead of toilets— that sort of thing."

"So you've got nutty-crunchy hippie types next door?" Rae peers into the dark as if hoping to spot a flower child in its natural habitat.

"Not exactly. Wakea Ranch has its own story."

She glances back at him. "Go on. I like stories."

"Well . . ." David looks reluctant to spill, as if he's not quite sure of the impression this tale might make. "Back in the seventies, that property was purchased by a religious group. It was a pretty self-sustaining community from what I understand. They farmed, lived off the land, didn't really mix with the rest of the world. That was how they chose to live."

"Are they still there?" Rae asks.

"No," David says. "The leader ran into some trouble with the law in the early nineties and everyone disbanded. His daughter ended up marrying a local man, and she inherited the place. Naomi Yoon."

Rae cocks her head to one side. "Wow. What's *she* like? I mean, growing up in a cult and living without electricity . . . that's unusual."

"Yeah, she's a character," David says. "I don't know her well. Naomi lives out there with her kids, and they mostly keep to themselves. I doubt you'll run into the Yoons."

Something in a nearby tree begins to chirp, adding its refrain to the night's song. "What is that noise?" I ask. "Are those bugs?"

"Little frogs with a big voice," David says. "The coquí. They hitched a ride in from Florida a couple decades back and they've taken over this side of the island. That's their mating call you hear. Loud, aren't they? But they're only about the size of a quarter. They're white noise, as long as you don't start listening to individual frogs."

I stare out at the tree line, comforted to know that racket is coming from frogs and not a bunch of large, unholy insects. The woods are off-putting enough as is. The image of that boy at Wakea Ranch, his face white and strange under the glare of the headlights, will not leave my mind.

I turn to David. "Your neighbor Naomi . . . does she have a son?"

"Three of them," David replies. "Two teenagers and a little one. No daughters, though." He steps off the balcony and back into the guest bedroom, as if to avoid further questions. "Is there anything I can get you? Some water, maybe, or iced tea? I'm sure you're both tired from all your travels."

"I think we're good." Rae follows him to the doorway. "You and Thom have a lovely place. Thanks so much." She smiles broadly as she watches him leave, and then turns to me. "Feel better? The kid we saw at Wakea Ranch must have been one of Naomi Yoon's boys. Nothing sinister."

"Yeah."

Rae gestures to my room. "Nice little place." She's not wrong. An airy yellow with green accents, the Bamboo Room possesses the same clean simplicity as the rest of Koa House. A pair of potted bamboo plants flank either side of the bed and elegant Japanese-style prints reveal David and Thom's good taste. "I love that we're next door to a cult," Rae says. "It adds a little, I don't know, ambiance."

If anyone else were to utter these words, they'd be heavily laced with sarcasm, but I know Rae. She probably *does* love being next door to a cult.

"It's not a cult anymore," I protest. "David said they disbanded, remember? Now it's just some eccentric family with a weird origin story."

"Super-religious with no electricity? That's a cult."

"Oh, come on. By that definition, the Amish are one big, giant cult."

"Well, duh," she says. "Didn't you ever see that show *Breaking Amish*? Point is, if you want followers to mindlessly obey you, electricity is the first thing to go. You have to keep people away from television and the Internet if you want to maintain authority."

She speaks like someone who has given a great deal of thought to best brainwashing practices.

"Congratulations," I say dryly. "I think you're ready for that dictatorship. Now can we talk about tomorrow? I'm supposed to meet Dr. Nakagawa at nine. Are you staying here or coming with?"

"Of course I'm coming! I want to get a peek at the volcanologist, don't I? Mr. Ironman? I bet he's fit." Rae gives me a loose hug and air-kisses my cheek. "Wake me up for breakfast if I'm still snoozing."

"I love you, Rae. Thanks for coming with me."

"Love you, too, Charlie-girl. Don't look so worried. We'll have a good time."

As I sit alone on the balcony, drinking in the immense sky, I can almost believe her. Here, on this remote island in the Pacific, I am safe from prying reporters, thousands of miles from anyone who might recognize me as that crackpot on the news. There is no laundry to be done, no meals to be made, no whining or sassy children requiring intervention. Just me, untethered from so many of the roles that have come to define me.

The night swells with the calls of amorous coquís. I think about my interview with Dr. Nakagawa tomorrow and wish I'd had more time to prep. Mentally, I review what I've learned in the last couple days about volcanology, run through the terms that will help me to speak Nakagawa's language. Somewhere between thermal plumes and harmonic tremors, my mind begins to drift. My eyelids grow heavy; my thoughts tangle in senseless strands.

And then I feel it. That insistent pull, both dangerous and familiar.

Not now. Not again.

Shades of night. Warm, dense forest. A teenage girl, alone in the woods.

I become someone else. Wear his eyes like a pair of sunglasses. Hear his thoughts, louder and more insistent than my own.

Crouched behind a shrub, I watch the girl. Rocking in her hammock. Signaling with her flashlight to someone who never comes. I watch her, like I have so many times before, and I want her. But this time is different. This time I don't fight my urges. This time I give in.

It's just us now, I say. *What are you going to do about it?*

You'll regret this, she tells me, and that's probably true. There will be consequences, but they don't matter in this moment. Only my need. Only the satisfaction of my desire.

When it all begins to fade, when I'm safe at Koa House again, there is nothing but relief. My eyes are no longer his, thank God. My thoughts are mine alone. I don't want to see what he saw, don't want to know what happens next. I can still feel the buttons of her shirt against my fingertips, still smell her baby-powder skin and the fragrance of her hair.

This was not supposed to happen. My time on this island was supposed to be a reprieve, not a disturbing reminder of my abilities. I hurry into the Bamboo Room, shaken. Who was that girl in the woods? What exactly have I seen, and why? Most importantly, whose gaze was I inhabiting? Someone who lurks in bushes, secretly watching young women in the dark. Someone who doesn't care who he hurts.

I remember the boy Rae and I saw prowling around earlier and draw my arms across my chest, suddenly cold.

I'm not an idiot. That tropical jungle-scape of my dream was not in Arizona. It waits for me here on the Big Island, a dark and ugly secret. I don't know what it means, not yet, but I know that it portends trouble.

Something happened to that girl, I think. *Something terrible.*

Rape? Kidnapping? Murder? She could've met any number of bad fates. I thought I'd faced the full power of human cruelty in my dreams, but what I saw tonight was different. It was his eyes, the way he forced me to look at her.

Maybe I can ignore it. The vision was so vague, after all—an Asian girl in a hammock, a tense encounter in the woods. No names, no words, no landmarks. I could let it go, tuck the dream into some forgotten corner of my mind, and just kick back. Hang with Rae, write my article on Dr. Nakagawa, and studiously ignore any mention of dead or missing girls, any hint of sexual assault. I could enjoy Hawai'i.

There's just one problem. My dreams are not always of things past. Sometimes they warn of what's coming. I spent an entire day wandering through Sabino Canyon because I knew there was a chance that Alex Rocío was alive, that he could still be saved. What about this girl? What if she's out there, too?

You're going to hurt a lot of people, she told the guy in the woods, and I'm afraid she's right. Can I let him do that? Can I really sit this one out, cause another family pain through my own inaction?

Not after losing a child. Not when I have two daughters of my own.

I sit on the edge of the bed and groan. This is not the "dream" vacation I had in mind when I came to Hawai'i, but what choice do I have? I know what I've got to do.

I need to find that girl.

monday

five

The smell seeps into my bedroom, smoky and alluring, but I don't want to get up, not even for bacon. Facing the day means confronting a host of issues I desperately prefer to avoid: a predatory guy, a girl in danger, and let's not even mention the whole psychic exposé that blew up my life last week. I did not sleep well.

When I finally haul my sorry ass downstairs, Rae's sipping coffee on the front porch. If I'm hollow eyed and disheveled, she's ready for her close-up, skin glowing and makeup expertly applied. A breeze catches the scent of a nearby tree in bloom and scatters a few white petals. I pour myself some coffee and plop into a chair as a green gecko skitters across the edge of the table.

"What's with you?" Rae asks, amused by the state of my hair.

Thom emerges from the house with a plate of muffins before I can answer. Today his T-shirt says, *Never trust an atom. They make up everything.* "Lemon poppy seed," he says, presenting the muffins with a flourish. "Fresh from the oven."

Rae grabs a muffin and taps the seat next to her, indicating Thom should join us. "Did you make these?" she asks before inhaling a mouthful.

He nods. "I bake, and David cooks. Helps me stay kosher."

"Oh yeah?" Rae washes down her muffin with a swig of coffee. "My husband's Jewish," she says, "but not kosher-level Jewish. He eats cheeseburgers. Did David convert for you?"

"Convert? No." Thom balks at the idea. "He's very committed to the culture he grew up with. Which I respect. I wouldn't be on this island if I didn't."

Rae licks a muffin crumb from her finger. "What did you guys do before opening Koa House?"

"I was a history teacher," David announces from the doorway, a tray of breakfast balanced in one hand. "Over at the Kamehameha school in Kea'au."

I detect a glimmer of pride when he speaks of his former job. "Is that a private school?"

David nods. "The Kamehameha schools are specifically for students with native Hawaiian ancestry. They were founded in the nineteenth century by Hawaiian royalty." He sets down his tray, which includes bacon and thick orange slices of papaya. "Part of their mission is to pass down Hawaiian cultural values to another generation."

"David's half Hawaiian himself," Thom says. "And a bit of a radical, too, sometimes, aren't you?" He gives his husband an affectionate pat.

"A radical?" David chuckles. "I wish I had the energy. In college, maybe; I was into the whole Hawaiian sovereignty movement. But it's been a while."

"It must be strange, operating a B & B here." Suddenly I'm aware of how ignorant Rae and I must appear. "All these outsiders parading through your house, your island, and we don't have a clue. I mean, I don't remember learning *anything* about Hawaiian history when I was in school."

"No, I'm sure you didn't," David says as he distributes plates. "The tourism industry sells you quite the happy picture of colonization, but these islands weren't all hula and surfing and lūʻaus. In the nineteenth century, the Hawaiian kingdom had one of the world's highest literacy rates. Today? Native Hawaiians are undereducated, over-incarcerated, and—" He stops himself. "Sorry. Once a teacher, always a teacher."

"Don't apologize," I say. "I want to learn. It sounds like you were really passionate about your work."

"David's still in denial about his early retirement," Thom says. "I guess that's the difference between a job and a calling. Me, I've never looked back. A few decades of teaching trigonometry, and I couldn't *wait* to leave the classroom."

"You were a teacher, too?" Rae asks, charmed.

Thom pushes his glasses back up the bridge of his nose. "Fifteen years in Oregon and another twelve over at the School for Free Thought."

I remember the sign last night over by Kanoa Drive. "The School for Free Thought—what is that, exactly?"

Thom laughs. "I know, I know. The name's a bit heavy-handed. Free Thought is a boarding school here in Kalo Valley. An ecological bent and cripplingly expensive tuition. The whole town pretty much built up around it. Honestly, half the guests we get at Koa House are Free Thought parents visiting their kids." He turns to Rae. "And what do *you* ladies do for a living?"

"I'm a sales rep for a chemical company." Rae makes a gagging noise. "Kill me now. Charlie, here, though, is a journalist. An author, too. She wrote a book about the kidnapping of Gabriel Deveau."

Thom's eyes light up. "I remember that case! I saw a TV special about it once. The little kid in Louisiana, right? Still unsolved? Wow, so you write true crime?"

"I write lots of things."

"Charlie's working on a big magazine piece right now," Rae says, as if letting the guys in on a scoop. "She's got an interview this morning."

Thom leans forward on his elbows, intrigued. "With who? Someone on the island?"

"Victor Nakagawa," I say. "Do you know him?"

"Victor! The Ironman himself!" David smiles as he arranges our silverware and napkins.

"Dr. Nakagawa is the one who recommended Koa House to me," I say, making moves on the papaya.

"Nice of him to support a local business," David says.

"Well . . ." Thom smirks. "He certainly seems to like this area. Victor makes it out here quite a bit."

"Really?" Rae asks. "Does he train out here?"

When Thom's smirk broadens, David gives him a warning look. "No, no," he says. "He's friends with our neighbor, that's all. He comes by to visit Naomi and her boys sometimes."

I have a million questions as to how Victor ended up friends with a cult woman, but David glosses over the subject. "So what are you writing, exactly, Charlotte?" He hits me with a bright smile. "Something about Victor?"

Thom scratches his bald head, his face now sober. "Must be Victor's daughter, right?"

I look up from my hunk of papaya. The juice runs down my hand, drips from my wrist onto the table in watery orange drops. "Why do you say that?"

"Oh. I just thought, you know, true crime . . ." Thom trails off uncomfortably and I see David shooting him daggers.

My mind races through all the articles and web pages I've seen about Victor Nakagawa in the past few days. Geology sites, triathlon finishing times and interviews, a talk about volcanic eruption preparedness. Was there something else buried in all those results, something I missed?

"What happened to Nakagawa's daughter?" The tips of my fingers have begun to buzz. I curl them into fists. It's her, I know it's her. The girl in the woods.

Across the table, Rae has stopped chewing. I can see her antennae going up now, too.

"Nothing happened," says David. "She ran away."

"Oh, come on," Thom protests. "You really buy that? Lise Nakagawa has been missing six weeks, David. Something happened to her."

"Nobody knows what happened," David returns. "A sixteen-year-old girl—she could be anywhere. Let's not get carried away with crazy theories that have no factual evidence, okay?" He gives Thom a strained smile. "You'll scare our guests."

Thom takes the not-so-subtle hint. "So what's your interest in Victor, then?" he asks me with forced cheer. "The whole Ironman thing?"

"Yeah, the Ironman thing." I clear my throat. "And his work with volcanoes. I write for *Outdoor Adventures* magazine. Our readers love physical challenges and exotic locales, so this story checks all the boxes." It takes every bit of self-control that I have to refrain from asking further questions about Nakagawa's daughter. David obviously wants to avoid the topic, but I make a mental note to catch Thom alone later.

I can't help but wonder about David's choice of words. *You'll scare our guests.* What exactly are these crazy theories about the Nakagawa girl that Thom harbors?

There's a story here, a much darker one than I bargained for. A missing girl, an obsessed guy—I didn't come to this island looking for trouble, yet that's precisely what I've found. One good thing, at any rate: tracking down the girl from my dream will be easier than I anticipated. I serve myself some bacon and munch slowly on the crispy tip.

Now I know her name. Now I know where to begin.

AFTER BREAKFAST, Rae follows me back to my room and corners me. "A missing teenager, huh?" she asks, one eyebrow raised to convey her skepticism. "And Dr. Nakagawa's daughter, no less. What are the chances?"

I know how this must look to her. Like I've dragged her out here in pursuit of some hot new case while lying to her about my motives. "Rae, I swear I had no idea."

"Right." She folds her arms against her chest. "You just happened to pick this Nakagawa guy for the subject of your article, and the fact that his daughter mysteriously vanished six weeks ago is a total coincidence."

"Yes! It is!" Even I can see how implausible that sounds.

"Don't insult my intelligence. If you wanted to hunt down this Lise Nakagawa girl, you should've just said." Her tone is acid. "I don't know why you brought me along at all if you're going to leave me in the dark about everything. What am I, some prop to justify the trip to Noah?"

"No!" I'm crushed that Rae could think so little of me. "I told you, I had to write this article, and I was coming up empty. I happened to mentioned to my editor that I was looking for a story in Hawai'i, and he suggested . . ." My face clouds over as I realize what's going on. "Isaac. This is Isaac's doing."

Ever since the story of Alex Rocío broke, the man has been trying to capitalize off my newfound celebrity, pushing me to do another book for Meyers Rowe.

"That son of a bitch." I grab my phone and furiously pull up his number. "He has some explaining to do."

Sensing this will turn into a fight, Rae plunks herself in a chair and kicks up her feet. Her anger has evaporated; now she wears an expression normally reserved for watching *Real Housewives*.

Isaac answers his phone on the second ring and does not seem the least bit surprised to hear from me. "Charlie! How's it going?" His barely repressed excitement confirms all my suspicions. "Did you meet Victor Nakagawa yet? Anything interesting happening?"

I don't mince words. "That was low, Isaac. Really low."

"You aren't getting on with Dr. Nakagawa, I take it?"

"You might've *mentioned* his missing daughter! That would've been really useful information to have. And here I thought you were actually trying to help me."

Isaac lets out a giggle, not at all dismayed to be caught out. "I *was* helping you," he says. "I was helping us both. What do you think? Can you dig up some new info on this girl? Will her father cooperate?"

"I haven't even met him yet! It's eight a.m.!"

"Oh right, time zones. Sorry, I'm in London now. My math's not good."

"I'm not writing you a book, Isaac," I growl. "There is no way. What were you thinking? Even if I wanted this, I'm only here for a week! What kind of sources could I possibly come up with in that amount of time?"

"Who said anything about sources?" Isaac scoffs. "As far I'm concerned, anything you learn about this girl is psychic insight sent to you from the great beyond." His flippant tone is infuriating. Isaac doesn't for a moment believe in my abilities—he just goes where the money is.

In spite of my irritation, I can't help but be impressed by his knack for sniffing out a story. "How did you even find this Nakagawa guy? Did you call up every major police station in the state of Hawai'i and ask them about their unsolved missing-children cases or what?"

"My assistant is looking to move up in the world," Isaac says, as if the raw ambition of his subordinates explains everything. "I gave her the parameters. Missing child, Hawai'i, an outdoorsy angle. At first, she gave me a missing six-year-old on O'ahu, but ten to one the pervy uncle was responsible; not much of a story. And then this turned up. I mean, a volcano guy? That's on the mark, am I right?"

"Yeah," I concede. "Except I came here to get away from missing children. I'm trying to have a vacation." I glance at Rae to make sure she's getting this, that she understands my innocence, but she's already engrossed in her phone. Evidently my tantrums are not over-the-top enough to maintain her interest.

"You are definitely still on vacation," Isaac says, taking a more conciliatory tone. "And I hope you have a wonderful time. Maybe you find this girl, and maybe you don't. If it doesn't work out, I get it.

But I figured, can't hurt to get you in the right place at the right time, can it?"

Wrong, I think. *On every level.*

"No book," I tell him. "I'm going to write a stirring article about volcanoes and triathlons, and that's it." I have no intention of telling him just how effective his plan was, that whether I like it or not—and I don't—I've already seen this missing girl. Something else occurs to me. "Does Dr. Nakagawa know about your little scheme? You didn't promise him anything, did you?" The last thing I want is to disappoint a desperate parent.

"I haven't said a word," Isaac promises. "You know me, I'm very low pressure. I like to let things unfold naturally."

I snort. This isn't the first time Isaac's played a dirty game.

Four years ago, he sent me to Louisiana to write a true crime book about a tragic kidnapping in a wealthy Southern dynasty; when I showed up at the family's sprawling estate, I was instructed to lie about the subject of my book to the family matriarch. I don't normally approve of subterfuge in journalism, but I'm glad Isaac didn't mention my abilities to Dr. Nakagawa.

"You are far too devious for me to keep up with." I sigh. "I need a new publisher."

"Now, that isn't fair," Isaac complains. "Who else would go to such lengths for you?"

He's right about that much. I may disapprove of Isaac's machinations, but they require an uncommon level of commitment. In the end, this one's on me. I should've known better than to accept his advice at face value. I should've exercised due diligence before galloping out here with Rae.

"Charlotte." Rae holds out her phone. "You're going to want to see this." She's pulled up an old article from the *Hawaii Tribune-Herald*, and though I can't make out the words, the headline is unmistakable: KALO VALLEY TEEN MISSING SINCE THURSDAY.

Even from a distance, the accompanying photo of the girl looks all too familiar.

I hang up as Isaac begins pitching a contract for another book and take the phone from Rae's outstretched hand. The small photo displayed is black and white, like the page of an old yearbook.

"This is her? Lise Nakagawa?"

She nods.

I enlarge the photo of the girl and study her face: the long black hair, the curve of her chin. The thin, delicate nose, the way her dark, thick eyebrows hang like marks of punctuation above her seemingly pupil-less eyes. Unmistakable, this face.

It's the girl in the hammock. The girl from my dream.

As I imagine the girl behind the picture, words like "serious" and "quiet" come to mind. According to the brief newspaper item, however, Lise is not the well-behaved child her photo would suggest. *Nakagawa is a junior at the School for Free Thought,* the *Tribune-Herald* notes, *where teachers describe her as "bright but troubled." Her mother, Suzumi Nakagawa, states that her daughter went missing once previously, but returned home forty-eight hours later. The sixteen-year-old was last seen by her boyfriend, who reported walking her home at approximately nine thirty on Wednesday evening. Her mother discovered her missing the following morning.*

I hunt for some mention of Victor, but his name doesn't appear anywhere in the article. That at least explains why Lise didn't surface in any of my search results for him.

"That article is dated early October." I stare at the pale wood floor and let out a deep breath. "Oh God, Rae. I'm so sorry to drag you into this."

"You've seen her, haven't you?" Rae murmurs. "You've dreamed about her."

"Last night. I didn't know what it meant."

Her eyes widen. "Is she okay?"

"I don't know."

Remembering that scene in the woods and the disturbing perspective thrust upon me makes my stomach hurt.

Who was watching Lise that night? Who was touching her hair, unbuttoning her shirt, inhaling her scent with such creepy intensity? Is it possible I witnessed the final moments of this girl's life in that vision? Or perhaps she's still alive, being held somewhere by her stalker. What the hell did Isaac get me into?

"There are a couple other articles," Rae tells me, rising from her seat. "More recent ones." She hits the back button on her browser, and a list of search results appears.

I click through them quickly.

In that first article, one can almost feel the boredom of the beat reporter. Another runaway teen; snooze. The possibility of foul play changes all that, however. Subsequent articles focus on the boyfriend, described only as "a fifteen-year-old juvenile."

According to police interviews, the boy admitted that Lise had broken up with him that night but denied any wrongdoing. Searches of his home turned up nothing. It is obvious from the progression of articles that law enforcement is gunning for this kid, and equally obvious that they don't have a single scrap of evidence to substantiate their suspicions.

"They're wrong, Rae." I return the phone to her. "It wasn't the boyfriend." I don't know whose eyes I was seeing through, whose ugly thoughts I took as my own, but it was someone on the outside. Someone who had seen her with her boyfriend and watched resentfully. Someone who waited, patiently, to get her alone.

"What exactly did you see?" Rae looks torn between fascination and alarm.

"She was in a hammock," I say slowly. "This guy was hiding in the woods, watching her. It was dark. I think she was waiting for someone—it looked like she was signaling with a flashlight—but they never showed up. And then the guy in the woods . . . he surprised her."

"Did he . . . hurt her?"

I shake my head. "I didn't see that part. But Lise knew him. She definitely knew who he was."

I let Rae absorb this for a few seconds. She tugs on one of her curls, twists it around her finger with a frown. "So . . . what do we do?"

In that moment, I love Rae more than anything. I am not alone in this. I am part of a *we*.

"Well," I say, "we can't go to the police. Even if they believed me, I don't have anything specific to give them. And we sure as hell don't tell Noah. He'd freak out if he thought I was up to something. He'd try to make me come home."

"Ditto for Mason." Rae shrugs. "So we don't tell them. It's Girls' Week, what do they expect? What happens on the island stays on the island."

"If we don't get involved, there's nothing to tell anyway." Part of me hopes that Rae will absolve me of all moral responsibility here.

"Oh, we're getting involved. Are you crazy? We can't let this go. What about Lise?"

"She could already be dead."

Rae's hands go to her hips. "Even if she is, that guy is still out there."

"We're only here a week," I protest. "And I'd be playing right into Isaac's hands. This is what he wants, for me to run around inserting myself into—"

"Charlie. This is bigger than your jerkwad editor."

I fall silent. Rae's right. I can't spend this week hiking through lava fields and strolling along black sand beaches, not now. As long as I am on this island, I am bound to Lise Nakagawa—and any other girls that stalker guy might go after. Only one course of action remains.

"We'd better leave."

Indignation floods Rae's face. "*What?* No! Are you seriously suggesting we leave the island? We just got here!"

"I'm seriously suggesting we keep our appointment with Dr. Nakagawa." I slip on my shoes and grab my bag. "You know. Lise's dad."

six

At eight forty-five a.m. there is no line whatsoever at the modest guard shacks that mark the entrance to Hawai'i Volcanoes National Park. Only a few people mill about; the visitor center hasn't opened yet. Somehow I expected more excitement, more bustle, but the innocuous brown sign seems more suggestive of summer camp than the fury of nature. The morning air is steeped in fog. As Rae drives deeper into the park, the eerie, swirling clouds move in ever thicker, concealing whatever geological marvels wait for us.

I'm not entirely clueless. I know the park houses two active volcanoes within its boundaries, that we are meeting Dr. Nakagawa by the summit of Kīlauea, the youngest of Hawai'i's five volcanoes. At one time, visitors could walk across its summit caldera, a two-mile-wide, four-hundred-foot-deep depression created when the ground collapsed into the magma chamber hundreds of years ago. In recent years, Kīlauea's activity has rendered that kind of tourist access inadvisable. Large portions of the park are now closed to the public. Victor Nakagawa is presumably one of the few who gets to breach those boundaries, but I'm still not sure I want a backstage pass to this show.

"It's kind of weird, isn't it?" I wonder aloud. "This Nakagawa guy agreeing to see me."

Rae's eyes remain on the foggy road. "Weird how?"

"How is the man even functioning? His daughter has been missing for more than a month. You'd think he'd be a basket case, wouldn't you? Seems like a strange time to be accepting interview requests. I mean, *I* couldn't do it."

There's a silence as Rae and I remember Keegan and the mess I became in the wake of my son's death, unable to perform my job or keep up with the most basic household duties.

"Maybe he's hiding in his work," Rae says. "A lot of people do that. And Lise is missing, not necessarily dead."

"I guess." But I'm not convinced. If anything, not knowing seems worse.

Per Dr. Nakagawa's instructions, we follow signs to the Jaggar Museum and park in the lot. Through the mist, I can make out the museum and the Hawaiian Volcano Observatory, which connects off to one side. The fog rises up from the ether, eddying around us in damp and ghostly tendrils. It has a faint smell, I realize. Not unpleasant, just vaguely mineral.

"Vog." Rae puts her hand up to the milky white air as if to grasp it, and I feel stupid I didn't realize it sooner. This is no ordinary mist but volcanic fog, clouds of sulfur dioxide and water vapor that mark our arrival at the legendary home of the volcano goddess, Pele. Usually the trade winds sweep the vog away—the breeze must be blowing the wrong way today.

"We're a little early," I tell Rae. "I guess we'll just hang out a bit."

We approach the scenic viewing station, where a handful of tourists peer out into the murky terrain. Not much to see with such poor visibility—I can't make out the caldera or the infamous Halemaʻumaʻu crater within it—but I sense the gaping space before us. I remove the camera from my backpack and snap a few pictures. At this elevation, the morning is a chilly one, and I'm glad I have my sweatshirt. After a few minutes, the vog starts to disperse, revealing dark patches of land that stretch out to the horizon. The white wisps recede with surprising speed. Within ten minutes, the vog has all but disappeared from the parking lot and the viewing area, leaving us with an unobstructed view of the caldera and its crater.

"Beautiful," Rae breathes, but I find it unsettling, the precipitous drop, the wasteland of hard black rock below. From the mouth of the Halemaʻumaʻu crater, a plume of smoke rises up. Like soup in an enormous iron pot, the earth is bubbling before us.

"Charlotte Cates?"

I whirl around, startled to hear my name, and find myself face-to-face with a lean yet muscular Asian man who is more than a little attractive. "Oh! Dr. Nakagawa."

"Call me Victor."

One look at Victor Nakagawa, and I know Rae must be glad she came. With his rugged face and runner's build, the man is like a mail-order cover model for *Outdoor Adventures.* He has a sharp but well-proportioned nose, serious eyes, and no wedding ring. Though not all men can pull off facial hair, Dr. Nakagawa has nailed the scruff quotient to achieve maximum sexy. In jeans and a long-sleeved plaid shirt, he looks ready to rumble, fully prepared to navigate molten lava while operating expensive seismographic equipment.

He does not look like a worried father.

"Victor." I mask my questions with a smile. "So great to meet you. This is my friend Rae."

Normally, I'd move in for a handshake, but Victor's arms remain folded across his chest. He acknowledges Rae with a solemn nod, the corner of his mouth and eye twitching upward in a brief facial tic.

"You look just like your photos," he tells me.

"Photos?"

"You're all over the Internet," he says. "That boy in the desert."

"Oh, God. You saw that."

"Of course. When you contacted me about the piece for *Outdoor Adventures*, I looked into you." His tone reveals nothing about the conclusions he drew, but I can imagine. This is a man who demands hard data and peer review. I must look like an incredible flake.

"I'm surprised you agreed to meet after reading all that nonsense," I say.

"Well, I read a number of your articles." His gaze travels over me, as if he's searching for signs of quackery. "They were thoughtful, well researched. Frankly, I was intrigued. How could a seemingly intelligent journalist like yourself turn around and make such a patently absurd claim to psychic abilities?"

Rae sees me bristle and touches my back, a gentle reminder to stay calm.

I lean against the overlook railing. The caldera yawns behind me, an expanse of nothingness that ends in rock. "I hope you didn't let a bunch of Internet rumors color your opinion of me, Victor. For the record, I'm not out there claiming to have mystical powers. If you've been reading these stories closely, you'll notice I haven't spoken to any of these news outlets."

"Some people might mistake your silence for approval," Victor observes.

I force a laugh. "Some people might, but not you. I'm sure we're on the same page when I say the reporting on the Alex Rocío incident has been . . ." I struggle to find a word that's not an outright lie. "Irresponsible," I conclude.

Victor smiles, pleased with himself. "I did suspect the whole psychic angle was a media fabrication to attract readers. How *did* you find that boy? Some source you couldn't name?"

"A source, yes. I had a very reliable source, which is more than I can say for publications like the *Squealer*." I don't feel overly guilty about misleading him. The man seems unnecessarily harsh, mocking my methods for finding missing children when he has a missing child of his own. "Can't do much about the tabloids, can you? I ignore the stories and stick to my job."

Rae gives me side-eye, but my answer seems to satisfy Victor.

"Of course," he says. "Personally, I maintain a healthy skepticism of the media, but you have to admit, they know their audience. The average person seems to prefer wild conjecture to thoroughly vetted facts." His disdain for the "average person" reads loud and clear. I bet he reads Richard Dawkins and laughs conspiratorially at Bill Maher. "I enjoyed your articles, anyway," Victor continues. "The one about the survivalist who developed an immunity to scorpion stings—very insightful. The parallels drawn to the vaccination process raise some intriguing questions."

His compliment temporarily disarms me. "Yes! Thank you." I spent several weeks working on the story about Tucson's self-proclaimed Scorpion King, a man who injected himself with trace amounts of venom for years. Victor might be obnoxious, but his approval is still gratifying.

"You're sure you want to write an article about me?" he asks. "Usually people's eyes glaze over when I talk about my work or training. And I'm afraid I can't drive up your readership with claims of clairvoyance."

I ignore his smirk. "It's not your job to be interesting, it's mine. I have so much respect for your work and athletic achievements—really, I'm just excited to see you in action."

"Me, too," Rae says with such feeling that I nudge her with my foot.

He glances at her with mistrust, as if she might be making fun of him. "Well, I'm happy to show you around and answer any questions you might have."

"Can't wait," Rae tells him. "And thanks for recommending Koa House. We love it. David and Thom have been so welcoming. Do you know them well?"

Victor shrugs. "I see them around town. They live in a pretty area. I have a friend out that way. Good bird-watching."

I nod and smile as if I'm a bird-watching enthusiast, but the casual mention of his "friend" doesn't escape me. Thom did say Victor spent a fair bit of time visiting Naomi Yoon. Could Victor be *dating* her? Or is their relationship more innocent? He's a good-looking man, but I'm also getting a strong geek vibe. I could buy him having bird-watching buddies.

"Charlie and I have just been admiring the vog this morning." Rae gestures to the empty air around us. "Is this normal? For it to move in and out so fast?"

"It's not *abnormal*. It all depends on the wind." Victor begins to walk abruptly away from us. "Come on. I'll show you the observatory." We leave the tourists by their protective railing and pass the Jaggar Museum.

Rae pauses in front of the HVO building, taking in another stunning view of the caldera. "Quite the place to work, Victor," she says, and we all stare at the smoking crater for a second until I come to my senses and break out my camera.

"Do you mind if I get a few pictures?"

Victor flushes. "Of me? For your magazine? Sure."

I attempt to make chitchat while he poses stiffly. "Do you ever train in the park? It looks like there are trails you could run or bike."

"I try to keep my work and training separate." Victor doesn't crack a smile for any of the photos I'm taking, but I don't mind. Stoic looks good on him.

"Quite the time commitment, isn't it?" I ask. "Your family must never see you."

"It's not a problem," Victor says. "My wife stays busy, and my teenagers aren't looking to spend more time with me."

So he does have a wife, I think, revising my earlier guess about his relationship with Naomi. Maybe the absence of a wedding ring is just a practical choice. At any rate, the mention of his children gives me my first entry point to discuss his daughter.

"You've got teenagers, huh? How many?" Might as well play dumb and see what he offers of his own accord.

"Two girls." Victor pauses before grudgingly offering up their names. "Jocelyn and Lise."

"Pretty." I get one more picture and slip the camera back into its case, done playing photographer for the time being. "Are those family names?"

"No," Victor replies. "My daughters were named for physicists. Jocelyn Bell Burnell and Lise Meitner."

"Burnell . . ." Rae sifts briefly through her memory bank and snaps her fingers when she gets a hit. "Radio pulsars, right? She's the one who discovered them."

Victor nods. "As a graduate student, yes."

I toss Rae a sidelong grin. With her fashionable clothes and obsession with celebrity gossip, it's easy to forget my bestie is also a whip-smart nerd. I myself have zero idea what radio pulsars are, much less knowledge of their discovery.

"Burnell should've won the Nobel Prize," Rae informs me. "But it went to the men she worked with that year instead. Same deal with Meitner."

For the first time, I see a hint of appreciation on Victor's face. He likes Rae. "Lise Meitner helped to discover nuclear fission in uranium," he adds for my benefit. "Her male collaborator received the Nobel that year. It was 1944, and she was both a woman and an Austrian Jew. Amazing she achieved what she did, with so many factors working against her."

I'm already scribbling these tidbits down in my notebook. "So, naming your daughters for women overlooked by the scientific world . . . would you say you're a feminist?"

He brushes off the question. "My wife chose their names."

"Ah. What does your wife do?"

"She's a professor in UH-Hilo's department of astronomy and physics."

Jesus, I think. If Lise Nakagawa is anything like her overachieving parents, she must be quite the brainiac. Or *was* quite the brainiac, until the guy in the woods got his hands on her. I don't know what tense to use when thinking of her. Don't know if she has a future to live or nothing but a terrible past to unravel.

"Sounds like your daughters have big shoes to fill," I tell Victor.

"Jocelyn's up to the task." He turns his back on me, begins walking briskly toward the HVO building. Lise's name does not leave his lips.

FOR A FIELD that studies the creation of the Earth and the destructive powers of nature, volcanology looks surprisingly mundane in practice. The observatory lobby is as white and clean as a hospital, with gleaming tiled floors and glaring fluorescent overheads. My eyes are drawn to a jumble of monitors set up in one corner—eight on the wall and six on the desk—that depict various graphs and seismic readings as well as live video of the Halemaʻumaʻu crater. I take several pictures of Victor studying the monitors. *Outdoor Adventures* will eat it up. If I crop out the rest of the lobby, there's a hint of Hollywood situation room in all those screens that will play well with readers.

The remainder of the floor, however, boasts little in the way of drama. Most of the scientists at the Hawaiian Volcano Observatory are physical volcanologists, attempting to learn about how and where eruptions are likely to occur. They collect samples and map the volcano's rock formations, Victor explains, hoping to uncover information about its history. Whatever exciting fieldwork transpires outside the observatory, inside it's all business. People staring at computer screens, gazing at topographical models or charts tracking changes in chemical composition.

Victor leads us from office to office, pointing out a handful of scientists whose names and specialties I jot down for future reference.

Everyone we meet is cordial and happy to talk volcanoes. They joke about Victor's becoming a celebrity or good-naturedly razz him, which he handles with that odd stiffness.

None of the other scientists strike me as terrifically athletic. When I ask about their hobbies, I get answers like reading, knitting, and playing guitar. One woman mentions an interest in hiking and kayaking, but Victor and his Ironman accomplishments are a clear anomaly amongst his peers.

"It must be a lot of training," a coworker remarks, solidifying my impression that despite two decades at the observatory, his coworkers scarcely know him. And it's not hard to see why.

Although Victor has much to say on the subject of his work, he clams up whenever I steer the conversation to his personal life. His office contains a framed picture of flowing magma but not a single photograph of his family. And he hasn't asked any questions of Rae and me, made any attempt to be conversational. I'm beginning to suspect the man's social skills are rather limited. Not good news for my article.

Nevertheless, Rae and I pry facts from him one by one. He was raised in California and came to the Big Island in the midnineties. His mother is dead and his father lives in Japan, but they aren't in touch. He met his wife, Suzumi, through a work acquaintance.

"What first attracted you to Suzumi?" I ask.

"We had an interesting conversation about telescopes," he replies.

I want to bang my head against the wall.

How am I supposed to write an article about a man who makes a habit of not discussing himself? How am I supposed to help his daughter and heal his family if he never reveals his pain?

The only visible emotion he displays comes when a young woman accosts him in his office with a thin manila folder.

"It's not a good time, Jessica," Victor mutters.

"I'm sorry." Her tense smile only barely manages to stay civil. "I need you to sign my internship papers. I can't get university credit if you don't sign off."

He waves a dismissive hand. "Put them on my desk."

"They've been on your desk for a week. I sent you email copies as well." Jessica thrusts the folder at him. "Can you sign them now, please? It's a few signatures. It'll take five minutes."

Victor stares down at the folder in her hand, the corner of his mouth and eye twitching in that distinctive facial tic. "I have visitors now."

"Oh no, go ahead," I urge. "We're in no hurry."

He hesitates for a moment, searching for an excuse. Finding none, he snatches the girl's folder away and begins signing papers. Jessica waits, her resentment palpable, and eventually collects her materials.

"Finally," she says, and leaves without a thank-you.

Rae watches her go with raised eyebrows. "So. That's your intern?"

He grimaces. "Her father works at the university with my wife. I took her on as a favor. What a nightmare. She needs constant supervision. Any time I want something done, I have to train her. It takes so much longer than just doing it myself."

"That's frustrating," I say, although I fail to see how it's unreasonable for an intern to expect training.

I take dutiful notes when he launches into a detailed explanation of the equipment he uses, but I just can't match Rae's enthusiasm for geological minutiae. What kind of person does not possess a single photo of his wife or kids at work? My gaze drifts toward his office door, seeking escape. After several arduous minutes, I spot Jessica heading into the ladies' room across the hall. It's a chance I can't miss.

"Would you excuse me a second, Victor? I need to use the restroom."

By the time Jessica emerges from her stall, I'm innocently washing my hands. "Oh, hey." Cue my sympathetic One of the Sisterhood face. "Did you get your internship papers sorted out?"

"We'll see." She squirts an excess of soap into her palm. "If Victor gives my adviser another crappy report, they could still withhold my credits."

"I'm sorry. Sounds like he's not used to supervising people."

She rinses the bubbles from her hands and grabs a paper towel. "You're a journalist, right? You're writing some article about him?"

I give a rueful laugh. "Well, I'm trying to write an article. It's a little challenging finding my angle. Victor isn't really . . . communicative. Not about himself, anyway."

"That's an understatement. I'm pretty sure the guy has Asperger's or something." She sighs. "He's really good at his job, don't get me wrong. I just wish someone else had stepped up to be my supervisor. You've probably noticed, people are not Victor's forte."

"I guess he's had a lot on his mind lately," I say. "I heard his daughter went missing."

Jessica softens. "I know. I've been trying to cut him some slack, I really have. It's not like the guy doesn't have feelings. But I really need these credits."

"You think they'll find her?"

"Not alive." Jessica has dispensed with all her business in the bathroom, but she doesn't leave. She leans against the sink, only too happy to linger now that she has my ear. "If Victor wants to tell himself she just ran away, then fine. Whatever lets him sleep at night. But that's wishful thinking."

"Why do you say that?"

"You don't know the story?"

I shake my head. "Just what was in the papers."

"It's pretty cut-and-dried. Lise met up with her boyfriend, Elijah, in the square one night. He admits she broke up with him but says he walked her home. Nice story, except no one ever saw her make it into her house. She hasn't been seen since."

"You think Elijah killed her." I file his name away; the papers didn't use it, since he's underage.

"*Everyone* thinks Elijah killed her. He was the last person to see her. Look, I live in Kalo Valley, where all this went down. And that Elijah kid is weird. I've seen his older brother around, and he's weird, too. The whole family is just off."

"It's an open investigation, isn't it? If he did it, they could still find something to prove it."

"No body, no blood. Right now they have no case." She speaks with the confidence of someone who has watched her share of *Law and Order* reruns. "The police can't prove Lise didn't just run away. He's gonna get away with it."

"That's gotta be tearing Victor up inside."

"Nope. Victor's in total denial. He bought the whole runaway story hook, line, and sinker, doesn't think Elijah had anything to do with it. But of course he wouldn't, given Elijah's mother. It's a lot more convenient for him to think—" She stops, turning ashen as she finally realizes who she's talking to. "Wait, you won't put me in your article, will you? I mean, you won't use my name?"

"No, no," I reassure her. "I'm not here to write about Victor's personal problems. Just morbidly curious."

"Right. Sure." She smiles, cautious now, and edges toward the
bathroom door.

I try to reel her back in. "You said Victor knows Elijah's mother?"

Hesitation, followed by an uneasy laugh. "He's known her for
years. They're . . . close." She sees my questioning look and explains.
"Kalo Valley is a small town. You hear things."

"Victor's married, isn't he?"

"Sure is."

"So maybe these are just rumors?"

Jessica gives me a pitying look. "Naomi's a nice-looking woman,
her husband's been dead for ages, and Victor goes over to her place on
the regular to 'help out.'" She finger-quotes the words "help out," lest
I mistake Victor's visits for actual helping. "You fill in the blanks."

"Naomi . . ." A chill runs up my spine as I repeat the woman's
name. "You mean Naomi Yoon?"

"Yep. That's Elijah's mom."

I remember what Victor said earlier, that he had a friend who lived
out by Koa House.

Is Jessica right? Is Naomi Yoon really his mistress? Rae is going to
love this.

"So, if I have this straight, Victor and his daughter Lise were both
involved with members of the Yoon family. That's a little . . ."

"Gross?" Jessica supplies. "Yeah, no kidding. But you can see why
Victor refuses to believe Elijah Yoon killed his daughter. It would put
him at serious odds with his lady." She moves to the door, done with
our little gossip session. "Good luck with your article. I don't know

how much you'll get out of Victor, but no one can say that man lacks stories."

Alone in the bathroom, I stare at my reflection in the mirror. My dark hair is puffing out in the humidity; my green eyes have that glazed, glassy look I get when I'm thinking hard. Isaac's cunning plot to land me smack-dab in the middle of another missing-child case has been more successful than he ever could have imagined: I am literally living next door to Lise's suspected killer.

A coincidence, or cosmic opportunity? Does it matter?

For the next six days, I am uniquely positioned to figure out what happened to Victor's daughter. Whether he wants me to or not.

seven

After a couple of hours of following Victor around the Hawaiian Volcano Observatory, I'm getting impatient. On another day, perhaps I'd be as enthralled as Rae by the file cabinets of seismographic reels, the boxes of lava samples, the panoramic view from the observatory tower. Today, however, it all seems beside the point. Victor is hiding behind science, speaking in that condescending tone about geological history when what I really want to know about is the man himself, his family, his child.

"I'd love to get more outdoor photos for the magazine," I tell him, trying not to fidget. "Any chance we could accompany you on some fieldwork today?"

"Fieldwork?" He looks taken aback. "I'm primarily working on a computer model right now, I don't see how . . ."

"Please," I beg. "I want *Outdoor Adventures* to run this story. Great photos sell magazines."

Victor thinks this over. Whatever failings he has in the emotional intelligence department, he's become rather invested in my profile of him. Being the subject of a feature article appeals to his ego. "I suppose I could take you out to see the park," he says. "Have you seen the steam vents yet? Or the Thurston Lava Tube?"

Rae shakes her head.

"Come on, then. We'll get the photos you need. We don't want your editor canceling the whole thing."

Rae and I exchange amused glances. This man likes attention.

Outside, the sun has come out and the vog has all but vanished. Victor slips into the passenger seat of our rental and directs Rae down Crater Rim Drive to the lava tube. Unlike the scrubby, rocky land around the HVO, the lava tube is situated in a full-on rain forest. Everything seems coated in green, be it moss or leaves or twisted vines. Tree ferns rise up from the dark earth, tall as a house. The air feels heavy in my lungs as Victor explains what, precisely, a lava tube is: the underground tunnel that magma travels through. This particular tube was emptied of magma hundreds of years ago, he says, but its stability and size—twenty feet high in some areas—makes it quite the tourist trap.

Although the gaping entrance is draped in greenery, the inside is all rock, with dripping walls and a dim, puddly path. The lighting gives everything a strange yellow hue. I get several photographs of Victor, who seems to enjoy posing in a space once occupied by two-thousand-degree magma. And the camera loves him. If he reads as peculiar in person, his face and bearing communicate depth, intelligence, and mystery in photographs. I still have a shot at making the cover.

On our way back to the HVO, we stop at the steam vents. No rain forest here, just gashes in the craggy land that release warm plumes of steam. I stand at the edge of one such crevice, letting the moisture gather on my face, inhaling its earthy odor.

"Feels kind of like a facial, huh?" Rae jokes. "You could stick your face down there and open all your pores."

"A park ranger tried something like that once," Victor says. "It didn't end well."

"What happened?"

"She lost her footing and fell about twenty feet down. It was too muddy to climb back out. When they found her the next day, her body had essentially been cooked."

I withdraw from the edge of the crevice. "It doesn't feel that hot."

"Twenty feet down? It's hot." He steps onto the concrete path. "Come on. I'll show you my favorite place."

Victor leads us down a trail that runs parallel to the rim's edge. There are no railings out here, nothing to prevent people from plunging four hundred feet off the side except common sense, and the shrubs are tall and thick enough in places that the line between land and air isn't entirely obvious. I stop when I see a delicate purple blossom quivering alongside the path.

"Is that a wild orchid?" Even my plant-loving fiancé has probably never seen one of these.

Victor nods. "They survive off the moisture from the steam vents." But he has more on his mind than the park's horticultural wonders. He leaves the footpath and begins winding through gaps in the grass and shrubbery, a clear destination in mind.

A few minutes later, I see what he's after. Just inches from the perilous caldera cliff, two large stones are embedded in the dirt, each dipping in the center to form a natural seat. Victor settles himself in one, cross-legged, his knees jutting out into space.

Rae takes the rock beside him, terror and delight playing across her face in equal measure as she surveys the vertical drop before her.

Something shifts inside me. I feel my hands buzzing, my spine tingling as I move closer.

"Best view in the park." Victor gazes out at some distant point deep in the caldera. "I used to take my daughters here. This was our special spot."

It's the most intimate thing he's shared today, and yet I scarcely register his words. My body has turned hard and leaden. The buzzing in my hands rises to a stinging crescendo. For a few terrible seconds, my vision blinks out and there is nothing, nothing but a chilly breeze and the sudden pressure of two hands on my back, fingertips pressing, pushing, urging me toward the edge. *Fall*, they tell me. *Fall.* I scramble backward, adrenaline surging as my sight returns.

"Did someone die here?" My question is a blight upon the peaceful scene, terse and ugly, but I need to know the answer.

Victor glances over his shoulder at me. "No deaths here that I know of. We don't get many fatalities in the park, just the occasional idiot chasing lava into dangerous places. The ranger that died, that was an unusual exception." He hesitates, as if worried that he's being too boring. "There are stories, of course, if you think your readers would be interested. I've heard there was a lover's leap into the crater back in the 1930s, some mixed-race couple that couldn't be together. And in the sixties, a man rappelled—"

"It would've been a child," I cut in. "A teenager, maybe. Someone young."

"No deaths at this spot since I've been working in the park," Victor says matter-of-factly. "If someone fell, we'd know it. The results would be hard to miss."

My stomach lurches at the picture that conjures up. I try to shake it off. I must be picking up traces of something very old, something that predates park records. Or I could be sensing an event that hasn't happened yet.

"This place is dangerous," I murmur. "Don't bring your girls here, Victor. Someone could get hurt."

He prickles at the unsolicited parenting advice, but I don't care. I hurry back toward the path, anxious to escape the sensation of someone looming behind me, the feeling of fingertips guiding me suddenly over the edge.

BACK AT THE PARKING LOT, Rae and I try to make a graceful exit while Victor attempts to further engage us with fun science facts. He shows us bits of pumice and tells us of a volcanic explosion in 1790 that killed some four hundred people.

"The records say about eighty," he says, "but the actual number was much higher. The Hawaiians only tallied the lives of their soldiers. Women, children, and others who perished weren't counted. I can show you their footprints, if you like. They're preserved in ash outside the HVO."

I politely decline, not in the mood for visions of terrorized children assailed by burning rocks. "We should probably be on our way," I say. "But I'll be in touch. Also, do you know any good resources for Hawaiian volcano mythology? It might be nice to offset all the science with some ancient legends." Anything to jazz up an article that could devolve into quite the snooze fest.

"I'll send you a link to some archives online," Victor promises me. "They have the best collection of ancient Hawaiian chants that I've found."

"You read Hawaiian myths?" It hardly seems in keeping with his precise, fact-based nature.

"Of course," he says. "You're aware of the myths surrounding this caldera, aren't you?"

"I know the summit of Kīlauea is supposed to be the home of Pele, but that's it."

Victor clears his throat, pleased to have my attention a little longer. "So, according to the ancient Hawaiians, Pele, the volcano goddess, was looking for a home. She traveled island by island, searching for a place to spread her fire." He pauses, relishing his role as storyteller. "On the island of Kaua'i, she met a man named Lohi'au, and they had a passionate affair. But Kaua'i wasn't quite the right home for Pele, so she promised the man that she would send for him later and continued on her way."

"Thatta girl, Pele." Rae grins. "Love 'em and leave 'em."

Victor ignores her. "Eventually Pele settled here, at the summit of Kīlauea. She asked her little sister, Hi'iaka, to bring her lover home. Hi'iaka agreed, but only if Pele would take care of her lehua forest while she was gone."

"What's lehua?" I ask, furiously taking notes.

"An indigenous tree." Victor pivots slightly on the pavement, his gaze now fixed on the smoking crater in the distance. "Pele gave her sister forty days to retrieve Lohi'au. Well, long story short, Hi'iaka found him, but it was a difficult journey, and she didn't get him back in the allotted time. Pele was not happy."

"Uh-oh," says Rae. "I don't think I'd like her when she's angry."

"No," Victor agrees. "When Hi'iaka finally returned to deliver the man, she discovered that Pele had destroyed her lehua forest. Hi'iaka was furious. And so in revenge, she brought Lohi'au here, to Pele's crater. And here, in full view of Pele, she took him as her lover." Victor's ears pinken slightly as he relates this development.

"Nice to have powerful women fighting over an incidental guy, instead of vice versa," I remark. "I'm guessing that stealing Pele's man didn't go over well?"

"Pele was not pleased," Victor confirms. "She killed Lohiʻau and buried him here. Hiʻiaka was devastated. She went digging for his body. She dug, dug, dug, and then she had to stop. She knew that if she dug too deep, she would reach the water that put out Pele's fires, and that would destroy her sister."

Rae crosses her arms. "That's it? Hiʻiaka just decided to be the bigger person and move on?"

"There's a happy ending, I think," Victor says. "Hiʻiaka and Lohiʻau remained together in spirit. Or something like that." He coughs. "Anyway, that's the story of this caldera. It was formed by Hiʻiaka's digging."

"Not the explanation I expected to hear from a geologist," Rae says with a laugh.

Victor bristles as if she's mocking him. "It's a very important story for a geologist," he says. "For years, geologists thought the caldera was formed by the explosive event in 1790. But we had it wrong. If we'd studied the old Hawaiian chants, we would've known the caldera predates 1790. Today, the geological evidence bears that out." He frowns at Rae. "Oral traditions can tell us a lot about the natural environment. Hiʻiaka's decision to stop digging—that means ancient Hawaiians understood about the water table."

"They understood about sisters, too," I say. "I have two daughters, and there are days when Micky would definitely burn down her sister's lehua forest."

"For the record, I'm with Pele on that one," Rae announces. "She gave her sister a clear deadline. Why is it so hard for some people to be punctual?"

Once again, I attempt to separate from Victor. I thank him for his time and suggest we meet again later in the week. "Maybe outside of your work hours," I say, "so we can discuss your training and your family in a little more depth."

Victor's eyes move from me to Rae and back again, unwilling to let us leave. He likes being in the company of women who hang on his every word. That will work to our advantage.

"You could come for dinner," he says. "Sue and I don't have a lot of guests, but . . . she wouldn't mind." His mouth and eye tic upward. "You could come tonight. At seven o' clock. I'll email you directions."

"Tonight?" The sudden invitation startles me, but Rae doesn't miss a beat. I suspect she's been waiting all morning for this.

"Tonight would be great, Victor," she says, beaming. "Thank you so much."

Back in the car, Rae and I compare notes.

"What a weirdo." I turn the key in the ignition. "I can't believe I have to write about this guy. He's all blah, blah, blah, science, triathlons, and the moment you ask him about his personal life, he turns into a brick wall. Did you see how rude he was to that intern? And his poor wife and kids. He sounds like a totally uninvolved father."

"I don't know." Rae snaps her seat belt into place. "He's almost like this big, brilliant kid. I don't think he means to be a blowhard, he just gets kind of carried away with his own ideas. When you were in the bathroom, he started telling me about the creation of landmasses on Earth—it was like poetry, no joke."

"Oh God, was he seriously wooing you with geology?"

"No . . . he's just really into what he does. I respect that."

"Hmm. Not sure what Mason would think of that. I better keep an eye on ol' Victor." I'm only half kidding, given what Jessica told me earlier about Victor and Naomi Yoon. If Victor has no regard for his marriage vows, who's to say he wouldn't pursue Rae? Not that I'm placing all my faith in a bit of tantalizing intern gossip. I struggle to imagine Victor, with his dearth of social skills, navigating a romantic relationship with one woman, let alone two.

Rae shrugs off the suggestion that she might find Victor attractive. "Mason's got nothing to worry about unless Channing Tatum comes knocking on my door. I mean, Victor's good-looking and all, but . . ."

I pull out onto Crater Rim Drive and head toward the park exit. "He's not just good-looking, Rae. The man's crazy smart."

"Yeah, but he's a Darcy. Too intense and brooding. I like a man with a sense of humor." She peels off her jacket and throws it into the backseat. "I noticed you were in the bathroom for quite a while there. How'd that work out for you?"

I break into a large smile. Rae misses nothing. "As a matter of fact, I had an interesting conversation with Victor's disgruntled intern. You'll never guess who the guy's supposedly been knocking boots with."

"Not Annie the geochemist, I hope."

"No one from the HVO. This is even juicier." I pause dramatically before delivering the news I know Rae will appreciate. "Naomi Yoon."

Sure enough, her jaw drops. "Cult Lady? Our neighbor?"

"Yup. Naomi Yoon and Victor. Supposedly they're a thing."

"Best. Vacation. Ever." Rae thumps the dashboard with her hand. "So we're going over there, right? We have to meet her. You can interview her or something, can't you?"

"Nah, we can't just show up at his mistress's house unannounced. Anyway, it's a little more complicated than that." I tell her about Elijah Yoon and his relationship with Victor's daughter.

"So let me get this straight," she says. "Cult Mom spawned some sick little dude who killed Victor's daughter, and this creeper lives right next door to Koa House on that spooky ranch without electricity? Charlie, this cannot be happening. I mean, did we really just land in the middle of Hawaiian *Murder, She Wrote*?" She sounds delighted at the prospect. "Oh my God, that boy we saw lurking around in the trees last night—you think that's him? Lise's boyfriend?"

"Maybe. David said that Naomi has three sons. Who knows how many Yoon boys prowl the woods at night." We've reached the park exit. I give the ranger a distracted wave and turn onto Highway 11. I try to focus on the road, but it's hard when my mind is bubbling over with unseemly possibilities.

"You said before that you don't think it was the boyfriend," Rae says. "But the dream you had about some strange guy hiding in dark woods . . . that would fit with Elijah Yoon."

"I don't think so." I bite my lip. "It's hard to explain, but I got the feeling this guy had been watching her awhile. That he'd seen Lise with her boyfriend and resented it."

"How do they work, these dreams? You never really said." Rae leans back in her seat and waits, as if I might deliver a clear and concise answer to a question I've spent years wrestling with.

"I don't know. It's not like there are rules." I squirm in my seat, embarrassed to discuss my abilities with her. "How is it you even believe in this stuff? You have a science background."

She makes a disapproving click with her tongue. "Are you implying that if science can't explain something, it isn't real? Because, breaking news, DNA existed long before Watson and Crick. Gravity worked before Newton. The Earth was orbiting the sun before Gal—"

I throw up my hands. "Yeah, okay, I get it."

"My point is that science always begins with a series of unanswerable questions. We shouldn't be afraid of the things we can't understand. We should be drawn to them." She takes a stick of gum from her purse and pops it into her mouth. "Now back to these dreams of yours. How do they operate?"

"Right. Um . . ." I run through what I know, which isn't much. "Places can trigger them, or objects. And they aren't always dreams." I watch the tree-lined road. "Sometimes I get impressions of things while awake. Things that happened. Things that are going to happen." *Like that feeling of being pushed into the caldera*, I think with a shudder.

"So you see stuff?"

"It changes." I'm aware of how infuriatingly vague I must sound. "Sometimes . . . well, it's like a connection I form. I see what they see. Hear their thoughts, feel their feelings." I swallow. "The dream about Lise was like that."

"You dreamed you were Lise?"

"Not Lise. Someone else. That dream was . . . different."

"Different how?"

"It's always been kids, Rae. Kids and teenagers, dead or in danger. When I make a connection, I become the victim. That's the way it's always worked."

Rae hugs herself as if she doesn't like what's coming. "And this time?"

"This time . . ." My stomach clenches into a knot as I remember his hungry gaze, the way he undid the buttons of her shirt one by one, slow and purposeful. "This time I think I was the bad guy."

eight

By the time we make it back to Kalo Valley, Rae and I are starving. Figuring the village must have something in the way of food, we follow Kanoa Drive to the center of town. There we discover a charming public square reminiscent of small-town Vermont, only with a tropical flair. The trees and flowering shrubs in its center seem poised to escape, tendrils creeping over the edges of their container, and judging from the crooked angle of the cement blocks, the roots will have their way eventually. It's strange to go from the desert, where growth is so painstaking, so efficient, to this florid island with all its wild excesses.

At half past two, the area teems not just with plants but with teenagers. School must have let out. Clusters of students lounge on benches, and pert girls in sundresses and shaggy-haired boys in flip-flops slouch around the flowering trees. For a few seconds I wonder which of the local businesses might be attracting this crew, but then I spot the handful of buildings across the street, note the sign at the entryway.

"So that's the School for Free Thought?" Rae asks. "Thom said it was a ritzy boarding school. That doesn't look like the kind of place rich people hang out."

"Well, it's an eco-school," I remind her, but she's right. Though it's hard to see much of the campus through the tree line, the two or three visible buildings are almost deliberately modest, single stories, with painted wooden exteriors and solar panels lining the roofs.

As we pass through the square, I catch the unmistakable odor of marijuana and incense. *Hippies*, I think, but then I begin to notice other, conflicting details about the student body. Fendi sunglasses perched upon a young woman's head. iPods with expensive headphones. Designer athletic wear.

"There's money here," I tell Rae, eyes scanning the shops for somewhere to eat. "It's not totally in-your-face, but it's here."

The town center consists of about a dozen businesses, including a real estate office, a convenience store, and a crystal shop offering psychic readings—no doubt the one Rae was going on about at the airport yesterday. Next door to the crystal shop, an unlit restaurant called Ono Place attracts my attention. I wander over, hoping they might have a menu posted, or at least store hours, but the exterior is devoid of helpful signage. I peer through the window, note the bistro-style tables and laid-back décor.

A cool breeze rustles my hair. A cloud passes over the sun, throwing us suddenly into shadow.

"Can I help you?" An elderly woman with bright black eyes and a long white braid stands wedged in the doorway of the crystal shop.

"We were just looking for a spot to get some food," Rae says. "I guess this place isn't open for business?"

"Not yet." The woman joins us outside the restaurant window. "Permits. They keep delaying my permits. I planned to open in September, but all this bureaucracy is holding me up."

"It's your place, then?" That surprises me. The woman looks seventy, easy, a little old to be starting out on a new restaurant venture.

"If it ever gets off the ground, it's mine." She jerks a thumb at the crystal shop behind her. "That's my real store. I've had it fifteen years, and it's done pretty well. Ono Place was just . . . a side project. The students have been telling me for ages they wanted somewhere to eat, somewhere comfortable and not too expensive. Somehow I got it into my head that I could be the one." She winces. "Don't know what I was thinking."

Given this woman's apparent inability to pass inspection, I feel fortunate to have missed dining at her establishment. "I hope it all gets sorted soon," I say politely, but she's no longer paying me any mind. She smiles at a clump of girls in the square who are waving wildly in her direction.

"Marvel!" one calls. "You were right! I dumped his ass. He didn't deserve me!"

Her girlfriends respond with a round of cheers and insulting remarks about the ex.

"Good girl," the woman says with an approving nod. "Know your own worth, Callie."

Rae glances at the crystal shop and back at the woman, her eyes lighting up with recognition. "So you're Marvel Andrada? The psychic?"

"I am."

"I can't believe we ran into you like this!" Instantly, Rae goes all fan girl, bouncing on the balls of her feet in anticipation. "I've been dying to see you! I heard your readings are *amazing*."

"Well, that's sweet of you."

With her snowy hair and swishy purple dress, Marvel looks the part of psychic adviser far more than that of restaurant proprietor. Give her a crystal ball and a wart, and she'd be booking Halloween parties for years in advance.

"Are you free now?" Rae asks, apparently forgetting her hunger.

"Tomorrow," Marvel says. "You can make an appointment for tomorrow. In the morning, maybe."

As the two negotiate a time, I can't help but entertain snarky thoughts about Marvel's stalled restaurant and the quality of her psychic advice. *She should've seen those permit troubles coming,* I tell myself, before realizing that is exactly the kind of smart-ass comment Micky would make. I, of all people, know how difficult it is to see— and correctly interpret—one's own future. Not that I buy into Marvel's abilities. The idea that someone could flip their powers on the moment that money is exchanged strikes me as dubious. If I could turn my visions on and off, focus them at will, life would be easy.

"Oh, for heaven's sake," Marvel mutters, suddenly breaking off her conversation with Rae. She's staring over Rae's shoulder at a boy walking through the square. "There's going to be a fight."

At first, I think Marvel has had some kind of premonition about the kid. He doesn't look like a troublemaker: a skinny Asian boy with floppy hair and a ratty T-shirt, who walks with his eyes fixed firmly on the ground. Soon, though, I become aware of the way the other kids are staring at him, the way conversations die in his wake and faces turn, stony and unforgiving, toward his.

"Who is that?" I whisper, but I already know, feel his name lodge in my throat.

"Yoon! Yo, Elijah!" From a nearby bench, a short and stocky boy rises to his feet, radiating ill intent.

Elijah lifts his head. He pauses, seems to judge the distance to the convenience store, assessing the danger that the stocky boy presents. His calculations come to a halt, however, when two more boys stand up beside the first. The trio approaches him, slow but menacing.

Get out of there! I think, but Elijah doesn't move, paralyzed perhaps, or else the kind of kid who just won't cut and run.

Led by the stocky kid, the three boys form an aggressive cluster around their prey. "You got some balls showing up here, Yoon," one says. "I'll give you that." Another shoves him, sends him sprawling to the pavement.

"Not this again," Marvel grumbles, and she flies away from us, diving right into the group without a second thought.

I brace myself for the sight of a seventy-year-old woman getting slugged, but the boys fall back at her arrival. Like angry dogs suddenly tethered, they await their cue.

"Back to school," Marvel orders them as Elijah stands and dusts himself off. "Go on, go on! You want me to tell your principal you're out here making trouble, Garrett? Come on, now!" She shoos the three away, ignoring their baleful stares and the collective gaze of a dozen other high school kids. When she comes to Elijah, her expression turns to one of exasperation. "And you! What did I tell you? You can't keep coming 'round here. It's not safe for you anymore." She nudges him toward the road. "Go on home."

Elijah brushes a swoop of dark hair from his eyes and says nothing, but from the sullen line of his mouth, he is less than grateful for Marvel's intervention. Shoulders hunched, he sets out for the main road.

"So that's Elijah Yoon," Rae observes when Marvel returns to us. She purses her lips. "He should know better than to show up here, what with all these little vigilantes running around. You go looking for trouble, you'll always find it."

I watch Elijah go, a solitary form plodding along the curving road. "His family lives at Wakea Ranch, right? We're staying next door to him. Maybe we should give him a ride."

"Ah, you're at Koa House," Marvel says. "No, no, don't you worry about Elijah. He's in no hurry to get home. Probably best to let that family keep to themselves." She changes the subject quickly. "You said you were looking for some lunch?" She points at the convenience store. "They've got sandwiches over there, nothing fancy."

"That's the only option?" Premade sandwiches that have been sitting in a fridge for days are not my top choice of meals.

"It's that or the Rainbow Drive-In, a few miles down the road," Marvel says. "You see how we need Ono Place? The kids have nowhere to go." She surveys the bands of teenagers, who all seem newly animated by the Elijah spectacle. "Well. I'd better get back to the shop." She pats Rae's shoulder. "I'll you see tomorrow then. Eleven o' clock, yes?"

"Fantastic! I can't wait!"

"Good, good." Marvel takes a few steps toward her store and then stops in her tracks. She peers back at me and without prompting offers her counsel. "You're not going to make a connection with Elijah Yoon, if that's what you're after," she says, as though all my hopes were tattooed plainly across my face. "He doesn't trust adults."

I'm so startled, I don't know what to say. Am I really so transparent? Maybe this woman really does have a gift.

I barely hear her parting words, spoken to herself as much as me: "If you want to help, you'll need to come at it from another angle."

nine

Victor and Suzumi Nakagawa live in a modest blue house about a mile from the center of town. Though the jungle hovers at the edge of their property, their yard has been completely cleared and filled with chunks of ugly black cinder. A single, extra-wide paved walkway leads from the carport to the house. I'm so taken aback by the lack of landscaping—Noah would disapprove—that I don't think twice about the ramp up to the front door. Then Victor's wife appears to usher us inside, and the low-maintenance yard makes more sense.

She's in a wheelchair.

"Sue Nakagawa." She tucks the bottle of wine that I brought into her lap and gives me a curt handshake. "You must be Charlotte, and you, of course, are Rae. Come in. Victor so enjoyed meeting you two this morning." She doesn't appear to share in his enthusiasm.

"Nice to meet you, Sue," I say. "Thanks for having us on such short notice." I try to meet her gaze with a friendly smile, although my mind is racing to accommodate her pale, unmoving legs. This is no temporary injury, not if they've got a ramp, and the island does not strike me as an easy place to negotiate in a wheelchair. How has Sue managed to raise two children while disabled? Parenting is hard enough without adding physical obstacles to the mix.

Rae notices the stack of shoes by the front door and scrambles to remove her flip-flops.

"You can leave your slippers on if you like," Sue says. "My chair tracks muck around the house, so you can't expect much of our floors, unfortunately."

It's hard to guess her age. Her short, stylish black hair frames a plain, square face without makeup. Still, there's something about her that makes me want to keep looking, a quick intelligence, a knowing twist to her mouth as she sizes me up.

She moves briskly through a space that the Nakagawas have made wheelchair-accessible with unusually low light switches, wide doorways, and large pathways between furniture. No high shelving or cabinets—all the storage is within Sue's reach. Even the photos are hung relatively low, as if Victor couldn't be bothered and left Sue to it. All these subtle alterations to the home only serve to highlight the difficulties Sue must face the moment she leaves it.

"Victor's out on the lanai lighting the grill," she says, wheeling across the tiled living room. "I should warn you, though. Once he gets talking, it's hard to make him stop."

I ready my notebook and pen with a laugh. "I can see how that might be annoying for his wife, but for a journalist, it's gravy."

I pause on the way out, taking notes on the house and inspecting pictures on the walls. Unlike Victor's strangely anonymous office, the Nakagawa home boasts an array of personal photographs— and all appear to be of Lise. I recognize her school photo from the newspaper article I read earlier, but Lise's face is distinctive in the others, too. Even as a little girl, she had those same thick brows, that thin nose. I wonder how Jocelyn feels about this, if her sister's pictures have always monopolized these walls or if they serve as a reminder in Lise's absence—an eerie memorial meant to call her back home.

Only one picture tells a different story: a wedding photo in a bamboo frame that sits atop a bookshelf. In it, a long-haired Sue poses in a simple white dress, while Victor stands behind her in a tuxedo, hand placed stiffly on her shoulder. I'm struck not by their youth or the Glamour Shots–style soft lens used, but by Sue's confident posture. She's *standing*. Whatever might've happened in the intervening years, back then, she could walk.

"Doesn't even look like me, does it?" Sue's sharp gaze follows mine. "The years have not been kind."

I have no idea what she means by that, but I'm afraid to bring up her daughter or her injury. Am I supposed to express sympathy? Marvel at her indomitable spirit, her strength? I fumble for something polite, something innocuous. "You were a lovely bride. How long have you and Victor been married?"

"Too long."

A joke or an uncomfortable truth? I can't help but think of Naomi Yoon and wonder about her role in this marriage.

Out on the lanai, Victor mans the grill and pours wine, which I decline. He seems more relaxed at home than at work, though he proclaims the house "an estrogen den" and describes himself as "a slave to the shifting whims of women."

Sue's hackles go up. "The way I see it, you can use a little shifting now and then," she says. "You're too set in your ways, old man."

"My husband's the same way." Rae sighs. "He won't try anything new. Food, music, clothing—nope. I'm lucky I have Charlie here, because there's no way I'd coax *him* out to the Big Island. He likes to know exactly what he's getting, no surprises."

"Sounds like we married the same man." Sue wraps a hand around her wineglass without taking a sip. "Victor has his routine, and God forbid anyone ask him to change it."

"Because I know what works." Victor flips the meat on the grill with a flourish. "I know how things should be done."

"Oh yes, he takes a firm stand on some very important issues." Sue rolls her eyes. "For example, if you make the man a cup of coffee, you'd better put the cream in first."

"Cream first?" Rae turns to Victor, mystified. "Why?"

"It slows the rise in temperature," he explains. "That reduces the chance of curdling. Ask any good barista. If you see someone putting in the coffee first—you are dealing with an amateur. Don't drink it."

"Wow." Rae gives Sue a consoling pat. "You have my sympathy."

Sensing he's lost the crowd, Victor changes the subject. "Where's Jocelyn tonight?" he asks his wife. "Shouldn't she be getting home soon?"

"She's out with Kai. They'll come by later."

Victor frowns. "Is Kai driving? You know I don't like her riding in a car with him."

"Oh, calm down," Sue says, as if this is a topic she finds tiresome. "He's a perfectly good driver." She sets down her wineglass and casts him a shrewd look. "I think you're less concerned about what happens when that car is moving than what happens after they park."

It takes Victor a few seconds to understand what she's getting at, and then he flushes. "We don't have to worry about that," he says, more to Rae and me than his wife. "I had a talk with Jocelyn the other day, and . . . she's a strong-minded young lady. She wouldn't let Kai pressure her."

"No, he wouldn't pressure her," Sue agrees. "Jocelyn's got him wrapped around her finger. Whatever happens between them is entirely consensual, I'm sure."

Victor's mouth and eye twitch upward. He does not want to be having this discussion in front of guests, and Sue knows it. "I spoke to Jocelyn about the risks," he tells Rae and me. "I told her, forty percent of sexually active adolescent girls contract STDs. Those are not good odds."

I cover my mouth with my hands, trying not to cringe as I imagine the awkward, data-driven sex talk he and his daughter must have had.

"Jocelyn does not take unnecessary risks," Victor tells his wife. "She's not like Lise. She makes good decisions."

Sue laughs sardonically. "Well, I haven't found marijuana in *her* drawer yet, if that's what you mean. But I wouldn't, would I? Jocelyn cares enough to cover her tracks." She glances at the notebook in my lap. "That's off the record."

"Of course." Now that the Nakagawas have finally begun to discuss their children, the last thing I want to do is put them on their guard. "I have two girls myself. Give me a few years, and I'll be in the same boat, worrying about sex and drugs and—"

"I don't worry about Jocelyn," Victor insists. "She's a good girl."

Sue folds her arms across her chest, disgusted. "Oh no, you're not going to do the Good Girl, Bad Girl thing. Come on, Victor. It's time to join the twenty-first century. Smoking pot and having sex does not make a young woman bad. Curious, maybe, and imprudent, given all the risk factors. But I think we can avoid moral judgments."

Though I admire Sue's defense of her daughters, I highly doubt that Victor has kept his opinions a secret from his children. They must know where they stand with him. What was that like for Lise, I wonder, being the "bad" daughter, the foil for her "good" sister?

It's time to address the elephant in the room. "So Lise," I begin. "Is she out tonight as well?"

Sue bites her lower lip and watches Victor, waiting to see how he'll field this. His face turns sullen.

"I wouldn't know," he says flatly. "We haven't seen Lise in weeks."

"What? *Weeks?*" Rae does an admirable job at conveying shock.

"She ran away," Victor says. "This isn't the first time, just the longest."

"But . . . why would she do that?"

Victor answers with unsettling composure. "Sue and I do not share Lise's vision for the future. We've had some disagreements. She's chosen to associate with some troubled people and missed a lot of opportunities as a result."

"You think she's all right, though?" I ask.

"Of course," Victor snaps, shutting down any further conversation on the matter. "At some point she'll get tired of rebelling, and she'll come home." He returns to the grill, poking at the meat with his tongs and then placing each cut on a plate. "These turned out well. Give me five minutes in the kitchen, and I'll have dinner on the table."

His absence does little to alleviate the tension that now permeates the air. Having remained silent throughout her husband's account, Sue now seems depleted. Her shoulders sag; her head is bowed in private thought. I can't tell if she concurs with Victor's version of events or not, but the subject is clearly an upsetting one for her.

Rae tries to steer the conversation to more neutral waters. "Did I hear you're a professor, Sue?"

"Over in Hilo, yes." Sue barely looks up.

"It's a state school, right? What are the students like?"

Sue massages her temples. "The undergrads are a mixed bag. Some are incredibly bright, some are not, and some are just woefully ill prepared by our failing public schools."

"The local schools aren't up to par?"

"No." She makes a face. "There are a few decent charters from what I hear, but private education is by far the best option. In Puna, definitely, but statewide, too. If there were strong public schools, I wouldn't be shelling out tuition money to Free Thought, believe me. But of course we want the best for our children."

I don't reveal that I'm the product of an unexceptional public school system myself. Her snobbery, though, does not go unnoticed. "So you sent your girls to the School for Free Thought? How have you liked it?"

Sue shrugs. "Expensive but sufficient."

"Do you know Thom Marcus over at Koa House?" Rae asks. "He used to teach there."

"Thom Marcus . . ." Sue turns to Victor, who has returned to gather his wineglass. "Thom and his partner bought that place over by Naomi's, didn't they?"

At the mention of Naomi, Victor's face remains impassive. If this woman is a source of contention between him and his wife, he's not about to let on.

"Yes, that's the place," he says. "Thom and David did a solid job with their renovations. They seem to be doing well with it."

Nobody mentions Naomi again. And nobody mentions Lise.

k

AFTER A SUPERLATIVE BARBECUE DINNER, Victor and Rae move on to a second bottle of wine. Lips stained purple, they converse with Sue about the ethics of building a new telescope on sacred Hawaiian land. I don't understand the Nakagawas, can't read the vibe in the room. Victor seems content to expound upon local politics while ignoring his own family drama. Sue reluctantly follows his lead, but there's obviously more on her mind. Throughout the evening, I've caught her looking at me, her gaze intense but inscrutable. Is she trying to tell me something? Is she warning me against delving too deep? I don't know, but I'm glad when my bladder gives me a pretext to get away.

Inside the bathroom, I can't resist nosing around, peering into the medicine cabinet and under the sink for some evidence of the girls. I discover allergy medicine, eye drops, and a whole lot of extra toilet paper, but nothing to indicate a teenager's presence. Jocelyn and Lise must have their own bathroom.

From the hallway, I can hear Victor mansplaining out on the lanai, his words slower and sloshier than they were during this morning's scientific ramblings. Rae laughs, although I can't tell whether it's with him or at him. I should join them, listen to his stories, poke good-natured fun at him, be a gracious guest, and yet I hesitate.

My eyes fall upon a pair of closed doors to my left. They can only lead to bedrooms, and I'm pretty sure the swimsuit dangling from the nearest door handle does not belong to Victor or Sue. If ever there were a chance to go sneaking around, it's now.

I weigh the alternatives. Prowling through someone's house? Bad. Failing to find Lise? Potentially worse. Perhaps if I enter her space, I'll sense her, see something more than that uncomfortable scene in the woods.

I open the door.

It's dark inside, but when I flip on the light, I find evidence of both sisters. The small, purple room has just enough space for two beds, two dressers, and a plush white rug Sue would be hard-pressed to navigate in her wheelchair.

As I look around, it's clear where one girl's space ends and the other begins. One side of the bedroom is sparse and impersonal, with white bedding and hanging bookshelves. I glance at the reading material: Stephen Hawking, Carl Sagan, Margaret Mead, Jared Diamond, Maxine Hong Kingston, Malala Yousafzai. *Has to be Jocelyn's*, I think. *Does she actually read this stuff, or just keep it around to look smart?*

Lise's half of the room has no such pretensions. Her dresser is littered with knickknacks: hair elastics, bottles of black and blue glitter nail polish, an iPod Shuffle with earbuds, a pack of tarot cards, and a collection of polished stones and crystals. Piles of clothes spill out from under the bed, and an orange bra dangles from her bedpost. I'm irrationally bothered by the bra. It must have been like this for weeks, Lise's undergarment out there for anyone to see. I resist the impulse to toss it in the laundry hamper.

I pick up one of Lise's stones, a polished black sphere that looks like onyx or obsidian. Micky would like this piece. I roll the ball around my palm, trying to feel the girl who once owned it, the girl in the hammock with the long hair.

I feel nothing. Only darkness. Only cold.

"I thought I might find you here."

Startled by Sue's voice, I drop the black sphere. It falls to the floor with a loud thunk and then rolls under Lise's bed. Internally cursing, I turn to face Sue, who sits just outside the doorway wearing an enigmatic expression that rivals the *Mona Lisa*'s.

"I am so sorry. I didn't mean to snoop, I—"

"Of course you meant to snoop." She cuts me off before I can embarrass myself with an implausible excuse. "You think I don't know why you're here?"

"Wh-what?" I blink. "What do you mean?"

"I'm not as trusting as my husband. I know what you're after." She wheels a little farther into the room, blocking my exit. "Missing children. That's your specialty, isn't it? That's why you chose Victor."

I wish that I could melt into the floor. "Sue. It wasn't like that."

"Don't insult my intelligence." Sue speaks with crisp displeasure. "You flattered my husband with false promises of some little article, wormed your way into our home, and now here you are, going after the thing you really want. I've been watching you all night, wondering how you'd come at it, but this? You're a novice."

I can't argue with that. "I really am writing about your husband," I say meekly. "I wasn't lying. What happened is, my editor, he—"

"Save it. I don't want to hear a story."

I stare at my feet, ears burning.

"I have just one question, one question for you to answer, and we'll forget about the rest of it." Sue leans forward in her chair. "Can you find her? Can you find my daughter?"

IN THE KITCHEN, Sue and I work side by side, washing and drying dishes. I scrub barbecue sauce from plates that she then wipes clean with a dish towel. The task is mostly for show, an activity that explains our absence to Rae and Victor, but I'm glad to have something to do with my hands. Our busyness forms a barrier between us that makes it easier to speak.

"I have to say, your CV is a bit of puzzle," Sue says. "*Outdoor Adventures*, a true crime book, and then your work for that awful woman's magazine . . ."

"*Sophisticate*."

She takes a wet dish from me. "You're all over the map as a journalist."

"I like to think of that as versatility."

She snorts. "I imagine you do. And now you have a metaphysical bent, it seems."

I reach for another plate and attack it with my sponge. The woman is getting under my skin. "Finding that boy in the desert had nothing to do with my career," I tell her. "I don't know where you get your information, but I've never claimed to be a psychic."

"Good. I'd avoid that word, if I were you." She glances at me. "It's a loaded one in our home. I can't even count all the fights Victor and Lise had."

I stop scrubbing. "Fights about psychics?"

"Well, Marvel, mainly. Victor wanted Lise to stay away from Marvel Andrada. She's a crazy old woman with a business near the school."

"Lise spent time with her?" That would explain the tarot cards and crystals in her room.

"Too much time." Sue nods. "The woman is a swindler. Marvel had my daughter ready to drop out of school and open some little restaurant. It was ridiculous, and Victor told them so. We were not about to see our child throw away her future on the advice of some charlatan." She places her dish on the counter behind us and waits for me to finish with another. "For the record, *I* don't believe in fortune-tellers, either."

"If you think I'm full of crap, why are you asking me for help?"

"You get results," she says. "Three children are alive because of you, that's what the news reports say." She points a finger at me. "I still don't believe you have magical powers. But your methods are irrelevant. I just want to know about Lise. I want to know what happened."

"I don't know what I can do for you, Sue. I'm only here for a week." I put down the sponge and hand her the final dish. "Even if I found some kind of answer . . . it might not be the answer you're looking for. It could be bad. She could be—"

"Dead?" The word falls hard from her lips, and I can see the woman bracing herself against its impact. "I think she is." Sue wraps her soggy towel around the dish, refusing to meet my eyes. "They haven't found her yet. Maybe they never will. But I know my daughter. It's the only thing that makes any sense."

"Then you think Victor's wrong about her coming back."

"Of course Victor's wrong. He doesn't live in reality, haven't you realized that by now? Anything difficult or ugly—he ignores it. Carries on like nothing's wrong." Sue can no longer suppress the edge in her voice. "Let me tell you about my husband. Lise had been missing two weeks, the police were calling us in, rumors were flying around town about Lise's boyfriend—I thought I'd lose my mind. What does Victor go and do? The Ironman triathlon, just like he'd been planning. And he places!" She's caught somewhere between fury and admiration for this feat. "Nothing gets in *his* way. He believes what he wants to believe. And what he wants to believe is that our daughter ran away."

"She's sixteen. Isn't that a possibility?"

Sue dismisses that out of hand. "Not for Lise. Jocelyn, maybe, she's a planner. But not Lise. She'd never make it this long on her own." Her hands curl into fists. "My daughter's dead. I just want to know why."

"Closure," I murmur, trying to be sympathetic, but the word seems to leave a bad taste in Sue's mouth.

"Closure?" she repeats with an incredulous laugh. "Damned if I know what that is." She runs a hand down one of her pale, bony legs. "In my dreams, I can walk, you know. Run, climb, kick—all of it. Eight years in this chair, but in my mind, in my sleep, I've still got use of my legs." She shakes her head. "There is no closure, no tidy endings. There's what you have and what you wish you had and how you live with the distance between the two."

Before I can respond, Victor pops his head in from the patio. "Sue? Are you almost done washing up?"

"We were just about to join you." She wheels over to me and grasps my arm, pulls me in close. "Tomorrow evening. Five o' clock." Her voice is low. "Drive up to the UH-Hilo campus and ask for the Sciences and Technology Building. We can speak in my office. There are things I need to tell you." With that, Sue pivots her chair neatly toward the lanai and resumes her role as hostess.

I pull the plug from the sink and watch the soapy water drain, not sure what to make of the Nakagawas. There are too many secrets in this house.

I'm dumping the sink sludge into the garbage when I hear something. The front door opening, footsteps on tile. A female voice. I glance over my shoulder and freeze.

In the foyer, a teenage girl stands kicking off her shoes. Her gaze sweeps the home for signs of people. At the sight of me, some stranger in her home, she wrinkles her nose. One eyebrow arches upward.

I know this face, this girl. It is the face that gazes out of every picture on the wall. It is the girl in the hammock, the one I dreamed of.

Lise Nakagawa has returned.

ten

L ise?" Her name catches in my throat. Is she real? Am I having a vision, seeing a ghostly projection so vivid I can no longer separate the living from the dead?

But the girl in front of me is very much of the flesh as she ushers her tall boyfriend inside and casts me a look of mild irritation. "I'm Jocelyn," she says. "Who are you?"

I put my hand to my chest, try to laugh at my thumping heart. "Of course you are. I just . . . I didn't realize you two were twins."

Identical twins. That explains Jocelyn's apparent absence from the photographs, at least. All this time I thought I was surrounded by images of Lise, I've been looking at two different girls. Odd that they never appeared together, though.

"I'm Charlotte Cates with *Outdoor Adventures* magazine. I'm writing an article about your dad."

"Cool." Jocelyn almost pretends to care. "Well. Me and Kai are going to hang out in my room." She grabs her boyfriend by the sleeve and moves to leave, but Victor ducks back into the house before she can make her getaway.

"You're home." He rubs his chin. "It's getting late. I hope your homework is done."

"All of it," Jocelyn reports. "And I finished my history paper tonight, which isn't even due until Friday."

"Good." Victor eyes Kai, and I know he's remembering his earlier conversation with Sue.

Despite his Hawaiian-sounding name, Kai is the whitest of white boys. Brown hair, startling blue eyes, and, apart from a light dusting of freckles, incredibly pale skin. If he were my son, we'd be buying sunscreen in bulk at Costco. Caught in the middle of a father-daughter moment, Kai stares at the floor and rubs the back of his neck, a Noah-like gesture that makes me feel irrationally protective of him.

Victor, meanwhile, squares his shoulders as if trying to imitate the Authoritative Dad in a fifties sitcom. "Where did you two go tonight?"

"I had swim practice after school and then we just hung around the library and did homework," Jocelyn tells him patiently. "It was not, like, a big, exciting evening."

"Did you have dinner?"

"At the cafeteria. Ember let us use her meal card."

Ember? I think. *Do the GMO-hating parents of San Francisco now send their children to private schools on the Big Island?*

"And how was the swim meet?" Victor has no intention of letting his daughter disappear with her boyfriend.

"It was just practice, not a meet, Dad, and it was fine. The meet's on Thursday, remember? Four o' clock. You said you'd be there."

"Oh. Yes." His facial tic makes a brief appearance. "You know it's a school night, Jocelyn. Kai should get back home."

Kai glances at Victor and then his girlfriend, trying to figure out if he's been officially kicked out.

"Don't make him go," Jocelyn pleads. "His mom is there with Brayden, and they are *so* gross together." When Victor seems unmoved, she tries another tack. "Come on, Dad. You're always telling me to make good choices and hang with good people. Shouldn't that apply to Kai as well? He's trying to make a good choice. Brayden's a drug dealer. Do you really want Kai spending time with drug dealers?"

"He sells weed, Joss," Kai says, half under his breath. "Not heroin."

Victor scratches his head, already exhausted. "It's almost nine o'clock, and we've got company tonight," he says. "You two can catch up at school tomorrow."

"No problem, Mr. N.," Kai says, already bolting. "See ya, Joss."

His departure does nothing to quell Jocelyn's resistance. This girl may have lost the battle, but she's not done waging war.

"Dad." Her voice turns calm and rational. She knows her father, knows how best to sway him. "Can we talk about this, please? I think you've been making some knee-jerk decisions about Kai without considering all the evidence."

Sensing this is not an issue that will be quickly resolved, I slip out onto the lanai and extract Rae. By the time we retrieve our shoes and make it to the door, Jocelyn has begun to argue her case in numbered points. Victor stands transfixed as she runs through the list of reasons her separation from Kai constitutes a grave injustice.

Her arguments are threefold. One, despite his deadbeat mother, Kai is struggling to be an upstanding citizen and needs the support of families like the Nakagawas. Two, Jocelyn has proven through a long history of academic success and personal integrity that she won't allow her relationship with Kai to negatively impact her schooling.

Three, her father's concerns stem from issues he's had with her sister and have no bearing on how she, Jocelyn, has consistently behaved.

Sue wheels inside during the third point and quickly shuts her daughter down. "This is not a debate," she says. "When your father tells your boyfriend to go home, then he goes home. No discussion required. Now go to your room. I don't like how you're behaving around our guests."

Jocelyn's mouth forms a thin line of fury, and for a few seconds I think all hell will break loose. But the girl knows better than to go toe-to-toe with her mother, at least in front of Rae and me. Without a word, she marches off to her bedroom, leaving the four adults to make our awkward good-byes.

"All that girl needs is a briefcase," Rae remarks as we walk through the dark toward our car.

"Right? Victor and Sue have their hands full."

"You know we're next. Bad teenagers can happen to good people."

"Ugh. I know."

Rae and I exchange apprehensive glances, imagining the years to come, wondering how adolescent hormones will transform Zoey and Micky and Tasha into young women we can scarcely recognize, young women with bodies and minds largely beyond our influence, young women with unknowable thoughts and needs and desires.

Young women who could, like Lise, disappear without a trace.

THAT NIGHT, I see her again. The girl from the woods.

His gaze slips over mine, pulling me along. A parade of images drifts by like a daydream. Watching her. Always watching. His thoughts are my thoughts, and that thought is, *I wish.*

She sits on a park bench in the square, bent over a textbook, her mouth twisting upward in one corner when she's thinking hard. *I wish.*

She relaxes on a beach, digging her toes into the sand, surreptitiously adjusting her bikini top so that it falls evenly across her small breasts. *I wish.*

She leans against a car, chatting with the young female driver through an open window, thumb hooked into the pocket of her ass-hugging short-shorts. *I wish.*

She is everywhere. Her bare shoulder, her earlobe, that pale strip of torso when she stretches. Sometimes I'm close enough to touch her, but I can't. I know I can't. Those are the rules.

Never mind the way her smile seems to invite it, the way her leg tilts open, almost imperceptibly, in my direction. I know the rules, of course I do, but in time I begin to wonder, *So what if I break them? So what?*

And then the images change. She's still on her park bench, still relaxing on a beach or leaning against a car, but I'm no longer thinking, *I wish.* Because I've made up my mind. Now I know, *I will.*

I wake up in the dark of Koa House, my sheets damp with sweat. Released from his stare, I now feel sullied, his desire dark and viscous on my skin. I sit up in bed and turn on a light. Sift through my vision for something useful, something telling. Find nothing to identify this boy or man. I still don't know whose gaze I've been inhabiting, and there are other questions now, just as burning.

I thought some terrible fragment of the past had revealed itself in that first dream, was pointing me to Lise. But what if I'm not seeing the past at all? What if this scene has yet to come? What if the girl in the woods is still very much alive?

She could be Jocelyn.

tuesday

eleven

The day begins with a six a.m. text from Isaac, who still hasn't figured out time zones or simply doesn't care. *Have a good meeting yesterday? Feeling inspired?*

I throw my phone across the bed and watch it bounce on the plush mattress. "Bastard. You aren't getting a book from me."

I already regret this whole trip. They say running away from your problems doesn't solve them, but I tried anyway. Now here I am, more than two thousand miles from the nearest major landmass, living proof that you can't escape yourself. Not only have I dragged Rae into my personal disaster, but I've left Sue Nakagawa clutching to the possibility that I might uncover something about her missing child. Could I have handled this any worse?

I step onto the balcony and inhale the fresh air. *It's still Hawai'i,* I remind myself. *No reporters, no kids, and you've got plenty to get started on the Victor profile.*

The morning is cool and gray. I find myself glancing periodically at the woods, searching for some sign of the elusive Yoons. Rae is still asleep, her body amazingly resistant to jet lag. I hope she'll understand if I spend much of my day at work, trying to spit out the basics of my article.

From the patio below me, Thom and David's voices float up. The couple who was supposed to arrive today has canceled their stay in the Paradise Suite with no advance notice; David intends to charge them full price. He and Thom run through the items they will need for breakfast, and after a brief debate about fruit, David tasks Thom with picking up a pineapple from the market.

I lean over the balcony, seizing the chance to catch Thom alone. "Hey! Can I tag along?"

Thom squints up at me. "Sure!" When he lifts a hand to his forehead, I can just make out the words on his T-shirt: *Hyperbole is the best thing ever.* "Can you be ready in five minutes?"

I can and I am.

Though Thom drives his little Yaris one-handed most of the way to the market, I don't feel unsafe with him at the wheel. He seems to know every curve of the road, and he shares trivia about the town residents as we pass by.

Enoch Keely is a Jehovah's Witness. Keoni Carvalho and his wife breed rare exotic orchids. Marijo Sato's childhood home in Kalapana was claimed by lava back in the eighties.

That last fun fact gets my attention.

"Is there any danger of volcanic activity here?" I ask.

"Oh, sure," Thom replies. "We're in Lava Zone 1, the highest-risk area."

"That doesn't worry you?"

"Nah. It's actually worked out well for us. We have B & B insurance, but the big hotels can't get insured out here. That pretty much limits development permanently."

"But . . . you're still in the path of an active volcano." His lack of concern confounds me. "Is there any way to divert flowing lava, if it came to that?"

"Divert it? Oh, no." Thom shakes his head vehemently, as if I've said something offensive. "You have to understand, to Hawaiians like David, Tūtū Pele is an honored guest. That's not just lip service. When the lava comes a-flowing, people clean their house, tidy up the yard, prepare a nice meal—they welcome her. Pele's the creator of these islands. You can't stop her fire. All you can do is get out of the way."

"Huh." I have to admire how Thom, a Jewish boy from Oregon, has come to embrace these practices. But I guess welcoming Pele isn't as strange as, say, drinking the blood of Christ.

"So how was your meeting with Victor yesterday?" Thom asks, ready to drop the subject of fiery goddesses and the destructive forces they unleash.

"Oh, I learned a lot," I say. "And I met Victor's wife. Sue's an interesting woman."

"She's an iron lady," Thom says. "It's amazing, all the things she overcame after her accident. Victor's got nothing on Sue when it comes to mental toughness."

"Yeah, what happened to her? She mentioned she'd been in the wheelchair for eight years, but I didn't feel right asking about it."

"It was something weird." Thom's forehead crinkles as he tries to remember the particulars. "Fell out of a tree, I think? Me, I'd be a lonely, bitter person in her place, but not Sue. She keeps on keeping on." Ahead of us, a rather grimy pedestrian saunters down the middle of the road. Thom slows the Yaris and lowers the window as we approach. He honks at the man, but as a greeting, not a complaint. "Ziggy! Howzit?"

The man raises his hand as we pass, sticking out his thumb and pinkie to salute us. He's older, and his grizzled face suggests hard drinking and homelessness, but Thom returns the "hang loose" gesture with genuine goodwill.

It seems that Thom knows everyone in this town, that he's the perfect person to extract local gossip from. "So . . ." It's time to broach the subject of Naomi with him. "I heard quite the story about Victor yesterday. Sounds like he's a rather controversial figure here in Kalo Valley."

"Controversial?" Thom raises his eyebrows. "In what way?"

"Not everyone is overly impressed with his moral character."

"Ah," says Thom. "Well, it's a small town. There are always rumors." His words are measured and professional, but I can see how badly he wants to blab, how much it's killing him to keep his mouth shut.

"You don't think it's true? About Victor and Naomi Yoon?"

"That's not . . ." Thom exhales. "Look, Victor was nice enough to refer you and Rae to Koa House. I don't want to gossip about him."

"Off the record," I say. "I'm not planning on writing nasty things about him. But I get the sense he's holding back when he talks to me. And I'd like to know what we're all tiptoeing around." I ask him point-blank, "Are Victor and Naomi an item?" I pause, let him struggle with how to answer. "Better I ask you than Sue Nakagawa, right?"

"Oh God," Thom says. "Poor Sue. She must know."

"So it's true."

"They're definitely friends," Thom confirms. "Have been for years. David and I see him heading over to Wakea Ranch now and then—I think he stops by when he's on his runs. Now, whether it's crossed into something more than friendship . . . I mean, I haven't personally seen anything. But if Victor's not the father of Naomi's youngest, I think everyone in Kalo Valley would love to know who is."

My eyes widen. "Naomi had his *baby*?" This is even messier than I thought. "Jesus."

"Naomi has a four-year-old son," Thom says. "And Peter Yoon, her husband, died ten years ago, so . . ."

"Does the kid look like Victor?"

"Kind of. Naomi's a *haole*, a white woman. And the kid is clearly *hapa*. Mixed race, definitely an Asian dad." He shrugs.

We've reached the "market" by now, which proves nothing more than a convenience store attached to the local gas station. "We go to Pāhoa for full shopping runs," Thom says apologetically. "The fruit here is fresh, though."

I grab a bag of lychee nuts, still working through what I've just learned, while Tom sniffs the bottoms of pineapples. Fathering a child with Naomi would certainly intensify Victor's desire to believe Lise is alive. The accusations circulating about Elijah Yoon test Victor's loyalty on multiple fronts. I had no idea his responsibilities to this woman—and to her family—could run so deep.

Like Thom, I can't imagine that Sue isn't aware of all this. She's too smart to remain oblivious to something everyone in Kalo Valley knows. But it would be wrong to assume that she's a victim here. Maybe she gave Victor permission to pursue the affair. I have no idea if, following the accident, Sue even had any interest in sex. Perhaps she allowed Victor to find refuge in Naomi's arms. Perhaps she knows about this love child he's fathered.

But how on earth did Lise Nakagawa begin dating Elijah Yoon? Wouldn't Victor have objected to his daughter's taking up with his baby mama's son-by-another-man? The whole thing sounds vaguely incestuous.

Thom can see me doing mental calculations and winces. "Seriously, Charlotte. These local rumors about Victor better not make an appearance in your magazine."

"No, no, of course not." The idea of publishing this stuff makes me blush. "I don't work for a tabloid. My readers want inspiring stories, not sordid investigations into some guy's personal life. I'll just have to . . . write around this."

Thom prods a few mangoes and drops two into his basket. "Are you going to mention Lise?"

"Probably. A missing daughter is hard to avoid in a human interest story." I take a shot in the dark. "Lise wasn't one of your students, was she? Back when you taught?"

He shakes his head. "I left the school before she hit upper math. Never knew her."

"What about Elijah Yoon?"

"You *are* writing a true crime story!" Thom wags a triumphant finger at me. "I knew it!"

"I'm considering it," I lie, "once I finish this profile of Victor. It really depends on how much I can find out about this case."

Another customer enters the store and Thom goes pointedly silent, as if warning me against a public discussion of the Yoons. In a town as small as Kalo Valley, everyone has ears. I take the hint and begin to inspect some papayas.

"Those are Puna grown," Thom informs me. "If you buy any local fruit, make sure you wash it thoroughly. You don't want to mess with rat lungworm."

Rat lungworm does sound like something I'd prefer to avoid. I put the papaya back in its stack and we go to make our purchases. I can tell Thom is still thinking about the Yoons, dying to dish. He remains heroically silent all the way through the parking lot, but the moment we're back in the Yaris, he spills his guts.

"So here's what I know about Elijah Yoon," he begins. "The kid is homeschooled. All Naomi's kids are homeschooled. It's a religious thing, but I have no idea if the kids are legitimately receiving any education."

"How does she have time to homeschool? She doesn't work?"

"Oh, she works. Naomi's a home aide. Pulls a lot of nights. That's how she got to know the Nakagawas. She worked for them after Sue's accident."

I let out a low whistle. "Damn."

"Yeah, I know." Thom glances over his shoulder and backs out of the parking lot onto the road. There are too many bizarre possibilities in the Nurse Naomi scenario for us to unpack them all. He doesn't even try. "So there's three boys. Adam—that's her oldest—is pretty much an unpaid nanny to the little one. And Elijah . . . well, he just runs wild."

I peel back the shell of a lychee and pop it into my mouth. The shape and texture approximates that of an eyeball, which makes it both disgusting and strangely satisfying to eat. "Wild how? Is Elijah wild enough to kill his girlfriend?"

Thom sighs. "You don't want to think that about your neighbors, but . . . maybe? You have to understand, Naomi Yoon is not a normal woman. She grew up on this very insular religious compound, and she married young, some guy more than twice her age."

"Did you know her husband?" I ask.

"No. David and I didn't move out here until after Peter passed away. I heard he was a good guy, though. Not part of her religious sect."

"Sounds like Naomi's had a rough go of things. Poor woman."

"I guess . . ."

I laugh; Thom's naturally expressive face cannot feign even a modicum of sympathy.

"She's that bad, huh?"

"She's something," he says. "Naomi's definitely something."

BY EIGHT A.M., I've set up shop on the back patio, downing coffee as I bang out the article about Victor. Rae misses breakfast and doesn't wake until almost ten—all that wine she drank with Victor last night caught up with her. After downing a glass of water and a couple of Tylenol, she plans her own version of a low-key day while I work: a reading with Marvel and then a little community recon at Kehena Beach, a "clothing optional" spot I am happy to miss.

"I can do topless," she tells me as she packs a beach bag. "If people see my ta-tas, it's no thing. Bottoms, though? That's a whole 'nother level. My bottoms are staying *on*. You have to know your limits."

As someone whose swimming gear has become increasingly Puritan in recent years, I agree.

With Rae gone, there is nothing to do but slog through my draft. I run through my notes of the evening, transcribing the best quotes and couching them in solid prose. I detail Victor's exercise regimen and his cutting-edge research on the origin of the island, share stories of the boyhood that foreshadowed his current passions, and even work in a few Hawaiian myths using the site he shared with me. The article finds its shape, and yet my mind keeps wandering to Lise, Jocelyn, and Sue. They are a central part of this narrative, but I don't know how best to incorporate them. More about parenting twin girls? Too mundane. I need drama, I need heart. I need the story of Sue's accident, to show how it reverberated throughout the family.

Which brings me to Naomi Yoon. I can't write about her, of course, but her presence has become palpable, a shadow that twists through Victor's life. His wife's nurse and now his possible mistress, the mother of his child. What kind of woman would raise her children in such isolation and settle for a relationship with a man as emotionally distant as Victor?

An orange tomcat nuzzles against my ankles, seeking a head scratch.

"I bet *you've* seen her," I say, getting him behind the ears. "The crazy lady who lives through the woods. What's she like?"

The cat keeps his opinions to himself. He jumps onto the table beside me and parks himself in front of my laptop.

I nudge him aside. "Gotta work, buddy. Sorry."

But with a couple thousand words of my article down and holes that require more research, working has become hard. The tree line that divides Koa House from the Wakea Ranch property now emits a magnetic pull.

Did police ever conduct a thorough search of the land? Did they have enough evidence to get a warrant?

I stand up from the table. I've been at this for more than five hours now. Might as well take a break, stretch my legs. No harm strolling through the woods a bit. It's broad daylight . . .

At first, the trees appear impenetrable, too dense to enter, but as I get closer, I see a few cracks in the foliage, trails carved through the branches and leaves. Someone's been wandering around back here, pruning.

I wade into the maze of trees, waiting for something to guide me, my elusive sixth sense to direct me to a place of evil. But it's unfailingly pleasant, full of birdsong and the kind of rich, extravagant green I never get in Arizona. An emerald swathe of leaf and shadow, dappled light playing across the forest floor. If Tucson desert botanicals bring to mind a postapocalyptic survival tale, this is a story of competition, thousands of plants springing up across the forest floor, each one vying for its own patch of sunlight.

Leaves brush against my bare arms and calves. The soil is dark and rich beneath my feet, a shallow but fertile layer atop solid volcanic rock. I move in deeper, hoping one of the winding trails will lead to a break in the woods, offer up a glimpse of a house or vehicle—some sign of the odd family living on Wakea Ranch.

What I get is a sound. Humming. A soft tune that seems to hover in the air above me.

I stop. Listen. The cheerful, meandering melody breaks off for a few seconds and then resumes. I try to trace its source, but the song seems to come from the sky, spritely, childlike. As I head north, parallel to the property line, the humming gets louder.

When I look up, I finally see him, perched on the slim trunk of a fallen tree. The tree has wedged itself between two others and hangs suspended from the ground, about fifteen feet up. Far too precarious to bear the weight of an adult, the trunk is just strong enough to hold a child, although the wood trembles as the little boy scuttles across.

He sees me and stops humming. Peers down, on hands and knees, curious but not frightened. His bowl cut and collared white shirt seem hopelessly dated. He can't be older than five.

"Hey, buddy," I call. His shaky perch unnerves me. I do not want to watch this child plummet down to a broken bone or worse. "Are you out all by yourself today?"

He disregards my question. "I'm climbing."

As he turns his head, I can see the interplay of Asian and Caucasian features in his dark eyes and faintly reddish hair. *Hapa haole,* Thom said. White mother, Asian dad. No doubt about it: I am staring at the youngest Yoon.

"Where's your mom, honey?"

"Sleeping."

From somewhere in the woods I hear a male voice. "Raph? Where'd you go?"

The child looks at me but doesn't respond.

"Is that you?" I ask. "Are you Raph?"

He climbs a few inches higher, still not answering, and hugs the rotting tree trunk.

"Raphael!" There's rising concern in the male voice now.

"He's over here!" I call back.

I hear footsteps, leaves crushed by hurried feet. It takes a few more shouts, but eventually I see a figure moving toward us, a boy in a light blue polo shirt and rumpled khakis. He's a variation of his brother, with slightly less European features and an equally bad haircut. He exudes a sweet, almost bewildered youngness. *So this is Yoon Boy number three.* I can't remember his name. Something biblical. Abel? Aaron?

The young man takes one look at the child crouched pantherlike above him and rushes forward. "Get down from there, Raph! It could break!" He holds out his hand. "I'll help you jump, okay?"

"It won't break," the little boy says, but he begins to back himself down the tree, bit by bit, until he can reach his brother's hand. His dirty paw clamps onto the larger one, and he leaps the final four feet through the air.

The older boy turns to me, his head bowed. "I wasn't watching him closely enough. I should've been watching better." He's a delicate, waifish kid, pale with dark strands of hair flying around his head at different lengths.

"Are you Naomi's son?" I ask.

"Adam," he says.

"Of course." I squint at him. He must be the eldest Yoon, but I'm hard-pressed to imagine him Elijah's senior. "I thought you were older."

"I'm nineteen."

I try not to convey my shock. This kid is legally an adult, and he barely looks old enough to get into a PG-13 movie.

"Nice to meet you, Adam. I'm Charlie. I take it Raph here is your responsibility today?"

"He's my responsibility every day." He draws the boy to his waist as if afraid I'll take his brother from him.

"It must be hard work, keeping up with this little man. How old are you, Raph? Four?"

Raph nods.

"Your mom is lucky to have you," I tell Adam. "Not a lot of guys your age could handle this job."

His grip on Raph relaxes slightly at the compliment. "Are you staying at Koa House?" he asks.

"Yeah. Sorry if I'm on your land. I didn't mean to trespass."

"I don't mind," he says. "I mean, it *is* our land. But I'm not . . . I'm not mad." He brushes some hair from his eyes. "You must be traveling. On a vacation. Where are you from?"

"Arizona," I reply. "Tucson." I wait and then can't resist amending the statement. "That's where I live now. Before that, New York."

He gives a wistful sigh. "That must be nice. New York, Tucson. I'd live anywhere that's not some little island."

"Hey, I traveled thousands of miles to see your little island. It's pretty beautiful."

"I guess. I've never been anywhere else. Not even O'ahu." His mouth lifts in a self-conscious smile. "That's weird, isn't it?"

"Nah," I say, although it does seem pretty weird to me. "I bet there's plenty of people around here who don't leave the island much."

"I don't know." He lets go of Raph, and the little boy skitters off, dancing in excited circles ahead of us. "I don't know what other people do. My mother . . . you might have heard about her. She's not like other people. She . . ." He trails off, unwilling to complete the thought. "She's just different."

The observation is saturated with sadness. He doesn't know *how* Naomi is different exactly, probably doesn't know why. But he knows that she is. That he, by extension, is different, too.

I'm dying to hear more about his mother, of course, but it's a little soon to start prodding old wounds. "What do you two have planned for today?" I ask. "Now that Raph is safely on the ground."

"Nothing." Adam's shoulders droop. "We never do anything. Just hang around the ranch and play in the woods all day. My mother doesn't like me to use the car."

It breaks my heart that a nineteen-year-old should be living life essentially under house arrest. "You don't have a job or go to school?"

"No." He frowns. "The schools all brainwash you. They teach you a godless history and they don't let you pray. Anyway, someone has to watch Raph and help with all the chores."

Aha! I think. *Bring on the crazy!*

I make a mental note to tread carefully. "You have another brother, don't you? Does he help babysit, too?"

"Elijah? No. Almost never. He's not responsible like I am."

We watch Raph crash through the leaves, pinballing off tree trunks, snapping off a low branch and brandishing it like a sword. Whatever sad and isolated life Naomi Yoon has subjected her boys to, she hasn't broken Raph's spirit. He has the same boundless energy you'd find in any four-year-old, and as I watch him battle a fern, I can't help but think of my own son, the same age when he died, the same boisterous temperament. How long can Raph live this way until he becomes like Adam? Self-aware. Yearning for more. Rae's comment the other day about how cults maintain obedience nags at me.

"Is it true your family doesn't have electricity?" The moment the words leave my mouth, I regret uttering them. Stupid, revealing to Adam that other people have been talking about him, pointing out his family's eccentricities. Stupid and cruel.

He jams his hands in his pockets. "Who told you that?"

"I just . . . the woods look very dark at night from over here, that's all. Doesn't seem like you guys have any lights on."

"We have electricity," Adam says. "We have a generator. If we need it."

I nod, trying to put him at ease. "Most people use a lot more electricity than they need. We get lazy, I guess. Your family must be very resourceful."

"Yes. We are."

I wait for him to drift away, to herd Raph back toward their house,

but whether from boredom, awkwardness, or just plain social starva-
tion, Adam makes no move to leave my side. I can't lose this opportunity to get an in with the reclusive Yoon clan.

"You guys could come hang out at Koa House, if you want," I find
myself saying. "Maybe Raph would like a change of scenery. They
have some pretty friendly cats roaming around if he likes animals."

Adam hasn't learned to mask his emotions. I can see caution bat-
tling loneliness on the poor kid's face. "Raph loves animals," he murmurs. "So do I. We used to have horses, Solomon and Malachai. But
my mom sold them last year."

"Horses are really expensive."

Adam's gaze turns cloudy, as if he's heard that excuse before and
finds it insufficient. Whatever reservations he had about visiting seem
to evaporate. He puts a hand to his mouth and calls to his brother.
"Raph!"

The little boy stops his assault on a shrub and looks up.

"Do you want to go next door? Do you want to see some cats?"

"Cats?" Raph's mouth drops open as though Adam has just pro-
posed a Disney vacation. "Yes! I wanna see the cats! I wanna see
them!" He charges back to us, grabbing his brother's hand and swinging it back and forth with anticipatory glee.

He's just a kid, I tell myself. *They always act like this, like some small
thing is the highlight of their year.*

But what if it actually is? What if cats are the most exciting thing
Raph Yoon—or Adam, for that matter—has on the horizon? I lead
the boys back toward the warm, buttery yellow of Koa House, hoping
the cats will tolerate the clumsy groping of an overenthusiastic four-
year-old, wondering if David or Thom will mind the company, and
starting to really, truly dislike Naomi Yoon.

twelve

Raph Yoon has an instinct for animals. When he discovers the orange cat sleeping on a patio chair, he doesn't tackle the creature the way Keegan would have. Instead, he touches the cat's head with one finger, rubs the base of his ear in small circles. "Hi, kitty," he whispers. "Are you having nap time?"

The cat opens one golden eye but reads no danger in the little boy crouched before him. He turns on his side and allows Raph to stroke him gently around the neck.

"He's purring," Raph marvels. "I feel him purring."

"That means he's happy," Adam says. He hovers around the lanai, too nervous to sit even when I offer him a chair, but he smiles shyly at me now. "Solomon and Malachai, our horses, they liked Raph, too. I taught him to always go slow, so he didn't startle them. They ate right out of our hands."

"You must miss them." In a world as limited as Adam's, his horses must have seemed like people. Like family.

"I miss riding," Adam acknowledges. "I miss it a lot."

"Maybe you could get a job working with horses someday."

"Raph is my job." He kicks at the grass with his shoe, a canvas sneaker gray with age, the rubber liner peeling at the edges. "I can't shirk my responsibilities."

I don't argue, but inside I'm raging at the woman who indoctrinated Adam. I have no doubt Naomi's upbringing was a twisted one, but she's free to make her own choices now, to roll back the religious dogma and raise her sons with something better. She's already forsaken at least some of those values by having a child out of wedlock—and with another woman's husband, if the Victor rumors are true. Surely she can loosen her iron grasp on her kids.

"What about when Raph gets older?" I ask. "Is there a job you'd like to do then?"

"I could be a driver," Adam says, so quickly I know he must have thought about it before. "I could pick people up at the airport and take them places. I bet I'd meet a lot of interesting people doing that."

It's such a quaint ambition, so humble, so achievable, I want to hug him. I bet he's never even heard of Uber. And little Raph, kneeling patiently by the orange cat, whispering into its ears while he strokes the creature's sleek fur—I want to hug him, too. They are innocents, pure and simple, and now I understand why Elijah Yoon would almost inevitably rebel, why he had to be the wild one. What fifteen-year-old boy could compete with these two?

No wonder Lise and Elijah found one another. They'd both spent a lifetime in the shadow of some goody-two-shoes sibling. There was no living up to Adam or Jocelyn, so why try?

"You know, I haven't come here before," Adam says, gesturing to the Koa House lawn. "You think it's okay?"

"Wait, you haven't met David and Thom?" The scope of these kids' seclusion grows more and more disturbing.

"Well, I've seen them before. But I don't talk to them."

"They're very friendly, Adam. I can't imagine they'd have a problem with you being here. You're a neighbor, after all."

"Yes, but . . . do you think it's safe?" He peeks back at the large yellow house. "For Raph, I mean."

When I stare at him blankly, he flushes.

"The men who own this house, they're homosexual," he says, as if sorry he has to break the news to me.

I take a deep breath, trying to extinguish the flame of anger I feel on David and Thom's behalf. "I don't know what your mother's been telling you, Adam, but you live next to a really great couple. You'd like them."

Adam can't quite conceal his doubts, but he's not exactly raring to return to Wakea Ranch, either. He bites his tongue—a good thing, since Thom shows up not two minutes later.

Once he recovers from the initial surprise of finding the Yoons in his yard, Thom's reaction to them proves similar to my own. Like an indulgent grandparent, he looks for ways to spoil them. He plies them with ice cream, teaches Raph to play Angry Birds on his phone, and offers Adam the use of his extensive library.

The little boy is in heaven, and I suspect Thom is as well. Perhaps he wanted children of his own, once. Even Adam, on guard for any hints of a homosexual agenda, seems to cautiously enjoy himself.

Thom drags out a storage bin stocked with lawn games and lets Raph select one. The boy picks horseshoes, even after Thom explains that there are no actual horses involved and the horseshoes are plastic. Raph cheats outrageously, running to drop his horseshoe directly on the stake as Thom and I laugh.

Embarrassed, Adam tries over and over to correct him.

At some point, I touch Adam's shoulder, release him of the obligation to fix his brother. "It's okay, hon," I say. "He's only four. Let him have fun. Just for today."

By the time Rae returns from her adventures, Adam and I are sipping lemonade on the lanai while Thom and Raph kick a soccer ball back and forth across the grass. She looks at the two boys and then at me.

"Hey!" I greet her. "How was your reading?"

"Good," she says. "It was good. Marvel's pretty dead-on. She said my day job is killing my soul, one day at a time. Hard to argue."

"And the beach?"

"Black sand, rough water." She taps her boob. "Nice to let the girls get some air, though. And I met some *very* interesting locals. Looks like you did, too . . ."

Praying she won't say anything embarrassing about cults, I introduce the boys. "This is Adam Yoon, and his brother Raph. They live next door."

"The mysterious residents of Wakea Ranch!" Rae grins. "So nice to meet you, Adam. I hear your family has a lot to teach the world about sustainable living." Her phone begins to ring, and she sighs. "So I hate to leave a party with new friends, but I promised I'd do a call with Zoey before she goes to bed. Maybe I'll catch you later, Adam?"

Adam watches her leave, speechless, and I take it he has never met an adult quite as bubbly as Rae . . . which isn't saying much. He hasn't met too many adults, period.

I stifle a yawn, my early morning catching up to me. "I should call my kids soon, too. Make sure no one has burned the house down."

"Kids?" Adam snaps to attention. "You have children?"

"Two daughters. They're in Arizona with their dad."

"How old are they?"

"Three and nine." I pause for a moment, and then find myself adding, "I had a son, too, but he passed away a few years ago. A brain aneurysm." I don't normally mention Keegan to people I've just met—it makes them uncomfortable—but something tells me normal rules of social etiquette don't apply with Adam. "He was four."

"Like Raph." Adam watches his brother sprint across the grass after the soccer ball. "He's four, too." His eyes meet mine, and I see for the first time that they aren't brown but hazel, tiny flecks of green and gold at the outer ring. "I bet you're a good mother," he says.

"Who knows? We all just do our best." But the phrase stays with me. *A good mother.* What metrics would a boy like this even use to evaluate that? I take a sip of lemonade. "Adam, you said before that your mom is different. What did you mean by that?"

His shoulders tense up at the mention of Naomi. "I don't know. Nothing. It isn't bad to be different. She . . . she gave me the gift of life, and I follow the word of God. Honor thy father and thy mother."

"And Elijah? Does he honor your mother as well?"

Having seen how protective he gets of his family, I don't expect an answer, but Adam's resentment toward his brother cuts razor sharp. "Elijah is a child. All he cares about is his friends."

"What friends?"

"Well, it *used* to be Lise and Jocelyn and Kai." His arms fold tight against his chest. "He was always hanging around them. He met up with them at night. Sometimes he went to parties. And he hung around the drug pushers, too. Kai's mother and her boyfriend." His nostrils flare with indignation. "It made my mother sick with worry, but Elijah never thinks about our family, only himself." His anger flickers out, replaced by a certain satisfaction. "Now Lise's gone, and Jocelyn and Kai, they don't even speak to him. So I guess he'll learn."

"Learn what?"

"That family is what matters."

A chill moves up my neck. There's a righteousness to his tone that feels dangerous, and I know exactly who he's channeling. *Did your mother want to teach him a lesson, Adam? How far would she go to bring Elijah back into the fold?* But I can't ask that. Can't imply anything untoward about Naomi. Family is what matters, after all. If I went after Adam's family, I'd lose all of his trust in me.

I struggle for a tactful approach. "Did you ever think that, well, maybe—"

"Oh no." Before I can fully form my question, Adam jumps to his feet. "Raph!" he calls. "Raph! It's time to go!"

He jogs over to his little brother, who is using both hands and his entire body to try to steal the soccer ball from Thom's expert dribbling.

"Come on!" Adam grabs the boy's wrist and jerks him away from the game. "We need to leave now."

For a second, I think that I've pushed him too far, that my inquiries somehow crossed a line. But then I see her.

A woman with long, red hair stands at the edge of the woods. Despite the eighty-degree weather, she wears a blue dress that extends to her wrists and ankles. If the idea is to make her less sexual by covering her body, it isn't working. The fabric hugs her curves. Even from several yards away, I can tell she has those broad hips and full breasts that men seem biologically programmed to behave stupidly around. And her hair seals the deal. The flaming curls tumble down to her waist, calling to mind an Irish travel brochure. I can see why Victor might have overlooked all the crazy rumors that swirled around Naomi Yoon and yielded to his baser needs.

"Adam?" I say. "Is that your mom?"

If I'm hoping for an introduction, I'm disappointed. The boys take off toward the woods like a pair of spaniels summoned by an inaudible dog whistle. I wave, trying to catch Naomi's eye, but she doesn't spare me a glance. The three of them disappear into the leaves.

Tucking the soccer ball under his arm, Thom moves to join me. "She's a strange one, Naomi," he says. "I've never been able to figure her out. Those poor kids."

"Did we just get them in trouble?"

He shakes his head. "Maybe. I have no idea what goes on at Wakea Ranch."

"That family's messed up, Thom." I know I should stay out of their affairs, but it bothers me. "Adam Yoon is nineteen years old. He shouldn't be at the beck and call of his mother. And Raph . . ."

"What a sweet kid, huh?"

"Yeah, but the way he was playing with you . . . he was just so blissed out to be with an adult that could cut loose. Little guy needs some fun."

"So does Naomi," Thom murmurs. "So does Naomi."

A QUICK CALL home reveals that no one is suffering too greatly in my absence. Tasha misses me, but Noah's been pulling out all the stops—pancakes for dinner, unlimited screen time—and she seems to have warmed to the idea of a Daddy Week. Micky is less enthusiastic. She has a cold, and her asthma has been acting up. Noah made her use her nebulizer, which she detests. Moreover, her one friend at school was absent today, leaving Micky without a lunch buddy or partner for group projects. I make sympathetic comments and send the children my love.

Noah asks how my article is progressing and how Rae and I are getting along. The news truck, he reports, is gone, although a few re-porters have dropped by and we're still getting calls on our home line.

"You enjoyin' your time away?" he asks.

"Enjoy" is hardly the right word for what I'm feeling, but I'm not about to reveal that I'm already entangled in another missing-child case, that my accommodations are next door to a suspected mur-derer, that I've been having visions through the eyes of a creepy stalker and potential rapist/killer. This is not information that Noah can handle, not while I'm here and he's there.

"It's really interesting," I say. "I've met . . . some interesting people."

"Interesting?" Noah echoes. "Uh-oh. You stay outta trouble now." His tone is joking, yet the underlying message is not. "Whatever hap-pens, you gotta make it home at the end of the week, got that? I can only hold down the fort for so long."

"Roger."

"I love you, babe."

"Love you, too."

Only when I've hung up do I notice the time. Slightly after four. I'll have to hustle to make it to Hilo by five. Don't want to miss my meeting with Sue.

There are things I need to tell you, she told me in her kitchen, things she didn't want to discuss in front of Victor and Jocelyn. I grab my sunglasses and wallet, collect the car keys from Rae.

There are things I need to ask.

thirteen

As I drive around the UH-Hilo campus searching for Sue's office, I'm struck by the discrepancies in its buildings. Some are worn and outmoded, with chipped paint and a damp look that screams cockroaches. Dorms, I'd guess. Others are sleek and glassy nods to modern architecture. Nestled atop a green sloping hill on the edge of campus, a row of international observatories reminds me that the astronomy department here is no trifling thing. Mauna Kea, the Big Island's tallest mountain, hosts more telescopes than any other peak in the world. To teach at this school, on this island, must be an astronomy professor's dream.

I finally locate the Sciences and Technology Building, a pristine structure that can't be more than a few years old. Inside, a merciful undergrad sees me wandering around and escorts me to Sue's office.

Sue has an evening class at six. When I spot her through the doorway, however, she's not preparing or correcting papers, but staring vacantly at a painting on her wall. I rap lightly on her open door, and she snaps to attention.

"Come in. Have a seat."

I shut the door behind me, taking note of the artwork she was staring at. An orange woman stands atop a mountain, her hair made of fire that trails to smoke at the tips. Below her, the ocean swells. At the crest of a wave, another woman rises up, her hair made of sea foam.

"That's beautiful," I say. "Who made it?"

"A local artist." Sue wheels away from the painting. "Victor bought it for me years ago. It's Pele and her sister, the goddess of the sea." She takes a bag of baked goods from her desk. "Would you like a stone cookie? They're a local treat."

I take a proffered cookie and, with one careless bite, nearly break my teeth. The name is no exaggeration; one could build another Great Wall with these so-called cookies. As Sue rummages in her desk for a plate, I spit the cookie back into my palm and surreptitiously deposit it in the nearby garbage can.

"Those are pretty intense," I say.

"Mmm-hmm." Sue pauses, as if she's forgotten what she was doing.

I detect a nervous edge to her tonight, a skittish energy magnified by the confines of her small office. We sit stiffly, surrounded by astronomy and physics books that underscore my own ignorance. Like her husband, she has no visible photographs of her family. Except for the painting, the room is sterile and forbidding, and the fluorescent lights overhead have an annoying tendency to flicker.

I don't know where to begin, and Sue isn't making this easy. "How—how are you?" I ask, like her circumstances might've dramatically changed since I saw her yesterday.

"Busy, I guess. Or trying to be." Her fingers skim the side of her wheelchair.

"And Jocelyn? How's she?"

She studies me, trying to decide if this is idle chitchat or a more purposeful line of questioning.

"It must be very hard for her," I say, "with Lise being gone."

"Lise's her other half." Sue picks at her cuticles. "Jocelyn doesn't talk about it, but she's struggling. She seems to be clinging to Kai more. I suppose that's a coping mechanism."

"There are worse ways to cope," I say.

"Well, her grades haven't suffered," Sue acknowledges. "Jocelyn had a little hiccup early on—she got a D on a math test the day we realized Lise was missing. But she's mostly pulled it together." Sue says this like only the most emotionally disturbed of children would get a D. "Jocelyn's like me. Resilient."

"Sounds like." I clear my throat. "Sue, I want to apologize for yesterday. You and Victor were kind enough to invite me into your home, and . . . I should've been more up-front about my motives. I'm sorry."

She picks up a pen, absently taps it a few times on her desk. "Honesty wouldn't have got you anywhere with Victor," she says. "You're here, and maybe that's a good thing. I don't like lies and subterfuge, but I do like competence. Save your apologies and give me that."

"I can't promise to give you anything."

"You can promise me plenty. Promise me this conversation is off the record, that you'll mention none of it to Victor. Promise that you'll write your outdoor fluff piece about him like nothing's changed and keep him happy."

"You really think it's best to keep Victor out of the loop?"

"Absolutely," she says without hesitation. "He'd prefer it. Some of us have to live in the world, but not Victor. Let him have his work, his training. It's safe there."

"You must feel very alone."

"I *am* very alone." She continues to flick her pen against the desk. "When I had my accident, and the doctors were telling me I wouldn't walk again, you think Victor was any help? 'Just give it time, Sue,' that's what he told me. 'Medical technology will improve. They're making great advancements with spinal cord injuries.'" She lays her hands across her thighs. "He couldn't face it."

Sue doesn't like the pitying looks I'm giving her. She returns to the topic at hand. "I don't know what you've heard about Lise," she says, "but if you're going to look into this properly, you might as well hear a few things from me. Since we both agree it's problematic to get information secondhand."

"The Yoon family." I lift my chin. "I need to know about the Yoons."

Sue doesn't balk at my bluntness. "I take it you've already heard the gossip about Elijah."

"I've heard a lot of people think he's responsible for whatever happened to Lise."

"Yes, well, a lot of people don't know Elijah."

"You're saying you do?"

"I've known Elijah for a long time. And he's not a bad kid, no matter what Naomi thinks." There's no malice when she says Naomi's name. "Victor and I were happy when Lise started dating Elijah. They'd been friends for years, and he was respectful—of us and of her. Much better than the other boys she took up with—she wouldn't even introduce us to them."

"What other boys?" I make a mental note: maybe her stalker was a frustrated ex.

"I never knew their names," Sue says. "Local kids. No future, no ambition, into drugs. But Elijah . . . Elijah loved my daughter."

"You felt he treated her well?"

"Yes. It was pure, sweet puppy love. Nothing violent about it."

"She did break up with him, though, right? He could've had . . . a strong reaction."

"He wouldn't have hurt her," Sue insists. "In fact, if I'd known she intended to end the relationship, I would've been worried about his safety, not hers."

"She didn't tell you that she was planning to break up with him, then," I observe.

She rolls her eyes. "Lise's sixteen. There are a lot of things she doesn't tell us."

The overhead lights stutter, as if on the verge of an outage. A storm, maybe. I stand up, approach Sue's intimidating bookshelf.

She's a smart woman, but how can I trust her to fairly evaluate this boy? She permitted his relationship with her daughter, encouraged it even. She has a vested interest in believing him innocent.

"Elijah was the last person to see her." I slip a textbook off the shelf and pretend to read the back.

"Yes. That's why the police have been so focused on him. But I talked to Elijah myself, that first day we couldn't find her. His story hasn't changed."

"And his story is what, exactly?"

"He walked her home from school at about nine thirty. She seemed upset. And then she broke up with him, with almost no explanation. 'I don't want to be with you anymore.' That was it." She takes a breath. "The police think Elijah is lying about taking her home, that she never made it back into our house that night. It's part of their whole timeline of how he killed her."

I close the astronomy text and push it back into its narrow space on the shelf. "You think the police are wrong?"

"I heard Lise come in a little before ten," Sue says. "That's just when Elijah says he left her. I was in bed reading. I heard her moving around her room—she was alone; I could hear the footsteps. I yelled to her and she yelled back, but . . . it's difficult for me to get out of bed and transfer to the wheelchair. And I was caught up in my book. We didn't really have a conversation."

I know Sue will regret that conversation they didn't have for the rest of her life. It's what happens when you lose a child: a cataloging of opportunities missed. I fold my arms, remind myself not to overidentify with this woman.

"If you never saw her, how do you know it was Lise? I mean, could that have been Jocelyn you heard coming in?"

Sue shakes her head. "I asked her, 'Lise, is that you?' And she said, 'Yeah, I'm home.' Jocelyn was at school with Kai studying for her math test. She got home a little later, maybe ten thirty, and popped into my bedroom to tell me that she was back."

"Did she see Lise?"

"No." Sue sighs. "She saw the empty bed and thought Lise had snuck out to see Elijah, so she didn't say anything. She thought she was covering for her. You know how it is with sisters." Above us, the fluorescents dim with an inauspicious buzz. Sue glares at them. "These stupid lights. The building's only four years old, and already the wiring is starting to go."

"So there's a half-hour window between when you think you heard Lise get home and when Jocelyn got back and found her missing."

She nods. "Lise must have left the house in that period of time."

"You didn't hear her leave?"

"I . . . I don't know. I *think* I heard her go out on the lanai, but I wasn't really paying attention. She liked to sit out there at night—it wouldn't have made an impression. And I dozed off for a bit."

"But you think she left of her own accord."

"There was no one with her when she came in. I listened to the footsteps just to make sure Elijah wasn't sneaking in. She came and within half an hour, she was gone. It didn't look like she took anything with her. As far as we can tell, all her clothes and belongings are still there. But she left her sweatshirt."

"What sweatshirt?"

Sue opens a drawer of her desk and produces a neatly folded black shirt. She spreads the fabric across her lap. A grinning white skull design peers back at me, more than a little eerie, given the circumstances.

"When Lise left for school on Wednesday, she was wearing this," Sue says. "She wore it to her classes. She wore it in the cafeteria that night at dinner. And Elijah told me she wore it when he walked her home. Thursday morning, after she'd gone missing, I found it on her bed. Lise was here that night, just like Elijah said."

"Still," I tell her, "maybe Lise stopped by the house and went back out with him."

"No." Sue grips the handrails of her wheelchair and leans toward me. "Elijah hitchhiked home that night. Alone. Nathan Mahoē says he picked him up at ten and dropped him off at Wakea Ranch. Naomi and Adam Yoon both confirmed that. They said he was up half the night crying about the breakup."

"Ah." I'm not gunning for Elijah here, but Naomi and Adam Yoon are not the most credible sources in my mind. Surely they would lie if they knew what Elijah was being accused of. As Adam said, *family is what matters.*

"There's no way Elijah had time to kill my daughter and . . . and stash her somewhere before he made it home." Sue sees my doubt and tries to squash it. "Whatever happened to Lise, it wasn't Elijah's doing."

"If all that's true, why are the police so hung up on him?"

"They have their ideas about what happened, and they adjust the facts accordingly. They say Lise must've left the sweatshirt earlier in the day, that she never came home that night at all. It doesn't help that I fell asleep. As far as the police are concerned, my whole exchange with her was probably a dream." Her fingertips trace the white lines of the skull on her daughter's shirt. "People in Kalo Valley don't love the Yoons. That makes them an easy target. But that doesn't necessarily make them the right target."

Something occurs to me now in her version of the night's events. "Where was Victor in all this? Wasn't he home?"

"He was visiting the Yoons, actually," Sue says, so awkwardly I feel embarrassed for her. "He and Adam were rebuilding the kitchen shelves. That's how I *know* Elijah came home when he did. Victor saw it. He confirmed everything that Naomi and Adam said."

Now I understand. Sue is desperate to believe in Elijah because she is desperate to believe in Victor. Allow herself any doubt, and the whole house of cards comes tumbling down. But seriously— rebuilding the kitchen shelves? At ten p.m.? Surely Victor could come up with a more convincing story. Though I say nothing, Sue sees my look of pity.

"I know what people say about Victor and Naomi," she tells me. "It's not true."

How can I respond to that? It seems that Victor is not the only one with a tremendous capacity for self-delusion. "It's great you have that kind of trust in your husband."

Sue doesn't let my deflection stand. "Naomi helped us after my accident," she says. "She cared for me. I wanted to die back then, but Naomi didn't let me give up on life. She's an unusual woman, and I certainly don't share her religious views, but I will always be grateful to her. Always." She jerks her wheelchair backward a few paces. "If people in this town want to gossip, let them. But I'll tell you the facts. Victor goes over there to help that family as a sign of friendship. He goes because I tell him to go, because Naomi needs a helping hand. Does he enjoy getting attention from a pretty woman? Of course he does. But he isn't sleeping with her."

Then who is Raph's father? I want to ask. *One of her patients? Is she running an escort service on the side? Having Tinder-assisted one-night stands?* Given Naomi's rigid beliefs, Victor seems the most likely possibility by a wide margin. I'm not cruel enough to poke holes in Sue's little bubble of denial, however. She has enough on her emotional plate without confronting Victor's probable infidelity. Instead, I move back toward the painting of Pele and her sister.

"Fire and water," I say. "Kind of like your girls, huh?"

"Victor thought so. He always said that Jocelyn had a cooling influence on Lise. That she was the only one who could put out her sister's fire."

"Is that normal? For identical twins to be so different?"

"They aren't so different. Not really." Sue folds Lise's sweatshirt in her lap, hood down, sleeves tucked into a neat rectangle of black cotton. "They're both determined, passionate, competitive. Lise could've been like Jocelyn. She just chose not to be. I suppose there were lots of reasons for that. Some were my fault."

"How so?" I'm still intrigued by this painting Victor picked. The yellow glow Pele casts upon the sky. Her jet-black eyes, like hardened volcanic rock. For a man like Victor, it's surprisingly fanciful. "Do you think you treated the girls differently?"

"Intentionally? No. But there were complications with my pregnancy. Selective intrauterine growth restriction." Sue's voice is factual and devoid of affect, like a doctor's. "The blood flow in the umbilical artery was inhibiting Jocelyn's growth, while Lise developed normally. I had them very early, at thirty-one weeks. Jocelyn weighed barely two pounds and spent a long time in the NICU. She needed so much more from us early on—maybe I just got into the habit of tending to her first."

"Understandable."

"Jocelyn was so tiny. She had to fight so hard. When she finally met her milestones, I was always so excited, so relieved. With Lise, I just assumed she would do it. There was no celebration." Sue purses her lips. "I look back, and I see how Lise was always chasing the limelight, looking for her share of attention. But at the time . . ."

"It must be very hard to have twins."

"You have no idea. The girls have always been close, but they never stop comparing themselves."

I find myself grateful for the six-year age gap between Micky and Tasha. The sibling rivalry has—so far—been minimal. With such different needs, they have always had highly individual relationships with Noah and me.

"Lise could've been so much more," Sue tells me. "Jocelyn now, she's an excellent swimmer, wins competitions, sets records. But for years, Lise was the better swimmer."

"Oh? What happened?"

Sue puts her daughter's black sweatshirt into a drawer. "The summer they were thirteen, Lise broke her arm. She couldn't train for months, had to go through physical therapy up in Hilo. Jocelyn got better than her, and so she quit." For the first time, Sue's voice betrays her emotion. "She threw away all her talent and took an art class instead. Made some new friends, started smoking pot." Her grief, I note, is laced with anger. "She has all her sister's intelligence, drive, ambition, and for what? I shouldn't have let her quit. I should've pushed her harder."

I have no idea how to respond. I understand her loss, understand the self-recrimination she must feel, although I'm far from convinced what Lise Nakagawa needed was *more* parental pressure in her life.

"When I think of all the energy I've diverted from my career to those children . . ." Sue looks regretfully around the office, as if its narrow walls are a reminder of all she's failed to achieve. "I should've at least got parenting right."

"Oh, come on. No one gets parenting right." I smile. "If you wanted an easy job, you should've stuck with astrophysics."

"I didn't even want to be a mother," Sue confesses. "I was on birth control when I got pregnant. Twins! Can you imagine? How different my life might've been . . ."

This conversation is taking an ugly turn. If Sue is sorry she became a parent, I'm not sure I want to hear it. I step away from the painting, finally facing her. "Why am I here today? What is it you want?"

Again, her mouth forms a tight line. "You want to know what happened to Lise," she says. "And so do I. I wish I could be out there myself asking questions, but . . ." She gestures to her unmoving legs. "Always fighting this damn chair, aren't I?"

"So, what? You're looking for a surrogate?"

"That's right," she says. "You're able-bodied, and you have a history of getting things done. Much as I'd like to, I can't run around this island shadowing people, spying on Lise's so-called friends. But I can point you in the right direction."

This is getting weirder by the minute. "What direction is that?"

"Don't waste your time chasing after Elijah Yoon. There are other people you should be looking into. People Lise knew. Her drug friends. Marvel Andrada. Talk to them. Watch them."

"Sue, I'm not a private investigator. I write for *Outdoor Adventures*, for crying out loud."

"You used to work for *Cold Crimes*," she counters. "And you wrote a book, a whole book about that missing child in Louisiana. You can do this." Her upper body is ramrod straight in the chair. "Please. I'll pay you for your time. You find something, you tell me. That's all I ask."

I need to get the hell out of here. Something about this woman and her urgent, unblinking stare troubles me. "No money," I say. "I don't work for you. And I'm not following anyone, either. I'll talk to a few people, that's it." I make a beeline for the door.

Outside, it's getting dark. Students move briskly across the campus, on their way to evening classes. Soon, Sue will teach her students about the night sky, about planets and stars and black holes, explaining in precise terms the mysteries of the universe. What kind of hubris drives a person to try to understand a world beyond the one we live in, a world already replete with mysteries we can see and smell and touch?

Sue herself is a mystery, one I'm half afraid to unravel. Is she a distraught mother, searching for answers, begging me to be her legs? Or was this whole meeting some underhanded attempt to keep tabs on me? There are many reasons she might wish to steer me away from the Yoons, and they don't all concern Naomi and Victor. I don't trust Sue. For now, anything I learn, I'll keep to myself.

BACK AT KOA HOUSE, I find Rae reading in the dim light of the rear patio. We've scarcely talked today, each of us caught up in our own activities, and she must be wondering about my visit with the Yoon boys earlier.

"Hey, lady." I flop down in a chair, tired though it's only seven thirty. The coquís are deafening tonight, a chorus of lonely-hearts searching for a froggy hookup. "You got a minute?"

Rae looks up and drops the open book onto her lap. It's a romance novel, some shirtless man looming over a woman who hasn't learned to manage her own cleavage.

"Your heroine could use a good bra fitting, huh?" I joke. "Must be that heaving bosom. I hear they're hard to contain."

She doesn't crack a smile. "You sound like Mason," she says. "But you know what? I read my Neil deGrasse Tyson on the plane, and I've earned this one. Heaving bosoms and throbbing members are vastly underrated."

I sit across from her in a white wicker chair and kick up my feet.

"That explains your interest in Kehena Beach. Were there a lot of naked people running around today?"

"Actually, the nudity wasn't the most interesting part of the experience."

"No?"

She flashes me a secret, knowing smile. "I met some very nice, friendly people at that beach. Kalo Valley folks, in fact."

"People who don't have jobs to go to on a Tuesday afternoon? Must be hippies."

"Quit being so judgmental. It was a welcoming and open group. Anyway, I made us plans for tomorrow. We're going to South Point," she says. "It's the southernmost point in the United States. I met a guy who's going to take us."

My eyes narrow. "You picked up some weirdo at the beach?"

"He's a local guy, not some weirdo I brought home from a bar. We hit it off. I told him we'd pay for gas and food." She's toying with me, holding something back, but I can't tell what.

"I'm not sure Mason would love this. Hanging out with some stranger you picked up at a 'clothing optional' beach—that doesn't pass my sniff test, Rae."

She laughs. "Oh, he's definitely not a love interest."

"Well, who is he then?"

A slow grin spreads across her face. "Guess."

"Wait . . . you're saying I should know this guy?"

"If you've been paying attention to all of the details of Lise Nakagawa's life? Yes."

I'm momentarily stumped. "Elijah Yoon?"

She shakes her head.

"Um . . . Jocelyn's boyfriend? Kai?"

"Getting warmer."

"I have no idea, just tell me."

"Brayden Goerlich." She waits for my look of shock but gets nothing. "Come *on*. The drug dealer, remember? Brayden! The one dating Kai's mom?"

"Oh." I still don't see what she's so excited about. I barely remember Kai and Jocelyn mentioning this guy. "That's odd. You just ran into him?"

"It was a highly orchestrated run-in. I got his name from Thom, and lucky me, turns out Brayden has a habit of making very public plans on the Twittersphere."

"*That's* why you went to Kehena Beach? You stalked him on Twitter so you could stage a meeting? And now we're all hanging out tomorrow?"

"Correct."

I'm tempted to tell her we might be taking this Nancy Drew thing too far, but the truth is, I'm impressed. "Damn, woman. You're turning into quite the detective. I mean, undercover topless—you're all in."

"Well . . . I was wearing a shirt when I met him." Rae gives a modest shrug, but she's clearly proud of herself. "Sue said she found marijuana in Lise's drawer, right? I figure she probably got it from this guy. And when Brayden and I got to talking, he said he knew her, that he hung out sometimes with Kai and Lise and their friends, so . . ."

I wrinkle my nose. "What's some old guy doing hanging out with teenagers?"

"Brayden's not old," Rae tells me. "He's, like, twenty-two? Twenty-three? Kai's mom must be a total cougar."

I think it over. This is exactly the kind of person that Sue just instructed me to go after, and Rae's people instincts are good. This Brayden kid might actually know something. But would he tell us? What kind of guy are we dealing with here?

"Are you sure we want to burn a whole day on this dude?" I ask. "What if he thinks he's on a date with you? He obviously has a thing for older women."

"It wasn't like that," Rae assures me. "He's very Peace, Love, and Recycle. So he moves a little weed on the side, who cares? And South Point sounds awesome—big, windy cliffs and a green-sand beach. We'll have a good time."

I have mixed feelings about that, but it's Rae's vacation, too. I blew her off today to work, and she didn't give me crap about it, not once. I owe her.

"Okay," I say. "But I'm bringing pepper spray or something just in case Mr. Peace, Love, and Recycle turns out to be Mr. Duct Tape and Zip-Ties."

Rae sighs at my general lack of faith in humanity but doesn't object. "So tell me about the Yoon boys," she says. "Did you get anything interesting out of them?"

"Not really. Just felt sorry for them, mostly." I try to explain my protective instincts toward Adam and his brother. "The younger one, Raph—he reminded me a bit of Keegan. Rambunctious but sweet, you know?"

"And the older one, the one who was making goo-goo eyes at you?" She raises a delicate, insinuating eyebrow.

I laugh. "Oh please. If Adam was making goo-goo eyes, it's because he's practically a baby. You'd never know the kid was nineteen. He's so socially stunted, it's sad."

We gossip for a few more minutes and I fill her in on my meeting with Sue, but upon review, my day hasn't been enlightening so much as strange. I leave Rae to her novel, wondering how my coveted Hawaiian vacation has devolved into this: guilt trips from astronomy professors and day trips with drug dealers. And I still haven't finished my article on Victor.

Back in my room, I drag out my laptop and dutifully begin to type. I fall asleep within the hour, laptop still balanced on my thighs.

It's well past midnight when I awake. Through the doors to the balcony, the moon shines bright. I step outside and discover a light rain falling, cool, almost sensuous against my skin. The raindrops hit the surrounding trees in a soft patter. I imagine little Raph, slumbering in his bed at Wakea Ranch. The island is sleeping, I think. Everyone is sleeping except for me and those frisky coquís.

A light blinks in the dark.

"What the . . . ?" I move to the edge of the balcony, staring at the woods.

The light, a flashlight or a lantern, flickers off for a few seconds and then on again, like a giant firefly.

Off. On. Off. Three flashes.

It's a signal, of course. The same signal I saw one of the Nakagawa sisters making in my dream—right before her stalker revealed himself.

Could it be Jocelyn out there? I peer into the night as if my gaze might somehow penetrate the layers of jungle. Who would she be signaling to at Wakea Ranch? Elijah? Adam? Having seen Jocelyn's passionate defense of Kai the other night, I find it hard to believe she'd be out on a rendezvous with a Yoon brother. I've been a teenage girl. Kai is a babe who exudes social capital. The Yoon boys? Tolerable, if you like the wounded-bird thing.

Still, my stomach is in knots. This could be it, the events of my dream unfolding before me. Perhaps he's out there, watching in the night, waiting for her, Jocelyn or Lise or whoever she is. I consider waking Rae, the two of us dashing into the woods on some insane rescue mission, and cringe.

And then, another light, this one from somewhere across the woods. Back and forth they flash, two small beacons several yards apart, winking in and out as if in conversation.

I relax slightly. This isn't a stalker catching someone alone and unaware. It's a prearranged meeting. But of whom?

I watch one light move closer to the other in the dark, and then they abruptly die. This time, both stay out. *They must have found each other*, I think, and yet my uneasiness lingers. The more I see, the more I'm convinced that my dream was of these very woods. Which leaves two possibilities.

One, I saw a flash of the future. For whatever reason, Jocelyn will come out here for a secret meeting in the dark, and Stalker Guy will be waiting. Given what I know of Jocelyn, secret night meetings seem unlikely, but she's a teenager. One never knows.

Two, I saw a flash of the past. Lise Nakagawa came out here, presumably on the night she went missing, to meet up with her boyfriend. She stopped by her house, dropped off the sweatshirt, and walked the couple miles out to Wakea Ranch. But instead of Elijah, she found *him*. And she never came home.

The rain has slowed to just a whisper, wet air more than actual droplets now. I shiver. Sue told me her daughter was dead, and I'm starting to suspect she was right. But if Lise's gone, then who was out there tonight, signaling in the dark? How many people roam these woods at night, and why?

I crawl back into bed and burrow myself beneath layers of blankets, answers swirling through my head, none of them satisfying. It's hours before I fall asleep again.

wednesday

fourteen

I open my eyes to the day's first dim strands of sunlight and peer at the green and yellow bamboo décor. Home feels so very far away. I reach around the bedside table for my phone to check the time, but no amount of lazy groping produces the device. Reluctantly, I get out of bed. Gotta check my email, make sure nothing important has come in. I rummage through my purse, my luggage, yesterday's pockets.

Nothing.

I rack my brain for the last time I had the phone with me. My bedroom, definitely, when I called Noah and the girls, and I'm pretty sure I brought it with me to Sue's office. Less sure I had it on the patio when I was talking to Rae. Perhaps it slid out of my purse when I was driving, lodged itself under the passenger seat somewhere.

A quick examination of the car and patio turns up nothing, and both David and Thom deny any knowledge of my phone's whereabouts. Trying to stamp down my panic, I head for the Tree Fern Room. The simple way to solve this is to have Rae call me.

Rae, as it turns out, is lounging in bed and playing with her own phone. "Hey!" she greets me without fully looking up from her screen. "Brayden should be by at nine. Does that work for you?"

"Nine?" It takes me a second to remember our date with the weed dealer. "Yeah, sure."

"I'll stop by the store and get snacks before they come." Rae peers down at her iPhone. "Nice Instagram photo, by the way. Kind of arty. You should post some of the volcano stuff."

"Instagram photo?" I have no idea what she's talking about.

"That thing you posted." She flips her phone in my direction. I see my Instagram account name, *charcates4473*, followed by a picture. A red flower folded inward in the dark, its thin, veiny bloom illuminated by the flash. Hibiscus, maybe—I think they close at night. It posted approximately five hours ago.

I stare down at the image, my arms breaking into goose bumps. "Someone's messing around on my phone. I thought I lost it, but . . . somebody must have stolen it."

"Wait, you didn't post that?"

I shake my head.

"That makes zero sense." Rae wrinkles her nose. "Why would someone steal your phone and post *that*?" She peers over my shoulder. "Any chance that it was Noah? Maybe he's sending you a virtual flower." She doesn't actually believe that. We both know how strenuously Noah avoids social media, and flower photos are not his style.

"Noah doesn't have access to my Instagram." I frown. "I don't even know the password to that account. It's loaded on my phone, but I never use it."

"How could somebody get into your apps, though? Doesn't your phone have a security code?"

I chew on my lip. "I took it off for Tasha. She plays games on there." Noah will be on my case big-time for this. He told me I needed a security code, told me repeatedly, but I brushed him aside in favor of whine-free grocery runs. "Oh God, Rae, I'm so screwed." I do a mental inventory of all the apps on my phone, trying to gauge what the thief might have access to. Nothing financial, thank goodness, but my email and my personal pictures are up for grabs. I grab my laptop from my room and change the password to my email account.

"Some nice person probably found your phone and wants to get it back to you," Rae says, ever the optimist. "Here, I'll try calling you." She gets immediately bumped to voicemail. "Did you check with David and—"

"Of course I did. They haven't seen it." I stare at my laptop screen, trying again to mentally retrace my steps. "I could've left it at the university yesterday when I went to see Sue. They had hibiscus on campus, I think."

"It must be someone who knows you," Rae muses. "Why would a stranger hit you up with a cutesy flower pic? Sign into iCloud and try Find My iPhone."

She watches from behind as I fumble to input my ID and password. I'm so agitated I have to reenter them twice, and when I do, the news is disappointing. According to Find My iPhone, the current location of my device is unavailable, meaning my phone is dead, off, or switched to airplane mode. Annoyed, I request the last known GPS coordinates. I draw a sharp breath when I see the results.

Koa House or thereabouts, at 1:48 a.m. Around the time the hibiscus photo posted to Instagram.

Rae shifts uneasily. "Any you chance you've been sleepwalking?"

"No." I rake a hand through my hair as the pieces start to fall in place. "I must have left my phone on the patio out back."

"Yeah, but who besides David and Thom would possibly—"

"There were people in the woods last night," I tell her. "I saw their lights. One of them must have taken it."

Rae's dark eyes turn deadly serious. "Charlie. That would mean someone was roaming around the property outside."

I nod.

"If that's true, you need to tell David and Thom about this."

Downstairs, the table is already set with pineapple slices and a pastry basket. A pair of geckos scurry around the table's edge, smelling fruit. I can't reconcile the feeling of danger in my stomach with the sunshine and peaceful flora.

David pops in from the kitchen to greet us. "Morning, ladies! I was just about to bring in breakfast. Did you find your phone, Charlotte?"

"No, actually. Looks like it was stolen." I nibble at a fingernail. "Listen, I know this sounds bizarre, but . . . I saw some lights in the woods last night. It looked like . . . I don't know, like people meeting up."

David sighs. "Oh, that."

"You've seen it before?"

"It's been going on for months," David tells me. "I see those lights a lot when I'm up late. Thom and I figure it's probably just Naomi's boys screwing around. We thought about mentioning it to her, but . . . I didn't want to get her kids in trouble. They don't seem to be causing any problems. Unless . . ." He pauses. "You think they took your phone?"

"Someone did. It was here at one a.m. I must've left it out back when I was talking to Rae."

"Huh. I wonder." David puts a hand on his hip, considering.

"What?" Rae asks. "What are you thinking?"

David hesitates. "Nothing, I just . . . Naomi called us last night. She was a little upset."

I groan. "Let me guess. She wasn't thrilled about her boys' being over here."

"No," David confirms. "Not thrilled. I don't know if she would go so far as to steal, but . . ." He sees my horrified expression and tries to backpedal. "I shouldn't have said that. Naomi's difficult, but I don't think she's a thief."

"You said she called you?" Rae asks. "I didn't think she even had a phone."

David snorts. "Oh, she's got a phone, and she knows how to use it. If it's not her kids, it's music we played too loud or a party we shouldn't be having, or the albizzia tree we cut down that was technically on her property—never mind that albizzias are invasive and the branches are prone to invisible rot. I mean, they'll just drop on you, out of nowhere, destroy your roof, your car. A normal person would've thanked us for taking down that tree. But there's no winning with her."

"It must be her weird upbringing," Rae says. "She doesn't trust outsiders."

"Not Thom and I, anyway."

Though David's words maintain a tense neutrality, I can read between the lines. I heard Adam fretting about homosexuals yesterday. I have a pretty good idea of what Naomi feels for her neighbors, and it's not the love that Jesus preached.

"The best thing is to just stay off her radar," David says. "I know you had good intentions, Charlotte, but if you see those boys around again, they're best left to their own devices."

"Right," I say. "Speaking of devices . . . what do I do about my phone?"

"There's a Verizon and a Sprint store in Hilo," David suggests. "You could get a replacement if you don't mind burning half a day. Or just wait until you get home. You're only here through Sunday, right?"

Put that way, my technology dependence sounds ridiculous. I have a laptop to check email. Surely I can go five days without a phone. That's what people do on vacations, isn't it? Unplug? And Rae has her phone. Noah could still reach me in an emergency.

I set aside the nagging voice in my head that tells me I will be vulnerable. Remind myself that people survived plenty of years without cell phones.

"It's only five days. I'll be fine."

ALTHOUGH I MANUFACTURE tepid enthusiasm for Rae, I'm not looking forward to our trip to South Point. The morning's phone fiasco—and the resulting calls to Noah and Verizon—have drained me of my energy and optimism. I can concede the potential usefulness of this Brayden character, but I'm still annoyed at Rae for expending so much time on him. And leaving us without an exit plan today was a rookie mistake. If he's unbearable, if our day with him proves a bust, or even dangerous, we have no out. But of course, that's Rae. Go big or go home.

Her beach pal shows up half an hour late in the kind of rusty old van favored by kidnappers and child molesters. He's young and sunburned, with a nose that looks like it's been broken a couple of times and a tangled strawberry-blond mane that screams surfer dude. Hardly the boy toy that I'd been envisioning, but maybe his youth was enough to appeal to Kai's mom.

"Hey there, friends!" Brayden calls, flicking a lock of hair from his face. "You ready for the road?"

"This is our guide?" I mutter. The distinctive odor of marijuana wafts from his vehicle.

"He's not a guide," Rae corrects me. "We're covering gas and food, but we're not paying him. Just be cool, okay? Treat him like a buddy."

When the guy approaches and takes my hand, I think he means to shake it. Instead, he draws me toward him and puts his other hand on my back in a space-invading half hug. "You must be Charlie," he says. "I'm Brayden, and my buddy Frankie's in the car. I think we're gonna have a really joyful day."

At the phrase "joyful day," I want to stab my eyes out.

I turn to Rae, frowning. "You didn't say he was bringing a friend." One random guy was bad enough, but two feels like a safety risk. I cross my arms and look Brayden up and down. "How do we know you and Frankie aren't serial killers?"

"Whoa!" Brayden holds up his hands. "That's dark! Hey, I don't want you to do anything you're uncomfortable doing. Rae here said you guys wanted to see the island. I'm just trying to share the aloha, Charlotte. I'm not, like, a sex offender."

His rusted van begs to differ.

"Don't mind her," Rae tells him with a laugh. "Charlie's always like that. It's why we're here. To help her lighten up."

Rae's casual insult smarts. This Brayden kid is twenty-three if I'm being generous. We are both old enough to be his mom. What's her deal, cozying up to him? Is Rae having a midlife crisis? *And* he reeks.

I sniff the air loud enough to make my point. "You okay to drive, Brayden?"

He grins, unoffended. "Aw, that wasn't me. Frankie was trying to unwind on the way over here. It's medical with him. He's got this condition."

"Really?" I deadpan. "Glaucoma?"

"PTSD," says Brayden. "He's had a hard time since he got back from Afghanistan."

Rae shoots me a look that says, *What up, judgy bitch?*

Chastened, I make a little more effort to be friendly. "So where are you taking us today, Brayden? South Point?"

"Yup. Ka Lae, southernmost point in the United States. If you accept Hawai'i is part of the States," he adds, "which is debatable what with the illegal overthrow of the monarchy." He pulls out a map of the island. "So we're over here in the Puna district, right?" His index finger moves to the bottom of the map. "We're headed over here, to Ka'ū. Figured you guys might wanna check out the green-sand beach, and then Frankie can show you some cliff diving."

Green sand is admittedly intriguing, and I've never seen someone cliff dive before. "How long is that drive?"

"Less than two hours." Brayden shrugs. "It's pretty scenic."

"That sounds awesome," Rae says.

"All right, then!" Brayden raises one hand to the air. "Let's do this!" He raps on the rear window of the van. "Frankie! Wake up, brah! Move up front, we got company!"

I catch Rae by the arm. "You're sure this is how you want to spend your day?" I whisper. "Hanging with a couple stoner boys?"

"Brayden's not just any stoner boy," Rae reminds me. "He lives with Kai and he was probably Lise's supplier. With the whole drug angle, you can bet he hasn't shared whatever he knows about Lise with police. So."

"Okay, okay. True enough."

At that moment, the door of the van slides open, and Frankie steps out, half-asleep. *Naturally*, I think. *It's nine thirty, probably the earliest he's had to wake in months.* Then I see the scar running up his leg, a pink, jagged line across his tanned skin. I remember what Brayden said about Afghanistan, and I promise myself that I'll be kind, that I'll endeavor to understand these two boys, however different from myself they may be.

That doesn't mean I have to like them.

IF I HAD to bet money on it, I would've guessed that Brayden was a Bob Marley fan, but the ride to South Point and Papakōlea Beach is dominated by Beyoncé, or, as Brayden calls her, Queen Bey. Brayden sings along to an endless reel of hits, belting out high notes in an unabashed falsetto while Frankie stretches out in the passenger seat.

Frankie has close-cropped black hair and a face pockmarked by acne. He sits with one leg folded to his chest, the other stretched out in front of him, that long scar extending up the side. If it's not a battle scar, I bet he tells girls it is. Frankie's homely in a way certain women find attractive, none of his features lining up correctly, so you can't help but take a second look. Rock-star ugly, I decide, with the attitude to match. He watches Brayden's no-holds-barred renditions of Beyoncé with a faintly amused, cooler-than-thou expression.

Rae and I huddle in the backseat of the van and fight giggles brought on by Brayden's performance. Whatever tensions might have existed earlier have dispelled amidst the absurdity of the situation. Here we are, two women in our forties riding around in a stoner van and trying to solve a mystery like we're the kids from *Scooby-Doo*.

"So are you both island boys?" Rae asks when there's a break in the music.

Frankie jerks a thumb at Brayden. "Come on. Dat *haole* walk, talk, breathe California. Me, I grew up Hilo side, but I ain't *kanaka*. I'm Filipino and Portuguese."

"I'm from Santa Monica," Brayden says cheerfully. "I went to school a couple years over in Hilo, but then I dropped out."

Frankie chuckles. "Hey, you came fo' get schooled and your girl Sage schooled you, yeah?" His syntax and cadence are laced with pidgin, a legacy of the island's sugarcane plantations.

"Did you really serve in Afghanistan, Frankie?" Rae asks.

His smile shrivels. "Yeah, I wen serve. I was twenty. Fo' one year. Got hurt, got a medical discharge. Dat shit so fucked. Prescription weed da least dey can do fo' me."

"Is it any good, that medical dispensary stuff?" Rae asks.

"Not like Sage's one. I just lucky I gotta line wit Bray." Frankie brightens. "You like? Brayden hook you up. He gotta nice blend right now, make you feel super relaxed on your vacation."

Rae laughs. "Aw, I don't wake and bake. Maybe later, though. I hear that homegrown stuff is pretty good."

I can't tell if she actually wants to buy from Brayden or is just sniffing around for details of his business. Either way, the boys seem perfectly at ease with her. If they know anything about Lise Nakagawa, I'm confident they'll eventually spill. We just have to pace ourselves.

"You know," Brayden says, just one hand on the wheel as he drives, "I see good things in this day, I really do. When I met you yesterday, Rae, you had this amazing energy. I think it's so great how we're all, like, connecting today. The four of us, we're sharing an experience. I hope it's beautiful for you guys."

I'm not sure about all this "connecting" with complete strangers. What kind of shared experience is Brayden expecting here?

"If you guys are banking on a wild, stoned-out orgy, you will be sadly disappointed," I announce. "Just laying that on the table."

In the front seat, both boys guffaw.

Rae covers her face as if physically pained.

"No offense, auntie," Frankie says with a smirk, "but Brayden's spoken for, and I like my girls barely legal. You wanna piece a dis, you gotta shave offa couple decades."

"I'll keep my decades, thanks, and you can hold on to that . . . piece of yourself." I'm not joking, just trying to establish some ground rules for the day, but the guys are cracking up regardless. *Great,* I think. *I have become old-person funny.*

Outside, the barren land drifts by, craggy plains of hardened lava that belong on some other planet. The plants that survive here aren't much to look at, either. Colorless grass and withered trees that jut at odd angles—just occasional patches of life springing up from rock.

"Hey," Rae says, unzipping her backpack. "Anybody want a snack?"

"You read my mind!" Brayden beams. "What have you got?"

"I didn't know what you guys liked, so I got a little of everything." Rae begins removing items from her bag. "Pretzels, chips, cheese sticks, trail mix, granola bars, dried mango, and then Thom gave me some leftover muffins and stuff. Take your pick." She empties her entire haul onto the seat between us.

Brayden selects string cheese and begins tearing off strands with his teeth. Distracted by the intricacies of his cheese stick, he rounds a curve a little too sharply and all the snacks topple onto my feet. I reach around the van's floor and under the front seat to gather them. Am I the only one with doubts about Brayden's driving? I sneak a glance at Frankie and Rae. Survey says yes.

I stack Rae's nibbles back on the seat, now hungry. The chips and pretzels and trail mix offer little temptation, but it's hard to resist Thom's baked goods. I reach into a plastic bag of cookies that look pseudo-healthy and swipe one. The taste is not what I'm expecting— dry and somewhat burnt. I make a face as I swallow.

"Yuck! Thom made that?"

Rae glances at the remaining chunk of cookie in my hand. "That isn't Thom's. Where'd you find that?"

Frankie peers into the backseat and his eyes widen. "Brah!" He smacks his friend in the ribs. "She found your shit."

My heart sinks. *Please don't let that mean what I think it means.*

"Oh, cool." Brayden polishes off the last of his cheese stick. "Where did those turn up? I've been looking for them."

"Under the passenger seat. I thought . . . I thought Rae brought them." My own stupidity leaves me numb. What kind of dumbass eats items retrieved from the floor of a sketchy van? I knew it tasted off. Why didn't I spit it out?

"Was that a pot cookie?" Rae demands. "Did she just eat a pot cookie? What the hell, Brayden? You didn't tell us those were back here!"

Frankie dissolves into peals of laughter. "Dude, no can leave dose things around! Remember when Joe Boy wen eat like six a dem by mistake? When you gonna learn?"

Apparently, I am not the first victim of Brayden's carelessness. I don't ask about the unfortunate Joe Boy. No sense scaring myself over nothing. I only had a mouthful, not half a dozen cookies. How bad could this be?

"I don't get it." Rae throws her hands up, exasperated with me. "There were, like, forty things for you to eat, and you chose the one thing in this entire vehicle—the one thing!—that had marijuana."

"It was just a bite," I say. "I mean . . . it won't really do anything, will it?"

Frankie titters. "Sage's stuff? Oh, dat going do something. Wait a half hour. Little longer if you had breakfast."

Brayden, on the other hand, downplays the mistake. "No biggie," he says. "That's not a real intense batch. You'll be fine, Charlie. Have the whole cookie, if you want. On the house."

"She's never even smoked before!" Rae hisses, like I can't hear her talking about me. "We don't know how she'll react. She could wig out!"

"First time? Really?" Brayden takes that in, momentarily startled. "Wow. All right, all right. Maybe don't eat the whole thing, then, Charlie. No worries, though. I mean, I'm honored to be with you on this. You're with friends here."

Frankie scratches his head, unable to conceive of a lifetime without marijuana. "You nevah smoke?" he asks me. "Nevah?"

I shake my head.

"Fo' what?" he presses. "I mean, alcohol, dat's poisonous, fine. But weed? Shit's natural."

"Is it, like, a religious thing?" Brayden asks, genuinely curious.

"It's an addiction thing. Runs in my family." I drop the partially eaten cookie back into its bag and pass the batch up front. "I don't want to end up like my parents, so no drugs, no alcohol, nothing that messes with my head."

"I hear you," says Brayden. "I respect that, I do. Sorry for the mix-up. And hey, thanks for sharing your truth."

My "truth" is a little more complicated than the pat narrative I just sold Brayden. My existence has not exactly been substance-free. I smoked cigarettes like a chimney in college. When I worked in publishing, I drank enough coffee to give the average person heart palpitations. And I *still* love me some Ambien on a sleepless night. I haven't avoided drugs or addiction—I've simply gravitated toward a more socially acceptable variety.

"So . . ." The thought of bugging out and embarrassing myself in front of these guys is not an appealing one. "What happens now? How long is this going to last?"

"It's an edible," Brayden says. "Takes some time to hit you, and then it'll linger. We'll see where it takes you, okay? Try to stay open. Look for love and beauty. You don't want to be in a negative mindspace."

His advice, while probably sound, does little to calm my nerves. How do I avoid a "negative mindspace"? I've been fixating on someone's missing daughter, dreaming I'm a stalker. Last night some creeper stole my phone. Who knows what kind of crap my brain might unleash without the strict boundaries of sobriety? Not to mention all the things I could reveal about myself if my personal-sharing meter's off.

I hunker down in my seat, ignoring the apologetic looks from Rae, wondering if I'm destined for a pleasant high or a freak-out.

Yet whatever their faults, the boys are not anxiety-producing company. Frankie puts on some Jawaiian music—Hawaiian-style reggae—and jams contentedly in the front seat. His hand follows the guitar line as he listens, intently working through all the finger positions. Brayden chats with Rae about his two years in Kalo Valley and

all the people he has come to love. The community of artists and arti-
sans. The "very chill" members of his drum circle. An eccentric senior
citizen named Davey, whom Brayden refers to as his "spiritual
mentor."

"Is that your girlfriend's crowd, too?" I ask, wondering just how
nutty-crunchy Kai's mom is and what Jocelyn must think of that.

"The drummers, not so much," Brayden replies, "but Sage has in-
troduced me to a lot of great people. She's super connected. I met her
a couple years ago at this tea ceremony, and she totally blew my mind.
Just so powerful but *contained*, you know?"

"Sounds like a catch," Rae says. "How old is Sage?"

"Old," Frankie states. "Real old."

"Forty-three," Brayden says, but I can't tell if he's confirming or
denying Frankie's statement.

The idea of trying to keep up with a twentysomething sounds like
the stuff of nightmares, not fantasies. I'm six years older than Noah,
and discussing our favorite music or films in high school makes me
feel ancient. I can't imagine throwing another decade between us.

"Forty-three, huh?" Rae slaps the back of Brayden's seat. "Damn,
boy. You got some mommy issues?"

Brayden smiles, a silly, lopsided grin. "I like a woman who's seen
things. Wisdom and experience—that's sexy. That's what drew me to
Sage."

"And da mommy issues," Frankie mutters. "She got a kid in high
school."

"Wow," I say. "So the age difference between you and Sage, does
that get a little . . . weird? Her kid's practically your age."

"Weird? Nah." Brayden peels a strip of dead skin from his sunburned nose. "Kai's cool. We hang out. I take care of him and his

friends, hook them up at parties. His crew's pretty laid-back. They go to that weird private school in town, the Free Thinkers or whatever."

"You said you knew that girl who went missing." Rae leans against the van door. "Lise Nakagawa. I heard she went to that school, too."

"Yeah, we knew her." Brayden sighs. "She was one of Kai's friends. Nice girl."

"Mo' nice den her sister," Frankie says.

"Aw, come on," Brayden objects. "Jocelyn isn't that bad."

"Brah, yeah she is. She so safe, even Kai no can stand her."

"I met Jocelyn the other day," I say. "You guys aren't fans?"

Brayden slows down the van, allowing another car to pass us. "See now, that's hard. I don't want to tear somebody down. Jocelyn and I, we just exist in, like, a different space. She looks to *control* the world, and I look to experience it."

"What does that even mean?"

"Okay, so . . ." Brayden releases a breath. "The Jocelyn I see, she's never really present in herself. All she ever talks about is her grades and how she wants to go to Stanford. She's living for the future. But the thing with the future is, it's always ahead of you. You never get there."

Rae slumps back in her seat. "Sometimes you get there," she says glumly. "You get there, and it's not all that. You run out of things to chase, and when you finally stop to look around, you realize that chemical engineering degree has landed you in sales, kissing up to a bunch of assholes in suits who will use your products to further pollute the planet."

"Yeah, exactly." Brayden casts her a sympathetic glance. "The future is hard on dreams, for sure. I tell Kai, you can spend your time chasing dreams or you can go ahead and live them. And I think he gets it. But Jocelyn? She's just always looking for another carrot to go running after." He tilts his head toward the half-open window, lets the breeze play with his hair. "Contentment exists only in the present, that's what the Buddhists say."

I have spent too much time with these guys, or else the weed is kicking in, because Brayden is actually starting to make sense.

"You hear dis guy?" Frankie chuckles. "He one philosopher. Me, I dunno what da Buddha say, but I know da world ain't fair. Da Jocelyns, dey step on other people, dey go to Stanford, make a billion dollars, buy up half our island. But da Lises, da cool girls . . . life shits 'em out."

"Huh." I slide down in my seat. "You think Lise's dead?"

"*Ma-ke*," Frankie says with a nod. "Elijah Yoon wen kill her. Everybody knows it, and nobody gonna do shit."

"You're wrong, brah." Brayden shakes his head, and his strawberry-blond locks tumble about his shoulders, slower than I expect, like a shampoo commercial. "We met Elijah a bunch of times, and he isn't dangerous. He used to run ahead to open doors for all the girls, remember? He wasn't a bad dude, just . . . quiet."

Frankie shrugs. "If such a good kid, where Lise stay?"

"Maybe she just ran off," Brayden suggests. "Got tired of her folks telling her who to be. They were always on her case about the future. Like, her dad got in this whole epic battle with Marvel Andrada about it."

"With Marvel? Really?" Rae scrunches her nose. "That's so weird. I just had a reading with her yesterday. I swear, everyone in Kalo Valley is connected."

"True dat," Frankie says. "Everybody know everybody and dey business. Especially Marvel. She been around foreva."

"She and Lise were kind of pals," Brayden explains. "They had this whole idea to start a restaurant in town, right? Ono Place. So Marvel leases a building, they do all this work together to get it going—even Elijah gets in on it. Then one day Lise goes home, says she wants to work at the restaurant. Like, full time, instead of going to college in a couple years. Her dad totally lost his shit. Then the mom, that professor lady, made some complaint with the health inspectors so Marvel couldn't get her permits."

"Really?" I find myself giggling. Sue left out that little nugget yesterday.

Brayden nods. "That mom plays dirty."

I press a hand to the window, examine the fingerprints my greasy digits leave behind on the glass. My head feels strange. Light and slow and calm. The landscape is changing around us, no longer black rock, but fields of golden grass swaying in the wind, each blade sharp against a startling blue sky. It feels like Montana or Nebraska or one of the Dakotas. Or at least what I imagine them to be.

"So what was Lise like?" I ask. "Her dad seems to think she was this bad girl."

"Bad? No. Kinda moody." Frankie climbs halfway into the backseat and snatches the bag of dried mango. "She's all kine fun and den, alla sudden, she pissed off. But dat's just girls, huh?"

"Did the police call you guys in when she went missing?" Rae asks. "Did you have to make a statement?"

"They had me in one time," Brayden says. "I told them I didn't really know her. Don't need the po-po breathing down my neck, that's for sure."

I yawn. "They didn't give you any trouble?"

"Nah. They were going hard for Elijah, and Lise never really advertised to her folks who she was hanging with. She just snuck out all the time." Brayden holds out his hand to Frankie and receives a leathery strip of mango. "Sage is really cool about letting Kai's friends kick it at our place when it's late." He takes a bite of mango, and his chewing noises reverberate throughout the van as he continues to speak with his mouth open. "Lise used to come around a lot. Not so much once she started dating Elijah, though. Then they hung out over his way, with Kai and Jocelyn. Like a little couples' retreat or something."

"On Wakea Ranch?" The memory of those lights in the night comes drifting back. "Did Naomi know about that?"

Brayden makes a face. "No way. You've seen that place. They've got a ton of land. Easy for someone to hide if they don't want to be found."

"Maybe Lise doesn't want to be found," I murmur. "Maybe she *is* in hiding."

"She could be hiding in plain sight." Rae looks up. "Lise's an identical twin, right? Could anyone tell her and Jocelyn apart?"

Brayden seems a little thrown by the question, as if he forgot that the Nakagawa girls came from the same genetic material. "Okay, so Lise and Jocelyn *looked* the same. Their voices were the same. But . . . I don't know. They were really different."

"Different style, different vibe," Frankie explains. "You not going mix dose two."

Rae doesn't back down. "But what if they wanted you to? What if they switched?"

Frankie looks up from his half-eaten strip of mango. "You think

Lise and Jocelyn wen pull a twin swap? Dat's some conspiracy-level shit."

"Okay," Rae begins, "so I'll admit I read a little too much Sweet Valley High when I was a kid. But maybe, just maybe, Lise got tired of being the bad girl. Maybe Jocelyn wanted to live a little. Maybe they switched. Jocelyn ran away, Lise took her place, and no one's dead, they're both just . . . taking a break. Living a different life for a little while until they're ready to go back."

I expect the boys to make fun of her theory or at least ask what Sweet Valley High is, but Brayden's expression in the rearview mirror is surprisingly tender. "That's nice," he says softly, the way one might respond to a child who has just blown out their birthday candles and wished for peace on earth. "That's really nice."

And it *is* nice. So much nicer than my visions, all the images I'd happily forget. I set aside my own nagging skepticism, let it drift away like a cloud. Breathe in Brayden's calm, which feels warm and all-encompassing, like a blanket in winter.

Love and beauty, I tell myself. *Love and beauty.*

fifteen

With no paved roads, the green-sand beach of Papakōlea is accessible only with a two-and-a-half-mile hike through highly eroded pasturelands. I'm game to walk or hitch a ride with the enterprising locals who chauffeur visitors in their truck for a fee, but Brayden, bafflingly confident in his old van, insists on driving us himself.

Any other day, I would nix this idea. The chances of our tires getting stuck are much too great. In my current state, however, the prospect of stranding a vehicle that isn't even mine does not seem particularly worrying. I feel floaty and detached, hovering between the real and the possible. Gazing at the ceiling of the van, I let my body absorb the bumps.

"How are you doing?" Rae studies me. "You feel okay?"

"I'm good." The words sound strange when they come out. "Really. I feel like . . . everything's going to be okay."

Rae bursts out laughing. "You're high," she says. "My God, I never thought I'd see the day." She roots through her backpack. "I'm sorry, but I gotta get a picture."

I offer her a hazy look as she snaps a shot on her phone. I don't like the sound it makes. I don't like the feeling of her watching me on her screen. The thought of my own missing phone moves over me like a shadow, harshing my mellow.

Eventually, Brayden stops driving, and we all file out of the van. He leads us on a winding path down steep, layered rock—a volcanic formation, probably, but I'm too focused on the ground, the pebbles shifting beneath my feet, to ask. Below us, the ocean feeds into a small bay. Dark rocks of hardened lava dot the cliffs, and streaks of a greenish mineral gather at the base to form a beach.

"Boogers," I murmur when I see the color. If the sands of Papakōlea Beach are not the shade of green I pictured, they are still unlike any shores I've seen before. I scoop up some sand, rub it between my fingertips, examine its alien color.

"That's olivine," Brayden says. "There's only a couple green-sand beaches in the whole world, and you're on one of them. This is the cinder cone of an old volcano." He gestures to the peculiar half circle of rock that encloses the little beach and bay. The waves are unexpectedly powerful.

"Can we swim?" Rae asks.

"I wouldn't go out deep," Brayden says. His hair has taken flight in the wind and it makes my own scalp tingle. "That current will sweep you out and you'll never make it back. We can splash around the shore, though."

The idea of swimming, coordinating my limbs in an organized fashion, seems quite farfetched at this moment. I sink into the sand at the water's edge. The wet green silt slurps at my toes. I snatch my feet back, alarmed, and shield my eyes from the blowing sand. Why did Frankie and Brayden bring us here? A looming volcanic cinder cone and an ocean with a deadly riptide—this isn't where you bring new friends. And there's no one else on the beach today. Did they know it would be just us? Were they planning for this? I hug my knees, the largeness of the land and sea suddenly overwhelming.

In the shallows, Rae and Brayden dart around with a Frisbee. She looks inexplicably happy chasing after it, although the waves keep knocking her over. I anxiously wait for the water to drag her out to sea, yet she rises, again and again, Frisbee in hand, unconcerned by the sand clinging to her skin.

"You doing okay?" she calls to me, but I can't tell her no, not with Frankie and Brayden listening. I nod.

Behind me, Frankie lies on his belly reading a slim volume of Pablo Neruda poems. While Rae and Brayden frolic like dogs across the beach, he turns pages, sometimes lingering on one, his lips moving.

"Don't read that," I beg Frankie. "You don't need poetry. *This* is a poem. The sand is a poem. My toes are a poem."

"You're baked," he says without looking up.

The ocean creeps up the shore beneath my legs, tickling my bare skin with its foam. Too cold. We are in Hawai'i. Why is it so cold?

I gesture to the stark white page of Frankie's book. "Do you really like Pablo Neruda? Or you just want to look smart?"

Frankie smiles and flips me the bird.

"Weird," I say. "Islands are weird." I kick at the tide. "There's water all around us. Everywhere you go, water. Like it doesn't want you to get away."

"I like da water."

"Water is dangerous," I say. "Brayden said the water is dangerous."

"Not as dangerous as people."

My eyes fall on the scar that runs down Frankie's leg. It's ugly, the lumpy pink tissue. I don't want to hear about the dangerous people Frankie has known. I've known too many myself. For all I know, he's one of them.

"She could already be dead," I whisper.

The pages of his book ruffle in the breeze. "Dead? Who?"

"Everyone. Everyone who's not alive is dead. And if you're not dead now, you will be later." The weight of that startles me. "I'll be like her. I'll be like Lise."

Frankie closes his book, resigning himself to social interaction. "You don't even know dat girl. Why you thinking about her so much?"

"I have these dreams about her. I think I'm supposed to help her. I think it's part of the plan, you know? On a cosmic level or whatever. It's why I'm here."

He smirks. "Whoa, lady. You wen eat dat whole cookie or what?"

I dig my fingers into the olive sand. "You shouldn't die if you're sixteen. You should do lots of other things first. Lise should've done the other things. Live first, die later."

"Everybody gotta die one time or another," Frankie says, and suddenly his own losses hover in the space between us. I can feel them, the people he's known, now gone. I study his pockmarked face, his greasy hair, the line of tattoos going down his skinny arm. He's just a kid, really. A kid hauling around too many shadows. Somebody should've protected him from whatever bad things he has seen, from whatever sliced up his leg like that. Somebody should've protected Lise, too. Not just Victor and Sue. Everybody.

I want to tell him all I know of death. My father. My son. The mother and the sister I lost before I even knew them. And the children, all the children that I see, the ones who speak to me in dreams.

I am on intimate terms with death, but I can't explain that to Frankie. Maybe he can feel it, though, feel the losses I carry the way I feel his.

"It isn't fair," I say, stirring the sand with my index finger. "Not for Lise, or her family. She was going to have . . . a life."

"What kinda life she gonna have here?" Frankie scoffs. "She just stuck on dis island wit da rest of us."

"Not *stuck*. This is paradise."

"Oh yeah, some kinda paradise." Frankie laughs, but without bitterness. "Unless you some rich asshole from da mainland, you poor as shit. Nobody Puna side got money, 'cause how you gonna get 'em? We got no jobs on dis island. State, tourists, and Walmart, dat's da big employahs. Bright fuckin' future, huh? And da local school's crap. You like your kid get ahead, you gotta pay for dese private schools, but how you gonna pay when you poor as shit?"

"Sage sends Kai to private school," I say. "Is she rich?"

"You got any clue da crap Sage gotta sell so she can afford dat school? Not just weed, huh. And Kai, you think he grateful?" Frankie shakes his head. "Get what you pay fo', I guess. Send your kid to a school wit little bitches, bumbye your kid going turn to a little bitch."

Like Jocelyn, I think, brushing sand from my lashes. Like me, maybe, too. I didn't attend a private high school, but at eighteen, I went to Columbia. Surrounded by students who seemed wealthy and urbane, I learned to dress like them, talk like them, be one of them. I became a little bitch, New York style.

"Lise went to Free Thought with Kai," I say. "Was she like that? A little bitch?"

"Nah." Frankie lies back on the beach, elbows splayed above his head. "Not Lise. Her parents try fo' polish her up, but she nevah bought in. Her sister now, she jump through every hoop like one circus dog. But not Lise. She da real deal." He closes his eyes, either to shut down our conversation or to take a nap.

Something snakes through the back of my mind, an unformed idea I can't lay my hands on. What if Rae is right? Not about the twins switching identities—that would last about ten minutes before someone figured it out—but about Lise wanting to escape her life. Perhaps something was happening to her, something she wanted to get away from. She could've gone into hiding. Or attempted to, and run into trouble along the way. True, Lise didn't bring any of her belongings, but maybe the situation was so desperate she was willing to leave everything behind. Maybe she wanted people to believe her dead.

But why? Who was the guy watching her in the night? What did he do to her?

Unable to hold the thought, I stare at my feet for a while instead. The longer I look, the stranger my toes appear, like deformed fingers incorrectly arranged. I wish the sky were not so big. I wish the sea were not so loud.

"Frankie?"

"Unh?" His grunt is almost lost to the crashing surf.

"You ever see anyone following Lise or Jocelyn around? Like, a weird guy with a creepy crush?"

His head rolls slightly in my direction. "Nah."

"Maybe he was normal on the outside," I say, "but inside, he had these secret pervy thoughts. Did you ever see a guy like that hanging around?"

"'Secret pervy thoughts'?" Frankie snickers as he turns away from me, grains of green sand stuck to one cheek. "Dat's every dude, lady. Every. Single. One."

ᛋ

IN TIME, a time I can no longer measure, the wind and waves and weed pull me under. I dream of Pele and her sister the ocean goddess. The dream is as flat as Sue's painting, lacking the sensory detail of my visions, but the images are vivid. Pele stands upon a gushing volcano, molten hair flowing to the sea. Her sister springs from the waves, frothy and graceful, hands outstretched. Then the lava pours. The sea begins to churn. Suddenly I realize that these aren't goddesses at all, but Jocelyn and Lise. Smoke billows from one girl's head. Her hands glow yellow and melt away; her body is consumed by flames. Below her, the other sister sinks slowly into the sea, silent, drowning.

When Rae shakes me awake, every fiber of my being screams *danger*. My arm flies out, striking her on the shoulder.

"Ow!" She pulls away from me. "What's with you?"

I sit up, push strands of sandy, windblown hair from my face. "Sorry. I was dreaming about the Nakagawa girls."

"Ooh. What about?"

"I don't know, but I'm scared, Rae." I chug from my water bottle, eyes roving the beach. An older couple has just arrived and stand discussing the color of the sand. "Whatever happened to Lise . . . it could put Jocelyn in danger, too."

Rae kneels beside me. "Oh my God," she says. "You're right. If some guy stalked and killed Lise, Jocelyn would be the next logical step. I mean, that's textbook."

I have no idea what textbook she's referring to—is there a *DSM-5* entry for homicidal stalkers who choose victims with identical twins?—but I nod anyway. "We need to keep an eye on Jocelyn." The feeling of the breeze against my back makes my skin creep. "I think she's been going out to the woods, the ones by Wakea Ranch. Remember the lights I saw last night? There was some kind of meeting."

"Brayden did say she and Lise and Kai used to hang out there with Elijah. You think she met up with Elijah?"

"No idea, but I don't want her in those woods. Not with these dreams I'm having. She's not safe."

I almost say, *And neither are we.* I almost tell her, *These boys are strangers and we need to get out of here,* but Brayden comes bounding across the shore, interrupting our conversation. His chest is a shade of Barbie pink, but he doesn't seem to notice. "You ready for South Point?" he asks. "Gotta show you guys some cliffs!"

I stare at Brayden, wondering who he really is and what he wants from us. Can he hear my thoughts? Does he know that I suspect him? Behind us, Frankie has already begun to ascend the cinder cone, attacking its steep slope with admirable vigor for someone in flip-flops.

Rae grabs me by the hand and drags me to my feet. "Come on. I'm not going home until I've tried cliff diving."

"Wait . . . what?" Standing has left me light-headed. I take a few steps, trying not to wobble. "No, Rae. No way. You're not jumping off a cliff. We can't trust those two. What if they're trying to get rid of us?"

Rae doesn't hear me. She's already running after Frankie, waving at me to catch up.

"Stop!" I shout, but the wind and surf muddle my words. "Rae? I don't even *like* cliffs. Rae? Wait for me, goddamn it!"

I struggle up the slope after her, afraid to be left behind, but also afraid to follow. I have the vague sense of being a teenager again, left in the lurch as a friend runs off to have her fun. Why does the party always move away from me? Even high, I'm not cool or funny. I'm just a raw nerve, uncomfortably alert, enshrouded in a cloud of dread.

Somehow Brayden's jolting van makes it back across the dusty pastureland. Everyone's talking, chattering, except for me. Like a turtle in my shell, I try to shut them out, to form a wall around my thoughts and fears so they can't hear me. The vehicle bumps along, and my gaze settles on the blue strip outside Rae's window. Water again. We can't escape it. It's always with us, always waiting.

Brayden turns left onto South Point Road, and suddenly the sea looms directly before us, our destination. "They say this is where the Polynesians first arrived," Brayden tells us, gesturing to the ocean. "Kinda blows the mind, doesn't it, going thousands of miles in a bunch of double-hulled canoes?"

As the road comes to an end and we all pile out of the van, my fingers can't stop worrying at the hem of my shorts. Rae keeps talking to the boys like everything's fine, but I don't buy it. We should've brought our own vehicle. Instead we're trapped, left at the mercy of two guys we barely know, and I don't even have a phone. Bad things are happening here. Why can't Rae see that?

The land only amplifies my fears. Brown craggy cliffs drop an abrupt forty feet into the raging ocean below. The rocks are sharp and cruel, ready to pierce flesh or shatter bone. To the west, rows of white wind turbines harness the power of such blustery heights and disrupt an otherwise stark display of nature. A lone fisherman sits perched on a rocky ledge, his line bouncing across the rough surf below.

I trudge behind Rae, watch the jarring movement of my feet across stone. We should just leave now, before they can get us. We should run. But I can't leave Rae on her own. I'm all she has. I will follow her like a lemming to my doom.

The closer we get to the brink, the more profound my anxiety spiral. The chill breeze, the cliff's edge, that sense of gaping space just beyond—they all carry an unpleasant sense of déjà vu. And then I feel a buzzing in my hands, my spine, a low-grade electrical humming, as if someone has plugged me in.

The vision comes in a rush.

Dark sky, grassy terrain, a mineral smell. I am standing not on the sunny cliffs of South Point, but in the blackness of Volcanoes National Park, gasping at the rim of the caldera.

I can't breathe. Can't resist the sudden pressure of two hands on my back, fingertips pressing, pushing, urging me toward the edge.

Fall.

"Charlie? You doing all right?"

I recoil from Brayden's touch like a scalded cat. "Fine! I'm fine!"

The details of my vision flutter away in the wind. The sunlight hurts my eyes. I scowl at Brayden.

"Okay, okay." Brayden puts up his hands like a hostage negotiator proving he's unarmed. "You were breathing a little weird, that's all. Just checking in. Weed can make a person kinda paranoid, especially your first time. You've got to remember it's just the Mary Jane messing with you."

"Maybe sit and take a few deep breaths, huh?" Rae says, but she's too fixated on the cliff to worry much about my mental state.

"We're all friends," Brayden reminds me.

I lower myself onto a rocky knob and sit tensely, not convinced he's right. *Is* Brayden a friend? Is Frankie? I don't understand what this vision means, who or what it's warning me of, but either one of these guys could've killed Lise Nakagawa. Are my fears paranoia or intuition? How the hell can one tell the difference?

Brayden approaches the cliff's edge and points to a rickety piece of metal protruding from the side. "So that's the ladder you use for diving," he tells Rae. "The jump itself is no biggie, but if you're scared of heights, going up that ladder afterward can make you a bit nervous."

"I can do it," Rae says, but she looks less sure of herself than before. "Where do you jump? Just off the side here?"

"Or can use da blowhole." Frankie leads her several feet back to a break in the cliff's rocky surface. A large hole drops all the way down to the sea. I can hear the sound of the ocean crashing below, and I gawp at Frankie.

"She isn't going to jump in there! Who would do that?"

"You can't see it from up here, but there's a tunnel through the rock," Brayden explains. "You jump while the water's coming in, and the current sucks you back out."

Rae peers down into the hole, her loose T-shirt rippling in the breeze.

"The blowhole isn't for beginners," Brayden says. "Stick to the cliff."

"What if she can't get back to the ladder?" I demand.

"She's gonna do fine," Frankie says.

"But the undertow!" I'm not at all sure of Rae's swimming abilities. "What if the current catches her?"

"Dis South Point," Frankie says with the faintest hint of a smile. "Da current catches you, you not coming back."

Rae continues staring down the hole. "I've come this far," she says.

"Oh no," I tell her. "Nope. I'm not explaining to your husband and your daughter why I let you drown. Veto."

"She can handle," Frankie says. "What, you wen come all dis way, might as well." He strips off his shirt and steps down onto a small ledge inside the hole. "Watch."

And with that, he jumps.

His body careens down the center of the hole as if in slow motion, avoiding contact with the surrounding rock wall. There's a splash, but I don't get close enough to the edge to see the results.

"Show-off." Brayden grins in spite of himself. "Come on." He heads back toward the rickety ladder.

I remain in a squat, fighting off a wave of vertigo.

After an excruciatingly long wait, the ladder begins to shake with the weight of a climber. Frankie's dripping-wet head appears on the side of the cliff. He heaves himself back up onto solid ground and shakes off like a dog.

"You see? No sweat." He nods at Rae. "Going, girl!"

She walks back to the blowhole and slides down onto the interior ledge, inspecting it. "Damn. I don't know."

"Rae." I try to look stern and authoritative, like I'm not stoned and fighting off hallucinations in an awkward crouch. "Rae, this doesn't look safe."

"Dass da point," Frankie says, shivering. "Make you feel alive."

"But what if—"

"Hey," Frankie says. "I wen see plenny people make dis jump."

"Oh yeah? Like who? Someone *our* age?" I glare at Brayden. "You ever see Sage leap off this thing?"

Brayden whistles. "No way. She'd never."

"Yeah, I didn't think so."

"Elijah Yoon," Frankie counters. "He wen jump dis blowhole, and dat buggah scrawny."

"You came out here with Elijah?" My arms have turned to gooseflesh in the wind. "Was Lise here, too? Did she jump?"

"No, but Jocelyn wen jump. She wen jump in da *dark*." Frankie's voice is tinged with grudging admiration.

"Jocelyn jumped in there?" I glance over at the ledge where Rae now dubiously stands surveying the water.

"At night, with a glow stick," Brayden confirms. "It was insane. We were all shining flashlights down the hole, watching the water like, no way. We didn't think she'd do it. She's a really good swimmer, though."

"*Jocelyn?*" This goes against everything I think I know about the Nakagawa sisters. "Why? Why would she do that? I thought she had a good head on her shoulders."

Frankie points at my wrinkled-up nose. "Dat look on your face," he says. "Dass why." He smirks. "You da good-girl type. You know. Sometime you gotta break out, yeah?"

I search for a smart retort, something to remind him I'm a woman, not a girl, thank you, and fading into the background is underrated, especially when you've recently been featured in the *Squealer,* but before my addled brain can find the words, Rae makes a sudden, startling jump from the ledge.

Her leap is not nearly as graceful as Frankie's—one leg bent in front of her, both arms raised above her head—and she hollers on the way down. Then her voice cuts out, and there is only water. I don't hear the splash, just surf slapping against rock.

I turn to Brayden, stricken. "What happened? Is she . . . ?"

Eyes wide, he steps onto the ledge and gazes down at the water. "I don't see her," he says. "She must have caught the tide right." The uncertainty on his face is far from reassuring.

I crawl over to the ladder. Lie flat on my stomach and peer over the side.

"Rae!" I call, but the wind swallows her name. I imagine her body getting dashed on the rocks, wonder if I should go in after her, wonder how I can possibly face Zoey if I let something happen to her mother. Were the boys plotting this all along? Did Frankie and Brayden want her to die? Am I next?

When her dark head pops up, my whole body goes slack with relief.

Rae looks around, spots the ladder, and begins swimming hard toward it. Though the distance is not great, the current renders her strokes largely ineffectual. It's like watching someone on a treadmill.

"She's not getting anywhere," I tell Frankie, my voice rising.

"She's gotta ride it," he says, and sure enough, Rae stops fighting and lets the waves carry her in.

By the time she makes it up that awful ladder, I think I might cry. This could have gone so differently, could've ended so badly. I can't reconcile my own fears with her broad grin, her curls glistening and uncharacteristically wild, the light in her eyes. The breeze must be cold against her sodden T-shirt, but she doesn't care.

"Did you see that?" she breathes. "I can't believe I did it! I can't believe I made it."

"That blowhole is no joke," Brayden says. "That was pretty nasty." He holds out his hand for a fist bump, which Rae returns so enthusiastically it resembles a punch.

"Aw, Charlie." Seeing my disapproval, she hooks a damp arm through mine. "In five days, I'll be a mom and a wife and a good little worker. I'll play it safe again, I promise. Just give me this, won't you? These few days. Because *I* don't have psychic powers to keep life interesting."

My eyes dart toward Frankie and Brayden—has she blown my cover?—but they aren't listening. They're digging through Rae's backpack for snacks.

I huddle closer to her, feel her dripping shirt leave a wet mark on my own. There are many things I'd like to say about this day, about the boys and the weed and these petrifying cliffs, but right now all I can do is tug on her arm and beg, in a voice as small as Tasha's, "Can we go home now?"

BY THE TIME we make it back to Kalo Valley, the pot cookie has worn off and I'm officially done with Frankie and Brayden. True, they made no attempts on my life, but on the ride home, I was subjected to alarming levels of Taylor Swift. Dining with them was no picnic, either. Knowing that Rae and I were footing the bill, the boys ordered two dinners apiece at the restaurant in Nāʻālehu. Frankie repeatedly hit on a waitress who could not possibly have been eighteen, and Brayden consumed an entire dish of loco moco while chewing with his mouth open. Even Rae rolled her eyes as the guys descended into braggy stories about big waves and boozy nights. I found myself missing Noah and my daughters, yearning for the unglamorous life we led pre-*Squealer*. In the Koa House driveway, Rae and I thank the guys and heave a sigh of relief as their old white van pulls away.

No more pot, I think. *Ever, ever, ever.* If I'm ready to curl up in the outdoor bath with a book, Rae has other ideas.

"Let's go see Marvel Andrada," she suggests before I can even make it inside.

I collapse onto the porch swing. "We only have a few days left on the island, Rae. Do we really need to waste time getting psychic advice from some eccentric old lady?"

"You are something else. After everything you've been through, you're still skeptical about psychics?" She wags a finger at me. "Come on, Charlie. You really think you're the only one out there, the only one with a gift?"

"Some gift." I remember the sensation of hands on my back, pushing, pushing, and shudder. "Half of what I see makes no sense. Why would I want this Marvel woman confusing me further?"

Rae sits beside me and offers up a piece of unassailable logic. "Because she knew Lise."

sixteen

One look inside Marvel Andrada's crystal shop, and I can't help thinking that Sue Nakagawa might not be the only thing standing in the way of her restaurant permits. The place is a cluttered, musty mess, with too many shelves crammed into a small space, each brimming with polished rocks and crystals, new age books, incense, candles, tarot cards, and other mumbo jumbo I don't want to be associated with. Whatever Marvel's talents may be, organization does not appear to be one of them.

Marvel has just finished a reading when we arrive. The client stands by the front register, teary eyed, still trying to compose herself, while her two hyperactive children bounce around the store, sniffing candles and examining crystals. The woman dabs at her eyes, trying to assimilate whatever Marvel has told her.

"Thank you, Auntie. I got a lot to think about now."

"You have hard choices to make, Maile," Marvel tells her, "but you have the strength to do it. Good luck." She watches the woman leave and then turns to Rae. "Back again, eh? And you brought your friend, I see."

"I did!" Rae beams, an eager little matchmaker for her two favorite psychics. "Charlie, you remember Marvel."

"Rae tells me you're quite a talent," Marvel says. "That you've been recognized in national magazines for your skills."

"Oh." The wooden floor creaks beneath my shifting weight. "I wouldn't say that I'm skilled. I can't control it or anything."

"Control will come," Marvel says, "although not without some work. Like anything, you've got to practice." She sounds like a piano teacher. "Have you ever been surfing? It's a bit like that. You swim out into the waves and catch one. If you pick a good wave and time things right, you can ride it all the way back to the shore."

"That's what your visions are like?"

She nods. "I can't control the ocean. But I can position myself to catch what comes." She looks me up and down, assessing something, and seems to find me lacking. "I have some stones in the shop that can sharpen your sight, if you'd like. And I highly recommend tiger's eye for protection."

I squirm at the offer. The whole store makes me feel ridiculous. In contrast to Sue's academically rigorous library, Marvel's shelves feature titles that try to imbue new age concepts with a business feel: *The Chakra Solution, Intuitive Finance,* and *Right Mind, Right Action: Meditate Your Way to Success.*

"Uh, no thanks," I tell her. "I'm really not here about . . . that."

"I know," Marvel says. "You want to talk about Lise."

When my eyes bug at her accuracy, she laughs.

"David Kalahele said you've been asking about her," she explains. "He suggested I talk to you. Said you're a journalist, and you might be able to put some pressure on the police."

"David said that?" I had no idea my gracious proprietor even knew what I was up to, let alone that he was urging people in town to help me.

Marvel studies me with intelligent eyes. "I've tried talking to the police myself. They aren't interested in what I have to say. Maybe a journalist could get things done."

"A journalist with an amazing ability," Rae pipes in. "If the police follow your visions, then maybe—"

I cut her off. "I'm here as *just* a journalist, Rae. Poking around at what could be a story. The rest of it's irrelevant." I don't know why I feel compelled to lie. Marvel's the last person to judge me for my dreams, yet I feel exposed in front of her, embarrassed.

Marvel sits down on a stool behind the counter, leaving Rae and me to remain standing. "This story—what's your angle?"

"I don't know yet." I pick at a yellow thread on my shirt. "Elijah Yoon, maybe? I know a lot of people around here think he killed Lise, but Sue Nakagawa is convinced they're wrong."

"Then Sue and I agree on something, for once."

I ignore her animosity toward Sue. "I heard Lise was going to work for you. Were you two close?"

"Close?" Marvel tries to smile, but it's obvious that Lise is not an easy topic for her. "I like to think so. She came into my shop a couple of years ago, and then—she just kept coming."

"Did she get readings with you?"

"No," Marvel says. "She bought a pack of tarot cards, and then she'd come by after school, wanting advice on how to use them. Eventually we got to talking, and it was clear she was just looking for a place to get space from her parents. She'd buy a little something and then hang around for an hour or two. I always liked her. We got on well."

I remember the collection of crystals and gemstones in Lise's bedroom and imagine, with a pang, her selecting one each time she visited Marvel. "What did you talk about?"

"Whatever was on her mind, really. School, her friends, her family—they're a piece of work, let me tell you. I told her about the restaurant I always wanted to open for the students, and she had lots of ideas, ways to make it the kind of place that young people would like to spend time in. She convinced me to buy the place, really. Her enthusiasm rubbed off on me."

I dip a finger into a basket of cheap gold angel pins that Marvel keeps by the register. The pins are on sale for $9.99, which seems like a real rip-off. "So Ono Place . . . you were in it together, you and Lise."

"Yes." Marvel turns away, busying herself with something behind the counter, but not before I see her dark eyes glistening. "We had this plan. Lise would work for me once the restaurant opened and become the manager once she finished high school. When I died, the whole thing would be hers. We talked about it for months—Elijah, too— and then I finally got the lease next door." Marvel pauses. "I didn't realize she hadn't told her parents any of it. Soon as they got wind of the whole thing, I started running into trouble with permits."

"You think her parents were responsible?"

"Of course they were." Marvel doesn't bother to disguise her scorn for the Nakagawas. "Victor never liked how close I was with his daughter. It drove him crazy that someone else might have some influence with her. He and Sue, they had their girls' futures planned from the moment they were born. They didn't want any options on the table for Lise but college."

"You never felt like you were interfering?" I can't help myself. I don't excuse Sue's sabotaging Marvel's business, but if some strange woman started talking Micky out of higher education, I might react badly, too.

Marvel sees that I'm not on her side and grows defensive. "Look," she says with irritation, "Lise was gearing up for a showdown with her parents long before I entered the picture. They were on her constantly about her grades, her activities, her friends. If it wasn't the restaurant, it would've been something else."

"But Victor and Sue blamed you."

"Ugh, Victor." Marvel shakes her head darkly. "He comes in here one day, hollering about how he's the parent and I just better stay out of family decisions that aren't mine to make. I told him where he could shove it. Said if he really wanted her to go to college so badly, the best thing he could do was stop fighting her so hard. A kid like Lise is always going to do the opposite of what you push for, any amateur knows that."

"Ooh." Rae winces. "I can imagine that didn't go over too well."

"Look at my empty restaurant next door, and you see how well it went over. I'll never get that place open now. It's a huge financial loss for me, and I can thank Sue for it."

As topics of conversation go, the Nakagawas have proven quite the minefield. I move away from the counter, wandering the dusty shop. "It's been six weeks. What do you think happened to Lise? I mean, you must have tried to find her. To use your . . . your powers." I flush at the words "your powers."

"I try to reach her every day." Marvel touches the tip of her thick gray braid. "Sometimes she feels so close, but when I try to get a sense of place, I get nothing. Cold. Darkness. That's it."

I swallow. "What does that mean to you?"

She hesitates. "I'm a psychic, not a medium. I don't speak to the dead, but . . . I think she's gone. I think someone killed her. A man. Not Elijah, someone older."

Half-hidden behind a rotating display of incense sticks, I freeze. "How do you know? Did you . . . see something?"

I'm not sure how Marvel's powers are supposed to work, if she uses tarot cards, consults a crystal ball, or if her methodology is as vague as my own, but in that moment, I want to believe in her. Maybe our impressions align. Maybe she, too, has seen the guy in the woods. Maybe I'm not alone in this.

"I haven't seen a damn thing," Marvel says, dashing all my hopes. "God knows I've tried. No, I'm basing this on what Lise herself told me. Before she went missing, she gave me some . . . clues."

Rae and I wait, transfixed, while Marvel collects herself.

"It started in August, I think," she says. "We were getting the restaurant ready, her, Elijah, and I, still thinking we might open soon. Lise had always shared things with me, but that began to change. I could feel that she had a secret, something troubling her. An ugly thing," she adds. "I visualized it as a black oil, something that coated the skin, left her feeling soiled. Then one day—in early September, I think—we were stocking up the freezer, just her and me. And she started asking questions. Some very disturbing questions."

"About . . . ?"

"About rape."

The word falls hard and heavy in the little shop.

I have a flash of the guy in the woods, watching, waiting, obsessing over this girl. When he emerged from those bushes, advanced on that girl, I thought that was the end of her. In my heart of hearts, I thought she died that night. But what if I was wrong? What if that was not the last night of Lise's life at all, but the moment that changed everything?

"What did she ask you, Marvel?" Rae prods.

The woman's answer surprises me. "She wanted to know about statutory rape."

"What?"

Marvel hunches forward on the stool. "She asked if statutory rape was the same in the eyes of the law as other forms of rape. If someone convicted had to register as a sex offender, that sort of thing." She takes a breath. "Lise was speaking in the abstract, but the more she asked, the more personal it began to seem. She kept talking about the age of consent."

"Which is how old, in Hawai'i?" Rae says.

"Sixteen," Marvel informs us. "And Lise had just turned sixteen the month before."

"So she was trying to figure out if it was legal for her to have sex with an older partner," Rae guesses.

"No," says Marvel. "It wasn't like that. She wanted to know if an older partner could still be punished once the underage partner reached the age of consent. If there was a statute of limitations."

"She'd already been having this relationship, then," I murmur.

"Apparently. It sounded consensual, but she didn't give me any details."

I frown. This isn't what I expected at all. "All these questions—what did you tell her?"

Marvel shrugs. "That I'm not a legal expert. That we could look it up on the Internet together. I regret not pressing her on it now, of course, but at the time . . . she said she was all right. That she could handle things."

There's no need to point out Marvel's colossally bad judgment here. She knows. She will live with it the rest of her life.

"You really don't know who the older person was in this scenario?" Rae asks. "Not even a guess?"

"No." Marvel rubs the space between her eyebrows as if trying to stave off a migraine. "But she obviously had someone in mind."

My thoughts turn to Frankie. On our way to South Point today, Frankie bragged that he liked his girls "barely legal." He knew Lise, and by his own admission, he liked her. I could imagine a rebellious teenage girl going for a guy like Frankie: older, damaged, the kind who drags around his volume of Neruda poems to read on the beach.

Could he be the guy?

Rae plants herself cross-legged in the middle of the store as if no longer able to stand. "So you think Lise was threatening this older guy with statutory rape charges, and then he killed her?"

"Yes," Marvel says. "It didn't sound like a healthy relationship. I don't know if they were still involved or if this was something in the past, but . . . it's like she was trying to figure out what kind of power she had over him. Trying to find out how bad she could break him, and whether or not she really wanted to."

"You're sure the person in question was a man?" I ask, and Marvel balks.

"I don't remember her actually saying 'he' or 'she,'" Marvel admits. "But I don't think Lise was a lesbian if that's what you're asking." Her voice drops at the word "lesbian," as if such things should not be discussed at full volume.

"Just checking."

"Look, it's clear enough what happened, isn't it?" She bows her head, and I can almost see the guilt that weighs upon her shoulders, a crushing stone built of should've, would've, could've. "At some point before she turned sixteen, Lise had a sexual relationship with someone older. Maybe she regretted it later. Maybe she felt that it had been coerced, I don't know. But for whatever reason, she was upset with the man. She wanted to make trouble for him. And he . . . he didn't let her."

I run a hand through my hair, trying to process all of this. "You said you've tried to talk to the police?"

"Of course I did. I've been to them several times. They don't want to hear anything that contradicts their theory about Elijah." She gives a brittle laugh. "Big, bad Elijah Yoon. Have you spoken to that boy?"

"Just saw him that day in town," I say. "But I've met his brothers."

"Elijah isn't like his brothers," Marvel tells me. "He knows there's a world out there he's missing, and he wants to be a part of it. Lise's always been his connection to that world. They've been friends since they were kids, long before they were a couple. He wouldn't give up that friendship for anything. It's all he has."

He doesn't have even that anymore, I think.

"Did you know Lise was planning to break up with him?" Rae asks.

"No," Marvel says, "but I knew his family was wearing on her." She puts her hands on her hips, frustrated we are back on the Elijah track. "So she broke up with him. So what? That doesn't mean he hurt her. I'm telling you, you need to be looking at this other man. You say you're a journalist? Then write something. Tell people the truth."

"Marvel." Seeing her passion, I now feel guilty for concocting an imaginary article. "You know I can't substantiate *any* of this."

"But I bet someone could." Rae dusts off her butt and rises to her feet. "Lise couldn't have kept this older guy a secret from *everyone*.

She's sixteen. She had friends. Who would know, Marvel? Who did she confide in?"

"Well," Marvel says doubtfully, "I don't know if she'll talk to you. But if anyone knows who Lise was seeing, it's her sister."

BACK AT KOA HOUSE, I pace Rae's bedroom. "How are we supposed to get ahold of Jocelyn?" I grumble. "Even if she talks to me, there's no way Victor doesn't hear about it. And he won't like it. At all. You heard what he and Sue did to Marvel. I can't afford to get on his bad side."

"Relax." Rae lies in bed playing a Tetris knockoff on her phone. "You're just doing what Sue told you to do. She *asked* you to get involved."

"Yeah, behind her husband's back."

Rae doesn't look up from her game. "I'm sure Jocelyn and Sue are used to doing things behind Victor's back. This is not a big deal. We'll find a way to bump into Jocelyn when her parents aren't around and see what happens."

"Bump into her how?" For the umpteenth time, I wish I had my phone. "You think she broadcasts her whole life on Twitter, too?"

"No," Rae says, already several steps ahead of me. "She doesn't have an account. But she's on the Free Thought swim team, isn't she? I bet they meet every day. We'll just snag her after one of her practices. Tell her you need to interview her for the *Outdoor Adventures* piece. Victor won't object to that."

I stop pacing. I could legitimately use a few quotes from Victor's daughter to pad the piece, and it's the perfect excuse to approach Jocelyn. Rae's good at all this maneuvering.

"We could probably arrange a run-in with her tomorrow," I say.

"I'll just have to figure out how to bring up her sister without being too obvious."

I drop onto the bed beside Rae and watch a gecko dart up the curtains. Compared to my room, the Tree Fern Room is dark and claustrophobic. Instead of warm yellow walls, the wallpaper is a leafy green forest. Here, the low-wattage lamps seem to cast more shadows than light, and the large potted ferns at the foot of the bed remind me of the Wakea Ranch woods.

Rae lets a couple of colored blocks drift to the bottom of her screen, a little dreamy. "Do you think the Nakagawa girls have one of those special twin connections?" she asks. "Like, if Lise's dead, would Jocelyn feel it in her bones? Would she just know?"

Once, I would've laughed at all that metaphysical crap; now it's my life. I sigh.

"I don't know, but you should've seen their bedroom. So much for identical DNA. It was like college roommates, two strangers smooshed in a single room."

"Identical DNA can express itself differently." Rae returns to her phone, trying to clear the mounting Tetris blocks. "You've got factors like environment, diet, physical activity, drug and alcohol use . . . all those would lead to variations over time. And family dynamics. Maybe Victor and Sue needed them each to play a certain role."

"They sure did look alike." I shiver. "All those pictures on the wall at the Nakagawas' place . . . I didn't even realize that they were two different people."

Rae scrunches up her nose. "Yeah, that was weird how the girls never posed in photos together. Always individuals, never a team."

"Maybe Sue was trying to help them differentiate."

"Or maybe she was trying to inspire competition."

Having met Sue, I could believe that. Those girls have borne some high expectations all these years, especially Jocelyn.

"When Jocelyn first walked in the other night . . . I really thought it was Lise." I shake my head. "For a few seconds, I thought she'd come home."

"Hey, maybe she never left." The words GAME OVER flash on Rae's screen. She sets her phone down with a pout. "Like I said before, Jocelyn could be the missing one. Maybe Lise stole her identity. She got tired of living in the shadows and . . ." She raises her arm and makes a stabbing gesture. "That would be a hell of a Lifetime movie, right? '*Twin Swap:* The true story of a girl who stole her sister's boyfriend . . . *and her life.*'"

"It's not funny, Rae." Though I know her callousness is a defense mechanism, a way to protect herself from feeling Sue's pain, it still pisses me off. "These are real people, not characters on a soap opera. Twin swaps are not an actual thing."

"You don't have an identical twin. How would you know?"

"People would notice!"

"Would they?"

"Of course they would!" I can't believe I'm dignifying her theory with a response. "Lise's a lousy student. You don't magically acquire good study habits overnight. And Jocelyn's on the swim team. She's in peak physical condition. If there was a sudden change in her academic or athletic performance, people would notice."

"Well, maybe they have." Rae rolls onto her stomach. "Have you checked her report card?"

"Yes, actually. Sue said Jocelyn got a D on a math test right after Lise went missing, and she's been fine ever since. Academically, she hasn't been affected at all."

"Not at all?" Rae frowns. "Well, that's cold-blooded. You'd think she'd struggle a *little*. Maybe Frankie and Brayden are right about her."

I know Rae is just throwing out any theory that will stick, but I bristle nevertheless. "What is with everyone dumping on Jocelyn all the time? She can't do anything to please you guys."

Rae yawns. "Hey, I don't even know her. She just sounds a little uptight, that's all. The burning desire to go to Stanford? She's like that girl on *Saved by the Bell*, the one who popped pills to study harder."

Using early nineties pop-culture references to justify a low opinion of Jocelyn strikes me as unsporting. "What's so wrong with wanting to go to Stanford?" I demand. "So she keeps her eye on the prize. Good for her. Is she supposed to sit around letting family crap screw up her shot at a good future?"

Though I don't say so, I have a pretty good idea where Jocelyn is coming from. At fourteen, I lost my father in a drunk-driving accident of his own making. Instead of tears and an emotional breakdown, I hit high school with a vengeance, let the goals I'd long entertained become my driving force. Was I overly focused on external markers of success? Sure. But my determination to achieve wasn't just for me. It was for my grandmother, too. Her only son was dead. I was all she had left.

"Jocelyn is carrying the dreams of both her parents," I say. "She has been for a long time. Maybe she's not as fun or relaxed or likeable as Lise, but that doesn't make her a bad person. If she were male, how many people would be mocking her ambitions?"

"You're right," Rae says. "That wasn't fair."

I can see her looking at me, intuiting the ways in which I might identify with Jocelyn. *No*, I think. *We aren't going there.*

"The bottom line is that if Lise had a relationship with some older guy, Jocelyn might know about it," I tell her. "She might've seen something, overheard a secret phone call, who knows."

Rae picks up her phone, probably to launch another round of Tetris. "How does Marvel's story about the older guy fit into what you've been seeing?" she asks. "You think he's the creeper in the woods?"

"No clue." I slide off her bed and stand by the door to the balcony.

The night is a thick, black strip between the curtains. "I still can't be sure whether it's Jocelyn or Lise he was watching in those woods. Hard to know what to do when I still don't know which girl we're dealing with."

Rae's too intent on her phone to answer.

Watching her fiddle with it makes me again crave my own missing phone. "Hey, I should check my email. Maybe Find My iPhone sent me an update. GPS coordinates or something."

"Yeah," says Rae. "I think you need to do that." She's staring down at her screen, forehead wrinkled, with an uncharacteristically serious expression.

"What? Why are you making that face?"

"You'd better get a look at this." She holds her phone out to me.

Instagram, I realize with a sinking feeling. A new picture posted to my account about half an hour ago. Not a flower this time, but a person.

A woman with brown hair and a yellow T-shirt, her blurry face half-turned from the camera as she enters Marvel's store. I glance uneasily over my shoulder, wondering who's there, who's been watching.

I know the woman in that photo. It's me.

thursday

seventeen

I can't sleep. My stomach is a bundle of nerves. My body reacts to every sound, every shifting shadow. I check the lock on the door to the balcony twice, feeling naked without my phone. The questions come in a feverish loop: *Who's been watching me? Why? Is it the same guy watching Lise/Jocelyn? Is it the mysterious older guy in Lise's life? Exactly how many creepy men are out there?*

Frankie's voice plays in my head, offering up a chilling reply. *Dat's every dude, lady. Every. Single. One.*

So far, technology has proved more alarming than helpful in tracking down my stalker. Though Find My iPhone did provide me with new GPS coordinates, the location indicated only that the person was in the square this evening—something I already knew, given the photo of me. I should've paid more attention to my surroundings, inspected every dark corner for a lurking stranger. From now on, I need to be on alert.

When morning comes, I'm only too happy to leave the prison of my bed. I trudge off to the shower, noting in the mirror the strange angle of my hair and the pinkish-gray circles beneath my eyes. Not a face you'd expect to attract a stalker.

"Stalker," of course, could be a misnomer. Stealing a woman's phone and using it to covertly take pictures of her strikes me as a distinctly male activity, but I could be misreading things. Maybe the thief is female, and she's just trying to scare me. It wouldn't be the first time that I've come into a town in pursuit of a story and upset locals with my questions.

Rae is already guzzling coffee when I make it to the breakfast table. Though it's early, she's dialed up to about an eight, her enthusiasm the product of both caffeine and a discussion she and Thom are having about the recent *Magic Mike* sequel. She stops when she catches sight of me in the doorway.

"Good morning, sunshine. You look like death warmed over."

"Sleep is overrated." I sit down and pour myself a generous cup of coffee. "Have you checked Instagram this morning?"

"Nothing new."

Though she puts on a good face, Rae is stressing at least as hard as I am about that photo. Last night, worried that we were in over our heads, she insisted that I call Noah. The conversation did not go well. Noah, bless his heart, is a take-action kind of guy. He can comfort a crying baby or replace a broken AC compressor, but he cannot sit idly by when he feels my personal safety is at risk. News of my watcher had him ready to airlift me off the island. *Don't go taking dumb chances*, he begged me. *The kids and I, we need you home in one piece.* My assurances of vigilance were small comfort to a man who has seen me held at gunpoint.

This morning, Rae shares his doubts about how I'm handling things. "Did you turn off your cell service yet?" she asks. "Maybe it's time to just wipe your phone and be done with this."

"Hell no." On that one point, I'm firm. "Every time that jerk posts on Instagram, they have to turn on my mobile data. That means I get GPS updates on where they are. I'm going to find this person. I'm going to figure out who it is."

"Your call." Rae doesn't argue, but I can tell she doesn't approve. "On a positive note . . ." She gives Thom a friendly tap. "This guy helped me find the schedule for the Free Thought swim team. They have a home meet at four o'clock today, which means Jocelyn will have some time to kill once school lets out. Thom says we can probably catch her in the square."

"Great," I say. "Thanks, guys." I'm unsurprised that Rae's managed to recruit Thom to our cause. Still, I wonder at what cost. How much is she telling people about our activities? How much is she telling them about *me*?

I sip my coffee, trying to come up with the best strategy for approaching Jocelyn. Even if she does know about the older guy her sister was seeing, I'm not sure how to extract the information from her. As far as I can tell, Jocelyn has resisted telling both her parents and the police. Why trust me?

"Is someone at the door?" Rae asks suddenly.

Thom and I look up. Sure enough, we hear footsteps on the porch out front. It's not David—he's in the kitchen prepping breakfast. Thom steps into the hallway and opens the door to a sight that leaves Rae and me speechless.

Victor Nakagawa, clad in form-fitting exercise gear, stoops over a large bouquet of red hibiscuses. It's unclear whether he's putting them down or picking them up, but when he sees Thom, he snatches the flowers up, startled.

"Oh," he says, the corner of his mouth and eye jerking upward in that odd little tic. "Thom. Hi."

Bringing flowers might be construed as a kind and neighborly gesture, but the sheet of white paper wrapped around their stems tells a different story. In execrable penmanship, a single word is visible, large and loopy: "Charlie."

From our seats at the dining table, Rae and I can only stare. Is Victor, a decidedly married man, bringing me flowers?

Thom is the first to recover. "Hey there, Victor." Although Thom's voice betrays no shock, his face can't quite keep up. "Leaving us a little gift?"

Victor's face reddens. "No, no," he says. "I just . . . I was out for a run. Thought I'd stop by to say hello."

"Ah." Thom smiles. "Come on in."

"I saw the flowers," Victor says quickly. "I thought—I mean, I didn't put them there. I found them. I thought I should bring them in." He stares down at the bundle in his arms, aware of how awkward this has become.

Thom tries to give him an out. "Did Sue send those over?"

"No, not Sue." Victor shakes his head vigorously. "Don't thank Sue. I don't know where they came from. I just came by to talk about the article. To see if there was anything I could do to assist you, Charlotte. If you had more questions."

I don't know if we caught him in the middle of what was supposed to be an anonymous flower delivery or Victor is simply thrown off by appearances. Either way, I've never seen him so nervous before.

"Why don't we go chat on the back patio?" I suggest.

Thom swoops the flowers out of Victor's arms. "I'll get these in some water for you." He purses his lips as he passes Victor, his bespectacled face half-covered by hibiscus blooms, and disappears into the kitchen. He and David will have a field day with this.

I give Rae a gentle push on the shoulder, silently urging her to follow Victor and me to the patio. There is no way I want to be left alone with Victor—especially not now. Because I recognize those hibiscuses, their veiny red blooms.

They're the same flowers pictured in that first Instagram photo.

"So. Victor. You didn't happen to bring my phone back, did you?" Though I pose the question casually, I watch Victor's reaction like a hawk.

"Your phone?"

"It's lost. I thought you might have it."

Either Victor's back on his game, or he genuinely doesn't know what I'm talking about. "I haven't seen it," he says. "Did you leave it at our house?"

"I don't know where it ended up. You'll return it if you find it?"

"Of course."

Rae plunks herself down beside me. "Nice morning," she says, fingers laced behind her head. "Out for a run, Victor?"

He nods, still standing despite several empty chairs. "I have a presentation this evening, so I thought I'd head in to work late, get five or six miles in. And I was passing Koa House anyway."

"Did you stop by Naomi's place?" Rae asks.

"Naomi?" Victor's face goes blank.

This is dangerous ground, and he must know it.

"You two are friends, right?"

"Oh," he says. "I suppose. She's got a big property to manage on her own, and I'm free labor. What woman wouldn't love that arrangement?" If he intends this as a joke, it falls flat. "I haven't seen much of Naomi lately. Adam has things under control."

"Adam seems like a nice kid," I venture, but Victor has no interest discussing anyone other than himself.

"I've got to finish my run," he says. "Did you need anything else for the article? I assume you'll run a copy of the story by me before you publish. I'd obviously like to fact-check. And I could weigh in on the photos you took, as well."

Charming. The man is trying to micromanage his own feature. There's no way a guy this self-involved came by with flowers for me this morning. Somebody else must have left them.

I clear my throat and avert my eyes from Victor's spandex running getup. "I guess the one thing I'd like to expand on a bit in the article is the parenting angle. A lot of readers will relate to that. The struggle to balance work and family and training, the challenge of raising teenagers . . ."

"I have no wisdom to impart when it comes to raising teenagers," Victor says. "As I'm sure you gathered from your visit the other night, it hasn't been an easy experience."

"No? Jocelyn seemed very responsible. Quite articulate, too."

"Jocelyn isn't the problem." His jaw tightens. "I don't want Lise mentioned in the article. She's embarrassed her mother and I enough locally without broadcasting her actions in a national publication."

"I'm sorry. I don't think I understand." With great difficulty, I choke back my anger. Victor is not a bridge I can afford to burn. "You find your daughter *embarrassing*? In what way?"

"Off the record? We all know Lise ran off with some boy. That's her modus operandi, these . . . casual relationships." He stalks around the dewy grass. "She's been on a bad path for a while now. Poor grades, questionable friends. I'm sure there are drugs involved. Marijuana and . . . and . . . meth, maybe." Victor has worked himself into a frenzy imagining all the sordid possibilities.

"Lise did *meth*?" That's a far cry from the weed Sue said she found in her daughter's drawer.

"I don't know what Lise did," Victor says irritably. "That's the point. She was sneaky. And to be gone all this time . . . her mother cries at night, you know that? She cries. She thinks Lise is dead. I tell Sue, that's what she *wants* us to think. She's trying to scare us, so that when she comes home we'll be so grateful we'll let her do whatever she wants. Drop out of school, run around with boys, anything. Well, it's not going to work on me. I am not going to abandon my rules in the face of this—emotional blackmail."

Rae raises her eyebrows, incredulous. "You're not worried? You don't think she was hurt or—"

"No." Victor shuts her down immediately. "All this speculation about Elijah is complete and utter garbage. I saw Elijah that night, after she ended their relationship. Lise hurt him just as much as she's hurt Sue and I."

"You saw Elijah?" Rae asks. "Where?"

Victor elects not to answer, no doubt aware the oddness of his presence at the Yoon home that evening vastly overshadows his defense of Elijah. He stands up. "I need to run home and shower before work. If you have any more questions—about me, not my daughter—then you can call."

"I don't have a phone," I start to say, but he's already off, racing across the grass toward the road.

"Well, that was weird," Rae mutters, watching him. "Victor's kind of losing it. And I can't believe he brought you flowers days after we all hung out with his wife. That takes some cojones."

I frown. "I don't think he brought the flowers. Someone else must have left them on the steps. Whoever took my phone. Whoever's been messing with my Instagram account."

"Charlotte." Rae speaks slowly, as if I am a slightly senile senior citizen. "That is pretty clearly Victor. I don't know if he's a nutso stalker type or just socially inept when it comes to making advances, but he's got your phone stashed somewhere."

"Victor isn't attracted to me," I protest. "There's no way. You saw him."

"I saw that he got flustered when he came to the door. That he was quick to distance himself from Naomi and didn't like talking about his wife in front of you. He's a science nerd. They aren't exactly known for their smooth pickup techniques."

"He wasn't trying to pick me up!"

"No, I guess he wasn't." Rae pauses. "Maybe he prefers to watch you from afar," she says, and then neither of us speaks because somehow that's worse, much worse.

WITH NOTHING TO do until Jocelyn gets out of school, Rae and I spend our morning on a scenic drive-turned-hike. The road to the island's eastern tip takes us past the remnants of an old Hawaiian village, through prehistoric forests and lava quarries and a cemetery with gravestones half buried from an old eruption. Pele's path across the earth has ruthlessly transformed lush growth into barren rock. And yet, paradoxically, it is this same destructive force that forms new land, expands the island inch by fiery inch.

We end up on the jagged black coast. Standing on hardened lava, my face to the purple-blue sea, I find myself exhilarated by this strange and volatile island. I have never experienced a place with such raw power, never felt creation and annihilation so inextricably linked.

Rae raises her arms above her head as if the breeze might catch her and grant her flight. "Nothing between us and California but a little water!" she shouts. "Twenty-five hundred miles of it . . ."

"Water and wind!" I call back. "You feel this?" I bat my blowing hair from my eyes, suddenly giddy. "We need a kite!"

I wriggle out of my windbreaker and hold it over my head by the hood. Gusts flow through the chest and sleeves, lifting the jacket like a wind sock. I sprint along the lumpy black ground, flying my make-shift kite up and down the shore. Rae jogs after me for a couple of laps, laughing.

"Don't let go!" she tells me. "The ocean will get it! You might as-phyxiate a hungry turtle."

I reel in my flapping jacket and stop to catch my breath. "I am *so* the kind of person who would kill marine life with her outerwear."

"You think I'm kidding? That jacket could be dangerous!"

My voice drops an octave as I go into announcer mode. "An in-nocent turtle. The temptation of nylon. Will Shelly survive an en-counter with Patagonia's finest?" I stuff the windbreaker into my mouth and do my best impression of a choking turtle.

Rae dissolves into giggles. "Environmental protection is no laughing matter!" she exclaims. "But that turtle face, my God, I can't even . . ."

Following our hike, we head south to the Ahalanui warm springs. Enclosed from the ocean by a circular rock wall, the springs are geo-thermally heated to a pleasant ninety-one degrees. With enough room to swim or snorkel, we float through the blue waters, laughing as the fish tickle our feet. Rae strikes up a chat with a pair of friendly Danish tourists, and I find myself unwinding, trusting for just one moment the goodness of strangers.

Then a woman arrives with a child in orange floaties. The little girl dog-paddles eagerly around the springs, calling to her mother over and over again in the universal words of childhood: "Mommy, look at me! See how fast I can go? Watch, Mommy! Watch!" An insatiable need to be seen, like every child.

Like Tasha, I think. Like Keegan. Like Lise Nakagawa once, I'd wager.

The thought of Lise kills my happy mood. I picture Sue crying at night, struggling to hold herself together day after day, and the weight of it nearly breaks me. How does Sue do it? I lost my son more than four years ago, yet even now when I see curly-headed boys of a certain age, I ache for him. Keegan is a loss I may never fully accommodate. But to live as the Nakagawas do, indefinitely suspended between despair and hope . . . how does one go on? Life for Sue—and Victor, and Jocelyn—must be an endless open wound.

I wipe at my eyes, hoping that my dripping hair conceals my face. "This water's kind of gross," I tell Rae as I clamber from the springs. "Probably full of pee, and it's not even hot. I can feel the bacteria proliferating." I leave her floating in the enclosed pool and find solace by the ocean's edge.

The waves pound the black and rocky shores with breathtaking force. I watch the ebb and flow of the water, let it dull my sadness as it might smooth a stone. I think of Keegan and Alex Rocío, of Lise Nakagawa and Elijah Yoon, and a line from a self-help book I read last year pops into my head: *In helping others, we heal ourselves.*

On some level, I suppose I believe that, or else why bother? Why trek through Sabino Canyon in search of a boy I don't know unless a part of me, however tiny, believes that it might make me whole again? Or, if not whole, at least a little less broken. As much as I long to be normal, my dreams and impressions do provide a kind of opportunity. They offer me a purpose. I wouldn't have made it through that first year without Keegan if I hadn't had another family, another child depending upon me to use my gift for good.

But it's a double-edged sword. In helping others, I expose myself to all their fears and losses.

"Hey. Are you okay?"

Rae stands behind me, a towel draped around her shoulders.

"I'm fine."

"You were getting a little bitchy there before," she observes. "What's your deal?"

I slump forward, realizing I will have to be a grown-up and explain myself. "Sorry. Just thinking about the Nakagawas, I guess. It kind of brought up Keegan for me." I swallow back the ball of emotion in my throat. "I miss him so much."

"Oh, honey." She drops to her knees beside me. "I miss him, too. That little blond mop of his . . ." She cocks her head to one side. "There are still days I swear I see him. In a park or on a train . . . I get this flash of curls in the corner of my eye, and I think, *Hey, it's Keegan*. Takes me a second to remember."

"I thought that was just me."

"Nope." Rae smiles. "Even Zoey says she still dreams about him now and then."

"Zoey? Really?" Rae's daughter was just five when she lost her playmate. It surprises me to know that Keegan has lingered in her mind all these years. "What kind of dreams does Zoey have?"

"I don't know. She mostly dreams about him when she's scared about something. She said he doesn't really talk. He just sits with her, and she feels better."

"Aw. That's sweet."

We stare at the waves for a moment in silence. So easy to forget, I think, that your child is never yours alone, that a child belongs to a whole big web of people, each one carrying different memories. I tilt my head back, catching the breeze off the water.

"Maybe we shouldn't be going after Jocelyn today," I murmur. "I know we're trying to help, but . . . she's just a kid. Do we really want to stir things up for this family?"

Rae fluffs her wet hair with her towel. "We'll snag her for a quick chat, that's all. Harmless enough."

"Is it?" I frown. "Jocelyn lived her entire life with Lise. Same parents, same bedroom, same face. You and I, we can't imagine that kind of closeness. To lose that, suddenly and without any answers . . ."

Rae points and flexes her toes, letting her flip-flops fall away from her heels. "Don't do this to yourself, Charlie," she advises. "It's not going to help you find that girl."

"Do what? What am I doing?"

"Don't go taking on their pain." She stands and wraps her towel around her waist. "I know you. You've got plenty of your own."

RAE AND I arrive in the town square around three o'clock, after the School for Free Thought has let out for the day but before Jocelyn's swim meet. We position ourselves on a wooden bench and I scan the waves of students, keeping an eye out for anyone who seems out of place or overly interested in me. There are no obvious red flags. A group of four noisy girls who walk, elbows linked, half bent over with giggles. A PDA-prone pair who keep stopping to suck face. An athletic guy with dimples and his less dashing friend, whom I remember as one of the guys harassing Elijah on Monday. It doesn't take long to spot Jocelyn and Kai . . . and to realize Jocelyn's not in a chatty mood.

She walks briskly, chin tilted upward, as Kai jogs to keep up. His mouth is running, but whatever he says fails to make things better. Though Jocelyn's face is expressionless, her speed and silence convey her anger. Kai is in trouble.

As they cross in front of our path, Rae catches Kai's eye and waves. He recognizes her at once—there are very few black people on the island, and Rae is pretty enough to stand out anywhere. Grateful for the excuse to stop chasing his bad-tempered girlfriend, Kai stops in his tracks.

"Hey! How's it going?" He has the kind of overly sincere, I'm-speaking-respectfully-to-an-adult face I don't fully trust.

"Good!" Rae grins. "Where you off to?"

"Oh . . ." Kai glances at Jocelyn, who has continued walking, but at a much slower speed now that he's stopped chasing her. "Nowhere special. You guys still writing that piece about Jocelyn's dad?"

"Among other things," Rae says. "There's been a little work, a little play."

Kai chuckles knowingly. "Yeah, I heard you guys were hanging out with Brayden and Frankie yesterday."

I wilt inside when I realize that a seventeen-year-old boy knows about my getting stoned with a pair of local bros, but Rae can withstand the teasing better than I can.

"Well, I heard little-boy Brayden's dating your mom," she says. "Tough break, kid."

Kai laughs. "It's cool. Bray's kinda my friend."

"Hey, no judgments here." Rae holds up her hands. "You're an open-minded kind of guy, I dig it."

Across the square, Jocelyn has stopped walking altogether and now stands, arms crossed, trying to pretend she isn't waiting for Kai to pursue her. She looks so lonely, standing by herself in a sea of students. Though she pulls out her phone, feigning nonchalance, she can't resist a quick glance in our direction.

"What's up with your girl?" Rae asks. "You in the doghouse?"

"Yup. I *live* in the doghouse."

"Maybe you should go talk to her, Kai," I say. "You really want to let her stew?"

He ruffles his hair, indifferent. "There's no winning this."

I wonder what he did to put her in a state like that.

"I think she's coming over here," Rae observes.

Kai groans when he sees Jocelyn approaching but makes no move in her direction. He seems to have decided that our presence will make it harder for his girlfriend to really let loose on him.

"Hey, Jocelyn!" Rae greets her with a sunny smile that even I believe. "How's it going? Did I hear you have a swim meet today?" She's trying to connect with Jocelyn, to show interest, but the question does nothing to lighten the girl's mood.

Jocelyn casts Kai a long look. "Yes, actually. I *do* have a meet today. A very important one. It's a shame some people can't make it. My mom, my dad, my boyfriend . . ."

Kai tugs on the neck of his T-shirt as if it just got very tight. Now I see the mess we've landed in, why Jocelyn's upset with Kai. In ordinary circumstances, I would find a pressing excuse to go and leave them to it, but the chance to learn what makes these two tick overrides good manners.

"I can go to your meet another day," Kai says, squirming. "I have plans today."

"Of course you do." Jocelyn offers him a sympathetic smile. "Really urgent plans. With Brayden, who you literally see every day, to smoke yourself into oblivion. I understand perfectly."

"Joss. Come on, don't be mad."

"Mad?" Her eyes widen in mock surprise. "Why would I be mad? I *get* it, Kai, I do. A person has to have priorities. Forget my little swim meet. You said you'd go last week, but whatever. You and Brayden are sure to advance your life goals out there today. I won't hold you back. You do you."

I sink a little deeper into the bench, wondering if Kai realizes he's just had his ass handed to him.

Yet even faced with a vastly superior opponent, the kid still won't acknowledge defeat.

"Bray and I are going diving," he objects. "We're not just going to sit around and get lit."

"If you're with Brayden, getting lit will be a prominent feature of your day," Jocelyn says.

"Yeah, but it *helps* me," Kai says. "I can't dive without a little something. It helps my asthma. Keeps me chill so I don't have an attack underwater."

Despite my best efforts to stay out of their squabble, my motherly instincts kick in. "Kai!" I sputter. "You can't go scuba diving while stoned! That's so dangerous! My daughter has asthma, and I would never, ever—I mean, what happened to using an inhaler?"

"Thank you!" Jocelyn folds her arms, triumphant. "Do you even *have* your inhaler with you right now, or did you leave it in the car again?"

"Weed isn't dangerous," Kai says, ignoring the question. "Honestly. It's super relaxing. My asthma's really bad. If I get stressed out, I have all these breathing problems. But if I smoke a little, I'm good."

Jocelyn and I exchange glances that bemoan his immaturity.

"There's actually research on this," Rae states. "In an asthma attack, your airways constrict and swell. But cannabis is an anti-inflammatory drug. It expands the airways, just like an inhaler, but without all the side effects." She turns to Kai. "You should use a vaporizer, though. It's easier on your lungs long-term."

My mouth drops open. Is Rae honestly advocating medical marijuana to a seventeen-year-old boy? I could kill her right now.

Kai, however, appears ready to adopt her as his new best friend.

"My mom got me a vaporizer," he says. "It's way better than my inhaler." He grins at Rae. "Brayden said you're really cool. You should come dive with us."

The compliment/invitation does not include me. I am not cool. No one has made that mistake. Jocelyn and I are two of a kind: The straight-edge girls. The ones who stand around stone-cold sober at parties, the ones who never miss a deadline, the ones who don't like to lose control.

Seeing her boyfriend get friendly with Rae, Jocelyn scrunches up her nose. "Wow, Kai, are you hitting on old ladies now? You really *are* turning into Brayden."

He shrugs. "What's wrong with being like Brayden?"

"Nothing, if you don't want to accomplish anything in life."

"I accomplish plenty of things." Kai sounds weary, as if he knows this is an argument he cannot win.

"Like what? Smoking all the time?" For the first time, I hear a shade of neediness creep into Jocelyn's voice. "I have the chance to beat a school record today, and you can't even be bothered to come. Seriously, do you have any idea what I've been through lately? I just want you to be there."

I can't help but pity the girl. She's played by the rules as they were taught to her, excelled in the areas she was told to excel in. But what good are all Jocelyn's achievements if they impress no one, if, at the end of the day, she's still standing solo?

"Sounds like you're quite the talent, Jocelyn," I say. "Good luck out there today."

"I'm trying to qualify for an athletic scholarship," she mumbles. "I guess my dad didn't mention that to you."

"He must have," I lie. "I'm sure it slipped my mind."

Jocelyn tucks a loose strand of hair behind her ear, avoiding my eyes. "Whatever." She knows her father. She knows Victor is too wrapped up in his own affairs to discuss someone else's.

"So your parents can't make your meet today?" Rae asks. "That's a tough break."

"My mother never comes," Jocelyn says. "The facilities are hard for her to get around."

For the first time, I imagine what it might be like to have Sue as a mother, the practical day-to-day details of living with a disabled parent. Helping her reach items on high shelves. Scouting out the accessibility of each new store or restaurant. Needing elevators and ramps, never stairs. Traveling less because of the hassle, perhaps missing out on social events. After Sue's accident, did the girls ever get to bring their mother to the beach? Accompany her on a walk in the woods?

"What about your dad?" Kai demands. "Why isn't he coming?"

Jocelyn fiddles with her ponytail. "He can't make it."

Kai frowns. "You said he'd be there this time. What happened?"

"He had a . . . a community meeting to go to. In one of the subdivisions. A presentation on disaster preparedness or something."

"He always has someplace to be, and it's never with you." Kai puts an arm around her, some kind of protective male instinct kicking in. "You work so hard to keep him happy. He should show up for you."

"Yeah, well, so should you." Jocelyn pulls away. "At least my dad has a legit reason. I mean, he's advancing science and working for public safety. I think his job is a little more important than getting baked with Brayden."

Kai's softness quickly returns to frustration. "Why do you always get mad at me? I went to your meet last week. Your dad's probably off with Naomi, and I'm the one catching flak just 'cause I want to check out some reefs?"

"He is not with Naomi." Jocelyn's words cast an icy chill in the air.

"No, of course not. He's 'working.'" Kai makes disdainful air quotes with his fingers. "He's always working or training, *never* screwing Naomi. That's some other guy, I'm sure. Raph's mystery dad. Couldn't *possibly* be the esteemed Victor Nakagawa."

Jocelyn whirls on him, her hand raised as if to strike him, but catches herself. "You don't talk about my family, asshole," she says through gritted teeth. "You don't talk about them ever." She spins away from the three of us and takes off through the square, a rapid walk that turns into a jog when she sees Kai trying to follow her. "Leave me alone! I don't want to talk to you! I wish I never met you!"

Her hands fly blindly around her face, warding him off. A few curious students glance in her direction to assess whether or not this is a scene worth watching.

I nudge Rae. "Get Kai out of here. He's only making it worse. I'll deal with Jocelyn."

Suddenly it doesn't matter what happened to Lise, what older man she might've been involved with. All I care about is Jocelyn Nakagawa. I do not want this girl's shitty little boyfriend to ruin her performance today. I do not want her unreliable father and her mother's physical limitations to bring her down. This kid deserves her shot.

"Jocelyn!" I run to catch up with her as Rae gently steers Kai away. "Are you okay?"

Jocelyn doesn't stop walking, but her hands are still clenched into angry balls. "I'm *fine*."

"Kai shouldn't have said that about Naomi. He was out of line."

She shrugs, but I can see the shine in her dark eyes, the tears she will not allow to fall. "Everybody says it. Not to my father, not to my mother. But they say it to me. You have no idea how long I've been listening to this crap about Naomi Yoon. And it's not even true."

"No, of course not." I wish I could believe her. "You live in a small town. People just like to gossip." I duck out of the path of two jostling teenage boys.

"My dad and Naomi are not a thing," Jocelyn says. "They never were."

I don't answer. She seems to be protesting a little hard for someone so convinced these are lies.

"My dad is just a nice guy, okay? He helps Naomi out because she needs it. Because her husband died and she doesn't have a lot of money and her boys all have the brain of, like, a five-year-old."

Even Elijah? I wonder. If that was her opinion of Elijah's maturity, maybe Jocelyn encouraged her sister's relationship with someone older.

"The Yoons are lucky to have your father's help," I say.

Jocelyn can sense I'm not sold on Victor's innate goodness. "Every time my dad goes to help Naomi, he brings me or Lise," she insists. "He's not alone with her. If something were going on with them, Lise and I would've known about it."

I am far from convinced of that. Victor's training regimen offers him plenty of opportunities to slip away from his family, as evidenced by his surprise visit to Koa House this morning. And wasn't he at Wakea Ranch, unaccompanied by his daughters, the night Lise went missing? The wrongness of what Jocelyn has just said is eclipsed by the weirdness, however. "Are you saying you and your sister chaperone his visits?"

She glares at me. "Kind of, yeah."

"Whose idea was that?"

"Dad's, probably. He wants my mother to feel comfortable with it. Because he *loves* her." She bridles at the judgment on my face. "I've been over to Wakea Ranch plenty of times with him, and it's not like he and Naomi were running off to get a room. He just helped fix her roof or whatever. And he tried to teach Adam how to take care of the property."

"Why not teach Naomi? She can't do things for herself?"

"I know, right?" Jocelyn throws up her hands. "She's totally living in another century with all the 'girls do this, boys do that' stuff. It's the religious crap she grew up with. The point is, Raph is not my brother. He's not. Maybe my dad has a little crush. So what? The way Naomi flaunts herself around, it's like she wants him to look. But he's never done anything with her. He wouldn't. My mother would have his balls."

I wonder if she's right about her mother. I don't know Sue very well, but it seems to me that if Victor did father a child outside his marriage, she is evenhanded enough not to punish the child. I can imagine her sending Victor off to Wakea Ranch to fulfill his parental obligations, one or both of his daughters in tow to keep things kosher. Perhaps Victor has been visiting as a father, not a lover, these last four years.

"I met Raph and Adam Yoon the other day," I say. "They seemed nice."

"They're weird. All the Yoons are weird."

"I've heard some stronger words than 'weird' applied to Elijah."

Jocelyn stops walking and turns to study me, her face hard. "Are you writing about my father or my sister?"

"Your father," I say. "*Should* I be writing about your sister?"

"No," she says. "You shouldn't."

"Hard to provide a full picture of him, though, without even mentioning you girls."

"You're writing for *Outdoor Adventures*. News flash: you're not going to win a Pulitzer." Jocelyn stops, as if suddenly aware of how belligerent she sounds. She tries another tactic. "Look, my parents haven't had an easy time lately. Cut them some slack, would you? My dad's a private guy. He doesn't want all this stuff about our family out there."

"You're very protective of him," I note.

Jocelyn waves at a tall blond girl in the gathering crowd of students, still trying to keep up appearances. "My dad has a hard time dealing with reality," she says. "Especially where Lise is concerned."

"He thinks your sister ran away. Do you agree?"

Jocelyn doesn't immediately reply. Her gaze rests on some point above my left shoulder. Ono Place, I realize with a backward glance. Lise's dream for the future, now empty and abandoned. How strange for Jocelyn to pass it every day.

"I love my sister," Jocelyn says softly, "but she's made some poor choices. A lot of them. It's like she *wants* bad things to happen."

"What do you mean by poor choices?" Is she referring to the older guy? Lise's drug use?

Jocelyn takes a breath. "You know that expression 'You reap what you sow'?"

"Yeah . . ."

"Lise didn't sow anything good."

I wait for something more, but that's all she'll give me, all she'll say about the secrets she still carries for her sister.

"I'd better get to my meet," she tells me. "Go gentle on my dad, would you?"

"I'm trying," I say. "I really am."

I watch her drift away through the students, a solitary figure as she heads back to campus. There will be no one in the stands to cheer her on today, but she'll push herself just the same. I hope she breaks that record.

"Hey, Jocelyn!" I call.

She stops. Glances back over her shoulder.

"Good luck."

She smiles, and in that moment I see a flash of the girl who jumped the South Point blowhole at night, see her chin lift and her eyes glint at the prospect of a challenge.

"It has nothing to do with luck," she says.

eighteen

Back at Koa House, Rae and I sip guava juice on the back patio and dissect our Kai and Jocelyn encounter. Kai, Rae reports, was immediately contrite after Jocelyn ran off. He regretted his mean comments about Victor, however true. Although tired of absorbing his girlfriend's bad feelings every time her father lets her down, he nevertheless had the self-awareness to acknowledge that he'd been a jerk. *I'll just go to the swim meet,* he told Rae, *since it means so much to her.*

"He's not a bad kid," Rae concludes. "Just in over his head."

I swirl the juice in my glass and take note of the gray sky. The clouds have moved in, hinting at an evening rain. "They're a weird couple," I say. "Kind of mismatched, aren't they?"

"Kai's mom sounds like a deadbeat. Maybe he likes having Jocelyn to boss him around." Rae shrugs. "Did you get anything from her? She seems like a pretty tough nut to crack."

"She knows something," I say. "Something about Lise. I think she's trying to keep it under wraps for the sake of her parents. But I got the sense—" My hypothesis comes to an abrupt halt when I spot a familiar figure emerging from the trees of Wakea Ranch. "Rae." My voice drops. "I think we have a visitor."

Naomi Yoon surges into the yard, her chest and her long red braid bouncing. The purpose in her stride doesn't exactly communicate warmth.

"Uh-oh," Rae says. "What did we do this time? Did Naomi find out Victor gave you flowers?" She settles back in her chair as if preparing to enjoy a smutty TV show, which, come to think of it, is sort of how this day has been playing out.

I search for what to say if she flies at me with accusations about Victor. When the woman does arrive, however, Victor's not the one she wants to talk about.

"Are they here?"

Rae lifts her head. This is not what she was expecting. "Your boys?" she says. "I thought they weren't allowed over here. Why? Are they missing?"

Naomi's jaw sets, and I can see her weighing her options, reluctant to involve outsiders in her affairs, but anxious about her sons. Fear gets the best of her. "Adam was supposed to be watching Raph, but he left him with his brother this morning," she says. "Now I can't find Elijah or Raph anywhere. I don't know where they went."

Seeing a mother worry over her child softens me somewhat. "Maybe Elijah went to see one of his friends?"

"He doesn't have friends," Naomi says, as if the notion were ridiculous.

"What about Jocelyn and Kai?"

She eyes me with displeasure. For a woman who's spent less than a week on the island, I know way too much. "Kai threatened to kill my son the other day," she says. "He isn't a friend."

"Kill him? Why?"

"You know why. This business with Lise. We've been getting

threatening notes, too." She touches her throat, and her voice turns faint. "What if someone hurt him? What if Raph got caught in the middle of all this?"

It's not an irrational fear, given what I saw of Elijah and those boys in town, but I try to calm her. "No," I say. "I'm sure he's gone off somewhere with Raph, and they're both fine. What is he, fifteen?"

Naomi nods.

"Kids do that at his age. They go off sometimes, and they don't tell you. But you could call the police if you're really worried."

"No!" Her voice turns harsh. "No police."

I can understand why Naomi would be ill disposed to trust law enforcement, given the way they've been gunning for her son. And David mentioned that the religious settlement at Wakea Ranch, the one Naomi grew up with, ran into its own trouble with the law a few decades back.

"Did you search the woods?" Rae asks.

"Of *course* I did." Naomi glowers. "I couldn't cover every inch, but Adam and I went calling for them. We've been looking for hours." She bites her lip. "I'm just so angry at him! Why would Adam leave that child with Elijah? He knows better!"

Because he's nineteen, I think. *Because he wants a life.* But Naomi is too distressed for me to quibble with her parenting. Besides, I have a better idea.

"Can we help you look for them?" I ask. "More eyes couldn't hurt."

"I don't even know where to start," she says helplessly. "I don't know where young people go."

"Why don't you and Naomi try the square?" I tell Rae. "We saw Elijah there the other day. Maybe one of the students has seen him around." I turn to Naomi, trying to sound sure of myself. "The kids like Rae. They'll talk to her. And I can help Adam check the woods. Two people will cover more ground."

Naomi hesitates, and I can see she doesn't want me alone with her eldest. But why? What's she afraid he'll say?

"Do you have a phone?" I ask her.

"Yes, I have a phone." Insulted, she produces a flip phone that is at least ten years old. Rae lends me her phone, and I promise to call Naomi if Adam and I discover something. She doesn't seem thrilled with the arrangement, but her concern for Raph overrides her reservations.

Rae herds her over to our rental car and, as Naomi steps into the passenger seat, casts me a backward look that is unmistakable in its meaning. *This is your chance*, she tells me with her eyes. *Don't screw it up.*

THE WOODS ARE beautiful and strangely terrifying. I plunge into the brush and follow the winding paths much deeper, much farther than I did that day I first met Raph. I don't call for the boys. If they're out here, maybe they don't want to be found. Instead, I let my legs guide me.

I don't know if I'm approaching the place I dreamed of or if it's something else that I sense, something bad that happened out here, but soon my skin is prickling, my fingers and toes beginning to tingle. I jog through the leaves, searching for that clearing, the hammock wedged between two trees.

Don't let me find her body, I think. *Please not that.*

I sniff the air gingerly but detect only plants. A good sign. Six weeks of decomposition would be hard to mask in this climate, especially when the layer of volcanic rock prevents deep digging. Still, a disturbing sensation of wrongness buzzes through me, stronger with every step.

I pause by a tree, no longer sure which way to go, the feeling of unease now too pervasive to track in a single direction. Ahead of me, the trees begin to thin. A well-worn path leads me toward the light. I spot a large field, a chicken house with several birds scrambling around the pen outside, and a dilapidated old wooden building. This must be Wakea Ranch.

I move through grass as tall as my thighs, misgivings mounting. *Something happened here*, I think. The land is steeped in ugly secrets—not surprising, given its history as a repressive religious compound. Nausea grips me in the gut, and it's not just the chicken stink. The birds cluck in agitation as I pass, feathers rustling, their wild eyes a warning. But I can't turn back. Not when Naomi is safely gone with Rae, when I have the shadow of an excuse to be here.

A raindrop strikes my ear. Another lands on my hair. I continue on toward the old wooden building, jogging now. I want to see where the Yoon boys have been living, and the stormy sky and impending rain provide additional incentive. Yet as I approach the sagging building, I realize it's not a house but a barn—probably for the horses they once owned, the horses whose sale so broke Adam. I spot the actual Yoon dwelling a few hundred yards back, half-hidden by trees: a boxy home with chipped white paint and a rusty metal roof that looks rustic but habitable.

The rain begins to fall more steadily, surprisingly chilly. I stare at the house, hesitating. When I look at the structure, I smell curdled milk, have the impression of being clasped too tightly to someone's chest, ribs squeezed in slow suffocation. I draw back into the barn, shivering.

Though worn and damp from the tropical air, the stalls remain intact, if empty. The pungent odor of horses lingers, a mixture of straw and droppings with a hint of leather. It would've been something, to awake each morning and feed these creatures. To saddle up and set loose across the fields. I peer in through the bars of a stall, imagining the animals who once occupied this space, and the grief the family must have felt in giving them up.

I flinch when someone touches my shoulder.

Too startled to scream, I whirl around and find myself face-to-face with Adam Yoon. He must've seen me come up from the woods.

"Hi." He pushes some hair from his eyes, smiling but self-conscious. He wears a white collared shirt and dark pants, like a Mormon preparing to knock on doors. "Are you looking for me?"

I don't know where he came from, how he came up on me so silently, but I try to laugh it off. "Wow. I about had a heart attack right there."

"Sorry."

"I was just trying to check in about your brothers. Any sign of them? Your mother's worried sick."

Adam wrinkles his brow. "My mother sent you out here?" He knows her better than that.

"She didn't send me. I volunteered. So, no sign of them?"

He shrugs. "It isn't a big deal. They'll be back. This is just what Elijah does. He disappears all day, sometimes all night, too. But he always comes back, and my mother knows that. She's only upset because Raph is with him."

"You trust Elijah to watch him, then?"

Adam looks uncomfortable, and I gather "trust" is not the right word. "Well, he's not going to *kill* him."

"Your mom wasn't too happy about you sharing babysitting duties. Where did you go?"

"I just . . . had things to do." Adam's not a good liar, and his attempts at evasion are anything but subtle. I let it go, though I file away the question for future consideration. No sense badgering the kid and making an enemy of him. I want him to tell me things, whatever secrets his mother fears his spilling.

"So these are the stables, huh? Where you used to keep your horses?"

"Solomon and Malachai." He runs his hand along the rim of the stall. "I was just a little kid when we got Solomon. He was a present from my dad."

"What was he like, your dad?"

"Nice. Quiet, but nice." Outside, the rain has transformed into a downpour. Sheets of water beat at the roof above us. Adam leans against a wooden beam, head tilted as if he likes the sound of it. "My dad was a lot older than my mother, and he never yelled. Even when my mother would scream and scream, he always stayed calm with her." He gives me a lopsided smile. "I try to be like that, too. It's hard, though."

"You must miss him a lot."

"Sometimes," Adam says. "Sometimes I'm just mad at him." He glances at me, and seems encouraged by my nod. "He was supposed to take care of my mother, you know? That was his job, that's why she married him. But he died, so now I have to."

I shouldn't intervene, I know I shouldn't, and yet I can't keep my mouth shut. "Your mother is not your responsibility, Adam. She's a grown woman. You deserve a life of your own."

The boy falls silent. For a second I think that I've offended him, come down too hard on the person he's been trained to love and respect.

When he turns to me, though, I see I've erred in the other direction. His shining young face isn't upset—it's hopeful. "Please," he says, "I need your help."

"Help? What kind of help?"

"I want to leave the island."

My eyes widen. "That's not . . . I can't make that happen."

"Why? I'm nineteen. My mother can't do anything if I go. I'm an adult."

He looks so unconvincing, so pale and fragile as he stands there, light-years away from the adult he claims to be.

"You need a job," I tell him. "If you really want to leave, you need a way to financially support yourself."

"Can you get me one?"

"No, honey. I'm leaving in three days."

"I could go with you. To Arizona. I could work for your family. Do chores and take care of your children. I would be good at that."

"Oh, Adam." It's painful to watch, those bright eyes fixed on me as if I might save him. "How would that be any better than the life you have now? Besides, you'd miss Raph."

At the mention of his little brother, he sinks down to the ground, deflated. "Yeah," he says. "It would be hard to leave Raph." He flicks at an old piece of straw. "Why do you have to go? You said you liked it here."

Is he for real? Is this kid really so oblivious?

"I have to get home to my children," I remind him. "This is just a visit. My life is in Arizona."

"But you want to help me," he says. "I know you want to help me."

He's right, of course. From the moment I laid eyes on this sad little mess, I've wanted to free him, to give him more than the life of servitude and guilt his mother has provided. It bothers me in some deeply visceral way to see a boy so warped by his upbringing, a boy who has borne the burdens of childhood far too long without ever enjoying any of its pleasures. But where does one even begin to help a kid so intellectually and emotionally stunted?

Before I can answer him, the sound of far-off whooping draws our attention.

"Raph." I hurry out of the barn, trying to catch a glimpse of the little boy. The rain streams down my hair and soaks the fabric of my shirt. I scan the tree line, listening, trying to trace the noise.

Adam trudges reluctantly behind me. "They're in the woods," he says without enthusiasm. "I'm sure Elijah's with him. I told you they'd be fine."

I hasten to the edge of the woods calling Raph's name. I want to see him for myself, to make sure both Naomi's sons are intact before I give her the all-clear. Adam sighs when he sees me tramping blindly into the forest.

"You're going the wrong way," he says. "Follow me."

We find Elijah first, a dark blur moving through the trees with astonishing speed. Somewhere behind him, Raph cries for him to slow down. "I'm hungry!" Elijah barks. "Hurry up! I want something to eat!" He stops his breakneck pace only when he notices Adam and me waiting for him along the path.

"What do *you* want?" Elijah's scowl is directed solely at his brother. I might as well be invisible.

Although Elijah is four years younger than Adam, he looks older in a side-by-side comparison. Elijah's taller, for one, and his shaggy haircut reads hipster, not just do-it-yourself project gone wrong. Even his tight T-shirt conveys a certain style, hugs his skinny frame and gives him the appearance of a musician or an artist. His arms cross in a sullen, challenging stance quite unlike Adam's puppylike deference.

"Where were you?" Adam draws himself up to his full if unimpressive height, assuming the role of older brother. The result is less than imposing.

"I took Raph to the beach," Elijah says.

"The beach? How'd you guys make it all the way out to the beach?"

"Walked some, hitchhiked some."

"Mama's going to be furious when she finds out."

"So don't tell her." Elijah shrugs.

"I can't cover for you. She's been looking for you. She'll want to know where you've been all day. You should've asked her, Elijah."

"I don't ask her for permission because she always says no. I'm trying to give him a life, which you and Mama never do."

"A sinful life," Adam counters. "You're teaching him disobedience. 'Honor thy father and thy mother,' remember that?"

"Yeah, well, Dad's dead. And I can obviously never honor our mother as much as *you* do, so what's the point? I'd rather be sinful than be her little puppet. Unlike you, I can still think for myself."

They continue arguing against the sound of steady rain, Adam getting more and more shrill and Elijah goading him with smirks and mocking comments. At some point I become aware that Raph has joined us, that he's watching his brothers fight, his mouth pursed into a tiny bud, his eyes tearing up at their open hostility.

I grab his hand. "Come here, sweetie. We're going to call your mother and tell her where you are."

I lead Raph away from his warring brothers. Adam must've said something that pierces Elijah's thick skin, because they're both yelling now, volleying insults at one another with abandon. This is the second personal argument I've landed in the middle of today. What is going on with the Yoon and Nakagawa families? They both seem on the verge of self-implosion.

Raph and I try to ignore them as we walk, but their voices follow us, just a few notches louder than the rain overhead. The thick canopy that protects us from the storm seems to trap their anger within the woods. And there's something else, something deeply unpleasant hanging in the air. I remember what Marvel said, that she envisioned Lise's secret as a black oil that coated the body. I know exactly what she meant.

I hustle Raph along, taking care not to trip over the plants that keep nipping at our ankles, the roots that burst up from the ground as if intent on upending me. Eventually we're out of earshot or Elijah stomps off—I don't know which. Beside me, Raph relaxes somewhat, but the quiet only increases the dark, swirling feeling in my gut.

Here, it says. *Here.*

A few yards ahead, something plastic hangs from a tree. My footsteps grow slow and heavy as I approach. Everything begins to tingle: toes, fingers, mind. A camping lantern, I discover. Someone drove a nail into the trunk of the tree and left it up there. But for whom? I flip the lantern on and off. The battery still works.

This place.

Suddenly dizzy, I grab a branch to steady myself. It doesn't help. The night descends on me, asking me to shed my sense of self, to see with other eyes. Raph tugs on my arm. I want to stay with him, to remain me, but I'm falling under. I stumble toward a shrub and then collapse.

The last thing I see is the hammock, stretched out between two trees like a net.

Skin, damp to the touch. Her body pressed against a tree. The acrid taste of sweat.

Her shirt dangles from the nearby hammock, illuminated by an eerie shaft of moonlight. A mosquito settles on my arm and sips my blood, but I don't care. Not with her standing there, arms above her head.

At last.

I place one hand on her wrists, lift her long black hair with the other. Lean forward and put my lips to her neck, knowing that I'll leave bruises.

This is better than any grainy video on the Internet. This is a moment I'll return to over and over again. At night, when I'm alone and hot with need, this is the image I'll resurrect. Her hair spilling from my fingers. Her bare back shuddering against my touch.

I'm jolted from this unwanted image by a shouting in my ear.

"Hey!" Raph's little forehead furrows with concern. "Hey, are you listening to me? I said I wanna go."

I blink. Rise to my feet and wait for the sickening rush of adrenaline to settle. "Sorry. Got a bit light-headed there for a minute."

Ahead of me, the empty hammock dangles, its fibers tinged with mildew. I think I might be ill.

"Raph," I murmur, "do you know this place? Do you know who comes here?"

His mouth twists into a slight frown. "I don't like it here. I wanna leave."

I glance at him. Can he feel something, too? Something bad?

"Why don't you like it?" I ask.

He shrugs, but I note the way his eyes scuttle away from mine, like two dark beetles anxious for a rock.

Does Raph know something? He certainly spends enough time exploring these woods. He might've seen things, things more concrete than the awful fragments I've been getting. In a perfect world, I'd leave the four-year-old out of it, but this world is far from perfect.

"You know Lise and Jocelyn, right?" I ask. "Elijah's friends? Their dad, Victor, comes to visit you sometimes?"

The boy nods.

"Did Lise ever come out here? With Elijah?"

Raph snaps a twig from a nearby branch and tears it into pieces. I can't tell if he's evading my question or simply losing interest. I sit down next to him, my eyes on the clearing. It's gorgeous here at dusk, sumptuous shadows and patches of pink peeking through cracks in the dense foliage, yet I can't appreciate the beauty. It all feels tainted.

I try again. "Did you ever see Lise or Jocelyn out here?"

Raph's lips press stubbornly together; he refuses to speak, but the anxiety on his little face tells me quite enough. He saw her, all right, and he didn't like what he saw. But was this months ago, or the last night Lise Nakagawa was seen alive? Could there be a shakier witness than a preschooler?

I keep my voice neutral, careful not to scare him. "Was she here with Elijah?"

Raph stares at the ground. "She didn't have any underwear," he says.

I don't react, though my insides are churning. "Did you feel scared?"

A nod.

"Why?"

He shrugs, and I don't blame him. How could a small child articulate the wrongness of what happened to that girl?

Somewhere in the woods I can hear the sound of terse male voices. Evidently Elijah and Adam have called a truce and are coming to collect their brother.

I don't have much time to pump Raph for info. "The night Lise had no underwear," I persist, "was someone with her?"

Raph frowns. "It wasn't Elijah. It was the Watching Guy."

"Who?"

"The Watching Guy." He peers slowly around the woods as if to ensure that we're alone. "He comes to the woods sometimes when it's dark. He waits in the trees."

Despite the relatively warm temperature, my arms break into goose bumps. "You've seen this guy?"

"Uh-huh."

"What does he look like?"

"Big. A big shadow shape."

Not the kind of description that would identify this guy in a lineup.

"Did you tell your mother about him, Raph?"

The boy shakes his head. "Adam says the Watching Guy's not real and I don't have to tell Mama. But he *is* real. I saw him when I was sneaking. Lots of times, right here." His voice falls to a whisper. "He likes this place."

Suddenly I am cold, so cold beneath my wet clothes. I think of the lights I saw in these woods the other night. The Watching Guy—was that him?

I run through other possibilities. Victor and Naomi are adults. They don't need to conduct their affair out in the middle of the woods. Maybe those lights were just Elijah, off to meet someone. But Lise's gone, and Kai reportedly threatened to kill him. Who would Elijah have been meeting?

I've already seen too much. Part of me doesn't want to know what happened or what might happen, doesn't want to dwell upon the violence that might be done to a young girl when I have two girls of my own. But I can't forget. Couldn't even if I tried.

I turn to Raph. "When you saw the Watching Guy with Lise . . . and she didn't have any underwear . . . what was he doing?"

"He turned off the light," the child says. "I didn't see, but . . ." He pauses, breaks off part of a nearby fern and mashes it between his fingers. "I think it hurt."

"Raph?" In the distance, a flash of white shirt signals Adam's approach. "It's time to go home. Come on!"

The little boy rises to his feet, grateful for the sight of his elder brother. "I'm here!" he calls, dashing off to greet him. "I'm here!"

Figuring Adam's got it handled, I take Rae's phone from my pocket and pull up Naomi's number. She needs to know her boys are all right. The rain has slowed to a trickle, and the first chirps of the coquís sound in the damp air, their two-note cry rising at the end like a question. I have questions of my own.

Who is this Watching Guy Raph says he saw? He has to be the one I've been dreaming as, the one lying in wait. The older man Lise mentioned to Marvel, perhaps. Maybe even the one who has been taking photos of me with my phone. He must know the property well, to navigate these winding jungle paths in the dark. He must have come here many, many times.

Something crashes down from one of the trees, causing me to start. A long white branch strikes the hammock with its tip before bouncing to the ground. An albizzia, probably, one of those invasive trees with the secretly rotting limbs that Thom mentioned. In the wake of its impact, the hammock sways back and forth, as if someone were reclining inside.

The image of that young girl sharpens in my mind, needles to the brain. Her body against a tree, her hair in his hand. Was that statutory rape, or something more? Sexual assault? Abduction? Murder? I find myself running, racing through this tropical labyrinth unable to stop until I've made it out, returned to the safety of Koa House.

Only then, standing in the dim drizzle of Thom and David's yard, do I finally call Naomi.

nineteen

That night, overwhelmed by the day's events, I go for a soak in the outdoor tub. Rae has gone to the Thursday night market with Thom and David, off to sample local music, food, and wares in what constitutes a weekly highlight of this sleepy town. Normally, such a cultural event would be enticing, but crowds of people are the last thing I want to face right now. I don't know who might be out there watching, snapping pictures of me. Tonight I just want to be alone.

The oversized tub promises the peace I crave. Located a few yards from the side of the house, the fenced-in bathing area boasts a spalike atmosphere. Inside its white wooden walls, an avocado tree sparkles with tiny holiday lights. David has provided me with a fluffy bathrobe, hand-crafted soap, fruity shampoo, floating candles, and plumeria-scented bubble bath. In theory, it should be glorious, a relaxing soak beneath the stars, not unlike the hot tub Noah and I have in our backyard.

The moment I let my bathrobe drift to the ground, however, I feel anything but relaxed. Despite the fence that encloses the tub and the sliding bolt on its door, I can't shake the sensation that I'm not alone, that my body is on display for unseen eyes, that pictures of me bathing will turn up on Instagram tomorrow.

I try to shake it off.

This Watching Guy is getting into my head.

I step into the claw-footed tub, grateful for the layer of bubbles that now conceals my naked body. Stupid, getting all paranoid. Nobody who stalks pretty teenagers would have any use for my old bag of bones. But still.

I nestle a little deeper into the bubbles, wondering what time it is. The floating candles bobble up and down in the water.

This is amazing, I scold myself. *Quit inventing things to worry about and enjoy yourself.*

But the theft of my phone is not an invention, and I don't buy Victor as the likely culprit. He wouldn't follow me to Marvel's and then photograph me, would he? He wouldn't leave me flowers. I swish the water with my foot. What if there's someone living in those woods, someone who knows the comings and goings at Koa House and Wakea Ranch? A stranger who saw my phone, forgotten on the back patio, and seized the opportunity.

Or perhaps he isn't a stranger. Victor and Adam and Elijah all seem harmless enough, but any one of them could have a dark side.

This bath is not working. Instead of calming me, it's making me crazy. I reach over the side of the tub, trying to find my towel. As my hand closes on the soft terry cloth, I hear a noise, something on the other side of the wall, just a few feet from where I'm bathing.

I freeze. Sit upright in the warm, soapy water, listening.

Maybe it was just one of the cats prowling around.

I step from the bath, water dripping from my skin, and quickly wrap myself in my bathrobe. As I lean over to blow out the floating candles, I hear it again: something grazing the wooden wall. Not a cat—it's much too high for that—but a person. Him.

The creeper who's been following me, taking my picture and who knows what else. He's out there.

My heart is in my throat, beating wildly. Can he see me? Is there some crack in the wall that I don't know about, a peephole he's been using? I pull my bathrobe tighter and scan the wooden slats. No obvious holes in the fence, but that's hardly comforting. And the bolt on the door is a flimsy defense at best.

I could leave, but what if he's out there, preparing to ambush me in the small stretch between the bathing area and the house? And I left the house door unlocked. He could wait for me inside. If only I had my damn phone, I could call Rae and Thom and David at the market. But he took care of that.

I have nothing. No one.

I think back to the women's self-defense class I took years ago. *If someone is following you from a distance, turn and stare them down,* my instructor told us. *Looking them in the eye lets them know you won't go easy. Most attackers don't want a real fight.*

This situation isn't quite the same, but perhaps the same principle applies.

"Hey!" I yell at the wall with a ferocity I don't feel. "I know you're out there!"

Silence, but for the chirping of the frogs.

"Don't think you can mess with me, asshole," I growl. "If you come near me, I will fucking break you."

More silence. I begin to doubt myself, wonder if I'm losing it, yelling at the empty night like a nutcase.

Then footsteps, the quick swish of grass. My worst fear confirmed: I'm not alone.

From the noises, I may have scared him away. Still, I'm not about to test that theory. Maybe he's simply retreated to the shadows, found a more strategic place from which to assault me when I leave the outdoor bathroom. The sliding bolt on that wooden door could be the only thing that separates us.

For two hours, I huddle on the ground, listening, waiting, worrying, until my friend and hosts return. When at last I hear their loud and punchy voices in the house, I burst from the bathroom. Thom and David don't know what to make of me, a distraught woman in a bathrobe rambling about "someone out there." They dutifully search their home for signs of intruders at my request and lock every door of Koa House, but it's clear they think I'm overreacting.

"It was probably a wild pig," David tells me apologetically. "They come sniffing around every now and then. I'll swing by the salon tomorrow and see if I can get some hair clippings. That always keeps the pigs away—they hate the smell of humans."

"Wild pigs, yessss!" Rae exclaims, too tipsy from her night out to take me seriously. "Brayden told me about those! He said they come and eat Sage's marijuana plants, that pigs wanna get high same as people."

And just like that, my terrifying brush with the Watching Guy turns into a discussion of feral pig encounters. I could scream. I look from Rae to David to Thom, each one eager to share what they know of the island's swine, each one sure that they are being helpful, and head upstairs without saying good night.

I know what I heard. And it was not a pig.

In my bedroom, I double-check the locks and draw the curtains to the balcony. I slip some cuticle scissors under my pillow just in case. Not an ideal weapon, but the curved metal could do some damage if it came to that.

I debate whether or not to call Noah. He'd believe me, even if Rae doesn't. Without a doubt, he'd be on the next flight to Hilo. But is that really how I want Girls' Week to end? I check the time. Two a.m. in Arizona. No sense alarming him with a middle-of-the-night phone call. There's no way I'm falling asleep without some help, however. I take a sleeping pill, let it suck me down into a thick and dreamless sleep.

In the morning, I wake up foggy headed but calm. I peel back the curtain, find the sun has transformed the backyard from a black, shadowy mouth to a light-filled meadow. I can see exactly what's out there waiting for me, and it's nothing worse than a field of dew.

Maybe they're right, I tell myself sleepily. *Maybe it was a pig sniffing around outside my bath, after all.*

I unlock the sliding door and step out onto the balcony. Rae's already there, ruminating. From her grim expression, I think at first that she's nursing a hangover, but when she catches sight of me, her lips form the kind of hard line that always brings bad news.

I yawn, still too drugged to feel worried. "Are you okay? Did something happen?"

She holds up a small white rectangle. "I found this on the railing over there. Safe to say you didn't put it there?"

I stare at the railing, an easy fifteen feet off the ground, and then at the object in her hand. Through the haze, I feel a slow, creeping dread.

It's my phone.

friday

twenty

"H e came back." Fear sweeps away any lingering effects of my sleeping pill as I realize what the reappearance of my phone means. "He came back in the night. The Watching Guy. He was right here, outside my room."

Rae bites her lip. For once, she has no ready joke, no trace of amusement lurking in her dark eyes. "I am so sorry, Charlie. We should've listened to you last night. I mean, God, if something had happened . . ." She doesn't complete the thought. "Who *is* he? Do we have any idea?"

"The same pervert hanging around my bath last night, I'd guess." I shudder. At some point, my stalker must have returned to Koa House. Somehow he hoisted himself up onto my balcony and left behind my stolen phone. He was just feet away from where I lay sleeping. "How did he even get up here?" I demand. "Look how high it is!" I glance over the side and get my own answer. "Oh. That frigging trellis."

Rae opens the Photos app and hands me the device. "You'll want to see this."

"Want" is the wrong word, but I swipe through the hundreds of new photos left on my device. One thing I'll say for my stalker: he has a good eye. Some of his pictures are actually quite beautiful. A papaya, sliced neatly in half. A wooden crate laid out in a shaft of sunlight. Various close-ups of brilliant green geckos. It's not as if I can actually appreciate his artistic soul, however, especially once I see the photos of myself.

Some, like the ones he took of me exiting Marvel's store, I can place at a specific time and location. Others are maddeningly unclear. His propensity to use the zoom feature produces close-ups of me talking or laughing with no real context, just something blurry and green in the background or vaguely wooden. From the time stamps, they weren't all taken at Koa House. But one was. A dim photo from early Wednesday morning depicts me sleeping in the Bamboo Room, face barely discernible against a grainy pile of blankets. From the strip of curtains at the edge of the frame, he didn't actually step inside my bedroom, but the knowledge that he confined his activities to my balcony is hardly comforting.

He was there. He was watching me.

"It's got to be one of the Yoon boys," Rae muses. "Or maybe Victor. David and Thom could've done it, obviously, but . . . I can't imagine they have that level of interest in their female guests. I'm guessing this dude's been watching you from the woods, waiting for your light to go off at night."

"Thanks, Rae. Way to help me sleep."

She shrugs. "It narrows things down, doesn't it? We're looking for someone who knows those woods."

"There could be a lot of people who know those woods. For all we know, there's a homeless guy from Wakea Ranch's cult days living out there. Some wackadoo Naomi grew up with."

"Possibly." Rae turns thoughtful. "I guess we can't eliminate Naomi from the list, either."

"Naomi? Why would *she* be following me around?"

"Maybe she knows you've been looking into what happened to Lise. Her son's suspected of killing this girl. Could be those protective mama instincts kicking in, trying to scare you off."

"So she posts flowers to my Instagram account and watches me sleep?" I pace the balcony. "That doesn't make any sense."

Rae leans against the balcony railing and frowns at the Yoon property. "This person who's been following you—maybe it's one of the people you saw signaling at night from the woods."

"Uh, it better be the same person. How many crazies can you have roaming around out there? Unless . . ." I stop. "Those light signals have to involve one of the Yoons, right? It's their land, after all."

Rae nods. "Naomi, maybe? It could be Victor's signal to her."

"No," I say. "If Victor wanted to visit, he could walk through the front door. Naomi has a phone. They can arrange their meetings like grown-ups. The meetings in the woods must involve Adam or Elijah. If Adam has any connections outside of his mom and Raph, I'd love to know about them."

"Elijah doesn't have any friends, either," Rae points out. "Not since Lise went missing."

"Exactly," I say. "Lise is his only friend. What if she's the one sending those signals?"

Rae's brow furrows. "I don't think Elijah's got her tied up to a tree somewhere and she's giving off SOS signals, if that's where you're going with this. David said they've been seeing lights in the woods for months, since long before Lise disappeared."

I let out a breath. "I'm not saying she's captive. We've been assuming she was killed or kidnapped, but what if she really did just run away? What if she's out there at night signaling to Elijah?"

"Brayden and Frankie did say she snuck out a lot," Rae murmurs. "She and Elijah could've developed light signals a while ago."

"Right. Elijah told the police she broke up with him, but he could've been lying. Maybe he and Lise had a whole plan. It wouldn't take much for her to live out in those woods. A tent, basically. Elijah could bring her food now and then, and she'd be set. Think about it. She flashes her light a few times, they meet up and hang out all night when no one can see them."

"Not a bad existence," Rae says wistfully. "Kind of like Thoreau, but with a romantic twist." She shakes her head, unconvinced. "Thing is, Lise wouldn't just up and leave without a good reason. Why would she take off without bringing any stuff? Why let everyone believe the worst, let Elijah take the blame?"

"I don't know." I'm not sure how to fill this hole in my hypothesis. Lise had friends, a good school, parents who loved her. Why would she be so anxious to leave her life? What could be so bad at home that she'd rather abandon everything than stick around?

"She was talking to Marvel about statutory rape just a couple weeks before she went missing," Rae says. "What if she was pregnant? She's a minor. She couldn't get an abortion without telling an adult, and that might've meant outing the father."

I shake my head. "I read an article about abortion laws recently. Hawai'i is one of a dozen states that doesn't require parental consent from minors."

"Well, something was not right in that girl's life. Maybe . . . it's a bigger something than we thought."

I swallow. Until now, I've allowed myself to believe that Lise was having a consensual, albeit illegal, sexual relationship with an older guy. But if that were true, why would she need to flee her home, her family? They should have been her safe place. She wouldn't run away from them unless . . .

Unless the threat was coming from within.

I remember what Marvel told us, Lise's odd questions regarding statutory rape. *It's like she was trying to figure out what kind of power she had over him*, Marvel said. *Trying to find out how bad she could break him, and whether or not she really wanted to.*

Statutory rape. Sexual intercourse with an individual too young to consent by law. Marvel imagined it to be a recent occurrence, a fifteen-year-old months away from being legal. But what if this relationship began when she was much younger? What if it was initiated by someone too close for her to refuse? A teacher, a coach. A parent.

I don't want to believe it, don't want to entertain such awful ideas that have no clear, hard evidence. Yet it would explain so many things. Her disappearance, yes, but also how she developed into such a different person from her twin. The drug use, the promiscuity. And it would explain why Lise's father has shown zero interest in discovering her whereabouts.

One look at the queasy expression on Rae's face, and I know we've arrived at the same ugly thought.

"Victor," I murmur. "Maybe she was running from Victor."

MY FIRST INSTINCTS are to stay out of it. If Lise really did flee an abusive parent, the last thing in the world I want to do is find her and send her back to Dad. But if we're right about Victor, nonintervention is not an option. Not with Jocelyn still living at home.

Victor has had ample opportunity to get acquainted with the woods of Wakea Ranch. That scene I saw by the hammock—what if those were his eyes through which I saw? What if he was out there spying on his own daughter and these unnatural urges he'd been nursing finally won out? The possibility makes me sick.

Rae and I need to help these girls. We need to find Lise and figure out what's going on, and we have just forty-eight hours left on the island to do it. Our options are limited: locate Lise ourselves, or find someone with information that can lead us in the right direction. Yet we have so many loose ends, I don't know how to begin tying them all together.

I grab a sheet of notebook paper from my bedroom and jot down our questions, Rae peering over my shoulder as I go:

Who's flashing lights at night in the woods?

Who stole my phone? Why did they give it back?

Who did Raph see lurking around the woods at night?

Why was Lise asking about statutory rape? Who was she involved with?

Where is Lise? Is she alive?

Who else knows where Lise is?

Isaac would be grinning ear to ear if he could see me now, totally immersed in this case, just as he planned.

"I say we go into the woods tonight," Rae suggests. "See if we can catch whoever's been sending signals. It's not a lock, obviously, but David said he sees them pretty much whenever he's up late, and you had a vision about flashlights, so . . ."

It's not the most attractive option, given our uncertainty about who or what we'll find—Noah would shit a brick if he got wind of this plan—but we have little else to go on.

"Okay," I agree. "In the meantime, we should have another chat with the people close to Lise. See if anyone had any suspicions about Victor."

I think for a moment about who to target. Those most likely to know about Victor—Sue and Jocelyn—are the least likely to say anything. Frankly, I don't know what to make of Sue. As intelligent as she is, could she really have remained oblivious to the sexual abuse of her daughter? Probably, given her blind spots about Naomi. For better or for worse, Sue has decided to remain in her marriage. She could've been passively complicit in something terrible.

As for Jocelyn, I have no idea what kind of dysfunction she's grown up with, but she's on her path to Stanford. Two more years and she can leave that house behind forever. If there's something off in her household, she has no reason to share it with me. We're better off finding someone more peripheral to Lise's life, someone who saw her when her guard was down.

"She might've said something while drunk or stoned," I tell Rae. "Something that hinted at problems at home or plans to run away."

"You want to hit up Frankie and Brayden again?"

"Might as well. They can at least give us the names of some people Lise hung out with." Above us, the wispy clouds have begun to disperse, revealing patches of blue sky. "Who knows? Maybe there really was an older guy she was seeing, and this whole Victor thing is bullshit."

"Maybe." Rae's fingers dance across the screen of her phone for a few minutes, hunting down her stoner friends. "Okay," she announces. "I've got nothing on Frankie, but according to Twitter, Brayden left half an hour ago to go surfing at the Isaac Hale Beach Park. If we hurry, we can still catch him."

"He posted all that on Twitter?" I roll my eyes. "Jesus. At least I make my stalker work for it."

twenty-one

It's cloudy when we get to Isaac Hale, and the air feels pregnant with rain. Rae quickly spots Brayden's beat-up van parked in the lot. We make our way down to the concrete pier where a few enterprising surfers are catching waves in the bay. Even I can see this is no place for novices; the dark lava rocks don't make for a welcoming shoreline and the rough waters rise up taller than a person, ready to have their way with the uninitiated.

Rae scans the whitecaps and soon hones in on Brayden's long locks and sunburned torso. "There." She points to a figure paddling out. "We'll get him when he comes in."

Not a bad plan, but Brayden shows no signs of returning to land any time soon. Rae watches him catch a wave while I craft a rather misleading text to Noah. *Found my phone outside this morning, yay! Will call you & kids tonight.* When Brayden begins paddling out again for another wave, I decide there's no point in our both waiting for him.

"I'm going to have a look around," I tell her. "Maybe Brayden's sugar mama came along today." Sage strikes me as a person who knows things, although getting her to share them could be a challenge. I don't know whether to applaud or frown at a woman in her forties who shacks up with a guy barely older than her son, but Sue did urge me to look into Lise's drug connections. From the sound of it, Sage has her hand in all kinds of cookie jars.

If Rae's a little miffed about being left behind as the lookout, she doesn't say so. She assumes a seat on the concrete pier and watches the surfers, her feet dangling into the choppy water.

I follow the path away from the bay to see what else is going on in the park today, but apart from a middle-aged man doing yoga, the scene is pretty tranquil. An empty playground. A bathhouse. A grassy area with picnic tables, palm trees, and a handful of feral cats. Some kid who must work for the county roams around collecting stray trash. Either Sage elected not to join her boy toy this morning, or she's out there surfing with him.

I'm about to return to the pier when the kid gathering trash looks up. His face, I realize, is familiar.

"Kai?"

He squints, taking a second to place me. "Oh. Hi."

Sage's son is not a bad find, not bad at all. He must have caught a ride over with Brayden.

"No school today?" I ask.

"Nah. It's Eco Day. We're supposed to get out in the community and do something to help the environment or whatever."

"And here you are. Good man." The mom in me can't help but observe that he should've brought gloves. I watch him scoop up a plastic bottle and stuff it into his trash bag. "How does the school know you actually did it?"

"The kids who board sign up for projects, and they get chaperones. But I'm a commuter, so it's mostly honor system. My mom just signs a paper." Kai shrugs, as if embarrassed to be caught doing work he could so easily get out of. "I can pick up trash for an hour, I don't mind."

I smile. "It's a nice thing to do. Can I help you?"

"I guess . . ." It's obvious that Kai doesn't want my company, but he's too polite to say so. He produces another garbage bag from his pocket and hands it to me. "Anything you see around, just grab."

We work in silence for several minutes, drifting to separate areas until I notice him struggling with some broken glass. "Don't touch that," I advise as he reaches for the tiny pieces with his fingers. "Let me get some wet paper towels from the bathroom."

Moments later, as he dabs at the last shiny splinters of glass, I know I've got him where I want him.

"No Jocelyn today, huh?"

"Nah. She's doing some recycling thing with the Environmental Club. She won't be back until the afternoon."

"How's she holding up?"

Kai looks as though he doesn't understand the question.

I press my advantage. "When I talked to her in town the other day, it seemed like the thing with her sister is hitting her pretty hard." Jocelyn, of course, said no such thing. But Kai doesn't know that. And he'll be more likely to talk to me if he thinks Jocelyn already has.

Kai stares at the glittery slivers on his paper towel. "Joss is okay. I mean, she *seems* all right."

"Yeah? From what she told me . . ." Though there's no one else around, I lower my voice, as if taking him into my confidence. "Well, there's obviously been trouble at home. She must have talked to you about it."

Kai's blue gaze flicks across me warily. "Aren't you a journalist? I thought you were writing something about her dad. Shouldn't you be talking to him?"

"I'm an *investigative* journalist," I say, although that's stretching the truth. "Sue Nakagawa has a lot of questions about her missing daughter. She wanted me to ask around."

Kai snatches a candy wrapper off the ground. "I already talked to the police."

"I'm not a cop, Kai, and I don't work with cops. I'm just trying to help a mother find some answers." I move squarely in his path, forcing him to look at me. "You and I both know there are things you couldn't tell police about. Things about Brayden, about your mom. Stuff you and Lise were involved in."

Kai fidgets but offers no denial, and I know I'm onto something. I push further.

"I already know that stuff, and I don't care. Neither does Mrs. Nakagawa. She doesn't care about who was selling or using or what. She just wants to know about her daughter." I nudge his elbow. "Come on. Let's go for a walk."

Kai puts down his garbage bag and complies, a sucker for authoritative females. He'd have to be, dating Jocelyn.

"You and Lise spent time together, didn't you?" I guide us to a path that runs parallel to the ocean.

"Yeah . . ."

"You liked her?"

To my surprise, his eyes fill with tears. "I don't want to talk about Lise," he says, wiping his face. "If you want to know what happened to her, go bother Elijah."

"You think Elijah knows where she is?"

"Yeah, he knows. He killed her."

Kai's conviction startles me. "You really think that?"

"I *know* that. We all know it." Kai sniffles into his hand. "She broke up with him, and then no one ever saw her again."

I can't tell if this kid is unusually sensitive or if I've just grown accustomed to dealing with the abnormally steely Nakagawa family. Either way, his softness is a point in my favor. "You hung out with Elijah a lot before Lise went missing, right? You must know him pretty well."

"I wasn't really good friends with him or anything." Kai sounds defensive. "Joss and I just hung out with him because of Lise. And he gave us a hangout spot. Somewhere to go."

"You mean the woods out by Elijah's place."

"Yeah. We went there a lot."

"So I've heard." I opt for the big bluff. "Sounds like you guys had a pretty good system with Elijah. Flashlights and all that."

Kai nods. "He didn't have a phone, so he used a flashlight to tell us when his family was asleep. And we'd flash back to let him know we were there." He hesitates. "Who told you about that? Elijah?"

I ignore the question. Let him wonder who's leaking info to me. "Did Elijah seem like a decent guy to you?"

We're wandering a concrete path now beneath some twisty, moss-covered trees, the ocean crashing to our left. Kai stares at his feet as he walks, hands jammed in his pockets. "I never really got why Lise liked him so much," he says. "I guess 'cause they grew up together. And maybe she felt sorry for him, with his weird family and all."

"Did Elijah's mother have any idea you guys were hanging around their property?"

"Nah. We stayed out of her way. The Yoons have a lot of land, and we always met up really late, after Naomi and Elijah's brothers had gone to bed. No one ever bothered us out there. It was a good place to go, sit around and just . . . you know."

"Smoke? Have a beer?"

He rubs his forehead. "Jocelyn didn't, but yeah. The rest of us."

"Couldn't you just do that at home? Smoking, drinking—I thought your mom was pretty laid-back about that sort of thing."

Kai makes a face. "You think I want to hang out with my *mother* all the time in that tiny house? Anyway, she and Jocelyn don't really get along."

"No? Why's that?"

"My mother thinks Joss is too uptight, and Joss thinks my mom is a loser." He pauses, offers a wry smile. "Neither one of them's wrong."

An orange feral cat dashes across the path in front of us carrying what looks like a chicken nugget in its mouth. For a second, I think of Tasha, how much she'd enjoy chasing this little critter, and I can't wait to get home to her and Micky. But how can I face my own girls knowing I failed to help someone else's daughter?

I stop walking and get a good, hard look at Kai, the windblown hair and deceptively wholesome smattering of freckles. He's not as innocent as he looks. Seventeen-year-old boys never are.

"How did you end up dating Jocelyn?" I ask. "No offense, but you guys seem so different."

He shoots me a quick glance, trying to determine if I mean this as an insult to his intelligence. "We had an econ class together last year," he says. "I don't know, I liked her. She was smart and pretty and you can tell she's going places. And she's local. She wasn't one of those rich boarding school girls always giggling or gossiping or whatever." He hooks his arm around the branch of a nearby tree. "Not to sound all high on myself, but most girls like me. Jocelyn was different. I really had to try with her."

"Ah. You like a challenge."

He sighs. "It was cool at first, but now? She's, like, *so* much work. And she's always busy with school and swimming."

He sounds like my ex-husband. One minute they're admiring our high standards and drive, and the next minute, they're complaining we're high-maintenance, that we don't pay enough attention to them.

"You must've had some time with her over the summer at least. Her and Lise and Elijah."

"When Joss wasn't working, yeah. We all hung out." He gets a faraway look, as if he wishes he could return to this happier, simpler time. "It wasn't just alcohol and weed, you know. Elijah set up a hammock, and we built this table thing with crates. Sometimes we just played cards. Elijah's a weird kid, but he's pretty good on a uke. He hears a song, and he can play it back to you. So we'd all be out there, you know, singing and goofing around, Elijah plucking away. It was nice." Once again, his eyes fill with tears. "I didn't think he would hurt her. I didn't think he was like that."

I don't want to rehash the Elijah Didn't Seem Like That thing with yet another person. As far as I can tell, Elijah *wasn't* like that. Kai's comment about the hammock interests me, however. If that hammock went up over the summer, as Kai claims, then my vision of the girl in it is definitely a recent event—if it's even happened yet.

"When's the last time you were out there?" The lights I saw on Tuesday night now seem important. "The woods, I mean?"

"We haven't all four been out there since August," he says.

I detect a slight dodge in his response. "The four of you haven't. What about *you*? Have *you* been out there lately?"

Kai's gaze drops. "Not lately," he says. "Maybe a few times in September."

"Drugs or sex?" I ask dryly, and Kai flushes.

"Look, it was a private place, and I could walk there. My house is really small. My mom and Brayden can hear everything. They don't care about that kind of thing, but I do. And the Nakagawa house wasn't an option. We weren't trying to disrespect Elijah by going out there, I swear."

Sex, then. Youthful hookups in the woods. *Good for you, Jocelyn*, I think. *If you're going to choose beauty over brains, you might as well enjoy it.* Their trysts might put to rest at least one mystery: Raph's Watching Guy. Raph must have spotted Kai hanging around the woods at night, waiting to get some. In all likelihood, it wasn't Lise the kid saw naked, but Jocelyn. I can see how a four-year-old might misinterpret a lustful teenage encounter as something sinister. Unfortunately, none of this brings me any closer to finding Lise, and there is no damn way a little player like Kai is my Instagram stalker. Maybe there *are* multiple weirdos lurking in those woods.

"Do you and Jocelyn still meet up there sometimes?"

Kai's ears are red with embarrassment. "I haven't been out there in weeks," he says. "I have my license now. Got a car."

"Oh. Yeah, that's a game-changer." I mull this over. "What about Jocelyn? Has she been out to visit Elijah at all?"

"No way. She wouldn't go alone. She hates the mosquitoes."

I feel a surge of excitement. If Kai and Jocelyn haven't ventured into the woods, then who has been out there with flashlights?

"Kai?" I sink into the crook of a tree. "Did it ever occur to you that maybe Lise's alive?"

He lifts his head. "Alive?"

"She ran away before," I prod. "She could've done it again. Maybe things got tough for her, and she needed some space."

"She wouldn't have left without telling someone," Kai insists.

"Maybe she did tell someone."

"Like who?"

The ocean rumbles in, breaking against the rocky shore with almost gleeful force. Even several yards away, I can feel traces of its spray. "You tell me. Who would she have gone to?"

He stares at his hands. "I don't know."

"Elijah, maybe? He seems like a pretty loyal guy. If she had wanted to disappear, would Elijah have helped her?"

"Yeah," Kai admits grudgingly. "He would've done anything for her. But Elijah . . . I mean, the cops brought him in a bunch of times. I don't think he could keep a secret like that. Not when everyone's saying he offed her."

"If he killed her, he's keeping an even bigger secret. Either way, Elijah's not the scared little boy everyone makes him out to be."

Kai bites his lip. "Yeah."

"What about Jocelyn?"

"What about her?"

"Did Lise ever go to her sister for help?"

"With school and stuff, sure. All the time. And Jocelyn's good at finessing her parents. She got them to ease up on Lise a lot. You never knew with those two, though. They'd be, like, best friends, and then super pissed at each other. Joss got mad 'cause Lise wasn't always responsible like her. And Lise kinda felt like Joss was babying her, trying to be her mom or something. So I don't know if she would go to Joss."

"How's Jocelyn at keeping secrets?"

Kai swallows. "Good." He folds his arms across his chest and stares down at his flip-flops as if they are worth serious scientific inquiry. "I mean, if that's what Lise was looking for . . . Joss could definitely lie to the cops."

"Yeah? Why do you say that?"

He exhales. "Because I've seen her do it."

"When?"

His body turns jittery. "I don't want to get her in trouble, okay? She was only trying to help me."

"I'm not working with the police on this," I remind him. "Not trying to stir up shit for you or Jocelyn, I promise. Just trying to figure out where Lise is, and give her mother some peace of mind."

I wait for a moment. Kai kicks at a rock, not happy about the turn our conversation has taken, but not shutting me down, either. He wants to know where this girl is, too.

"After Lise went missing, the police came around school asking questions. Who we were with that night, what we were doing, if we saw her."

"You told the police that you and Jocelyn were studying together."

"We *told* them that. And, for maybe half an hour, we legit were. But Brayden came by the school at seven thirty, and I . . . I went off with him for a bit. He had these 'shrooms. And I never did them before, and I was stressing about this math test, and I thought . . . I don't know, it would be fun."

"So Jocelyn lied about being with you that night."

"She was covering for me. If admin found out I was using on school grounds, I would be expelled. That would be it, no second chances. So she lied."

"That's quite a risk she took."

"She cares about me." Kai slumps against a palm tree. "She's a pain in the ass, but she cares. Here I am, some total fuckup with a mom who's gonna end up doing time sooner or later, and Joss is still here for me, putting herself on the line." Kai presses his face to his hand, and I see now that he is crying yet again. "I should be a better boyfriend. I should just . . . appreciate her."

I don't mean to ruin his tender feelings for his girlfriend, but I can't ignore the gaping hole in his selfless Jocelyn narrative. If Kai went off with Brayden at seven thirty, that's three hours Jocelyn hasn't accounted for. "You say she lied for you, Kai. But you might not be the only person she lied for that night."

"What do you mean?"

"If you weren't with Jocelyn, then who was?"

"No one. She was studying."

"No," I say, and it all makes sense now. "She wasn't studying. She got a D on her math test the next day. Does that sound like she spent the night studying to you?"

"A D? Jocelyn?" His surprise could not be greater if I'd told him she'd appeared in a porno.

"That's what her mom told me."

"Well, if she wasn't studying . . . what was she doing?"

"That's a great question. Her mother says she got home at ten thirty that night. Jocelyn claims Lise wasn't there when she got home, and from what I've heard, the police are assuming Lise never made it home at all."

"Right. Elijah said he walked her home, but he didn't. He killed her. And then he hitchhiked a ride home." Kai sounds impatient. "I know all this."

"Here's the thing. Mrs. Nakagawa swears she heard Lise come

home about half an hour before Jocelyn did." I take a seat at a picnic table just off the path. "Now, granted, Mrs. Nakagawa didn't actually see Lise. But she found her sweatshirt in their bedroom."

Kai follows me to the picnic table but doesn't sit down. "The sweatshirt Lise was wearing? She found that?"

I nod and let him chew that over. Back toward the playground, a woman strings up a clothing line between two trees and hangs a few wet garments. From her unkempt appearance, she's either camping or living from her car. A difficult life, I think, but in this environment, not impossible.

"So what does it mean?" Kai demands. "If Lise made it home, what does that mean? You think Jocelyn ran into her that night? You think she's been lying?"

"I think wherever Lise went that night, there's a good chance Jocelyn knows about it. Maybe Jocelyn even helped her go."

Kai holds his forehead as if trying to prevent his head from exploding. "But none of Lise's clothes were missing. She couldn't have run away without her clothes."

"Maybe Jocelyn gave Lise some of her own clothes to throw people off." Rae's twin-swap theory flits briefly through my head. "If Lise wore Jocelyn's clothes and styled her hair correctly, she might be able to walk around town passing for her sister without anyone being the wiser."

"You're wrong." The idea that Lise and Jocelyn might've duped everyone, duped him, makes Kai visibly angry.

"How do you know I'm wrong?"

"First of all, Lise and Jocelyn did not share clothes. Ever."

I give him a look. "That's it? That's the best you've got?"

"If Lise's alive, then where is she?" he asks. "Where did she go?"

"I'm shooting in the dark here, but you guys did spend all that time around Wakea Ranch. It wouldn't be a bad hideout, especially not if Elijah were in on it. He could bring her supplies until she figured out where to go next." I drop the final bomb on him. "Somebody at Wakea Ranch has been sending up light signals at night. Are you aware of anyone else Elijah used those signals with?"

"No." The blood drains from his face as he drops onto the bench beside me. "Fuck." Kai hurls the word with previously unseen viciousness. "Why are you telling me this? This . . . this is really messing with my head."

"Because we still have to answer the million-dollar question, don't we, Kai? Why. Why would Lise want to leave so bad? What in her life was she running from?" *Don't say Victor,* I think. *Please.*

"How would I know?" Kai stares at the ground. "If she had this big plan to sneak off, she sure didn't tell me about it." There's no disguising the hurt in his voice. For the first time, I wonder if Kai's feelings for Lise were something more than platonic. I could understand that. Long doses of Responsible Jocelyn might make a teenage boy secretly pine for a walk on the wild side.

"You were around Lise a lot," I say carefully. "Maybe she said something. Maybe Jocelyn said something. Maybe you noticed something off, something about their family . . ."

"Of course their family is off! Mr. Nakagawa is screwing that crazy lady, and the rest of the family is in la-la land about it." His hands are balled into tight white fists; there's nowhere for his fury to go. "The guy has a fricking kid with this woman, and they're all just pretending like it didn't happen. And then Lise starts dating that bitch's son? Yeah, something's off!"

"What did Lise think about her dad and Naomi?"

"She and Jocelyn always said it was just gossip. That it was a story people made up because they couldn't understand a man and a woman being friends."

"But you don't believe that."

"Of course I don't believe that," he says, disgusted. "Naomi got pregnant, didn't she? We're not talking about the Virgin Mary, here."

"If Lise found proof about her dad and Naomi . . . would that have been upsetting? Enough for her to leave?"

Kai turns to look at me slowly. "Maybe," he says. "Lise got in a lot of fights sticking up for her dad. If she knew he'd been playing them all this time . . . that would hurt."

It's a far more pleasant scenario than the one I've been entertaining. This feels like progress. "You've been really helpful, Kai," I tell him. "Thank you. Just one last thing." I'm still troubled by the girl's conversation with Marvel. "Did you ever notice Lise hanging around with an older guy?"

"What do you mean 'hanging around with'?"

"Hanging out, hooking up, whatever."

Kai frowns. "There were some local guys she met at parties, maybe. I don't know how old they were. And she was kinda into Brayden's friend Frankie for a while."

I raise my eyebrows at the name, a gesture Kai doesn't like.

"That was months ago," he says. "She wouldn't have gone off with one of those guys, if that's what you're thinking."

"Were any of these guys especially interested in *her*? Did anyone follow her around, call her a lot, anything like that?"

"Not that she said. The only one totally obsessed with her was Elijah."

"Okay. That's good to know." I don't call him out on the little crush

I suspect he nursed. Kai's been a good sport. No need to make things awkward. "Well. I'll let you get back to Eco Day."

I start down the path toward the pier. When I look back, he's still watching me. Those blue eyes and freckles make him look young, so young.

"Hey," he calls. "You really think she's alive?"

I pause. "I hope so. God, I hope so."

BACK ON THE PIER, Rae seems to be engaged in a rather intense conversation with Brayden. I can't make out their words over the lapping waves, but Brayden's brow creases as he speaks and Rae listens intently. Not wanting to interrupt what could be a useful source of information, I double back to the car and take some time to process what I've just learned from Kai.

On the positive side, nothing he told me hinted at any kind of abuse on Victor's part, and if Victor isn't about to win any upstanding-citizen awards, an affair with a consenting adult is a far cry from raping your child. Maybe Frankie is the mysterious older guy, after all. If Frankie broke Lise's heart and she was feeling vengeful, she might've flirted with the idea of statutory rape charges. Could Frankie have had a hand in her disappearance?

In the parking lot, a truck tows a huge metal boat to the edge of the grassy area, where a group of people with windbreakers and cameras now gather. A woman barks directions, warning people with injuries and heart conditions about the bumpy ride ahead. Tourists, I determine, preparing for a marine tour of the lava flow. I haven't seen this many tourists in one place since Volcanoes National Park. On this side of the island, the beaches are rocky and wild, the weather humid and unpredictable. If you aren't a surfer, charmed by the un-tamed sea, then lava is your only draw. Nothing to do here but sit back and watch the island burn.

I lean against the trunk of our rental. Kai has returned to his gar-bage collecting, ridding the park of refuse at his plodding pace. All those tears—who knew such a sensitive soul resided behind those baby blues? The kid certainly confirmed the level of self-delusion go-ing on in the Nakagawa family. My heart goes out to the girls, stub-bornly maintaining faith in their father when confronted over and over with the truth. I don't know about Lise, but if my conversation with her sister the other day is any indication, Jocelyn *still* hasn't ac-cepted what's staring them all in the face.

Jocelyn. I feel a prickle of anticipation.

Her busted alibi could be a promising development, a sign that she knows more than she's let on. Something must have happened that night her sister went missing, something that prevented her from studying for her test.

Did Lise call her, begging for help? Did they meet up somewhere?

You know that expression "You reap what you sow"? Jocelyn told me. *Lise didn't sow anything good.* But she didn't sound afraid for Lise's life when she said it. On the contrary, she seemed exhausted by her sister, bitter even. Like someone well versed in Lise's shenanigans, someone tired of running interference.

It would make sense for Lise to go to her sister in a time of trouble. Jocelyn has nerves of steel. She's a planner, an organizer. She'd know exactly what to do, how to handle any mess that Lise found herself in. And if Lise needed her, really needed her, how could Jocelyn turn her away? However different the Nakagawa girls might be, they're still sisters. Twins.

"There you are!"

I look up, see Rae jogging toward me.

"Man, I thought I'd never get away. That Brayden kid can yap." She opens the passenger-side door and tosses me the car keys. "Your turn to drive."

"Did Brayden say anything useful?"

"Nada. He was mostly sharing his philosophical insights about life." Inside the car, Rae quickly reapplies lipstick and adjusts a few curls. "He did say Victor was too controlling of his daughters, but when I asked for examples, he basically just objected to curfews and having to let your parents know where you are. Run-of-the-mill parenting stuff."

"I don't suppose he mentioned anything about Lise and Frankie ever being an item? Or any other guys who might've prompted the statutory rape questions?"

"I got nothing," Rae says ruefully. "How'd you make out with Kai? Collecting garbage together—nice way to build rapport, detective."

I'm in no mood for her lighthearted banter. "We need to find Jocelyn," I say as I start the engine.

Across the park, the tourists have begun to board the lava boat, eager to watch molten rock cool as it hits the sea, to witness the creation of new land. I wish that I could join them, but I need to be with Jocelyn now. I have to protect her—and her sister—from whoever has been prowling those dark woods. But I can't do that without some answers.

"She knows something, Rae," I say. "Jocelyn knows something big." I let the words sit on the tip of my tongue, testing their truth before I finally say them aloud. "I think she knows where Lise is."

twenty-two

According to Kai, Jocelyn is off saving the world with the Environmental Club, so I leave the girl to her recycling and wait until afternoon to make my move. In the meantime, Rae and I traipse half-heartedly around Hilo, a run-down town by the water that balances its touristy souvenir shops and art galleries with car dealerships and grocery stores.

At Liliʻuokalani Gardens, we ramble through a picturesque park with giant banyan trees, ponds, pagodas, bridges, and a Japanese tea garden. Populated mainly by *haole* tourists and a few homeless men, the gardens strike me as a peculiar tribute to their namesake, a queen who fought against colonialism and ended up under house arrest while white businessmen seized control of the government. Today, the rich white women in straw hats and swishy sundresses who stroll these grounds seem an affront to Liliʻuokalani's fierce Hawaiian nationalism.

I can't pretend I'm not one of them. When Rae and I end up sipping Frappuccinos in a local Starbucks, I know the American conquest of the islands is totally and devastatingly complete.

At three o'clock, I drop Rae off at the hot ponds for a couple of hours and drive over to the Nakagawa home. Though I feel bad about ditching Rae, my gut tells me I'll get further with Jocelyn alone. Two inquisitive adults might put her on her guard. Far better for me to show up at the house before Victor returns from work and pretend it's him I'm there to see.

As it happens, no one's at home when I pull into the driveway. The carport is empty, and I get no answer when I knock. Did I miss her? Is Jocelyn still out doing her project for Eco Day? Before I can decide what to do, a sporty silver car pulls up behind mine. Jocelyn steps from the passenger side, squinting at me.

I assume a Big Dumb Adult smile and wave.

Jocelyn sighs as she recognizes me. "It's okay, Ember," she tells the plump blond girl at the wheel. "Just someone here for my dad."

The blonde gives her a thumbs-up and pulls sharply out of the driveway, tires screeching.

Jocelyn trudges up the ramp toward me. "If you're looking for my father, he won't be home for another hour."

"Well, shoot. I was hoping I might catch him. I should've called." My cringeworthy performance will not win me any Oscars, but maybe Jocelyn'll buy it. "Hey, did I hear you were working on a project for Eco Day? Something with the Environmental Club?"

She eyes me suspiciously, as if displeased that I've been asking around about her. "As a matter of fact, we turned in three hundred pounds of recyclable plastics today."

"Wow! Impressive!"

"We're donating the money to the Conservation Council for Hawai'i," she says. "This was the first time we've done this, but I think we're going to make it an annual thing. And I pretty much organized it all, so . . ."

I grin. "You're building quite the résumé, aren't you? I don't see how Stanford could turn you down."

"They won't."

Sensing I've generated all the goodwill that I can, I make my request. "Listen, would you mind terribly if I hung around until your dad gets back? He'll be so disappointed if I miss him."

"Okay..." She unlocks the front door reluctantly. "I mean, I guess so." She holds the door open for me, pointedly removing her shoes when I forget to remove my own.

Now that I'm in, she can't get rid of me. "You know," I say, like the idea has just occurred to me, "maybe you could fill in some details for my article while we wait."

"Me?" Her body stiffens. "What do you want to know?"

"Well, I've heard all about Victor Nakagawa the scientist and athlete. But I've yet to learn what kind of dad he is."

Jocelyn stares blankly at me, but I know she must be remembering the scene I witnessed in the square yesterday, all the things Kai accused her father of. "My dad's busy," she says. "Obviously."

I follow her into the kitchen area. "So ... an absent dad?"

"It's not like I never see him," she objects. "When he's training, we work out together sometimes. We'll do laps at the aquatic center or bike. I tried to run with him a few times, but I can't keep up. He's really fast."

"That's great info." I break out a notebook and jot this down. "Do you and your dad share any other interests?" I want to put her at ease, get her relaxed before I steer the conversation to Lise.

"Just, you know, I think his work is really cool." Jocelyn opens the fridge and reaches for a pair of Diet Cokes. The refrigerator light flares bright and then winks out, its bulb suddenly dead. "Power surge,"

Jocelyn grumbles, offering me a soda can that I wave away. "Our solar panels have been a little wonky lately."

I follow her over to the sitting area, where she curls up in a chair with a teal cushion. I sit across from her on the wicker couch. "Has your father taught you much about volcanology?"

"Sure. When I was a kid and home sick from school, he'd bring me to the observatory with him." She smiles at the memory. "He'd give me these samples of volcanic rock. Pumice, reticulite, Pele's hair."

"Pele's hair?"

"They're these long, thin strands of volcanic glass that really look like hair. They form when lava hardens while flying through the air. Anyway, it was interesting, all the graphs and equipment and stuff. I used to fake sick sometimes so I could hang out with him."

It's a sweet confession that also strikes me as a little sad. "You must really admire him."

"He's achieved a lot."

"So has your mother."

Jocelyn pops the top on her can of Diet Coke. "My mother would've done more if she hadn't had her accident. She just teaches now. But that's not her fault."

Her comment seems to dismiss everything Sue has been through and all the work she's done for her students, but I hold my tongue. "Must have been quite an adjustment for you all after the accident."

"We adjusted."

"You sound like your dad," I tell her. "Stoic in the face of hardship."

"What are you supposed to do? Crumble when things go wrong? Accidents happen, things you don't plan for. My mom understood that." From her suddenly skittish gaze, this is not a conversation Jocelyn wants to be having. "She handled it. We all handled it."

"And your sister? She handled it, too?"

Jocelyn traces the rim of her soda can with her finger. "You're very interested in my sister."

"Why do you say that?"

"You were asking about Elijah the other day. I don't see what he has to do with my father."

"Your father is a complicated man," I say. "Just trying to provide a complete picture of him. I'd be remiss as a journalist if I ignored his missing daughter."

"You'd be remiss as a journalist if you printed rumors about Elijah."

So much for pleasant conversation. Jocelyn knows I'm up to something.

"Elijah was under investigation," I state. "That's not a rumor, that's a fact. It doesn't mean he had anything to do with Lise going missing. But it affects your father, who's the subject of my article." In truth, I have no plans to drag all the Yoon family garbage into my article for *Outdoor Adventures,* but I figure it's better to pretend my interest is professional and not personal. "This business with Elijah has weighed heavily on your dad, I'm sure, given his friendship with Elijah's mom."

"Honestly? I'm getting a little sick of having this Naomi conversation every time I see you." Jocelyn slams her can of Diet Coke on the coffee table, so hard that some fizzes out and drips down the sides. "If you put stupid rumors about that woman in your article, I will seriously sue you."

I have to bite my cheeks to keep from laughing. I have no doubt whatsoever that sixteen-year-old Jocelyn would march into a law office and secure an attorney if I published unflattering gossip about her family. Against my better judgment, I like this girl. She's feisty. I can see why Kai has stayed with her, why Lise would turn to her in times of trouble. Jocelyn is a good person to have in a foxhole.

"Relax," I tell her. "I'm a journalist. I deal in facts, clear and verifiable facts."

"If it's facts you're after, you can leave the Yoons out of it," she returns. "The police would've charged Elijah if they could support a case. There's no evidence anything bad happened to my sister, anyway. It's a missing person case, and she has a history of running away."

"I sense law school in your future."

"Maybe."

I try another tack. "You were friends with Elijah, weren't you? Hung out with him in the woods, listened to him play music. What did you think of him?"

"That's relevant to your article how?"

"Not relevant at all. Call it curiosity, pure and simple."

"Yeah, well, forgive me if I don't feel the need to satisfy your curiosity." She glowers at me. "I'm not an idiot, you know. I've read all about you."

"Did you?" There is no way I will let Jocelyn see how much it tears me up to be judged for some humiliating Google results. "I'm sure that made for interesting reading."

"Interesting? More like sad. No offense, but I really don't get the whole psychic thing. I mean, what, did Marvel call you out here? Do you people have some secret network?"

"I'm not here at Marvel's request. I'm a journalist. If you've been reading up on me, you know that."

Jocelyn grabs her hair and sweeps it over one shoulder. "You went to Columbia, didn't you?"

"Yep."

"That's a good school," she says. "And crazy expensive. Was it really worth all that tuition just to become a journalist? Seems like a lot of money to throw down." She pauses. "But I guess your parents helped."

If she thinks I grew up like one of the pampered rich girls at Free Thought, she's pegged me all wrong.

"I had a pretty good scholarship," I tell her. "I'm sure you'll get one, too."

"I can't go to school unless I do. Geology and teaching are only slightly more lucrative than journalism. Even with a scholarship, I'll have loans out the ass."

I study her for a moment, the tilt of her chin and the determined brow. She has her mother's perseverance and her father's ego, but there's another layer to Jocelyn, too—one I can't quite put my finger on.

"Why do I get the feeling that you're hiding something?"

"*Me?*" Her head whips toward mine at the accusation. "I thought you were after Elijah. What did *I* do?"

"I wish I knew."

"I don't think you want to talk to me that way, Charlotte. Not if you want my dad to cooperate with you."

I lean back against the wicker couch, impervious to her threats. The more this girl challenges me, the more I'm convinced she's covering for her sister. And I have my ace in the hole.

"You know, I had a chat with Kai today."

"Kai? Why?" She doesn't blink. If she's worried about anything her boyfriend might've said, it doesn't show. The girl should play poker.

"I wanted to know about Lise," I say. "And I wanted to know about you. Where you were the night she went missing."

"I *knew* you came here about Lise. I knew it." She waits a beat. "What did Kai tell you?"

"Nothing I didn't already know. That he wasn't with you. That you lied to the police."

Her jaw tightens almost imperceptibly. "Big deal. So I'm a loyal girlfriend. Kai was using drugs that night. I covered for him."

"Oh, I know what Kai was up to. What I don't know is how *you* spent your evening." I give her a reproachful sigh. "A D on a math test? You obviously weren't studying."

"Is there a point to this? Because so far all you've proven is that my boyfriend has a big damn mouth." Jocelyn tries to feign boredom, but I don't buy it. "If you want to say something, then say it."

"Okay, I will." I drop the friendly tone, let my voice turn hard as the rocky shores of South Point. "I think you know damn well where your sister is. In fact, I think you helped her get there."

For once, Jocelyn has no quick retort. She falls silent, the wheels in her head turning. "You don't understand," she says at last. "You don't understand me and Lise."

"Probably not. Enlighten me."

She draws her legs close to her chest. "What do you think love is?"

"I don't follow."

"I mean, what does love look like? How do you know someone loves you?"

Though still unclear about where she's going with this, I play along. "Their actions," I say. "How they treat you. What does this have to do with you and Lise?"

"I've always been the one who loved her most," Jocelyn says. "I watched out for her. After my mom's accident, there was no one else. My mom was learning to live her whole life again, and it was too much for my dad. He just . . . checked out. I was the one who took care of things. I did everything so Lise wouldn't have to."

"You've shouldered a lot of responsibilities for your family, Jocelyn. I know that."

"No, you have no idea. I do half her fucking homework so she doesn't fail out of school. I lie for her when she sneaks out to hook up with these stupid druggies who couldn't give two shits about her. She thought she might be pregnant last year, and you know who bought her a test? You know who stood there with her, waiting for a little minus sign to appear, telling her whatever happened, we'd deal with it? It wasn't my mother. It wasn't my dad. And it sure as hell wasn't the rando she'd been screwing."

"You've spent your life protecting her. I get it."

"That's love. Not touchy-feely, blab-about-it love, but real, get-stuff-done love. The kind that matters."

"Where is she?" I murmur. "Where did you take her?"

"Leave my family alone."

"If you tell me what happened that night, maybe I can make that call."

"It should be *my* call. I love my sister more than anyone. My actions prove it, don't they? So if I tell you to drop this, then drop it. Maybe you think you're helping my parents, but you're not. All you can do is make things much, much worse for them."

I try to imagine what situation Lise might've found herself in to make her want to run away forever, to make starting over the only attractive option. Is there a situation so horrible I would rather believe my child dead than know her true circumstances? I run through the possibilities. Prostitution? Addiction? Participation in a terrorist organization? I'd rather know. I'd always rather know.

"I know she came to you. I know she thought you could fix it."

Silence.

Jocelyn sits perfectly erect, awaiting my next move. When it becomes apparent she has no intention of answering, I appeal to her better nature.

"If you don't tell people the truth, Elijah Yoon will spend his entire life with a cloud of suspicion hanging over his head."

Jocelyn closes her eyes. "Yeah, well, that's the least of Elijah's problems."

"So that's it? You know exactly where your sister is, but you'd rather just sit back and watch your parents suffer?"

"My parents are the ones that I'm protecting!" She grips the arms of her chair. "Lise made her choices, and nobody can undo them. Not me, and not you, either."

For a second, I'm torn. What if Jocelyn is right? What if Lise's going into hiding really was the best thing for the whole Nakagawa family? The truth can be an ugly, unwieldy thing. Once unleashed, there's no going back.

But then I think of Lise. You can't throw an immature sixteen-year-old out into the world and expect her to float. Lise's vulnerable. Even if she's safe now, she'll eventually need help. Expecting Jocelyn to single-handedly shoulder this burden is unfair to everyone.

"I don't want to hurt anyone, Jocelyn. But people are already hurting."

She moves to the edge of her chair. "You didn't come here today to talk to my dad, did you?"

"No, I guess I didn't."

"You need to leave now."

"Jocelyn."

She shakes her head. "Don't bother coming back. When my father hears about this, your article is dust."

"You need to tell them. Whatever you know, you need to tell them."

"I'm not going to say a thing, and neither are you." She rises purposefully from her seat. "Not unless you want drug charges thrown at you."

"What?" I stare at her. "What are you talking about?"

"That cookie you ate with Brayden. It takes a long time for THC to break down in your system. You'd still test positive for marijuana."

My lips part, but no words come out. She's really going there. I can't imagine anyone in law enforcement caring if Jocelyn went running to them about one measly cookie, but the sheer audacity of it—that's a side of her I hadn't anticipated. She has all the ferocity of a mama bear, which is admirable up until the moment she's charging you.

I head for the door and gather up my shoes, warm feelings for this girl rapidly evaporating.

"Nice to see you, too," I mutter, and the door bangs shut behind me.

A FEW HOURS LATER, I get a call from Victor. I let it go to voicemail. The message he leaves is angry and rambling, but on three points, he is clear.

My profile of him will never see the light of day.

I am not, under any circumstances, to have contact with his daughter again.

I am a lying, manipulative "media whore."

I delete the message, a little regretful that I don't drink.

twenty-three

That night, sitting out on our balcony, Rae and I see the lights in the woods again. It's half past midnight; we've been fighting off sleep for more than an hour, hoping for—and half dreading—some sign of life in the dense growth. And now here it is.

Blink. Blink. Blink. Three flashes in slow succession, and then darkness. That same familiar pattern, although tonight I see no answering signal. Not yet.

"He's giving her the go-ahead," I say. "He's telling her that it's safe to come out of hiding."

Rae stands and leans against the rail, inspecting the woods. "You really think Lise's out there? That Elijah's been helping her all this time?"

"Him or Jocelyn, yeah. Maybe they're working together." Just thinking about Jocelyn makes me twitch. I have no doubt that she or Victor will soon be in touch with my magazine to register some kind of complaint. The fallout could be bad.

"Jocelyn basically admitted to knowing where her sister is and helping her disappear," I tell Rae. "She believes she's protecting the family somehow."

"You think she dumped her sister on Elijah? Just kind of handed her over and was like, 'Hey, she's yours now, I'm out'?"

"I think someone is in those woods right now and we need to know who."

The cloudless night sky stretches out above us, a vast well of stars. I have never seen the heavens so clear and so infinite, not even in the Arizona desert. No wonder astronomers from across the world flock to this island.

"Maybe they're signaling to us," Rae says, uneasy about the flashlight. "Could be some perv trying to lure us to our deaths. Your stalker, maybe." She shifts her weight. "It would be dumb for the two of us to go rushing out there."

"Very dumb," I agree. "Downright dangerous."

"Right." She lets out a sigh of relief.

"We can't both go. You need to stay here and keep an eye on things. To call for help if things get dicey."

Rae tugs at my shirt, alarmed. "You aren't suggesting you go in there *alone*, are you?"

I don't love the idea myself, but what choice do we have? I can't put Rae at risk, and someone needs to see what's going on. If Lise's alive out there, I have to know.

"It'll be fine," I tell Rae with more confidence than I feel. "I have my phone now. I'll call you and keep it on speaker while I'm out there. You'll hear everything that happens."

"Like the sound of someone attacking you from behind with a shovel? No way. No. Way."

The lights begin again from more or less the same position in the woods. *Blink. Blink. Blink.* Still, they get no response. Perhaps tonight's meeting went awry and someone didn't show up. I shudder.

What if it's Lise flashing those lights? Or Jocelyn? My dream could be unfolding this very minute. Someone could be crouched in a bush, ready to move on the unsuspecting twin. My final vision by the hammock comes flooding back in all its unwanted detail. Her hair spilling from his fingers. Her bare back shuddering against his touch.

I have to act now.

"I'll check in with you every couple minutes," I promise Rae. "I'll—tap on the phone three times. If you don't hear me tapping, then something's gone wrong, and you call the police."

"This is your life!" Rae protests. "We are not allowing for the possibility of something going wrong!"

She's too late. I'm already climbing over the balcony's edge, sliding my body over the rail and easing my grip downward. If Watching Guy can climb this trellis, so can I, damn it.

"Are you crazy?!" Rae hisses. "Charlie! Get back here!"

I find a foothold and descend. Once safely on the ground, I pull my phone out of my pocket, dial her number, and start jogging toward the woods. The next round of lights has begun to flash.

Blink. Blink. Blink.

Rae answers her phone with a squawk. "What are you doing? This is totally—"

"Shhh!" I whisper. "No talking, or I hang up on you!"

"If I hear anything weird, I'm calling 911," she warns, but she doesn't speak again.

I can picture her gazing into the field after me, certain she's sent me to my doom. Maybe she's right.

I shove the phone into my pocket, trying to keep the speaker exposed. Even in the dark, the field is bright enough to navigate, silvery grass beneath a pallid moon. The woods are a different story. I locate one of the pathways and enter, but the thick tree cover suffocates the moon and starlight. Not fifty feet in, I trip on a root and skin my knee.

"Charlie?" Rae's voice drifts up from my pocket, muffled but terrified by whatever thumping sounds I just produced.

I tap the speaker three times with a fingertip and she goes silent.

I have two choices: stumble wildly through the dark or use my phone as a flashlight, thereby alerting anyone here to my presence. Not a good pair of options. I knew going in that this wasn't my best and brightest plan, but it's got even bigger holes than I realized.

Before I can choose, the signal begins again several yards away from behind a tree. *Blink. Blink. Blink.* I can't see the person responsible from this angle, but if I get a little closer, I might catch them during the next round.

I move in the approximate direction of the lights, my footsteps not exactly ninjalike as they crash through the brush.

Whatever advantage I held through surprise has been lost with all my tramping around. The flashlight bearer knows I'm out there. For a moment, I think I see someone, a shadow ducking in and out of other shadows, though I can't judge the distance. I hold my breath. Against the night's resounding chorus of coquís, someone rustles invisibly toward me. My hand goes to my phone.

A light blinks on, this time directly at me, and does not flicker out.

"Who are you?" a male voice demands, but I can't see his face, not with the blinding white flashlight shining in my eyes. "What are you doing here?"

I shield my face, trying to dodge the intense beam. "I saw lights in the woods. I thought maybe someone was hurt."

He lowers the light. "You're that woman. The one staying at Koa House."

"That's right." As my eyes grow accustomed to the dark again, I begin to pick up some of his features: shaggy hair, a lean frame. "Elijah?" I wonder if Rae's getting this or if she's already panicked, hung up, and dialed the local police.

"This is my land," Elijah says coldly, "and you're trespassing."

I hold up my hands, assessing the threat this kid might pose. He's hardly friendly, but I wouldn't expect him to be, given the circumstances. "Not trying to stir up problems. I just wanted to make sure nobody was in trouble. Who are you signaling to, anyway?"

"That's none of your business."

"Is somebody out here?"

He pauses. "Have you seen someone?"

"Your little brother has. A guy who hides in trees."

"A guy?" Elijah's not expecting this. "When? Recently?"

"Hard to say. Raph's concept of time is pretty fluid." I steal a glance at my phone, realize the call with Rae is still connected. I tap three times on the speaker, relieved to know she's with me.

"Raph probably saw someone over the summer," Elijah says. "One of my friends."

"Kai, maybe?"

"Maybe."

"Any reason Kai would be sneaking around your land?" I'm curious if he knows that Jocelyn and Kai were using his hammock as a love den.

Elijah sweeps his flashlight across the surrounding trees as if searching for more intruders. "If Kai was here, it wasn't sneaking. We were friends. He was welcome here."

Welcome, I suspect, is an overstatement. "Your mom was okay with these visits?"

"My mom?" He snorts. "She doesn't want anyone on our land. Especially not you." He raises the light to my face again as if daring me to tell on him. "If you know what's good for you, you won't be back. There's nothing here for you, so just go home."

"Elijah, I'd like to help you." My words come out in a rush. "I know what people think you did to Lise, and I know that they're wrong. If she's out here, please, you need to tell someone."

"Tell someone? Like who? You?" His tone is a mixture of incredulity and anger. "Go home, *haole*. You can't help me, and you sure can't help Lise. Can't even keep track of your own phone, can you?"

A chill runs up my back. "That was you?"

"You're not the only one who can trespass on private property."

I shiver, suddenly reminded that we're out here alone, that I have no weapon, that this kid is widely suspected of murder. He doesn't seem like a stalker type, the kind who would be photographing me unaware and lurking while I bathe, but who the hell knows?

"What did you want with my phone?"

Elijah draws his lights across the trees in a slow loop as if he suspects someone might be watching. "Internet," he says. "I wanted Internet."

I play along—now is not the time to bring up those creepy photos. "Well, sure. That makes sense. You must feel disconnected, living way out here."

"Nobody ever tells me what's going on," he mumbles. "Lise always said you can find anything on the Internet. I just wanted to know if they're still looking for her."

I can't tell who *they* are. The police? Lise's parents? Either way, he doesn't sound like he expects her to be found.

"Elijah," I whisper. "Is Lise out here?"

"You think I killed her," he says. "You think she's buried under a tree somewhere, don't you?"

"No," I say, although it sounds terrifyingly plausible coming from the lips of this wild-eyed boy in the dark.

"I didn't hurt her," he says. "Something was going on with her that night, something weird. But she made it home safe. I saw her go inside." He pounds his flashlight against a tree, frustrated. "I just don't get why she broke up with me. She couldn't even give me a reason. How do you wake up one day and not love someone anymore? And then she just vanishes. Where would she even go? How does that make any sense?"

"It doesn't," I say. "I think you're right. Something *was* going on with her." If he's lying, he's doing a convincing job of it, confusing me further. "Why are you out here tonight?"

"The lights," he says. "I keep seeing the lights. I go out here, trying to find them, but I never do. Sometimes they get so close, and then . . . nothing. No one's there."

"You think it's her," I realize.

"I don't know who it is," he says. "I just know if she's alive, she'll come back. We had a plan, okay? We were going to work at Ono Place and rent a room together. She promised she wouldn't leave me here. And Lise never broke a promise."

The poor kid. Whatever mess Lise found herself in, whatever crisis she was running from, Elijah remains clueless. He may have loved this girl, but he didn't know her secrets.

"I'm sure she never meant to break her promise to you," I tell him. "I think she got herself in trouble and just didn't see a way out. I think she went to Jocelyn for help."

"Jocelyn?" He refuses to entertain such a betrayal. "No. That's not . . . if something was wrong, she would've come to me. You don't know what you're talking about." He takes a few aggressive steps toward me, brandishing the flashlight like a club. "Get off my land! *Now.*"

I take out my phone and flip on the flashlight, shining it in the direction I came from. "I'm leaving the island Sunday night," I call over my shoulder. "If you hear anything from Lise or find out who's been flashing these lights, let me know, would you?"

Behind me, Elijah's light blinks out. I can no longer see him, no longer tell exactly where he's hiding, but I hear his words, clear as a bell, from somewhere in the trees: "Screw you."

"That went well." Rae stands in the Tree Fern Room smiling when I return. "You and Elijah Yoon, what a nice little chat."

I topple onto her bed, one hand on my still-racing heart. "I almost peed myself."

"Yeah, that moment when I heard some random guy's voice calling to you in the dark? Coulda used a defibrillator. But of all the outcomes I was imagining when you ran off into the woods, this is by far the best."

"Except I learned nothing."

"You learned one of the parties responsible for those flashing lights," Rae points out. "Kinda sad, isn't it? It's like he just wanders around the woods at night all lovelorn on the off chance his ex-girlfriend is going to appear."

"I saw two sets of lights the other night. Elijah's not alone out there." I wrap my arms around a pillow, trying to fend off goose bumps. "Something is going on in those woods, Rae. Something . . ."

"Hey, we didn't come away empty-handed tonight. Elijah had some useful things to say." She begins ticking items off on her fingers. "He told you the guy lurking in the woods was probably just Kai. He told you Lise definitively did make it home that night. And he told you his mom totally has it in for you." Rae now wears a satisfied smile.

"What's Naomi got against me, anyway?" I ask. "I haven't *done* anything to her except help her find Raph."

"Maybe she found Elijah with your phone. Realized he'd been following you around. That's pretty sinful stuff in her world."

Thinking of crazy Naomi and her pitiful boys just depresses me further. "I'm going to bed."

"You sure you want to stay in the Bamboo Room tonight?" Rae asks. "My bed's a king. Maybe you shouldn't stay in a room where dudes snap photos of you sleeping."

I wave her off. "Elijah won't show up here again, not after tonight. But I'll lock the door to the balcony and make sure the curtain is closed, okay?"

Rae looks doubtful, but she shrugs it off. "You're a grown-ass woman. Suit yourself."

Back in the Bamboo Room, I start to see the wisdom of Rae's suggestion. I can't stop thinking about that unknown guy in the woods, the one that I've been dreaming of. Who is he? Adam? Victor? Frankie? Kai? I struggle to believe that any of them are evil. Could it be some stranger, then, who watches from the shadows, taunting Elijah with false promises of Lise's return each night? I curl up in bed, unable to warm myself beneath the blankets, too unsettled to turn off the light.

What will happen to Jocelyn? What has already happened to Lise?

I don't know when I drift off, but I awake in the dark to the sound of a light rapping. For a moment, I think I'm home, that it's Tasha come to drag me out of bed. Disoriented, I sit up. Take in my surroundings and realize that I have it all wrong.

The rapping sounds again—not the door to the hallway, but the sliding glass door to the balcony. Someone is out there. Again.

Probably just Rae, I tell myself, but my beating heart doesn't believe it. I snatch my less-than-intimidating pair of nail scissors and point their blades outward like a knife. Padding softly to the glass door, I take a deep breath. Try to steady my shaky hands. Draw back the curtain.

twenty-four

The pale face pressed against the glass door gives me a quick jolt of adrenaline. In the split second it takes to recognize the bewildered, boyish figure, my body prepares for an attack, increases my heart rate, and diverts all the blood from my digits to my muscles. Not the kind of reaction people usually have to Adam Yoon.

Seeing my fear, he withdraws from the glass, greets me with a sheepish, tips-of-his-fingers-only wave like a middle school boy at a crowded dance.

I don't open the door. It's two a.m.

"What the hell are you doing here?"

Adam blinks at me, wounded. I doubt he can hear me through the door, but my ire is obvious. He glances behind him into the dark and then back at me, evaluating whether he should leave. *Sorry*, he mouths, gaze dropped to the floor. He moves back toward the railing, ready to leap over it.

I can't let him go, not without an explanation. Cursing, I lift the bolt and crack the door a few inches. "Before you go running off into the night, maybe you can tell me why you're on my balcony."

"I saw your light on," Adam says. "I thought . . . maybe you wanted company."

"Company? My light is not an invitation. Adam, you scared the crap out of me."

"I—I'm sorry," he stammers. "I was looking at your window and the light . . . it seemed like you were having trouble sleeping. I thought . . . maybe you were lonely. Maybe we could talk."

It dawns on me now: Elijah wasn't the one following me around. "This isn't the first time you've been out here, is it? You were the one screwing around with my phone, taking pictures."

"I didn't steal it," he says quickly. "That was Elijah. I saw him with it, and I told him he couldn't do that. That you were nice, and we had to give it back."

"You took your time getting it back to me."

Adam hangs his head.

"The flowers—that was you also?"

"I wanted to give you something. A gift."

"So you left them at the front door without any indication of who they came from? I don't think I follow your strategy."

"I thought when you saw the flowers, you'd understand."

"Understand what?"

"That I want to be with you."

My grip tightens around the tiny scissors. He sounds more like a child than a mentally unhinged pervert, but I'm not taking any chances. No doubt that was him hanging around outside my bath. God knows what twisted fantasies this boy has been dreaming up.

"Is this how it was with Lise?" I ask softly. "You wanted to be with her?"

"Lise?" He sounds baffled by the name. "Lise is Elijah's friend, not mine. Why would I want to be with her? She's just a kid."

"You're telling me you didn't watch her in the woods?"

Adam remains puzzled. "Watch her do what? All they ever did out there was sing and smoke and drink alcohol. I wouldn't participate in that."

His self-righteousness feels a little misplaced, given his stalker tendencies, but I let it slide for the moment. "What is it you want from me, Adam? Spit it out." I'm fully prepared to plunge these nail scissors into his throat if he gets too close.

His eyes well up. "I just want to leave, okay? I just want to come with you. You've been so nice to me, and to Raph. We would be happier with you. I don't want to spend my whole life with my mother. Please."

I look him over. He's an inch shorter than I am, and scrawny. No weapon. Rae and David and Thom are all just a scream away.

"You're nineteen years old," I say, cracking the door open another couple of inches. "You don't need her permission to leave. You don't need me to take you with me. This is on you, Adam. Get a job and go."

"It's not that simple," he says. "I've got Raph. If I get a job, who will take care of him? I can't do this alone."

His devotion to his little brother does complicate matters—and leave Naomi with ample opportunity to exploit their bond. But if it's submission she's after, her repressive rules have backfired, leaving both her teenage sons desperately hatching exit plans.

"Raph is your mother's responsibility, Adam," I say, "not yours. If you're this miserable, you need to take care of yourself first."

"He has to come with me," he says stubbornly. "I can't leave him."

Mentally cursing my own bleeding heart, I open the door and join him on the balcony. Clouds have drifted in off the mountains, forming a wispy veil across the stars. I sink into a damp chair with a sigh.

"You're over eighteen. If you can make the case that your mother is an unfit parent, you could petition to be his legal guardian."

"What does that mean, 'an unfit parent'?"

"Is your mother neglecting Raph? Causing him physical or emotional harm?"

"No."

I think for a moment. "Elijah doesn't go to school, right? If your mom hasn't filed paperwork to meet the state standards for homeschooling, that might get Child Welfare in the door."

He dismisses the idea outright. "I don't want to get her in trouble." Adam tilts his head toward the sky. It has started raining again, tiny drops like gossamer in the air. "It would be better if me and Raph just left," he says at last. "She wouldn't follow us, I know she wouldn't."

"Adam, you could face kidnapping charges."

"No," he says, frowning. "She wouldn't do that. Raph is just as much mine as hers."

I stroke my forehead, wondering how it is I'm stuck explaining legal concepts to a kid who has spent nearly two decades living under a proverbial rock. "Look, I know you've been like a dad to Raph. You practically raised him, I get it. But in the eyes of the law, a brother is not the same thing as a biological parent."

Adam's gaze holds mine, and for the first time, I see something burning in him, a will to fight. "I'm not just *like* a dad to him," he says. "I *am* his dad."

For a second, I don't believe what he's saying. "But . . . Victor . . ."

"Victor, Victor. People never stop talking about Victor!" Adam laughs a little wildly. "He's been hanging around my mom for years, pretending to be so helpful. You think she doesn't know what he really wants? She knows, and she's never going to give it to him. But hey, if he wants to fix our roof for free, she won't say no."

"I don't understand. If you're Raph's dad, then who . . ." I can't finish the question, can't ask him the identity of Raph's mother. Because I know what's been going on, can feel it in my gut. "Oh God," I murmur, my stomach turning. "Oh, honey."

Adam twists away from the railing. "I don't want her to go to jail."

I run the numbers. Raph is four now, and Adam is nineteen. That means Adam was probably only fourteen, fifteen tops, when Naomi became pregnant. If this gets out, it doesn't matter whether Adam wants to prosecute or not. He was a minor when the abuse began, legally unable to consent to any sexual activity with an adult, let alone his own mother.

Suddenly Marvel's words come back to me. *She kept talking about the age of consent. She wanted to know if an older partner could be punished for statutory rape after the younger partner turned sixteen.*

Only now do I realize: Lise wasn't talking about herself. She knew.

I lean forward, fingers gripping the sides of my chair. "Is it just you? Your mom and Elijah, are they . . . ?"

"Elijah is just a kid," he says, as if insulted. "He and my mother have never been close." The fine rain settles on his hair and imbues his skin with an eerie sheen. He hunches over, hands tucked into his armpits, afraid to look at me.

"Just you, then." I'm dazed.

How did Lise know? Did Elijah tell her? Did she figure it out for herself or, God forbid, see something? More importantly, did knowing play some role in her disappearance?

My questions will have to wait. I need to be fully present for Adam. He will judge himself according to my reaction.

"Adam . . ." I begin, "I'm . . . sorry this happened to you."

It's the wrong thing to say, and he rushes to Naomi's defense. "Nothing *happened* to me," he says. "My mother needed someone, a man of the house. Someone responsible who wouldn't leave her. She deserves a man like that."

"You deserve things, too," I say. "Things she hasn't given you." *Like a childhood*, I think. *Like a healthy, functional parent.*

His face crumples. "I've tried," he tells me. "Really. But I can't be the man that she needs. I know it's selfish. I know I've failed her."

There's no arguing with this level of brainwashing.

I swallow back my feelings and keep a steady voice. "We need to call somebody, Adam. Somebody who can get you and Elijah and Raph out of that house." This now goes well beyond a simple call to Child Welfare. Only law enforcement can remove children from a home.

Adam paces around the balcony, his steps jittery and erratic. "I don't want anything bad to happen to her," he says. "People won't understand. She didn't do anything wrong."

"Yes," I say forcefully. "She did."

"I could've said no. I could've said no, and I didn't. I didn't ever. I love my mom. And she loves me."

I don't want to hear any more details, don't want to see the way this poor boy has been taught to empathize with his abuser. Recognizing he can't bear any criticism of Naomi, I try another approach.

"Adam, you're not happy in that house. Neither is Elijah. You told me how much you want to leave. You'd both be happier, right?"

He nods.

"This is how we have to do it. This is how we get you out." I move to the doorway, gesturing for him to come inside.

The Bamboo Room glows warm and inviting, offering refuge from the dark.

He hesitates. Brushes a few raindrops from his hair, but doesn't enter. It takes a moment for me to realize that he's weeping again. Arms wrapped around his own skinny body, he rocks back and forth, crying noiselessly. I wish that he would holler, let loose, make some noise. He has been silent for so long.

When he finally does speak, his voice is nearly lost to the sound of the rain. "I don't know if I can do this to her," he says. "She's my mother."

"Hey." I place a hand on his arm. "Forget your mother for a minute, and think about who really matters here. Who is it you should be protecting?"

He takes a breath, shoulders slumping. "Raph."

"That's right. Raph. He deserves a better life than the one you've had." I give his arm a squeeze. "This is how you give it to him. You walk into that room with me, and we make the call."

Adam closes his eyes and in that moment makes his decision. As a brother. As a father.

"Okay," he says hoarsely. "Okay."

saturday

twenty-five

The police cruisers show up at Wakea Ranch a little before noon. Rae and I have been lingering at the foot of the Koa House driveway for hours, searching for signs of activity down the road, wondering if Adam got cold feet after I dropped him off at the station. It's one thing to tell your story to a nameless voice on the phone, and—as I know from experience—quite another to sit across from some guy in an interrogation room and answer a string of unsavory personal questions. When the officers finally arrive, I know that Adam has stuck the landing.

If Rae and I are expecting fireworks, a showdown and a dramatic arrest, we get something else entirely. No lights, no sirens, no screaming or gunshots; just a pair of Hawai'i County police vehicles that arrive and depart from the property within half an hour. The lack of drama confuses me. Have they arrested Naomi? The cruisers' tinted windows make it impossible to see who's coming and going.

"You think they convinced her to come to the station?" I ask. "I mean, they wouldn't just leave her with those kids, right?"

"No way," Rae reassures me. "There were two cars. One for Naomi, one for the boys. It's going to be fine."

"Fine" is the last adjective I'd use to describe the Yoon family's situation right now, but I'm too exhausted to disagree. I call Noah to let him know the mystery of my stalker has been solved, news that somewhat eases his mind, although he's not as disposed to forgive Adam's creepy behavior as I am. That duty dispensed with, I trudge off for a four-hour nap. To my immense relief, sleep proves restorative, not frightening. I don't dream of stalking young women. I don't feel myself getting pushed off a cliff.

That evening, Thom learns through the rumor mill that Naomi is in custody. The news brings both relief and crushing guilt. I hope I didn't destroy lives. I hope I'm giving these boys something better.

Rae and I pick up some Chinese food in Pāhoa and treat Thom and David to dinner. The mood at the dining table is somber as we each struggle to process what has happened.

"I still can't believe it." Thom dips his chicken in duck sauce, shaking his head. "Naomi Yoon. All these years we've been living next door to her, so sure she and Victor were an item . . ."

"You weren't the only one who misjudged that relationship." Having dismissed all three Nakagawa females as credulous dupes, I feel more than a little guilty. "But Sue was right about Victor all along. He might've had a little crush on Naomi, but it never went beyond that. After her husband died, Naomi only had eyes for Adam."

Thom cringes. "The crazy part is . . . I'm not exactly *surprised*. If she were a man, living like she does with three daughters, someone would've called Child Welfare years ago."

David picks at his food, his forehead lined with self-recrimination. "We should've seen the signs," he says. "I've dealt with enough kids from abusive homes over the years—I should've gotten involved.

When I think about Adam living over there in isolation all that time . . ." He puts down his chopsticks. "What will happen to those kids?"

I play with the napkin in my lap. "I'd guess they'll be put in a temporary foster placement while Adam seeks custody."

"You think he'll get it?" Thom asks.

"I don't know. I hope so. He really loves Raph." My heart aches for all three boys. They face so many changes, and the foster care system isn't always fair or kind.

"At least this gives police free rein to search Wakea Ranch," Rae says. "Who knows what they'll find?"

Thom puts a hand to his chest. "If they find Lise out there, I swear I'll never sleep again."

"Don't," David says, blanching. "Don't say that. The Yoons have their problems, but murder? That's . . . no. I won't believe that."

"Naomi had motive," Rae points out. "Lise Nakagawa knew what was going on in that family. She'd been asking Marvel for legal advice, trying to figure out what the consequences would be if she reported it. She was trying to get Elijah a job at Marvel's restaurant, to give him a way out."

"That doesn't mean Naomi killed her," I protest. Frankly, I'm not convinced Lise is dead at all. Jocelyn sure isn't acting like it. She must know something the rest of us don't. I refrain from sharing my suspicions with David and Thom, however. No reason to go spreading unfounded rumors—not when Rae's doing such a bang-up job.

"I don't think Naomi *planned* to kill Lise exactly," Rae says. "But, back to the wall, what else is she going to do? My guess is, Lise felt bad about dumping Elijah that night. So she goes back to Wakea Ranch later, hoping to smooth things over. Only instead of finding Elijah in those woods, she runs into Naomi. They have words, and . . . Naomi realizes she's cornered. She's got to get rid of Lise. It's the only way to protect her secret."

Rae relates this tale like someone spinning ghost stories at a campfire, and if David and I respond skeptically, Thom seems spellbound.

"You think Elijah knows what his mother did?" he asks.

"No," Rae tells him. "Elijah's still out there in the woods every night, signaling to Lise. He really believes she might come back to him."

"You should talk to the police," Thom says breathlessly. "Tell them what you know."

I glare at Rae. "We don't know anything. This is all conjecture. We have no proof."

"What kind of proof would they need?" Thom asks. "I mean, short of a body . . ."

"A weapon," Rae suggests. "Naomi isn't a big woman. Someone should go over to her place and check out her tool shed."

"Oh my God, you're right." Thom covers his mouth, his imagination spinning out of control. I wince. He and Rae are a bad influence on each other. "There could be some blood-crusted thing hanging from a hook in the barn and nobody would be the wiser."

"Stop it!" David's legs hit the table as he jumps to his feet, knocking over his glass of water. "These are *real people*. Lise Nakagawa is a real person, and all this speculation . . . it's not right, Thom! She was just a kid. Have some respect."

Thom and Rae exchange guilty glances as David flees the room. Heaving a sigh, Thom hurries off to smooth things over with his husband. A puddle of water gathers on the wooden floor as the contents of David's glass flow steadily from the table.

"I wasn't trying to be a jerk," Rae says, chastened.

"I know."

"I really want to know what happened to Lise."

"Me, too." I grab a handful of napkins and mop up David's spill. "But it's different for us, isn't it? We get to fly in and out, leave tomorrow night, and never think about these people again. With David and Thom . . . this is their home. They have to see the Nakagawas around town. They have to watch Raph Yoon grow up. Whatever damage we do, they get left with it."

"Damage? Don't tell me you're having second thoughts."

"I don't know. I just broke up a family."

"Naomi Yoon does *not* need your pity."

"Not her. The kids." I begin dismantling an egg roll with my fork, mindlessly raking bits of cabbage across my plate. "Adam will have to prove paternity in order to get a shot at custody, and once he does . . . Naomi'll end up in jail, there's no way around that. And Adam will feel responsible."

"Charlie. In this situation, you had no choice."

"I know. I'm just saying . . . I understand why Lise didn't tell anybody. Why she didn't want to be the one."

"Do you think Jocelyn knows?"

I look up. "About Naomi and Adam? Why would she?"

"Lise could've told her, duh."

I contemplate that possibility for a moment. "No. No, I don't think she knew. Jocelyn's a problem solver. She would've tried to solve the problem. She would've . . . hired a lawyer or lodged a complaint with

Child Welfare. After all the rumors about Naomi and Victor, Jocelyn wouldn't miss a chance to take Naomi down and clear her father's name. I think it's safe to say Lise was on her own with that one."

I let that sit a minute: Lise, supposedly so dependent on her sister, weighing the fate of her boyfriend's incestuous family. Trying to get information from Marvel without tipping her hand. Listening to people joke about her father's supposed love child with Naomi when she knew the truth.

Jocelyn was wrong about her sister, I decide. Lise was not without a backbone. Perhaps that was why she broke up with Elijah: she was freeing herself from the burden of bearing his secrets, giving herself the space she needed to report it.

And what will happen to Elijah now? He clearly wants to connect with the outer world, but how will he ever learn to adjust when people still view him with such suspicion? If he's thrown into foster care, they'll make him attend public schools for the first time in his life. I've seen the way teenagers here treat him. They'll crucify the poor kid. And who does he have standing in his corner? Not one friend. Not one. This is the mess I'm leaving in my wake, and it's not right.

I push my chair back from the table. "I need to talk to Kai."

"Kai?" Rae echoes. "What does he have to do with this?"

"He's the closest thing Elijah had to a friend," I say. "And Kai turned on him. Kai needs to know that whatever happened to Lise, Elijah wasn't responsible." Kai strikes me as a decent person, and he just might have enough social capital to call off the Free Thought guys who have been harassing Elijah. Maybe Kai will take pity on the kid, let him tag along from time to time. Elijah needs any social support he can get.

Rae arches an eyebrow, and I can tell she disapproves. "You don't think that's getting a little overinvolved?"

I shrug. "It's a little late to worry about *that*. And honestly, Rae . . . if I can't leave things better than I found them . . . what good am I?"

KAI WASN'T LYING when he said his house was tiny. Tucked away in a lush patch of rain forest, the trailer he, Brayden, and Sage all occupy can't be more than three hundred square feet. I've seen these little eco houses on HGTV before and always thought them charming, perfect for a no-frills couple. They are decidedly less perfect, however, for a teenage boy living with his mother and her boyfriend. I can understand why Kai would spend as little time as possible at home.

The front door is dark when I show up, but I can see a light on inside the home. Beside me, a beat-up pickup truck and an old red Corolla occupy the driveway. Judging from the Free Thought bumper sticker and surfboard decals on the Corolla, the vehicle belongs to Kai. A Tibetan prayer flag hangs from one of the trees, its edges tattered. Large purple snails dot the moist ground.

I wonder if Sage cultivates her marijuana crop on this property or elsewhere. Situated at the end of a long and winding drive through barely tamed trees, the land is certainly private enough. Without Thom's precise directions, I would've missed the place entirely.

I knock on the door and wait for a response. I'm about to knock a second time when a flash of movement in the lower corner of the door frame catches my eye. A fat centipede, about eight inches long with a hard, shiny body, scuttles into the shadows. I let out a startled shriek just as a woman opens the door.

"Can I help you?" A middle-aged brunette in a red tank top blocks my entrance to the trailer.

I back away from the centipede, shuddering, eyes still fixed on it. "Hi," I manage. "Are you Sage?"

"Depends on who's asking."

"Charlotte. My name's Charlotte. I'm staying over at Koa House." I point at the creature, which has begun creeping up the wall. "Um . . . there's a . . . thing . . ."

The centipede proceeds up the door frame, just inches from the woman's bare knee. Its head and legs are red, but the many segments of its body are black and seem to ripple when it moves.

Sage glances down at it, unconcerned. "Charlotte, huh? Brayden told me about you." She reaches into the house behind her and grabs a wooden dowel rod. After poking at the creature a few times, she ignores all the writhing legs and lifts him up with the rod. I back quickly out of her path as she steps barefoot onto the stoop and chucks the centipede into the bushes.

"You stay away from my house, brother," she tells it.

Skin still crawling from the unwelcome encounter, I take a deep breath and finally get a good look at Sage. Kai's mother is nothing like I've pictured. The much younger boyfriend threw me off, way off. I imagined her bleach blond with a boob job, Malibu Barbie turned drug dealer, but instead of a spray tan, Sage has her son's clear blue eyes and freckles. She wears no makeup, and her crow's feet and strong shoulders project an earthy sturdiness.

"So, Charlotte," she says, "what brings you by?"

"Actually, I was hoping to talk to Kai—is he home?"

"He's resting out back on the lanai." She steps away from the door. "You can come in, though."

I follow her through six feet of kitchen, past the ladder to an overhead loft, into an area covered with cushions of all sizes, shapes, and colors. It looks like a small hookah den and the overpowering smell of incense gives me a headache, but Sage sits down cross-legged and waits for me to do the same. She's in no hurry to get Kai, and I can't fathom what she's after until she leans forward and says a little too casually, "So, Koa House. A lot going on with the neighbors, huh?"

I grimace. Apparently Thom's not the only one with connections. "What did you hear?"

"I heard Naomi lost her boys today."

"That's already making the rounds, huh?"

"My friend Lani fosters," Sage explains. "A caseworker just called her asking if she'll take Elijah and Raphael. Musta been big, if the county police bothered getting off their asses."

"Yeah," I say. "That's sort of why I'm here. Elijah's in a hard spot right now. He could really use a buddy."

"A buddy? And you thought Kai's the guy?" Her eyes crinkle with amusement, and I realize how foolish I sound, like I'm trying to arrange a playdate for a pair of toddlers.

"They used to hang out, right? I don't know who else to ask."

"Kai thinks that kid killed Lise Nakagawa," Sage says. "He's not gonna be his friend."

"Kai's wrong."

"Yeah, I know." She raises her right elbow above her head and grasps it with her left hand, stretching. She hasn't shaved her armpits in a while. "I've met Elijah plenty of times, saw him and Lise, how they were together. I told Kai, Elijah Yoon is a cryer and a begger, not a killer. If that girl dumped him, he'd be following her around for weeks, asking for a second chance. He wouldn't just snap on her."

I don't know what to make of this woman. With her freckles and bright eyes, she looks like an aging Girl Next Door, the type to bring you fresh tomatoes from her garden and share her special recipe for zucchini bread. Beneath the pleasant exterior, however, I sense someone who trades in information.

"Um . . . could I talk to Kai?"

"He's napping." Sage raises her left elbow, switching up the stretch. "I wouldn't wake him. His asthma's been acting up today. He could use some sleep."

I remember Kai arguing about the medical benefits of marijuana for asthmatics and wonder if he's lazing around, high on his mother's own product.

"My daughter has asthma," I say, trying to form a connection with Sage, however tenuous. "She starts wheezing every time she gets a cold, and we have to break out the nebulizer. What triggers Kai?"

"Oh, different stuff. If he gets really emotional. If he exercises too much. If the wind is blowing wrong and the vog gets bad." She crosses her legs and assumes the lotus position, uninterested in discussing her son's health issues. "How'd the police end up at the Yoons'? Did *you* call them? Is that why you're feeling so guilty about Elijah?"

The woman is smart, I'll give her that.

"Adam Yoon came to me for help. I did the best I could."

"Adam, huh? Good for him. I've been wondering when things would finally come out about him and his mom. She's a sick little puppy, Naomi. He couldn't have been more than thirteen when she started in on him."

My mouth forms a ring of disbelief. "Who . . . where did you hear that?"

Sage laughs darkly. "I've got a pair of eyes, don't I? And I've dated an abusive dickhead or two. Naomi checks off all the boxes. Won't let anyone near her precious baby. Elijah, she doesn't give a shit what he does. But Adam? She guards him like the Holy fuckin' Grail. I know a jealous girlfriend when I see one."

"You never told anyone?" Whatever goodwill I might've felt for this woman evaporates. "For six years?"

"Not my business." She shrugs. "The way she grew up, Naomi probably thought that shit was normal. Her daddy got busted twenty years ago for messing with underage girls on their little commune. Wouldn't be surprised if she was one of them." Sage leans back on her elbows. "It's a shame her husband died. She might've been okay if he'd stuck around. Pete was a good guy."

"Did Kai know about this? Do you think he had any idea what was going on in that house?"

"Nah. Kai's naïve. He doesn't think about stuff like that." Her abrupt laugh sounds like a hiccup. "Kid acts like he's had it so rough, living here with me and Brayden, but let me tell you, he's got it pretty good. Goes to a nice private school, has his own car, never gone hungry. Not a lot of kids in Puna can say that."

Providing for Kai didn't come free, I know. Whatever I might think of Sage, she loves her son. "You must've made a lot of sacrifices for him."

"He's my kid," Sage says. "That's what you do."

Having given up the goods on the Yoon family, I figure I should at least get a little something back. "You said you knew Lise. She came by sometimes, right?"

"Sometimes. You still writing that article on her dad?" Sage smiles, and I can't tell if she heard about my blowup with Victor or not.

"Possibly," I say. "What did you think of Lise?"

"Sweet kid," she pronounces, "still trying to figure out who she wanted to be. Used to read tarot cards for me. She wasn't like her tight-ass sister, anyway." Sage makes a face. "I keep hoping Kai will grow a pair and dump Jocelyn. He had a thing for Lise, I could tell. And they would've been good together. But Kai's a snob. He sold out for Little Miss Stanford."

"You think he regrets that?"

"Who knows? He's young. Can't tell the difference between a high price tag and a quality product."

I bristle at this description of the sisters. "I don't know. It sounds like Lise had a lot of personal issues. She might not have been a picnic, either."

"Who said love was supposed to be a picnic?" Sage demands. "It's a growth opportunity. A soul lesson. Anyway, Kai's path is his to choose, not mine." She eyes me for a second, as if deciding whether or not to tell me something. "I saw her, you know. The night she went missing."

"Lise?"

"Yeah. Sometime after nine o'clock that night, before she ran into Elijah. She was in town, coming out of Marvel's place."

"The crystal shop?"

"Ono Place. That restaurant she and Marvel were trying to get off the ground." Sage plays with the tassel on one of her pillows. "I was picking up a little something from Brayden and Kai over at Free Thought, and I saw Lise walk out. She seemed . . . I dunno. Spooked, maybe? In her own world. I yelled to her, offered her a ride. She just kinda stood there, all deer in the headlights."

"Did she say anything?"

"Nope. Elijah showed up then and insisted on walking her home. I don't think she was expecting him—she didn't look happy to see him. But off they went. Last I ever saw her."

"Wow." I pause. "Do the police know about this?" I've never heard any mention of Marvel's restaurant in connection with Lise's movements that night.

Sage waves me off. "No point putting myself on the cops' radar if I don't have to. Elijah said he met up with her in the square at nine thirty, that she was wearing a black sweatshirt with a skull on it. All that's true. I've got nothing to add."

I don't answer. Don't name all the things that her sighting could, in fact, change. I want her to keep talking.

"Looking back, I should've offered them both a ride home," Sage says. "But I didn't. I just thought they'd want to be alone."

"It isn't your fault, Sage. Whatever happened, it isn't your fault."

"No, I know that." She hesitates. "Still. It was too dark for a girl to be out walking alone."

"She wasn't alone. She was with Elijah. You had every reason to believe she'd be safe."

"Yeah."

I adjust the cushion I'm sitting on and let her wrestle with that for a beat. "Any idea what Lise was doing at the restaurant?"

"Helping Marvel, probably. They'd been getting some food shipments. Back then, Marvel was still figuring she could get her permits sorted and open in a week or two."

"But Marvel didn't see Lise that night. I mean, as far as I know . . ."

For once, Sage doesn't have the answer. "Maybe Lise was working alone? She was really excited about Ono Place. She was going to be a manager, get the hell away from her parents. It was her ticket out."

I frown. "I don't think the police know she was there that night. You should tell them. It could be important."

Sage brushes off the suggestion. "I don't see how it matters," she says. "I wasn't the last one to see her alive. Elijah was. Last thing I need is cops trying to work out all my movements that night. I had stuff going on." She gives me a long, hard look, and I know better than to ask about her business arrangements.

"Right, of course. You're a busy woman."

She straightens up, and I can see that I've worn out my welcome, that I'm being dismissed. "I'll tell Kai you stopped by, all right? Good to hear about the Yoon kids."

"Don't forget about Elijah," I remind her, rising to my feet. "Put in a good word for him, would you?"

"Yeah, sure," she says. "Whatever my good word is worth."

twenty-six

I don't go back to Koa House, although Rae is waiting for me. Instead, I stay on the main highway, follow it to Kanoa Drive. Sage's information could be the game-changer I've been looking for. I need to know what Lise Nakagawa was doing at the restaurant that night. Was she really unloading food shipments, or was she stocking up on supplies, preparing to leave?

I have to talk to Marvel. Lise couldn't get into Ono Place without a key, after all. Marvel must have let her in, and while the woman said nothing about Lise's whereabouts that night, that doesn't mean she knew nothing.

Was she in on it?

I've been assuming Lise made her escape with help from Jocelyn, but what if Jocelyn didn't act alone? What if Marvel has also been covering for this girl? She and Lise were obviously close, and Marvel had zero love for Victor and Sue. Maybe all her psychic impressions about Lise's being dead were an act, designed to throw Rae and me off the trail.

The square is nearly empty when I arrive, a row of mostly dark storefronts with only a handful of vehicles lining the road. I park beneath a streetlight, not sure how safe the area is at night, and survey the scene. Only the convenience store remains open for business, but they don't seem busy with customers. The clerk carries a stack of old boxes outside and disposes of them in a nearby alleyway. As he opens the Dumpster, a stray cat darts out of the shadows.

Luck is on my side. Though the sign in the window says CLOSED, I can see Marvel still inside the crystal shop, sweeping. Her long gray braid sways with each stroke of her broom.

I step out of my car, weighing how exactly to approach her. Above me, the streetlight begins to buzz, a quiet hum that swells to a more sinister crackle. I look up, unnerved. *What the hell is with the electricity on this island?*

As if in response, the light dims to brown, then bursts white, like the flash of a camera going off. I jump back, protecting my face. When I remove my hands, the light has returned to normal. My pounding heart has not.

I bolt across the street to Marvel's store, wondering if I'm making a mistake showing up here alone. Still, I rap on the glass window, catch her attention with a wave.

She props her broom up against the wall and lets me in with a wry smile. "I don't suppose you're here for a reading." She doesn't seem surprised to see me, but maybe surprise is not an emotion you express when you're in the fortune-telling business.

"I know it's late, and I'm sorry. I just . . . had a question for you." I lick my lips, trying to find a delicate way to handle this, a way that doesn't sound accusatory. "The night that Lise went missing, did she get the key to Ono Place from you?"

"From me?" Marvel's face registers mild confusion. "No. She had her own copy. Why?"

"So she could come and go in the restaurant as she pleased."

"Of course," Marvel says. "I trusted her."

"She went there alone sometimes, then." I linger by the door, not wanting to stray too far from an exit. Something doesn't feel right. Marvel, the store, or just something about this night—I can't tell what, but something's off.

"We spent the whole summer trying to get the space cleaned up and ready to go," Marvel tells me. "I still had to keep an eye on the store here, so I wasn't always available. Lise kept an eye on the contractors when I couldn't be there. Sometimes she brought Elijah by, and he'd help out." She stops. "Why are you asking me this?" Her shoulders have tensed, her eyes gone hyperalert, and I wonder if she feels it, too, a sense of foreboding gathering in the air like an electrical field shortly before lightning strikes.

"Bear with me, Marvel," I say. "This might be nothing." I swallow. "That Friday, the day after Lise disappeared . . . when you went in the restaurant, were there any signs that she had been inside?"

"I didn't go in the next day. It was days before I went by."

"Why's that?"

Marvel takes a breath. "Denial, I guess? Without Lise, the restaurant started to feel so overwhelming." Her fingers close around the folds of her long skirt. "To be honest with you, I've only been in there a couple times since September. My lease ends in January. I've just been letting it run out."

"Okay. But when you did eventually go inside, you didn't see any indication that Lise had been there?"

"Of course Lise had been there. She and Elijah had been setting up tables, scrubbing down the floors and counters for days. We took a food delivery in early September, too, the only order we ever made. God, it's probably still in the freezer. I should donate it."

The possibility of missing food strikes me as significant. If Lise's holed up somewhere, she has to be eating. "What kind of food?"

"Oh . . . bread, I think? Soup. Maybe some cheese and deli meat in the fridge? We didn't get lettuce or tomatoes or anything that would immediately spoil. Why?" Her voice rises in frustration. "What's the sudden interest in my restaurant?"

I lay my cards on the table and observe her reaction. "I think Lise might have stopped by Ono Place before walking home with Elijah that night," I explain. "It's probably nothing. Still . . . if you wouldn't mind me looking around . . . couldn't hurt, right? Just being in the space—who knows, maybe I'll feel something. Or maybe you will."

"You're welcome to try." She plucks a small key ring from her pocket and examines it. "I don't have the restaurant key with me now. Must have left it on the hook at home. I'm going to lock up for tonight, but can you come by tomorrow? Around noon?"

Tomorrow is a lot later than I'd like, given that my flight leaves from Hilo at nine p.m. But I can't politely demand that Marvel go home and retrieve the key, not for what is admittedly a long shot.

"Sure," I say. "I'll be here at noon."

Marvel turns off the store lights and locks the door behind us. It's nearly nine o'clock now. Even the convenience store is on the verge of closing, its tired clerk tossing a few final bags of trash in the Dumpster. I know that I should leave, return to Koa House, but the strange current in the air has me on edge, convinced I'm on the brink of something important.

"The key that Lise had," I say, following Marvel across the street to her car, "what happened to it?"

She glances at me sidelong, understandably uneasy about my chasing after her in the dark. "I don't know," she says. "It could be at her house somewhere. Or maybe she had it with her when . . . when something happened."

I cross my arms. "You really don't think she ran away?"

Marvel doesn't speak for a moment. We stand in front of her car now, an old SUV with a rusty bumper. "I don't know what I think anymore," she admits at last. "Not about Lise. I try to use my gift, but when you turn it on your own life, the people you love . . . you can never be objective, can you? The feelings always throw you off."

"But you didn't sense anything in the restaurant," I persist. "The few times that you've been back, you didn't get any impressions."

"Oh, that stupid restaurant!" She slaps at the door of her car suddenly. "I never want to set foot in it again. Of course I got impressions there. Tons of them. That's the problem with the place. Too many emotions, too much noise—like a dozen bullhorns going off in my head. I have half a mind to set the place on fire and collect the insurance money."

"Then let me do it, Marvel." I seize the chance. "I don't have a personal connection to her. Just give me the key. I'll go alone."

She shakes her head. "No. We'll go together. I . . . I should try. I owe Lise that." She unlocks her car door. "I'll see you tomorrow at noon."

I stand at the curb, watching in frustration as she drives away. Does Marvel know something? Is she just putting me off, knowing I'll be gone soon if she delays me long enough? For all I know, she's going straight to Lise, warning her to lie low.

My phone vibrates against my thigh with an incoming text. *U coming back soon?* Rae asks. *U r missing pretty epic Scrabble game over here.*

The constant search for cell towers has drained my battery to 11 percent. *Give me an hour,* I reply. *Looking into something.* I make a mental note to charge my phone when I get back. At least David and Thom are keeping her occupied. They're probably much better company than I am right now. I don't have it in me tonight, the requisite happy face for the final night of Girls' Week. This whole trip has been a colossal failure.

My sole accomplishment was to ruin my chances at a cover story for *Outdoor Adventures.* Now I'll have to slap together some fluff piece about Hawai'i Volcanoes National Park, something bland and impersonal. Even worse, I ruined this week for Rae. Hawaii was our dream vacation, and instead of enjoying sunsets and gorgeous waves, I turned it into an inane crusade to find a girl who'd rather not be found. A girl who might have a perfectly valid reason to disappear. What is wrong with me?

I haven't found Lise, haven't made sense of the visions that sucked me into all this. Who is that guy prowling the woods and what has he done? What *will* he do? I have no answers. As far as I know, he's still out there.

On the far end of the street, the bright lights of the School for Free Thought beckon. I hear the occasional laughter of students strolling around the campus, making the best of their Saturday night. Two months ago, Lise might have been one of them.

I wander along the fence that encloses the campus, searching for an entrance. Maybe I'll run into some students, get their take on this elusive girl. A two-minute walk proves this an impossibility. The Free

Thought gate is locked, a guard stationed at the entrance. Unless I check in and somehow score a visitor's pass, I'm not about to gain access to the school or its inhabitants. Another dead end.

I sink down onto the curb, let myself wallow for a moment in the shadows. The air is moist, swollen with impatient raindrops. The humidity has brought my hair to a state of unrepentant frizz, but Tucson will cure that in a hurry. I lay my head against my knees.

I don't know how long I sit there—ten minutes? twenty?—but at some point I become aware of movement somewhere in the square. I look up. A slim hooded figure steps out from the Dumpster area. I can't make out much at first, just a gray sweatshirt, athletic shorts, and a knapsack slung over one shoulder, but when the figure moves beneath a streetlight, I catch a glimpse of a familiar face.

It's Jocelyn.

Or Lise.

I know exactly where she's going.

twenty=seven

Sure enough, the girl stops in front of Ono Place. She produces a key and quickly lets herself in. I wait for a light to go on in the building, but the windows remain dark. Whichever twin has entered the restaurant does not want to be seen.

I rise from my place in the shadows, mind racing. Is it her? Is this how Lise Nakagawa has been subsisting these last six weeks? It's not a bad setup. Ono Place must have a refrigerator and bathroom. It has a roof to keep out rain and a constant supply of electricity—more amenities than Wakea Ranch could offer, certainly. And if anyone spotted her, she could claim to be Jocelyn. Lise couldn't pull off a twin swap for long, but a few minutes? Who would think to doubt her?

I jog across the street. This is it. My chance for answers.

The door is still unlocked when I get there. I turn the handle and push it open, fingers groping the wall inside for a light switch. Success. The restaurant lights up, illuminating tables, chairs, a pair of ceiling fans, and, partially obscured by the countertop, a Nakagawa girl.

She's crouched on the floor, staring in the direction of the door with the look of a frightened, half-crazed animal, her hood pulled back to reveal long, dark hair. The unzipped knapsack lies at her knees, along with a roll of garbage bags. Is she here to steal food?

"This is private property!" The girl stuffs the garbage bags back into her knapsack, frantic. "You shouldn't be here."

"That's right," I agree. "Marvel's private property. Which means you shouldn't be here, either."

She fishes a key out of her sweatshirt. "I think this indicates I do have permission to be here. And a reasonable expectation of privacy. If you don't want to face trespassing charges, you'd better leave."

The threat of legal action immediately tips me off. This isn't Lise that I'm dealing with.

I sit down at one of the tables, not about to let a teenage girl get the better of me. "Actually, Jocelyn, I think that key belongs to your sister. But I'd love to know how you got your hands on it."

Jocelyn's eyes dart around the room as she works out her options.

"Maybe Lise gave it to you?" I suggest.

"Maybe," she says, breathing harder.

"You're not out with Kai tonight," I observe. "Still pissed at him for blowing your cover?"

She peers at me, jittery and poised to flee, but does not reply.

"Kai won't keep lying for you, Jocelyn. You know that. He told me the truth, and he'll tell the police eventually, too. They'll come asking where you were that night, what happened, and sooner or later, you'll have to tell them. You can't hide her forever."

Her body goes still. "I don't know what you mean."

"Come on. You think I don't know about this place? It's the last place your sister was seen. I know why you're here. I know you're here for Lise."

Jocelyn stands and stares at me, fish-mouthed. She's used to being smarter than everyone else, but I've caught her out. There's nothing she can say, no ready deflection she can offer, and I know then that I'm right. She and Lise must've planned a meeting tonight. If I'm lucky, Lise will still show, and I'll finally get a crack at her.

"I'm not here to make things any harder on you, Jocelyn, but your mother needs to know where her daughter is," I say. "I know you had your reasons, but you can't carry this forever. You have to tell someone."

All the blood has drained from Jocelyn's face. "I can't," she says, not moving. "I can't do that."

"You've been sneaking around long enough," I say. "Lying to your parents' faces like you don't know what's what. At this point, wouldn't it be easier to just come clean?"

"No." Jocelyn's voice has shrunk to a whimper. She covers her face. "I can't."

I approach her and place a hand on her shoulder. "They'll be mad for a while, but they'll forgive you eventually. They're your parents, honey. Your mom and dad are always going to love you."

Jocelyn pulls away from my touch. "Not me," she says. "They forgive *her* for everything. She can slut it up with half of Puna, get drunk, get high, fail classes, run away, they don't care. But me? I don't get a free pass. If I'm not out there making them look good, I'm nothing."

Jocelyn grips the counter as if she might faint, probably imagining her tarnished reputation, the legendary chewing-out she will receive. Unlawful obstruction of an investigation, providing a false statement to a police officer—I bet this girl knows every law she's broken.

"Where is she?" I ask softly.

Jocelyn says nothing but her gaze drifts toward the kitchen door.

My heart beats a little faster. It hadn't occurred to me that Lise was already in the building, but it makes sense. She could've been camping out here the whole time. I take a few steps toward the kitchen and pause. What do I say to her? How do I convince Lise that she can't spend the rest of her life in hiding, when I don't even know what she's hiding from?

I lower my voice so that the girl in the kitchen can't hear me. "I need to know. Why did Lise run away? What happened?"

Jocelyn stares at me for a second and then she begins to laugh, a thin, incredulous sound. "You don't know," she says. "You don't know *anything*. You followed me over here, but you don't have a clue, do you?"

"I know you are a serious, responsible person who wouldn't have helped her sister disappear without a good reason. Is she in some kind of trouble?"

"Trouble," Jocelyn repeats. "Of course she's in trouble. Lise's always in trouble. And here I am again, handling it. Story of my life. When I screw up, it's my responsibility. When she screws up, it's still my responsibility."

Sensing Jocelyn's not about to clarify anything, I head for the kitchen. "I'm going to talk to her."

Jocelyn scurries after me, babbling incoherently about the future, about her good intentions, about how wrong it all went, but I'm done with her. I want to hear it from Lise.

I flip on some lights, discover a cramped room with a stainless steel food-prep area. A few finishing touches remain incomplete. The lack of a sink leaves a conspicuous hole in the counter, and half of the drawers in the room are missing pulls. On one counter, I spot a screwdriver, screws, and half a dozen matching drawer pulls, as if the job were only recently interrupted.

"Where is she?"

In reply, Jocelyn stops outside a large metal door. Although the door has a latch for a padlock, no lock is currently in place. Jocelyn's fingers hover above the handle, but she doesn't grasp it. Her half-dazed eyes rest on the screwdriver and drawer pulls.

Too impatient to wait for her to snap out of it, I brush her aside and tug open the door. A blast of cool air greets me.

Inside, the light blinks on, revealing a walk-in fridge, largely empty but for a few cartons strewn around the shelves and stacks of cardboard boxes marked SOUP in the center of the floor. And there, her back pressed to the boxes so that all I can see is her dark head, sits Lise.

But something is wrong. I feel it in my gut as I step into the fridge. It's too cold in here. Much too cold. I know even before I see her, see her flimsy tank top and the delicate slope of her bare shoulder. The face that greets me is pale and bloodless, the limbs gray and frosted. On the side of her head, beneath the long black hair, I see a gash, red and sparkling with ice crystals.

This is not a refrigerator, I realize, but a freezer. Lise is dead. Has been dead for a long time.

I turn back toward Jocelyn. She stands in the doorway of the freezer, and though her face is flushed, still very much alive, the resemblance remains uncanny. She and Lise look the same, even now.

"Jocelyn," I whisper. "What did you do?"

The pitch of her voice rises to that of a bitter child. "I helped her," she says. "I protected her. But she had to be Miss Popular, didn't she? She couldn't stand to think there was someone out there who liked me better. That for once, someone picked me, not her." Only then do

I see the screwdriver in her hand. "She had to go and fuck things up, like always."

She raises the screwdriver and I duck instinctively behind a box, no longer sure what this girl is capable of. Yet instead of advancing on me, Jocelyn steps backward, out of the freezer. "Sorry," she says, and gives the door a quick, decisive shove.

I leap forward and throw my body against the door. Too late. The metal latch catches. The light blinks off.

I am with Lise now, in the cold, in the darkness.

twenty‑eight

The darkness is absolute. No shaft of light beneath the freezer door, no windows—this place is sealed tight. I grope around for the door handle, jiggle it up and down, throw my weight against it over and over to no avail. Something's blocking me from the outside. The padlock? Something jammed into the locking mechanism? I remember the screwdriver in her hand, and my heart sinks.

There's no getting out of here.

I dig my phone from my pocket. No service. I dial 911 anyway. Nothing. Even my texts fail to send. And my battery has dipped below 10 percent, triggering a rush of LOW BATTERY warnings.

I flick on my phone's flashlight, trying not to panic at the thought of all the power it's draining. Casting the beam along the walls, I search for a light switch. Find only empty shelving.

I hold the phone above my head and peer up at the lightbulb in the center of the freezer. There *has* to be some way to turn it on, something other than opening the door. It looks as though there was a pull chain once, but the chain must've broken off at the base, leaving no way to trigger the switch. I grab a cardboard box filled with soup and climb atop it to get a better look, careful to keep the beam of my flashlight off Lise's body.

A careful examination of the lightbulb reveals nothing good. I poke at the hole where the chain used to be. Not even pliers could fix this. I'm really, truly screwed.

As I dismount from the box, my foot slips, sending me sideways into a shelf. Metal punches at my hip, but the pain means nothing. Or everything.

Pain means I can still feel. Pain is good. It's the inevitable numbness I must worry about. I've read about people freezing to death. Weariness and apathy—those are more dangerous than pain.

Over and over, as if on repeat, my mind keeps asking the same question: *How long?*

How long until my battery runs out and I'm plunged again into darkness?

How long can I survive here in subfreezing temperatures?

How long until someone finds me?

Rae will look for me, of course, but last she knew I was at Kai's. It could take hours for her to start worrying about my absence. If she and David and Thom are drinking together, she might not get to wondering until morning. And there's no reason she'd come looking for me here.

I should've told Rae what I was up to, should've included her, the way she's always asked to be included. For years, I've been trying to shield Rae from my abilities. I told myself I was protecting her, but Rae's not a child. She's an adult, fully capable of making her own choices—and given the choice, she would've been here with me tonight.

We should've faced Jocelyn together. She couldn't have taken the two of us. If I hadn't tried to go it alone, fallen into my old pattern of shutting people out, Rae and I would've had her.

Marvel's my only hope. She was the last to see me. She knows I wanted to get a peek inside the restaurant, and she's expecting me here at noon tomorrow. But if I don't show up, will she enter the building at all? It could be ages before she finds me—she obviously hasn't seen the inside of her freezer in a while.

More than anger toward Jocelyn, I feel anger toward myself. I should've seen what this girl was. Instead, I saw ambition. I saw a Strong Young Woman. I saw myself.

She had to be Miss Popular, didn't she? Jocelyn said of her sister. Maybe, in the end, their differences really were that simple. Lise Nakagawa wanted to be liked. She was fine with ceding the academic spotlight to her twin. She didn't need to please their parents with personal achievements the way Jocelyn did. And yet Lise was just as competitive as all the other Nakagawas. She was the fun one, the cool one, the one with all the friends. Surely that identity meant something to her.

But there was one thing Jocelyn had that her sister didn't, a status symbol Lise couldn't quite match.

She couldn't stand to think there was someone out there who liked me better. That for once, someone picked me, not her.

Kai.

If popularity was her chief aim, then of course Lise would be jealous. No matter how much she loved Elijah, she had to know how he appeared to the outside world. It must have stung to see a guy like Kai going for her sister, attracted, at least initially, to the dedication and drive that ordinarily made Jocelyn such a square. Lise couldn't let her have that one. Cute boys—that was *her* realm. She had to assert her power.

No wonder Kai was in tears when we spoke about Lise yesterday. All his meetings in the woods over the summer, all his sneaking around—it wasn't with Jocelyn. If I'd used my head, I would've realized that. Raph Yoon said he saw Lise naked out there, not her sister, and Jocelyn never did strike me as the type willing to brave mosquitoes for a hookup.

The Watching Guy in the woods, the visions I've been having?

That was him. Kai's eyes, Kai's thoughts.

For the first time, I consider the possibility that the encounter I've been seeing wasn't a rape or assault or some other violent act. Maybe it was just a hormonal teenage boy going after the girl he knew he wasn't supposed to have. All his lusty thoughts, his secret longings, the things that seemed so incriminating when I was inside his head... maybe these were, as Frankie said, the pervy thoughts of every guy.

I drop to a squat, arms and knees huddled against my chest in a vain attempt to conserve my warmth. Kai knew Lise met up with Elijah in those woods. Maybe he waited for her. Hid in the bushes, made sure her boyfriend didn't turn up. And then he made his move.

You'll regret this, she told him. *You're going to hurt a lot of people.* But she didn't tell him no, didn't remind him of Jocelyn or Elijah. What if Lise wanted it? What if that encounter, and the many that followed, were consensual—two selfish teenagers giving in to their desires? I thought my visions were showing me the crime, the perpetrator, but what if they were showing me motive?

My body begins to shiver violently. *Lise is gone now,* I tell myself. *Focus on you.* I rub my arms, hoping the friction will give me a couple of degrees, however fleeting. Why oh why didn't I grab a sweatshirt when I went out tonight? Another layer would buy me time, slow the rapid loss of heat. But it's cold, so damn cold, and my phone battery is down to 3 percent. Its precious light can't last.

I pull open boxes, frantic now, looking for something I can use to get the hell out of here. Packages of soup. Frozen loaves of bread. A lump of ham, hard as a rock. I throw the ham at the door. It makes a resounding thump but doesn't leave a dent. I hurl my body against the door a few more times for good measure and then slump to the floor. Fold myself into a ball again and feel the heat drain from me. Thoughts of Tasha and Micky and Noah race through my head. How can I leave them behind? How can my love for them amount to so little in the end?

What a pointless way to die.

My brain continues running in desperate circles like a mouse on a wheel, searching for ideas. A bomb to blow the door off? A fire to keep me warm? I'm not MacGyver. I can't turn my cell phone into an explosive device, and even if I could, that freezer door is pretty thick. I'd probably just be hastening my own demise.

I glance into the dark rear of the freezer. Lise is there, stiff and cold, still waiting.

"You were alone, weren't you?" I whisper. "Working to get this place up and ready, thinking about your future. And then she showed up. Confronted you."

I approach Lise gingerly, no longer able to ignore her. The gash in her head seems to glitter when I shine the flashlight over it, but I bite back my fear. This was a girl once, a kid, and I can't lose sight of that.

I'll never know if the act was premeditated on Jocelyn's part or just an argument that spun out of control. If Lise was dead or, God forbid, simply unconscious when Jocelyn dragged her in here. Either way,

Jocelyn did a solid job of covering her tracks. Whatever she hit Lise with, she was smart enough to remove the weapon. And she cleaned up pretty thoroughly. The front of the restaurant looks a bit dusty but shows no signs of a crime, nothing that would've alerted Marvel the few times she popped in.

I let my flashlight play across Lise's body. She's propped up against some boxes, legs bent, arms frozen at her sides. Her eyes are open but empty, the pupils fully dilated in death. She wears a black sleeveless shirt and cutoff jeans. I can make out a bump in the right pocket of her shorts. A lighter maybe? She seems like the kind who might smoke. Hand quaking, I reach inside.

No lighter and no phone—if she had one, Jocelyn must have taken it. Just a black wallet with pink trim. Not much in it. Six dollars. A debit card and a student ID with the same unsmiling photo I've seen in newspaper articles. *Lise Nakagawa*, the ID reads. *The School for Free Thought. Class of 2017.* A reminder of the future she'll never have.

I place the wallet on her thigh, shuddering.

"Why?" I ask her. "Did you love him, or was it just to hurt her?"

I grew up an only child. I'll never understand what it means to have a sister. But I can't imagine this is what Jocelyn wanted. She told me she loved Lise, and in her strange, self-centered way, I bet she did.

I doubt Jocelyn expected her sister to go undiscovered this long. She probably assumed Marvel would find the girl within days. And then? There were other suspects, other people who would take the hit for Lise's murder. Elijah was the obvious choice. But not Jocelyn. Even if her DNA turned up on the body, she had nothing to worry about—it was identical to Lise's, after all.

As I turn back toward the freezer door, my light sweeps across Lise's bare shoulders.

"The sweatshirt," I realize. "She took your sweatshirt."

That explains how it ended up in the girls' bedroom: Jocelyn pretended to be Lise that night. She ran into Elijah and let him walk her home, conveniently throwing off the timeline of her sister's movements. Broke up with him, to establish motive. Entered her house, still pretending to be Lise. Greeted her mother, even.

Sue didn't hear Lise come home that night. She heard Jocelyn. Twice.

A wave of sadness washes over me. Sadness for my family and for Rae, yes, but for the Nakagawas, too. They love their daughters, just like I love mine. To lose one at the hands of the other is unthinkable.

"You had a whole life to live," I tell Lise, my teeth beginning to chatter. "And now you're here."

Around me, the freezer hums, pumps its deadly cool air into the small, enclosed space. I glance down at my phone. The battery icon shows 1 percent remaining. I rise to my feet, cross back over to the door. Half-heartedly study its hinges, test the handle, run my finger around the edge, feeling for cracks. There has to be a way out.

I let out a long, ear-piercing shriek, bang on the walls, the door, scream for help over and over as if there might be someone outside who could hear me.

Nothing.

My phone blinks off, finally dead, hurling me back into darkness.

Despair sets in. I can no longer feel my fingers or toes. I regret every choice that led me to this moment, my decision to come to this island most of all. I came because I was a coward. Because I couldn't face other people's judgments of me. But I shouldn't have fled the scene like an embarrassed teenager, shouldn't have let a handful of aggressive journalists define me. I should've grown a spine. Now it's too late. Fuzziness has already set in. My scattered thoughts are slowing. The facts as they stand are simple. I will not last the night.

"Just you and me now," I tell Lise, and from somewhere in the dark I hear a reply, almost like an echo.

Just you and me, she says.

twenty‑nine

Something buzzes overhead. The lightbulb crackles on, bright and then dark, before settling to a dull orange glow. I glance into the rear of the freezer, wondering if I have lost consciousness. Maybe I am dreaming. Maybe hallucinations are common amongst people freezing to death.

"Lise?"

Her frozen body remains propped up against the boxes, not a hair out of place, obviously dead. And yet I sense that she's with me. Not in the frosted mass she once inhabited, but in the air, buzzing against my skin, humming in the filament above me. As I lose sensation in my body, she's the spark that remains, the one thing I can feel.

This is my fault, she says, and her voice is inside me, not just words and sound, but a kind of knowing. *You shouldn't be here.*

"Get me out," I beg. "Please. I have to get back to my children."

I can't. I'm sorry. The lights, that's all I can do.

I curl up on the floor, my hands now wooden, insensate. Better to die seeing my surroundings than in total darkness, I suppose. But not much better.

There's a pressure on my shoulder, as if someone were kneeling beside me, comforting me. My arm goes pleasantly numb. My violent shivering stops. Is this how dying feels? No pain, just nothingness.

"I've been trying to find you," I say, although it seems so silly now. "I thought maybe I could help you."

You did help. You helped Elijah.

"Elijah?"

You got him away from his mom. Raph and Adam, too. I was too scared to do it. But not you.

"Yes, but... Elijah?" After everything I've done, all the leads I've pursued to uncover Lise's whereabouts—was it really about Elijah all along? That floppy-haired fifteen-year-old who gave me attitude out in the woods last night? "No," I mumble. "No. That can't be right."

If my whole mission was to help the Yoon boys, then there was no need for me to show up at the restaurant tonight, no reason to put myself at risk. My death will be entirely senseless.

I love Elijah, Lise says, as if that might make me feel better. *I'll love him forever.*

But that's not good enough. There are people I love, too, people who need me. I struggle to my feet, anger cutting through my foggy thoughts.

"If you love him so much, then what was going on with you and Kai?"

Lise doesn't answer, which only ignites my fury.

"That's how you got here, isn't it? You and Kai." I kick at a box of soup. "That's what set Jocelyn off."

Still no answer.

"I'm not saying you deserved to die. You didn't. But of all the guys you could've chosen, why Jocelyn's?"

When at last it comes, her reply is maddeningly simple. *He made me feel . . . special.*

And then she shows me. Shows me that night in the woods, not through his eyes, but through her own. Kai emerging from a bush, startling her. That strange jolt of power when she realized why he was there, how much he wanted her. The intoxicating knowledge that, despite all the ugly consequences he might face, he had chosen her. Risked everything.

There are a blur of other encounters, breathless and forbidden, too exciting to resist. Not about love—not for Lise—but the thrill of winning over and over again. Yet there are softer moments, too, complicated feelings she can't name. Swinging in the hammock side by side, bare legs entwined, bodies sticky with humidity. Kai stroking her head, kissing her ear.

You're so hot, he says, but she only laughs.

You realize any compliment about my looks also applies to your girlfriend?

Kai turns toward her, flustered. *I didn't mean how you look. I meant how you are. You two are different. I don't see you as the same.*

Whatever. She's laughing again, prodding him with a teasing finger. *I know you get off on it, the whole twin thing. It's like a real-life porno for you or something.*

It's not like that at all, Kai insists, wounded. *I don't like you because of her.*

Okay, then, why do you like me?

Because of you, he says in a voice so husky it would give anyone shivers. *I like you.*

The woods melt away as Lise releases me from her gaze. Now I find myself standing by the empty tables of Ono Place. The scene is largely indistinct, a half-faded memory except for one detail. On the floor beneath the counter, bloodstains.

I didn't know, Lise says, and somehow she's beside me, a teenage girl in a black skull sweatshirt. *I didn't know it would end up like this.*

"Of course you didn't."

Look, I'm not a bad person. I used to flirt with Kai when Joss wasn't around, so what? I didn't think he would do anything. I thought we were just playing. Then he showed up that night. He said he couldn't stop thinking about me. He was so cute, so into me . . .

"Was Jocelyn lying about all the things she did for you?" I ask. "Getting you through school, covering for you with your parents? Was she just blowing smoke up my ass, or what?"

Lise jams her hands into the pockets of her sweatshirt. *She wanted me to be weak, and so I was. She wanted to be the good one, and so I let her. Jocelyn was always telling me what a screwup I was, that I self-sabotage. So fine.* She shrugs. *I decided to be the person she said I was.*

"How did she find out about you guys?"

Lise crosses the room and stops on a bloodstained patch of tile, her back to me. *I told her.*

"You *told* her?"

I told her we needed to talk, somewhere away from Mom and Dad. She showed up here at the restaurant, asked me, "What did you do this time?" And so I told her. I thought she should know. I'd ended stuff with Kai a couple weeks before, but I felt bad. She thought she had this amazing, loyal boyfriend, but she didn't. She had a right to know the truth.

I remember my ex-husband confessing his affair years ago, trying to pretend it was for my benefit and not some selfish cry for attention.

For a second, I actually feel sorry for Jocelyn, getting ambushed like that. At least I didn't know my husband's mistress. Jocelyn's betrayal was double.

"So you told her and then what?"

Lise turns to face me, and now I can see the gash in her head, the blood running from her scalp. Again, she lends me her eyes. Images of Jocelyn flutter through the space, silent and slow, as if underwater. Jocelyn clutching her temples, struggling to process. Jocelyn flushed, her mouth pinched and venomous as it all sinks in. Jocelyn unloading on her sister, screaming, her pretty features twisted by rage.

It seemed so stupid, how worked up she was getting. Lise runs her fingers over the edge of the counter. *She didn't even like Kai, not really. She was always trying to change him. I told her, maybe you're into the idea of him more than the actual guy. Maybe I did you a favor, showing you who he really is.*

"Did she hit you with something?"

She shoved me.

Suddenly the restaurant goes spinning. I'm knocked off balance, lurching backward, falling. A splitting impact to my skull, and then darkness. Cold.

My head hit the counter, Lise says from the void. *And that was it. No chance to fix things. Over so fast.*

This was not a premeditated killing, then, but an argument gone very wrong. Enough to exonerate Jocelyn, perhaps, had she not handled the aftermath with such careful precision.

"She took your sweatshirt. Pretended to be you."

Yeah.

I have to grudgingly admire Jocelyn's quick thinking. She was too smart to let herself be seen in the wrong place at the wrong time, to ruin her alibi with Kai. Did Jocelyn realize she was setting up Elijah as the perfect suspect when she pretended to dump him on their walk home? Was she really willing to sacrifice him for her own gain? She and Elijah were in the same boat, after all. Lise betrayed him, too.

"Elijah loved you," I say, and now I'm back in the freezer again, the lightbulb flickering overhead. "He's been wandering around the woods at night for weeks, signaling to you."

I know. Lise is just a voice again, an echo in my brain. *The woods are the only place he can see me.*

"What do you mean?"

He left a bunch of lanterns out there. I turn them on sometimes at night, do our special signal. So he knows that I'm still with him. Always, like I promised.

"Jesus Christ. That was you." Of all the explanations I had for those lights, ghostly love note never made the list. The image is as pathetic as it is romantic. Is this what I'll be reduced to, the only way left for me to tell Noah and my girls I love them? Silly electrical tricks that could just as easily be dismissed as faulty wiring? My daughters need a mother, not a poltergeist. If only I'd stayed away from Ono Place tonight. If only I hadn't followed Jocelyn inside.

"Why did she come back tonight?" I mutter, to myself as much as Lise. "Why did Jocelyn come here?"

Lise doesn't respond, but her sister's appearance at the restaurant doesn't sit well with me. Those garbage bags in her knapsack—did Jocelyn intend to move Lise's body? To where? Without a car, Jocelyn couldn't get far, and there's not a lot of options in the square except . . .

That Dumpster.

"Ugh." The thought leaves me queasy. The girl would do anything to hide a mistake.

It occurs to me that any sudden doubts Jocelyn had about the crime scene were likely my fault. I changed the game yesterday, told her that her alibi was ruined, that Kai had admitted he was doing 'shrooms with Brayden instead of studying math with her on campus. That left her wide open to questions. Where she was that night. Why she lied. Jocelyn must have weighed her options and decided that the body in the freezer was too easily tied to her.

This wasn't supposed to be about you, Lise says, and I feel her presence fading. The lightbulb begins to dim. *I didn't mean to put you in danger.*

"Danger?" I choke back the tears that my eyes are too cold to cry. "Lise, I'm going to die here."

No. You won't.

The freezer light erupts suddenly into sparks and then winks out. A shower of burning embers falls like fairy dust. I reach out my hands to catch them, their light, their warmth, but they die in midair. I'm back to where I started. Alone in the dark.

The freezer door rattles.

I stare into the black, edging toward the noise. Has Jocelyn returned to finish this? Will I get my chance to fight?

The door cracks open, and a wedge of light pours in. I tense up, ready to attack with everything I have. But it's not Jocelyn peering into the freezer with an expression of pure shock.

It's Rae.

thirty

W hat in hell?" Rae gapes as I burst from the freezer. "Charlie!? What happened?"

My skin burns as it hits the warm air. I lean over the stainless steel counter, shaking, trying to compose myself.

Rae holds up a screwdriver with her right hand. "This was stuck in the door. Did someone lock you in there?"

At the sight of the screwdriver, I can only shake my head. "That little bitch." I wince as the blood rushes painfully back to my digits. "What are you doing here? How'd you know where I was?"

"Find My iPhone. I used your Apple ID and password. I saw you type them in before." She looks a bit guilty at this admission, as if I might honestly be mad at her for tracking me down.

I'm so grateful to see her, so happy to be alive, I almost cry. "So you came out here looking for me? Just like that? Maybe I'm not the only one with a sixth sense."

"I was mostly pissed off you were prowling around without me," Rae confesses. "I mean, you sent me this cryptic text about how you were looking into something—I was ticked. It's our last night. We should be doing this together! So I looked up your location and had

Thom bring me over. I saw our rental car, and then . . . someone walked out of the restaurant." She peels off her cardigan and drapes it around my shoulders. "Was that Jocelyn?"

"Yeah, that was Jocelyn. Did you see where she went?"

"Kai picked her up about ten minutes ago. They drove off in a red Corolla. I came over here as soon as they left to see what was up. I don't think they saw me." She takes me by the wrist. "What's going on? Did Jocelyn put you in the freezer?"

"Not just me," I tell her. "Lise's in there, too."

Her jaw drops so hard it nearly detaches. "Lise?" Her startled gaze shifts to the freezer door. "Are you telling me—"

"She's dead, Rae," I say. "Jocelyn killed her. It was an accident, but the cover-up sure wasn't."

Rae looks ill at this revelation. "Oh my God. Victor and Sue . . . they'll be devastated."

I can't let myself imagine their pain, not now. Something else is gnawing at me. "Did you say Jocelyn's with Kai?"

"Yeah. You don't think—was he in on this?"

"No. But Kai's not safe with her." I cross through the kitchen, my misgivings multiplying with each step. "We've got to find out where they went."

Rae scrambles to keep up with me. "I don't get it. Why would Jocelyn hurt Kai? He's the one person on her side."

"He can blow apart her alibi," I say, "and she knows it."

She knows because I told her. I told her that he'd already begun to crack, to spill her secrets. I told her Kai wouldn't keep lying for her, that he'd go to the police, tell them what he knew. Unaware of who I was dealing with, I cemented Kai as a liability in her mind—and given his relationship with Lise, he is indeed a liability. He has the power to reveal both Jocelyn's opportunity and her motive for murder. If law enforcement ever got wind of his fling with Lise, suspicion would immediately shift to Jocelyn.

"Kai is a loose end," I tell Rae. "Just like I was." I sprint toward the restaurant door. "She's come this far. She's not turning back."

We jog across the square to where our vehicle is parked. This is it, I realize. The reason for the visions I've been having, why I've been seeing with Kai's eyes. That moment in the woods was where it all began. Where he and Lise sealed their fate.

I couldn't help her, but I can still save him. I hope.

"You think Jocelyn's going to off him?" Rae asks. "Just like that?"

"Probably." I hit the unlock button on my car key, and the car chirps back in response. "With Kai dead, she'd completely control the narrative. She could pin everything on him." I slide behind the wheel and close my eyes. "We've got to think. Figure out where she'd take him, how she'd do it."

"Kai's a lot bigger and stronger than Jocelyn," Rae points out. "It would have to be something sneaky. Poison, maybe? She could slip him some bug killer or something. Although it would be hard to make that look like an accident . . ."

"People are going to find Lise in that freezer. As far as Jocelyn knows, they'll find me there, too. There's no way to make that look like an accident."

"A suicide, then," Rae guesses. "She could spin Kai's death as a suicide. Kai killed you and Lise, but he couldn't live with the guilt, something along those lines."

I nod. "It's that or self-defense. She could say he attacked her."

Rae scratches her head. "So she kills him how? Beats him in the head with a tire iron? Pushes him off a tall cliff?"

I turn toward her slowly, palms beginning to tingle. *A push. A tall cliff. Of course.*

The sensations I had by the caldera come rushing back. Darkness. The pressure of two hands on my back. Fingertips pressing, pushing, urging me toward the edge of a four-hundred-foot drop. I dismissed the experience as noise, an unrelated fragment of the past or future. Now I see how wrong I was.

My impressions on this island haven't been random. They've been connecting me to Kai all along. I've seen with his eyes, felt with his body. Unwillingly shared moments of both his past and future. If Rae and I can't get to Jocelyn, that push is where his future ends.

I used to take my daughters here, Victor said as he stood on the summit of Kīlauea, legendary home of the goddess Pele. *This was our special spot.*

Special, indeed. I insert the key into the ignition, toss Rae the GPS.

"What?" she says. "Where are we going?"

"To a place with a tall cliff." I pull sharply away from the curb. The car squeals onto Kanoa Drive, already ten miles above the speed limit. "Volcanoes National Park."

ALTHOUGH THE PARK is open twenty-four hours a day, costs have evidently affected its staffing abilities. The guard shacks at the entry stand empty, and we pass through unobserved. I was hoping for a ranger, someone who could confirm that Kai's old Corolla has been by, but no such luck. We're left operating on blind faith.

The ride over—nearly an hour in the pitch dark—was a tense one, but at least I've brought Rae up to speed. She called the Hawai'i

County Police Department, alerted them to the body in the freezer at Ono Place, told them sixteen-year-old Jocelyn Nakagawa attempted to kill a visiting journalist who was looking into the story. Eventually, fed up with the dispatcher's many questions, Rae demanded they send someone to Crater Rim Drive at Volcanoes National Park and hung up. Now she sits clutching the door, uncharacteristically quiet, as she prepares herself for what might lie ahead.

For the first time since we began digging into the disappearance of Lise Nakagawa, this is no longer a game to Rae. Someone could die tonight. I very nearly did.

We see no other cars as we pass the visitor center, although I'm sure there are people out there somewhere, hikers hoping to catch a better view of the lava flows at night. At least the wind is on our side. The caldera itself is a bit hazy, but the clouds haven't yet drifted to the street.

I proceed down Crater Rim Drive, trying to remember the little nook by the rim that Victor showed us, exactly where it was situated. His favorite spot in the park, he said, and if I'm right, the place made an impression on Jocelyn. It certainly made an impression on me. I know what I felt standing at the edge. The end could come so quickly.

"What are we going to do?" Rae asks. "How do we find them?"

I think it over. Although the road follows the caldera rim all the way to the observatory, we're too far from the edge to see anyone while driving by.

"We'll park over by the steam vents," I say. "And from there . . . follow the path west, I guess."

"We'll be wandering around a mile or more in the dark," Rae warns me. "And you don't have a flashlight."

She's right. In the absence of a car charger, my phone remains dead. We've got nothing but the light on Rae's cell to guide us.

And what if I'm wrong?

That sensation I had on the edge of the caldera bore no time stamp. It could be weeks in the future, or months. If Jocelyn waits even a single night to dispose of Kai, Rae and I won't be here to stop her. I can point my finger and scream bloody murder—literally—but Jocelyn won't be easily defeated. As soon as she learns that I'm alive, she'll adjust her story, craft explanations, find ways to acquit herself.

Don't get ahead of yourself. I focus on the headlights, the winding road.

Fortunately, the steam vents are marked by signs. I turn into the parking lot, trying not to think about the story of the ranger who fell inside one, the pain and terror of that end. One thing is apparent: if Jocelyn intends to kill Kai, she has plenty of options out here.

"Charlie." Rae grabs my arm, interrupting my morbid train of thought. "Look."

In the corner of the parking lot, a single car. I drive closer, flashing my headlights over it. A red Corolla. No sign of the occupants, but the Free Thought bumper sticker leaves no room for doubt.

"They're here," Rae breathes.

I park horizontally across the Corolla's rear, blocking them in. Rae slides out of the passenger seat with her phone light on and shines it quickly into the backseat. She shakes her head. Empty.

I join Rae on the curb. A nearby steam vent catches the breeze, engulfing us in its telltale mineral odor. "What do we do? Just walk along the path yelling for Kai and hope we interrupt whatever Jocelyn has planned?"

"No," Rae says. "No way. For all we know, that kid is already dead and Jocelyn's lurking in the bushes somewhere. We don't want to give her a heads-up that we're coming. Not after what she did to you tonight."

"She'll see our light," I point out. "There's no surprising her."

"If she sees our light, she'll think we're just hikers and she'll try to wait us out. Remember, she still thinks you're trapped in that freezer. We have the upper hand as long as she's not expecting us."

I'm not sure if anyone ever really has the upper hand with Jocelyn, but I have no better plan. Rae charges ahead, locating a paved pathway that eventually runs parallel to the rim. My gut in knots, I follow the bouncing light of her phone.

It's chilly in the park tonight, and if I hadn't just experienced subfreezing temperatures with a dead body, I might be uncomfortable. As things are, I count my blessings. Even the dark is manageable compared to the total blackness of that freezer. The moon is more than half-full, awash in a sky of rolling cloud cover, and I can make out plenty of shapes: grass, shrubs, the crooked silhouettes of scrappy native trees. In the distance, an indistinct pink glow hints at the molten layer just beneath the surface of the Halema'uma'u crater.

Minutes later, however, the visibility deteriorates. Rae's light grows murky ahead of me, her figure dissolving into a cloud. The wind has shifted course. Now the vog drifts in, stealthy as a cat.

As we continue down the trail, it takes over, engulfs the rim area. Rae stops walking and looks back, searching for me in the soupy dark. I jog to catch up with her and trip on a bump in the hard-packed ground. Somehow I avoid a face plant, but the fall does not build confidence. How will we find anything in this mess? I don't know how far we are from Jocelyn's special overlook, and Rae's light only makes it worse, illuminating the floating vapor around us while blinding my eyes to everything else. For a helpless, hopeless minute, I think that all is lost, that under cover of night and vog, Jocelyn will surely get away with this.

But I can't let her win. The vog is my cover, too. I can use it just like she can.

"Turn your light off," I tell Rae.

"What?"

"Just do it."

The light in Rae's phone winks out. I wait, let my eyes adjust to the darkness. I think about being blind, learning to navigate the world with your other senses, how they get stronger when one is disabled.

I need to use my senses. *All* my senses. But how?

Marvel said that it's like surfing, choosing your wave and riding it out. But I don't have any waves to choose from. I can't focus my impressions, can't choose what I tune into—I've tried. My visions always come unbidden. The more I try, the less I get.

I focus on Kai, the way it felt to occupy his body, to stand gasping at the edge, two hands urging me over. Slow and silent, I wade through the vog. Listen for any sounds to indicate we're not alone. Nothing. Just the occasional whisper of fabric as I move and Rae's soft, labored breathing beside me. I scan the shadows for movement, some sign we're close. There are any number of trails leading off the path to the rim, trails of tamped-down ash and grass with nothing to distinguish them. How will we possibly know which one to take?

I clear my head and keep listening. Our padding shoes. Car key rattling in my pocket when I pat it. Rae's breaths, quick and shallow in my ear.

I pause, giving her a chance to rest, wondering when she got so out of shape. But instead of improving, her breathing worsens. There's a distinctive whistling noise when she exhales, a wheezing sound I recognize from the handful of asthma attacks Micky's had over the years—a reaction to the vog, maybe?

"Are you okay?" I whisper.

"Me?" Rae sounds surprised. "I'm fine. Why are we stopping?" Her voice is perfectly normal. For the first time it occurs to me that it's not her I've been hearing at all.

Kai, I realize with a jolt. Sage mentioned that the vog aggravated his asthma. I wave my hand through the thick, wet air, imagining what the sulfur dioxide content might be doing to his weak lungs.

"Do you hear that?" I ask Rae. "That breathing?"

She goes silent, listening. "No . . ."

Perhaps my senses aren't quite as useless as I thought. Perhaps I'm learning.

There's no way Jocelyn could've predicted the vog. She must've just lucked out. One thing's for sure: if Kai's wheezing like that, falling isn't the only danger he faces.

"Go back to Kai's car," I tell Rae. "Quick. If it's locked, break a window, I don't care how you get in."

"What? Why?"

"You're looking for an inhaler. If you can't find that, then look for a joint. I'm sure Kai has a stash in there. Please, Rae. I think he's having an asthma attack."

Rae hesitates for a second. "What are you going to do?"

"I'll keep going. I think we're close." I give her hand a quick squeeze. "Hurry."

As I proceed down the path, the wheezing sounds intensify in my ear. The labored intake, the whistling exhale—they're the only sounds I hear as I press through the creeping vog. Loud. Louder. The struggle to breathe.

And suddenly, like the unplugging of a headset, silence.

I stop. Let the stillness wash over me. Feel a wave of dread as I consider what it might mean.

To my left, the grass and brush part, forming another dirt pathway to the rim. Then, rising from the vapors like a miracle, coughing. Voices with a familiar timbre. A back-and-forth, male and female. I've found them.

I take a few tentative steps toward the caldera. Tilt my head, try to catch the wind just right.

"You'll be fine," Jocelyn's saying. "It's just down this path."

"No," Kai puffs. "I need . . . to rest."

"You already had a rest! Come on, we're almost there." She sounds preoccupied, terse.

"We should . . . go back." Kai coughs violently. "I need my . . . medicine."

As I move closer to the rim, the vog thickens. Between the mist and the dark, I can see almost nothing, but the emptiness of the caldera is palpable, a change in the air, a sense of oblivion looming before me. Though fairly sure I'm still a good thirty feet from the edge, I test the ground carefully with my foot before each step, make sure it's solid. Easing toward the rim, I follow the sound of their voices.

"It's a long walk back to the car," Jocelyn says from somewhere in the ether. "All the walking would make you worse. Just stick with me. The wind will change in a minute."

She's got him where she wants him, I think. *Weak. Vulnerable. So close to the edge.*

"I wanna . . . go," Kai says with difficulty. He takes a particularly ugly, gaspy breath and his voice turns pleading. "Joss."

"Okay, okay," Jocelyn says, and in that moment the vog parts so that at last I can see them, see their silhouettes against the night. Her smaller shape moves alongside his, nudging him forward. "We'll get you back."

For a second, I think I've misjudged the whole situation, think she might truly intend to return to the car. But there's something wrong about the way she's guiding him, one hand on his shoulder, the other nudging his hip, something off about the angle they're moving in, closer to the caldera rim, not away from it.

Kai knows something is off. "You're going the wrong—"

When her hands move swiftly to the center of his back, I know exactly how it feels, the fingertips pressing, pushing.

"Kai!" His name explodes from my mouth. "*Sit down!*"

There are two kinds of people in life: those who obey and those who question. For better or for worse, I have always been the latter. If my life depended on following a simple instruction without stopping to ask why, I would be dead. Kai, thank God, is cut from a different cloth.

He drops to the ground. Looks around in a daze for the person yelling at him, still fighting for a breath.

Jocelyn pulls away from him in alarm. "Who's out there?"

I dash across the tall grass, droplets of dew soaking my legs, an unexpected branch raking my arm. I must look like a ghost, the Romantic-British-novel kind that haunts desolate landscapes and wanders the night bemoaning her sad fate. Who knows? If I hadn't escaped that freezer, maybe that's exactly what I would've become.

I place a protective hand on Kai's shoulder and urge him away from the edge. Jocelyn watches him scoot to safety, completely paralyzed by the arrival of another person. For once, she has no contingency plan. This *was* her contingency plan.

"Hey there, Jocelyn." My voice does not betray the tension in my body, the blood coursing through my veins. "Remember me?"

thirty-one

W hat—what are you doing here?" Jocelyn addresses me in utter panic. "I don't—were you following us? How did you get here?"

Ignoring her, I lead Kai away from the vog-filled rim.

If I were Jocelyn, all my crimes unraveling before my eyes, I'd bolt. She must know I'll expose her, that the game is up. Lise has been found, I've escaped, and her rash plan to silence Kai has failed. What option is left to her but flight? Yet instead of taking off, Jocelyn remains glued to the spot, gibbering at us. The night has gone way off script, and she is out of ideas, unable to do anything but yell.

"Charlotte?" she shouts. "Where are you going? Stop! Come back! You have to tell me why you're here. *How did you get here?*" When I don't reply, she goes still, as if trying to regroup, and eventually comes trotting after us.

"Back off," I warn her, trying not to stumble under Kai's weight. His wheezing has grown too intense for him to speak. I don't think he understands what his girlfriend just tried to do to him, and that's probably for the best. Right now he needs to concentrate on every ragged breath.

"But . . . but I can help you," Jocelyn says, all her vinegar now turned to honey. "I can help you get Kai back to the car." She moves to shoulder some of her boyfriend's weight. As if we're all on the same team. As if she didn't just lock me up with her frozen sister or attempt to shove her boyfriend into a volcano.

I shunt her away. "You think I want your help?"

"Kai's heavy," she tells me. "You *need* my help. We can't let him overexert himself."

It's insulting, her aligning herself with me, pretending that we both have this boy's best interests at heart. I assume this whole innocent act is for Kai's benefit—she can't think *I'll* be fooled. I know what she is. I know what she's done. But Jocelyn is so rattled, so desperate, I'm no longer sure how rational her thoughts are. Maybe she truly believes she can still talk her way out of this one, ingratiate herself to me.

Either way, no point in challenging her on it, I decide. Animals are most dangerous when cornered. I let her support Kai from the left, aware of every movement that she makes.

"I've already called for help," I say. "They should be here any minute." In truth, I have no idea if the police will respond to Rae's call or dismiss her as a crackpot, and even if they do show up, they're unlikely to do much for Kai. I'm banking heavily on that inhaler. Still, the threat of "help" arriving should prevent Jocelyn from hatching any more spontaneous plans to exterminate us. One hopes.

"We're lucky you showed up when you did," Jocelyn says, clinging to the part of Good Girl. "I was trying to show Kai this cool spot on the rim, but then his asthma got bad and who knows what he did with his inhaler . . ."

Kai's airway whistles mightily in response, and I shudder. His medical crisis is frightening enough, but Jocelyn's trying to pretend the last two hours of my life didn't happen is all the more disturbing. This girl is the Meryl Streep of underage killers, so credible I'm tempted to doubt my own experience. Part of me wants to succumb to the comforting illusion that this night was all a misunderstanding, that she's just a scared kid trying not to get in trouble with Mom and Dad. But that scared kid was willing to take down anyone and everything in her path. I can't forget that.

"Kai," I say, "do you have a rescue inhaler in the car?"

"I . . . unhhh . . . dunno . . ." His helpless wheezing does little to quell my fears.

"We'll get you out of here," Jocelyn says, soothing him. "It will be okay, Kai, I promise."

I can't see her face in the dark, can't make out her expression of faux concern as she helps me support her woozy boyfriend, but I know it's there and I hate her for it. A hundred unspoken accusations burn in my throat. I force them down. Like it or not, Jocelyn's right. I need her now.

We lug Kai's wobbly frame down the path, through wisps of vog. In the midst of a full-fledged attack, Kai seems to be losing the battle for air. Though Jocelyn and I do our best to support his weight, his body goes increasingly limp as his oxygen level decreases and his tortured whistling far exceeds the severity of anything Micky has ever experienced.

After hauling him along for a few minutes, I stop. Exercise of any kind will only exacerbate his condition. The kid's in serious danger of passing out. I sit in the middle of the path and help him to lie down. His forehead is clammy.

"I can run ahead," Jocelyn offers. "Maybe I can find his albuterol in the car."

"No," I snap. "You stay here. We both stay here." No way am I letting her get her hands on Kai's medicine—she could chuck it into the caldera in a hot minute. "I told you, help is coming. Just sit tight."

I hope that I'm telling the truth, that help *is* coming, but if Rae can't find Kai's inhaler somewhere in that Corolla, Jocelyn just might get her way tonight. People die from asthma attacks every day, and who knows how far we are from the nearest hospital?

"So . . . who exactly are we waiting for?" Jocelyn asks. "When did you call them?"

Jocelyn's not just questioning my tactics for crisis management. She's trying to assess who I might've told about what happened tonight, to better fashion her defense.

I make no reply. The less information she has, the better.

My hand skims Kai's rapidly rising and falling chest. His heart beats much too fast, and though the temperature keeps dropping, Kai is sweating. Should I really just sit here, pinning all my hopes on Rae? If he goes into cardiac arrest, the kid could die in my arms.

"Hang on, buddy. Hang in there."

As I search the park for signs of life, someone, anyone who might help us, I keep a cautious eye on Jocelyn's shadowy figure. She seems committed to playing innocent, but at this point, I wouldn't put anything past her. She's like the glowing Halema'uma'u crater, with all the heat that one can't see by day on full display at night. Victor was wrong about her. Jocelyn was never the cooling ocean to her sister's fire. She has always been Pele, a cool black surface concealing molten rage.

In the distance, a tiny beacon of light catches my eye. Rae's phone.

Glowing, bouncing, up and down, up and down. She sprints toward us, a slim shape loping through mist and moonlight.

I call her name and wave frantically.

She pauses. Races toward my voice. Reaches me faster than I ever would've thought possible.

Panting mightily, she hands me Kai's inhaler.

I position the plastic in his mouth and squirt some puffs, praying it does the job. "Breathe, Kai," I tell him. "Breathe it in." If effective, it will take a few minutes to start working. I hold his hand. Listen to the awful, high-pitched sounds he makes as he seeks oxygen.

Rae calls emergency services and speaks impatiently with the dispatcher, who seems to instruct her to do things we're already doing. She explains the difficulty of getting him back to the car and asks about the nearest hospital. Leaving Kai collapsed against her, I pace around in anxious circles, waiting for some indication of how I might help.

"How did she know?" Jocelyn draws close to me, too close for comfort. "How did your friend know to bring his inhaler?"

I stop walking, use my body as a barrier between her and Kai. "I told her."

"But . . . how did you know?"

"I know lots of things, Jocelyn. As you're aware." I can't hold it in any longer, can't pretend this girl is anything resembling normal. "It's why you tried to kill me, isn't it?"

"I didn't!" she says quickly. "I just . . . I saw Lise and I freaked out. I wasn't trying to hurt anyone."

"You locked me in a goddamn freezer and left me to die."

"It wasn't like that."

"It was exactly like that." I'm no longer sure if Jocelyn is lying to me or to herself. "I know you're afraid. You don't want to disappoint your parents, don't want to jeopardize your future, I get it. But you can't keep hiding what you did. You're just making things worse, don't you see? Digging a hole you'll never get out of."

"I don't know what you're talking about."

"Jocelyn." I grab her by the shoulders. "Your sister is dead because of you."

She shrugs out of my grasp. "No. That's not true. I can explain everything."

"You knew where Lise was," I persist. "You had her key to the restaurant. You took her sweatshirt. How are you going to explain that all away?"

"The key doesn't prove anything," she insists. "I—found it, that's all. Tonight, in our bedroom. I knew Lise spent a lot of time working at the restaurant, and I thought . . . I thought I should check it out. Maybe she'd left some clue about where she went. It was . . . twin intuition. That's why I went over there."

"Right. And you just happened to bring garbage bags."

Jocelyn doesn't speak for a moment. Her hands have begun to tremble. She stuffs them under her armpits and begins to rock back and forth, yet she refuses to break. "Eco Day," she whispers. "Those were in my bag because of Eco Day."

"You were going to move her body."

"No." She won't look at me. "No. I discovered what was in that freezer exactly when you did."

God, I want to shake this girl. If Rae were getting any of this, she'd give her an earful. But Rae's still on the phone, embroiled in logistical discussions about what symptoms Kai is currently displaying and whether or not to send him an ambulance. Losing my temper with Jocelyn would only hurt me later, discredit me when I have to face investigators.

"And that screwdriver you jammed in the freezer door?" I say. "You think you can spin that? That's intent, pure and simple. A calculated choice."

She turns on me slowly, eyes flashing in the dark. "Intent?" she asks. "No, I think that's a pretty clear case of self-defense. You've been dogging me for days, harassing me. My father even called to demand you leave me alone. And then you followed me into the restaurant tonight. I was scared of you—who wouldn't be? When I saw Lise in that freezer, I thought you'd put her there and I was next. So I tried to protect myself."

"Nice try, but that story won't fly." I shake my head. "Lise has been dead six weeks. I couldn't have killed her. I wasn't even on the island when she died."

"It doesn't matter what you did," Jocelyn informs me. "It matters what I thought you did. State of mind is paramount when establishing self-defense. And who can blame me if I wasn't thinking clearly? I'd just learned that my sister was dead."

Her voice turns shrill at the end, causing Kai to roll over in Rae's lap.

"Dead? Did you say . . . Lise's dead?" He sits up slowly.

Only then do I realize that his breathing has improved, that his whistles have lessened in speed and intensity. My heart lifts just a little.

"You sound better," I tell him. "The albuterol's working."

Rae looks up from her endless back-and-forth with the dispatcher.

"Can you walk back to the car now?" she asks. "We should still get you to a hospital."

Kai pays Rae and me no mind whatsoever. "Is Lise dead?" he asks again, still wheezing on the in breath. "Please. You have to tell me. Did they find her?"

If my own attempts to unsettle Jocelyn were an abject failure, Kai's stricken voice does the trick. She does *not* want her boyfriend worrying over her sister.

"Yes!" Jocelyn hollers. "She's dead! She's been dead for a while!"

Kai breaks into tears. "Oh, no. No, no, no, no. It was Elijah, wasn't it?" His asthmatic weeping brings to mind a large, dying bird.

Jocelyn turns her back to him and doesn't answer, which he takes as confirmation.

"Oh God," he sniffles. "This is . . . my fault, Joss. My fault. Me. I can't . . . can't carry this around anymore. I need to tell you . . ."

"Kai." Rae pulls him to his feet. "This isn't the time. Come on." She informs the dispatcher that we'll be walking to our own vehicle and hangs up.

He follows her down the path, still crying.

I shoo Jocelyn along and bring up the rear, so I can keep an eye on her.

"It's not right," Kai moans. "I can't keep lying to you, Joss. It's eating me up."

Jocelyn wants none of his confession. "Don't," she tells Kai. "Whatever it is you want to say, don't. This night has been bad enough."

But her boyfriend will not be derailed. "I'm so sorry," he says, pausing only to gulp air. "I didn't tell you before because I didn't want to hurt you . . . and Lise made me promise . . . she made me promise I wouldn't say anything . . . and then she was missing and I didn't want to . . . didn't want to add to your stress. But now . . . now I have to tell you. I have to take responsibility."

"Shut up."

Her words fall on deaf ears.

Kai keeps talking through his tears, eager to unload and buffered by the presence of Rae and me. "I know why she's dead, Joss . . . maybe I knew all along . . . the thing is . . . Elijah killed her because of me . . . because Lise and I . . ." His sobbing intensifies. "We were together. Over the summer."

"She already knows," I tell Kai wearily. "Lise told her about you guys the night she died." I don't connect the dots for Kai, don't tell him he's got the Elijah part of the equation all wrong. The last thing this kid needs right now is to slip into another asthma attack when he realizes who he's been dating.

Kai wipes at his face. "Wait . . . what? Lise told you? That doesn't . . . make sense." He stops walking. "Is that true, Joss?"

Jocelyn pauses, her face just inches from his, and for an awful moment, I think he's done for. She'll charge him like a bull, run him the twenty yards to the edge of the caldera and finish what she started. Jocelyn never quite reacts as I anticipate, however. "Yes," she says without emotion. "Lise told me about you guys. In more detail than I cared to hear."

"But . . . if you knew about us, why didn't you say something? Why have you been pretending everything's okay?" Kai's guilt turns to indignation. "That's so . . . messed up!"

"Why have *you* been pretending?" Jocelyn retorts as Rae grabs him and directs him to keep walking. "You could've told me that you were sleeping with my sister, but you didn't, did you? Well, you know what? I was glad that you didn't. Because it's not something I really wanted to discuss! It's humiliating."

"I don't understand." Kai's hands go to his head. "Lise said we couldn't tell you, that it would hurt you too much. She *ended* things. I had to promise her over and over I would never say a word. After all that, why would she turn around and tell you about us?"

"To rub my face in it? To clear her precious conscience? Who cares?" Jocelyn surges ahead of him, no longer interested in the conversation. "You cheated on me, the both of you, and you can't take it back."

"I'm sorry, Joss. I'm really, really sorry." His tears have abated, and the albuterol is working its magic on his airways. Maybe honesty has finally bought the kid some peace. "I should've broken up with you a long time ago, I get that now. I was just . . . scared. Scared of how you'd react."

"A legitimate fear," Rae mutters.

"You deserve to be happy," Kai adds, a breakup line so unnecessarily cliché I wince. "You deserve more than I could ever give you."

The vog has receded somewhat, carried away by the fickle breeze.

Ahead of us, Jocelyn's shadow cuts a lonely figure against the brilliant night sky. "What is it about Lise, anyway?" she asks softly. "Why does everyone always like her better?"

Maybe it was her lack of murderous impulses, I think. *People seem to respond to that.*

"It wasn't that I liked her better," Kai protests. "I just . . . loved her."

"Loved her?" Jocelyn doesn't look back, doesn't change the pace of her walk at all. "You *loved* her?"

"I told myself I didn't," he says. "I told myself that you were better for me, focused and going places. But I couldn't stop thinking about her, Joss, no matter how I tried. I kept waiting, looking for a way to tell her. And then this one night, I finally got her alone and . . . stuff happened."

"That's fucking, not love," Jocelyn says flatly. "Don't you know the difference? Lise didn't love you. Not by a long shot. You know what she used to say about you? That you were shallow. A follower. 'Another dumb bro, just a little cuter than the rest.' She played you, Kai."

"You're wrong."

"What do you think she liked about you?" Jocelyn presses. "What made you so irresistible? Your personality? Your intellect? Your dimples? No." She shakes her head. "It's the fact that you were mine. She used you to screw with me."

For once, Jocelyn's telling the truth. The girl in the freezer worried about Elijah. She still simmered with resentment for her sister. But Kai? She gave him little thought.

Rae interrupts this unpleasant revelation before he can process the truth of it. "I think we're almost to the parking lot," she announces. "Kai, are you doing okay?"

"Okay" doesn't really describe the shell-shocked boy beside us, but he's breathing well enough. I give his shoulder a little squeeze.

Moments later, as we finally reach the lot by the steam vents, a pair of headlights swoops in from the main road. A car door slams and a high-powered light blinks on in our direction. Park ranger, I determine from the goofy hat. About damn time. The police must have contacted them.

"Hey," a male voice says. "I'm looking for a Jocelyn Nakagawa."

His light plays across Kai, Rae, and me—wrong gender, wrong race—and settles on Jocelyn. "That you?"

Showtime. Jocelyn steps forward, lies locked and loaded. "Yes," she says, and her voice is tearful and small, a vulnerable girl in need of protection. "That's me."

after

Kalo Valley, Hawai'i

thirty-two

On Wednesday evening, I sit on the back patio at Koa House waiting for Rae to pack the last of her belongings. It's five o'clock. Our flight, a red-eye to San Francisco, leaves in a few hours. Inside, David is welcoming his latest guests, a couple celebrating their twenty-fifth wedding anniversary. I can hear their happy exclamations as they describe their drive from Kona, how much they love the landscape, how thrilled they are to see the island.

I look down, discover a cheeky gecko nibbling at my half-finished papaya, and smile. "Enjoy your spoils, little fella."

After chatting on the phone with Noah and the girls for the last half hour, I'm feeling generous. Tomorrow, I'll be home again. There will be shopping with Tasha to accommodate her growing sense of fashion and a trip to the gem and mineral store to pick out new specimens for Micky's collection. Sipping tea with Grandma. Cuddling with Noah on the couch after the girls have gone to bed . . .

I can't wait.

One might think three extra days in Hawai'i would be a welcome treat. Three days spent speaking to investigators, however, proved a special kind of punishment. No one seemed to believe my version of events, that Jocelyn could be so treacherous. Maybe, they suggested, given the bad blood between Miss Nakagawa and myself, I had misread her intentions. Maybe I had inadvertently caused her to fear for her safety, leading to the unfortunate freezer episode. After admitting that Jocelyn had never fully confessed to killing Lise in so many words, what could I do or say? There was no physical evidence to support my claims, certainly nothing to show that she'd intended to kill Kai.

Jocelyn fed them an irresistible story about a guy Lise had been secretly seeing. She hadn't mentioned him before, she said, because she believed her sister alive, thought that Lise had in fact run away with him. Now she knew that he must be Lise's murderer. She blamed herself for not coming forward earlier. Naturally, the cops ate this tale right up. Easier to pin things on a menacing mystery man than to recognize a sixteen-year-old girl with a penchant for recycling could have such a dark side. *There are some sick guys out there*, one detective told the local paper. *We'll do everything we can to hunt this one down.*

If that weren't frustrating enough, some genius in the media got wind of my involvement in the Lise Nakagawa case. Though I refused to grant any interviews, the story received national coverage. Frankie got his fifteen minutes of fame telling the world that Lise had appeared to me in my dreams and I believed I had to help her— file that one under Things I Wish I Hadn't Shared While High. The headlines were brutal. PSYCHIC MOM ARRIVES TOO LATE, CNN reported, as if Lise's death were my fault, my failure. *Why do they label you a mom?* Rae grumbled. *You're a journalist! Your kids have nothing to do with this.*

But they will. Noah's had his share of reporters buzzing around, looking for a scoop, and it will be worse when I return home. Who knows how long I can keep them away from my children? If show-boating Tasha has her way, we'll land a TLC series in no time.

Thinking about the future makes me jumpy. I can't ignore the stories about me forever. Sooner or later, I'll have to make some hard choices. I hope it's later. I wander the yard, restless, snapping a few photos of the trees and shrubs that I think Noah would appreciate. He'll want to learn all about them: blooming cycles, root depth, growth patterns. My heart calms at the thought of Noah, and I finger my engagement ring. God, I love that man. It's time to set a date and tie the knot already.

The sun drops slowly in the sky, casting an eerie shimmer on the grass. For a moment, the lawn looks so inviting, I consider removing my shoes, reveling in it barefoot. Then I remember Hawaiian centipedes, rat lungworm, those slimy purple snails. To live in paradise, you must be tougher than I realized. Long-term, I don't know that I could cut it.

I'm not sure if I regret coming here. With its jagged shores, misty mountains, and lush tropical jungles, what I've seen of the Big Island has certainly been beautiful. Yet beneath the seemingly impenetrable black rock flows a hot and destructive force that will inevitably surface again. The ancient Hawaiians understood something I'm still trying to wrap my brain around. You can't stop Pele's fire. Sometimes all you can do is minimize the damage.

Isaac called almost as soon as the Lise story broke, positively giddy about the discovery of a body on what was supposed to be my vacation. "I had a hunch about this!" he chortled. "What did I tell you? Did Victor Nakagawa give you an amazing scoop or what? And you're in the news again! I know you aren't doing interviews, but I think being reclusive could work to our advantage. People will be that much more curious to read your book if you go all J. D. Salinger."

When I told him I had no intention of writing about the experience, he pretended to back off. "I know, I know. Too soon. You need time to process. That thing in the freezer, wow—you're going to need a good therapist and a night light."

I do wonder about that. Will I leave this island with a whole new set of phobias? Will I have flashbacks every time I feel the cold rush of an open freezer door? Probably not, but it's a hell of an excuse if I want to avoid cooking.

My eyes stray to the dense forest that marks the Yoon property line. Isaac, CNN, the *Squealer*—they will never know about the children I did help, and I'm grateful for it. Those boys deserve a fighting chance.

Thom heard through the Kalo Valley grapevine that Elijah's foster mom registered him for school today. Hard to say how Elijah will fare at a public high school. There's not a kid in Kalo Valley—and probably all of Puna—who doesn't know his story, that he's the boyfriend of the dead girl. But Jocelyn's preposterous Mystery Man story has at least shifted the blame from him. With luck, there will be another girl, a girl with a rebellious streak and an eye for wounded birds, who will see Elijah and fall hard. He strikes me as the kind who will always find someone to take care of him. And Raph's a scrappy kid. He'll turn out fine.

It's Adam I worry about, still living on Wakea Ranch without his brothers or a clue about how to survive in the real world. Nineteen makes you legally an adult no matter what scars you bear. How will he learn to join a world he's never been allowed to experience?

I walk a little closer to the tree line, debating whether or not to pay him a visit. I haven't seen him since the night he turned up on my balcony. Despite his pseudo-stalker behavior, I feel for the kid. His boundary issues aren't exactly surprising under the circumstances, and I'm the one responsible for all the changes in his life. To disappear without so much as a good-bye after pushing him to speak out against Naomi—that would be heartless. I should check in on him one last time.

Inside the woods, birds chirp and trill at one another. The dwindling sunlight slips through cracks in the canopy and falls in delicate shafts. Even with Naomi gone and Lise found, I'm apprehensive about roaming around this big green maze. I'm still not sure I can navigate these paths without getting lost, and a trail of cloven hoofprints in the earth looks suspiciously like wild pig tracks.

Fortunately, no roving pigs make an appearance, and the ugly, magnetic pull of Wakea Ranch proves enough to guide me out. I stand at the edge of the meadow, recoiling at the slick, suffocating waves that roll off the distant house. The sickness of its inhabitants cloaks the land in wrongness. Do I really want to go in there?

In the end, I don't have to. I find Adam scrubbing down the empty stables, his trousers muddy at the knees. He dips his rag into a bucket full of vinegar-smelling liquid and runs it over the wooden beams. The attempt to clean strikes me as a sad one. Those horses are never coming back, and he knows it.

"Adam," I call. "Hi."

At the sight of me, his face hovers somewhere between hope and wariness. "I thought you were leaving." He wrings out his rag and drapes it over the side of the bucket. "Did you change your mind? Are you going to stay?"

"I'm leaving tonight, actually. Rae and I got stuck speaking to the police a few extra days."

His face darkens.

"Nothing about your mom," I add quickly. "We were trying to sort out the whole thing with Lise. You must've heard about that."

"Oh. Yes. Marvel came yesterday to tell me." Adam drags the back of his hand across his damp forehead, leaving a dirt smudge in his wake. "I was sad but not surprised. Lise was a sinner, and God punishes sin. If you don't follow His teachings, you'll burn." He pauses. "I didn't say that to Marvel, though. I know she loved Lise."

"Good call." I'm glad he has that little bit of social grace. After a few years away from Naomi, maybe he'll drop some of the fire-and-brimstone talk. "Have you seen Elijah and Raph at all?"

"Not yet. The family court has to give me visitation rights. Maybe by the end of this week." Adam brushes mud and old straw from his trousers. "They're staying with Lani Chang. She sounds pretty nice. Raph says he likes her." He digs into his pocket and produces the most basic of flip phones. "I got this, so I can talk to them."

I grin. "Nice. You're part of the world now."

"It might take a while for them to come live with me," Adam says, not returning my smile. "I have to prove to a judge that I'm responsible enough to take care of them both."

"Of course you are. You've been taking care of Raph for a long time."

"I need a job, though. If I can just get a job, Marvel said the state should pay for Raph's preschool."

"Are you still thinking you want to be a driver?"

"Well," he begins slowly, "Marvel wants me and Elijah to help start her restaurant."

I'm taken aback. "The restaurant? Really? After everything that happened there, I thought she'd be eager to unload it."

"She said Lise told her not to."

My skin breaks into goose bumps. "When did Lise tell her that?"

"The other night," Adam says. "Marvel saw her hanging around the crystal shop. Lise told her not to give up on Ono Place, that Elijah and I could still make it happen. So Marvel came by to ask what I thought about that."

"Huh." I wonder if his religious upbringing can accommodate such an event. "Do you believe her? Do you believe she saw Lise?"

"Maybe." He looks torn. "Marvel said the lights in her shop were going crazy. I don't think she'd lie about that."

"Neither do I." I wonder how long Lise Nakagawa will be hanging around, unnerving people with her electrical displays. The idea of giving Adam and Elijah a job doesn't strike me as a terrible one, though. "Do you want to work at Ono Place?"

"Sure," Adam says. "I would get to meet people. That would be nice. I'm a hard worker, you know. And I wouldn't have to do it forever. Someday, maybe, I could work at a ranch."

"A ranch?"

"Marvel says there are ranches all around the island," he explains. "When my brothers get older, I could try to find a job on one. Maybe I could even board some horses here, if we don't end up selling the land . . ." He stares at the empty stables, the stalls where Solomon and Malachai once resided, and I imagine he's taking stock of his losses: the horses, the home, and of course, Naomi.

"You sound like you've done a lot of thinking about the future." I swallow down the lump in my throat. "That's great, Adam. I'm proud of you."

He doesn't accept the compliment. "They're going to send my mother to jail," he murmurs. "It could be for a long time. She'll never forgive me."

"There's nothing to forgive," I say. "You're not the one who did wrong. All you've done is tell the truth." I search for a relevant Bible verse to quote at him. "'The truth will set you free,' right?"

"It won't set her free," Adam says dully. "Families protect each other. Mama always said that. But I didn't protect her."

"Oh, honey," I say. "Families can do terrible things to each other. Look at Jocelyn and Lise. Look at what your mother did to you. Anyway, you did protect your family. You protected Elijah. You protected your son." The word "son" feels hard and strange in my throat, but Adam has earned it. Young as he is, he's raised Raph as dutifully and lovingly as any father.

"She said no one would ever love me like she does. Do you think she's right?" He lifts his gaze to mine and in that naked, pleading look I see, with some discomfort, what has always drawn him to me, the need that propelled him to follow me around.

I am the mother he always wanted.

"I think your mother is confused about love," I say. "Love is not about controlling someone, not about hiding them away from the world so they don't leave you. I don't know what happened to your mother growing up here on this ranch, but she's sick, Adam. She's sick, and she needs to get better."

He takes a few steps toward me, close, too close for me to feel at ease. I draw away.

"I need to go," I tell him. "Don't want to miss my plane. I just came by to tell you . . . that I'm rooting for you. You and Elijah and Raph. I hope you stick together. I hope you make it."

"Oh," he says, and his disappointment is palpable. "Okay." He turns away from me, despondent, a child that I've cruelly abandoned in his time of need. "Bye."

RETURNING THROUGH THE WOODS, I find myself in a losing battle with mosquitoes. Just one more tropical nuisance to add to the list of things I won't miss. By the time I emerge on the Koa House end of the jungle, my arms and ankles have gathered an impressive collection of itchy pink bites. I'm halfway across the yard, scratching myself like a flea-infested animal, when David pops out onto the patio.

"Charlotte! There you are! We couldn't find you." He stands nervously in the doorway, as if bearing bad news.

I rub a bite on my wrist. "Just thought I'd check in with Adam before I left. Everything all right?"

"Sue Nakagawa's parked out front. I told her you were gone, but she's been waiting for you."

"Waiting for *me*? Why?"

David shrugs, but I know we're both having the same thought. This can't be good, not after I've implicated one daughter in the other daughter's murder. I exhale deeply. Oh well. Might as well let her get it all off her chest. Anger and blame are part of the grieving process, and I can absorb whatever Sue decides to throw at me.

I find Sue in the driveway behind the wheel of a white Odyssey. She wears sunglasses, though it's no longer sunny—perhaps an effort to remain incognito, or else an indication of how oblivious she is to her surroundings right now.

I approach the car gingerly. Sue waves me into the passenger seat, silent and expressionless. Her lack of outward emotion frightens me more than any hysterics could. What terrible feelings has she locked away? How and when will they surface? I slide in beside her, closing the car door to give us privacy.

"I figured I'd be the last person you'd want to see right now."

For a few long seconds, she doesn't answer. When she does speak, her voice is brittle and faraway. "You did what I asked of you, I guess. You found her."

I bow my head and stare at what looks like a coffee stain on the upholstery. "I'm sorry, Sue. I had no idea. That wasn't what I hoped to find."

"No, I guess not. But we don't get to cherry-pick the truth." Her fingers flit across a metal lever that I imagine to be a hand brake or accelerator—some vehicle adaptation that allows her to drive. "It's strange. I knew I had a problem child, I just . . . I always thought it was Lise."

So Sue didn't come here to protect Jocelyn, to demand that I retract everything I told the police. This is even worse. Sue believes me.

I fumble for words and come up short. "Your daughters . . . had a complicated relationship."

"Complicated. Yes." She makes a noise that sounds almost like a laugh, something wild and unnaturally high. "She's not going to serve time, you know," Sue tells me. "Our lawyer says Jocelyn's an ideal witness. Young and sympathetic, no priors. He doubts they'll even press charges."

My blood boils at the thought, but I've seen Jocelyn in action. Her lawyer's probably right. "You and Victor must be happy about that," I say.

"Happy? Hardly. Victor's a wreck. He's barely functioning." She puts her hands on the steering wheel and stares ahead, eyes hidden behind the glasses. "He's been lying to himself about Lise for so long. But now? You can't tell yourself your child's coming home once you've seen her in a morgue."

I'm not entirely sure about that. Keegan has been dead four and a half years, and I still have moments when I see him running in a group of children or hear him calling from another room. I still have moments when, on the edge of sleep, I'd swear he's close. Is it better to see the world with Sue's clear and sober gaze, or to allow yourself the occasional comfort of delusion?

"Victor's lost," Sue says. "He's grasping, anything to stay afloat. You have to understand, Jocelyn's all he has left. He has to believe her. He'll defend her to the end."

"And you?"

Her head drops. "You must think I'm a fool. That I didn't know my own daughter. But I had a . . . feeling, maybe. Too nebulous to act on." She bites her lip. "Jocelyn's always had a temper. Both of the girls did."

Outside, Thom joins David on the front porch of Koa House. Though he tries not to stare at Sue and me too directly, his curiosity is obvious. Whatever conversation he and David appear to be having is just an excuse to keep tabs on us.

"You never asked about my accident," Sue says. "How I ended up in a wheelchair."

Her paralysis seems like an odd thing to bring up now, but I run with it. "If you're comfortable telling me, I'd like to know."

"Mangoes," Sue says. "I was picking mangoes."

I fight the urge to scratch my mosquito bites. "Mangoes?"

"We used to have a big tree in our backyard," Sue explains. "Mangoes were Victor's favorite fruit." Her voice is quiet now, remembering. "I was up on the ladder one afternoon, picking from the higher branches, when Jocelyn ran over. She was very upset. Lise had been invited to a birthday party, and she hadn't. Jocelyn wanted me to call the parents, to insist she get an invite, too."

"What did you tell her?"

"I refused. I've never catered to that kind of silliness. I said, 'Jocelyn, you and Lise aren't the same person and you won't always get the same things in life. Some people might just like her more than you.'"

"How old was Jocelyn?" I ask, wondering how many years Lise eclipsed her in the popularity department.

"Eight." Sue pauses. "Too young for that kind of honesty? I don't know. I've always been plainspoken. She didn't take it well, regardless." Sue sounds oddly detached from the story she's telling. Perhaps severing her mind from her heart is the only way that she can cope. "I don't know if it was a conscious effort to hurt me or just blind anger," she continues, "but Jocelyn kicked the ladder. She kicked it, and I fell. I landed exactly the wrong way." Sue runs a finger down her spine. "I'd still be walking if it weren't for her. Jocelyn knows it and I know it, and knowing that changed our relationship forever."

The brutality of her words startles me, even coming from Sue. "You blame her, then?"

"Oh, I forgave her," Sue says, so quickly I'm not sure I believe her. "She's my child. But it made her . . . indebted to me. Afraid to rebel."

"You think that's why she's pushed herself so hard? She felt she owed you?"

Sue nods. "Part of her always wanted to be Lise. To have friends, to slack off, to quit swimming. But she never did. Jocelyn thought she had to be my legs. She thought she had to do the things I couldn't. That she had to earn my love. And I let her think that. Because it was easier." Her voice has a noticeable tremor. "No wonder she hated her sister."

Now at last I understand how two identical girls could grow to be such different young women. Lise wasn't some sad, stunted version of her overachieving sister. All this time, Jocelyn has been the sad and stunted version of Lise, desperate for approval, desperate for absolution.

"You aren't the only factor in their relationship, Sue," I point out. "Lise didn't do herself any favors when she took up with Jocelyn's boyfriend."

"That's what I can't wrap my head around," Sue says. "That they would hurt each other like this for a *boy*. A stupid, nothing boy."

"He wasn't nothing," I say. "He chose Jocelyn, and that was everything."

"Boys." Sue pronounces the word like a curse. "They inspire so much passion, and for what? Kai wasn't worth it. They're never worth it. You think they're fulfilling your dreams when really they're just dimming your star. Why can't we ever see that before it's too late?"

She's not just talking about her daughters now. I wonder at the ways that marrying Victor derailed her life, how bright her so-called star might have been.

Sue turns on the car, which has grown rather stuffy, and cracks the windows. "I don't have any illusions about who Jocelyn is or what she did," she says. "I take responsibility for it. I raised her to succeed. I said, let nothing get in your way. And she didn't."

"No, she didn't." I'm growing impatient. If this is Sue's roundabout apology for my near-death experience in a freezer, it's falling short. I still don't know why she's here, what she wants from me. "Listen—is there something I can do for you? Anything?"

She takes a breath. The sky is a serene and deepening blue; soon the stars will be out. "Your story. The article you were writing on Victor."

"Forget about it." I start to open the car door. It's late. Rae and I had better be getting to the airport. "The article's dead, I promise. It wouldn't be appropriate now."

"Oh," she says. "I think it would." She finally lifts her sunglasses. If I was expecting waterworks, I fundamentally misjudged the woman. Her eyes are bloodshot and swollen but resolute. "A story about Victor, that would be a hard sell. But the story of Lise—that would be entirely appropriate."

"You want me to write about Lise?" This feels like a trap. "Why?"

"A human life is so little in the scheme of things," Sue says. "So fleeting, so easily forgotten. I accept that. But Lise was mine. She was my daughter. I want her life to mean more than nothing."

I'm still not convinced of the woman's motives. "You know I can't tell Lise's story without telling Jocelyn's. She's a minor. Even if I could manage the linguistic gymnastics to ethically pull off this story, why would you want me to? I'm hardly unbiased here. Whatever I wrote, it wouldn't do Jocelyn any favors. She tried to kill me."

"I know what she did. That's why you need to write this."

I shoot her a questioning look.

"I'm her mother. I can't say the things you can."

I raise an eyebrow. Is Sue attempting to exact journalistic revenge on her child, or is she trying to perform a public service?

"Anything I wrote could follow Jocelyn for the rest of her life."

Sue's gaze is hard and black, but I can still feel the heat that flows beneath the surface. "Yes," she says, "exactly."

thirty-three

On the flight to San Francisco, Rae trades seats to get a spot next to me. Days of dealing with law enforcement have left us both exhausted, and I'm more than happy to join her in watching a campy Channing Tatum sci-fi flick. We laugh at the bad acting, we whisper snarky comments about the nonsensical plot, and we lose ourselves. It's everything a Girls' Week should've been.

Afterward, I fall asleep and do not dream. I awake, disoriented and drooling, to find Rae smiling at me. "Here," she says, handing me a napkin.

Only on the ground, when we're about to part for separate flights, do I finally address the craziness that we've just shared.

"I'm so sorry about this week, Rae," I say as a trio of Silicon Valley types brush past us. "You know how much our Girls' Weekends mean to me. I didn't intend for it to go down like this."

"Sorry? Are you kidding me?" Rae looks genuinely mystified by the apology. "It was an incredible week."

"Incredible as in you can't believe it happened?"

"Incredible as in intense, unforgettable, amazing. I don't know, you're the wordsmith." She grins. "What I'm saying is, I'm glad we did this. I wouldn't trade it for the world. It was totally what I needed right now and it felt . . . important."

Now it's my turn to be mystified. "We destroyed that family, Rae." I step out of the path of an oncoming vehicle, barely aware of the hordes of people moving around me. "Sue and Victor . . . they'll never be the same. Sue lost everything. Not just one daughter, but two."

"How about what Sage didn't lose?" Rae reminds me. "Kai would've gone sailing off that cliff if you hadn't known where to go. And don't you tell me the Nakagawas lost Jocelyn. That girl has her story all lined up. A couple years, and she'll be phoning home from Stanford, just like she always wanted."

I kick at my suitcase. "This world is so messed up."

"But we tried to make it better," Rae says. "We tried, and I think we did. Naomi will end up in jail because of you; that's something. And Jocelyn might get away with it, but you changed the narrative. If you hadn't found Lise in the freezer, sooner or later someone else would've. And Elijah Yoon would've taken the blame."

"Yeah, maybe." I hadn't considered that before. It does make me feel a little better, to imagine the ordeal we might've spared Elijah. God knows he has enough other battles in his life right now.

"Seriously, Charlie, if I could do this every day, get out there and help families, look for bad guys—I mean, that would be the life. A job that meant something."

"You have a great job," I protest. "And you worked so hard to get it."

Rae sticks out her tongue. "Back in college, I thought I'd be working in a lab, creating something new. And here I am, some soulless corporate sellout. I have the house, the husband, the kid—and a job that makes me want to jump off a tall bridge."

"Oh, Rae."

"Yeah, yeah, we're not allowed to say that, are we? When you're gainfully employed and making bank, you're not allowed to say how boring it is, that your soul is withering away one day at a time. I mean, why do I do this? Am I really living my best life?"

I don't know what to say. I've been so focused on the Nakagawa girls, I missed the fact that Rae was having a midlife crisis before my very eyes. "If you need a change, then make one. No one wants you to be miserable."

"Yeah," she agrees. "This week with you really got me thinking. What would it be like to have a vocation? Not just a job you show up to and collect a paycheck, but something that gets you excited. Something that fulfills a purpose. I look at you, diving into this story, un-wrapping all the layers. You're doing what you want to be doing."

With all the chaos in our home, I have little time to reflect on how much I love my work, but Rae's right. I'm doing what I want to be doing—although whether that can last in the face of all this tabloid noise is anybody's guess. I wish that we could talk further, but according to the flight bulletins, my plane has begun to board thirty gates down. I've got to get moving.

I wrap my arms around Rae, the one woman in this world that I can hug without feeling awkward. "I love you," I tell her thickly. "Whatever you decide to do."

"I know." She casts me an impish grin. "And since you seem to be making a habit of these little investigations, just remember, I'm in the market for a new career."

"Don't even joke about that."

"Who's joking? We make a good team. Every Sherlock needs his Watson . . ."

"No. Hell no. Not in a million years." I take off down the terminal with a smile. "Keep dreaming, though."

"No, *you* keep dreaming!" Rae calls, and I groan. Walked right into that one.

When I glance back at her, she's studying the flight bulletin, one finger fiddling with a curl. Real life and all its attendant problems await, but I know she'll land on her feet. Jumping is the hardest part.

I ARRIVE HOME around lunchtime. Noah's at work, the kids are at school, and whatever reporters have been hanging around seem to have abandoned me for another hot story. Either no one got wind of my return, or they've ceased to care. There's just one mud-spattered station wagon parked in front of my house, a blond woman staring at the maps app on her phone, apparently lost.

Maybe I'll have a few days' peace, some time to enjoy Micky and Tasha and Noah. Life won't be normal exactly—they're out there, all these stories about me, still out there for anyone to see—but given time, surely I will fade into obscurity. I just have to stay out of trouble . . . which, knowing me, may be a tall order.

I'm halfway up the drive when I hear someone call my name. "Charlotte? Charlotte Cates?" The blond woman stands nervously by her car, door open, not sure she has the right house. She's five or ten years my junior, and her vehicle has Colorado plates.

My eyes narrow. "If you're writing an article, I have no comment."

"An article?" She runs a hand through her hair as if confused by the suggestion. "No. I'm not writing anything. I just . . ." She pauses, and then, seeming to make her decision, scurries across the pavement toward me. "Please. I need to talk to you."

I stand in the middle of my driveway, moving neither toward nor away from her. "About what?"

"I saw you on TV," she says. "I thought that maybe you could help me."

"Help you?" My words are hollow, a faint echo of her own. I see what's coming, see the choice that I must make. Why did I ever think that normalcy would be an option?

"My son," she says hoarsely. "I have to find my son."

I don't reply. I know, in this minute, that everything hangs upon my answer. Not just her future, and perhaps her child's, but my own.

If I agree to help her, some stranger I have never met, a desperate woman who saw me on television and hoped that maybe I was the one, her salvation—if I agree to do this, I can't go back. I can't live a quiet life, pretending to be the woman I have always been. If I help her, it will never end. There will always be another parent, drawing me into their pain, drawing me into their loss. Sometimes, perhaps, I will help them. Find their child, like I did Alex Rocío, and provide them with that perfect reunion. But there will be other times, as with the Nakagawa family, when I can offer only answers. Answers that might be worse than the questions themselves.

"I could pay you," the woman says. "I don't have much, but . . . whatever I have . . . I would pay."

"It's not about money," I say. "This isn't . . . a decision based on dollars."

I search the eyes of this despairing mother, unsure whether my involvement would offer her comfort or pain. Unsure whether exposing my abilities over and over to the world would offer myself comfort or pain. Twenty years ago, I chose journalism as my career because I believed in truth. But the truth is far messier than I ever imagined, and confronting my own truth is the hardest of all.

You see things most people don't, Charlotte, and that's a fact, Grandma told me when I agonized about my so-called gift. *Maybe it's time to stop worrying over it and just . . . settle into your own skin.*

Perhaps that's the real question. Can I settle into my own skin? Can I live my life as I am? Not as the person that I wish I was, but as my true and twisted self, one hand in darkness, one hand in light. Unafraid. No longer hiding.

I reach for the woman's hand, press her thick, callused fingers between my own two hands. There's a crackling in my skin, a small jolt, and I do as Marvel told me. I catch that wave. Feel the wind, snow-flakes biting my face, and know that her son is somewhere north. An icy branch. A baseball cap dangling from the tip, navy blue, an *N* and *Y* in familiar white stitching.

"Is your son a Yankees fan?" I ask, and the woman's bottom lip drops open, a perfect little O of astonishment.

"Yes," she says. "His father lives in New York. They go to games together in the summer." She stares at me, scarcely daring to breathe. "Is he alive? Do you see him alive?"

I don't know if I can learn to harness my visions, if I can be the woman that Marvel is, surfing, selecting the right waves and riding them all the way to the shore. But I can feel this woman's son buzzing at my fingertips, ready to speak, ready to show me things. If I don't listen, then who will?

I think of my grandmother, a lifetime spent concealing her

abilities. And I think of my girls, the women I hope they'll grow to be: confident, courageous, tough.

I can't settle for a life in the shadows.

I put a hand on the woman's shoulder, feel her quaking, afraid of what I might reveal. "Come inside." I lead her gently to my door. "We'll talk about your son. I don't know if I can help, but . . . I'd like to try."

acknowledgments

A huge thank-you to the folks who made this book possible. I fully own all factual errors, inaccuracies, or oversimplifications.

Don Swanson at the Hawaiian Volcano Observatory offered his invaluable expertise both in person and in email. I'm so grateful for all the information and inspiration that he provided. The work he's done connecting ancient Hawaiian chants to actual geological events—which Victor alludes to in this book—represents a beautiful marriage of culture and science that so befits this magical island. And the Hiʻiaka and Pele myth he shared with me shaped this novel in important ways.

Ingrid Johanson from the HVO was also generous enough to speak with me about research, fieldwork, and the life of a geologist on Hawaiʻi. I so appreciate her time.

My gratitude to Clifford Lim, who helped me with my pidgin while caring for his new baby and rocking his job as an elementary school teacher. Jenny Stulck and Charles Wu provided a small window into their Puna world. I admire their adventurous lives and trusting spirits. Woody Musson taught me much about the day-to-day challenges of life in Puna. I will wash my fruit carefully forevermore.

To my alma mater, the University of Hawai'i: thank you for allowing this *haole* girl to expand her horizons and get a little taste of Pacific literature. Passionate and knowledgeable professors coupled with an interesting and diverse student body made my grad school years one of the most rewarding experiences of my life, and taught me much about the hard legacies of colonialism that Hawai'i and its native people continue to face. I will do my best to share the fruits of my education with others.

I owe so much to Kerri Kolen, who first sent me on this journey with Charlie. Our own lives have evolved so much over the course of these three books. Kerri, I wish you all kinds of success and happiness as a mom and book wizard. It has been a pleasure to work with Danielle and all the great folks at Putnam and Cornerstone. Their commitment to books and authors brings so much joy to readers and writers alike. My agent, Esmond, also remains a valued guide.

Much love to my mama, Deb, for sharing a very special Big Island camping trip with me. Your patience and support—even when faced with some wild plans over the years—have been a great blessing. And I knew I could count on my dad, John, to explain the intricacies of walk-in freezers. He didn't disappoint.

Spencer Wise listened to my ideas, begged for new chapters, and never let me succumb to self-doubt. His enthusiasm and willingness to travel have made my writing life possible. Finally, a big thank-you to Paxton and Lyra for reminding me that, while I have the coolest job in the world, a job should never be what matters most. I'm honored to have a role in your stories.